NO STRAIGHT THING

NO STRAIGHT THING

F. NELSON SMITH

Bear Hill Publishing

No Straight Thing
F. Nelson Smith

Bear Hill Publishing
P.O. Box 50088
Edmonton, Alberta
Canada, T5Y 2M9
bearhillbooks.com

ISBN (paperback) 978-1-7750741-0-6
ISBN (hardcover) 978-1-7750741-2-0
eBook ISBN 978-1-7750741-1-3

To Tessa—who saved me lots of embarrassment

Southern Alberta, Early August 1936

"Wait for me at the end of the street," Cat whispered to Joe.

She approached Frieda Hoffman's house gripping little Charlie's hand, making him scurry along beside her to keep in stride. All the while, she watched Joe move up the street to the corner without her.

"Wait for me," she hissed at him again.

But Joe didn't wait. Her stomach fluttering like trapped butterflies, she deposited her young brother at the doorstep and gave a sharp rap at the door before turning to leave. Her mother wouldn't like that. Mrs. Hoffman had offered to take Charlie swimming with her own brood, and it was Cat's job to ensure he arrived. She wasn't fooled. The same trick had been played once before when her mother had shipped Alex off to a farm.

Cat left Young Charlie at the door and ran back down the street along the route Joe had taken. She found him three blocks away, looking at a bike, discarded in the schoolyard.

"You can't take it," she protested.

"It's already stolen," he said, and sat on it, trying it out for size. "Maybe you'd better go home."

Ignoring his command, Cat perched sideways on the bike's crossbar, gripping the handlebars while Joe began to pedal. Both rubber tires squashed against the rims under their double weight but picked up speed gradually, Joe's heavy breath sending puffs of air against her neck. Nearing Thomson Hill, he stopped and made her get off, then pushed ahead of her up the gravel road leading to the top of the cliff, as if by hurrying he could leave her behind. Afraid he might, she scrambled to keep pace. Once there, with the prairie expanse spread out before them, he relented and waited for her. They rode and walked through the short grass, scattering grasshoppers, until they came to the CPR siding near Macson.

Joe found this place upon the advice of a rail-rider weeks before. "Never flip a rattler in the town," the rail-rider had warned. His eyes raked over Joe, and his mouth turned down. "You fixing to go out of town, boy?"

Joe looked him straight in the eye and nodded.

The man sighed, shaking his head. "Stay away from men who are too friendly, or say they'll take care of you. What they do with young boys like you ain't pretty. You understand?" He waited until he saw Joe nod, and added. "If you have to flip a rattler, go to Macson. There's a switch there. You can jump the train when it slows. And don't try to ride the rods. You ain't strong enough."

At Macson, the tracks continued east or switched towards the southwest, to Lethbridge and beyond, through the Crow's Nest to Vancouver. Cat had tried to picture travelling on a train, through places with strange names like Crow's Nest, and forests thick with trees, under mountains so high the tips were snow covered.

Now, watching Joe as he assessed the location, her imagination faded along with the tracks disappearing into the horizon. She moved closer to him, reaching out for him, and struggled to breathe against the pain in her chest.

The never-ceasing prairie wind flattened their clothes, wrapping around arms and legs whose childish roundness had evaporated along with ample food. A tumbleweed of dead Russian thistle rolled past, hooking itself against the sagebrush. Cat shivered even as the heat of the day lingered into evening.

They walked a short distance more until Joe decided this was the best spot. He led her across the track, picking his way along the ties, mindful of spots a snake might snuggle against a rail for warmth. Cat held Joe's arm as he pulled away.

"Joe." Cat's amber eyes pleaded, worry lines creasing her small face. "Wait for Mr. Marchenko. Don't leave me alone."

Joe shook his head. "I have to find Dad. Go home, Cat. I shouldn't have let you come."

"But Vancouver's big. You'll never find him." Uninvited tears sketched through the dust coating her cheeks. "The train bulls will catch you. They beat up rail-riders. They'll put you in jail with the hobos and bums. If Mom knew . . ."

He yanked his arm from her hand. "Then why is she making me quit school? She doesn't care as long as I'm gone."

"It's not her," Cat said. "It's him. I heard them talking. They thought I was asleep."

Joe nodded. "I think he made her send Alex away too." They regarded each other.

"I hate cows." Joe blinked and swallowed hard.

"Please, Joe."

"I'll just follow the guys hitching," he said, ignoring her. "Dad will be in a work camp for sure. I'll tell him Mom can't manage. He's gotta know about Alex too." He took hold of her shoulders and bore into her with begging eyes. "Don't ever tell anybody I hopped the train. Just pretend Mr. Marchenko picked me up and I'm working on his farm." His voice broke, going deep and then without warning into a high tenor. It made him young, frightened.

"I'll be okay, Cat. . . . Get rid of the bike in the coulee behind the flour mill. By the time you get back, people will be gone from the mill, and nobody will see you. *Don't* tell Mom."

Cat answered with a weak nod.

"Cross your heart and hope to die?"

"Cross my heart and hope to die," she affirmed, feeling brave if only until the breeze picked up the words and carried them off.

They lifted their heads at the vacant echo of the train's whistle. The rails hummed. The freight train slowed for the switch. Joe had rehearsed his timing the whole last week—how he could grab the ladder on the boxcar. With luck, someone would reach out and pull him through the freight door. Another mournful whistle warned the train was closing in on the switch. Joe turned his face away, but not before she saw his lips begin to quiver.

"Bye, Cat. And keep our violin safe. Harley will sell it."

The big mountain engine rumbled at them before she could reply. *Is it coming too fast?* Her stomach flip-flopped.

They ducked low in the darkness, backs turned and eyes closed against flying cinders until the engine rolled past. Boxcars thumped, wheels click-clacking over the joins in the rails. Joe grabbed his small bundle, an extra pair of pants and shirt, with the jacket's sleeves tied to make a handle. She shouted goodbye, but he was running towards the train.

His figure got smaller, a thin arm reaching out for the ladder on the side of the boxcar. In spite of herself, there was a small thrill watching him. She's watched him before, a show-off, daring her to try. The timing was everything. First, grab the ladder, put his foot on the ledge below the boxcar, and climb. Easy, he told her.

Then he was gone, the sight searing through her eyes and into her head. She thought he cried out her name.

Overwhelming despair cemented her legs into the prairie. She put her hands over her ears to stop the thrumming noise, but it only increased. Her surroundings began to whirl in dizzying spirals, and she sank to her knees, closing her eyes waiting for her head to explode. Instead, a wave of nothingness surged through her, as though a hand had mercifully thrown off a switch. Welcoming the tranquil peace it brought, she opened her eyes.

The tail end of the caboose was already shrinking into the distance, its last mocking whistle echoing in her brain, repeating, *"Don't tell ... don't tell."*

1

AN eon ago, in Southeastern Alberta, a geological rift appeared along the South Saskatchewan River, spewing up fine sandstone and clay that formed into cliffs and coulees. What remained was a valley dotted with hillocks curving round the land and river.

Within this rift, the city of Cypress Landing developed. Sandstone cliffs contained the prime ingredients for manufacturing industries, and the city flourished with cheap heating, water, and electricity. Wheat prices soared, and five flour mills operated at full capacity. The CPR network of rail lines brought markets close. In the unblemished prairie air, the stars formed a golden halo over the city. Despite warnings, optimistic farmers in an area called the Palliser Triangle broke up progressively more land rooted with stable short grass to plant evermore wheat.

The reckoning began with a persistent drought followed by the stock market crash in October 1929. Then the winds came. Heartless winds scooped up all that rootless, arid dirt and blew it away from the earth.

Within the city of 9,500, prosperous people found themselves destitute. The CPR was the largest railway terminus between Winnipeg and Calgary, and as a consequence, there arrived a daily influx of train-riders; homeless, transients, and just plain hobos, seeking work or camping for a few days before moving on. And the city police chief, Captain Sam Embleton, and his force of eighteen men made sure they did. Transients got fifty cents for food and shown the way out of town.

The second Tuesday in August started out as expected that summer of 1936, hot and airless. As the day wore on, the heat radiating off roads and sidewalks dissolved into watery illusions. The occasional breeze wafted heat-laden air against people and buildings as if to suck out the last bit of moisture. Near four o'clock in the afternoon, a few wilting citizens remarked on the large ring around the sun, but experienced people sprang into action. Proprietors shut up stores, housewives slammed windows closed and stuffed rags or mats around thresholds. Mothers with shrill voices urged children into shelter while whipping the washing off clotheslines.

In the distance along the horizon to the east, a huge black cloud, roiling in on itself, tossed in silent fury as it moved toward the city. It covered the entire width of the horizon, growing larger with frightening speed. Sound arrived first, like the moan of a distant train, then small swirls of dirt, tumbleweeds and other debris danced along the streets.

The wall of dirt hit the city twisting and blowing the ground from under feet, stealing breath and loose items away, roaring against everything in its path. In minutes, the tall, dense cloud covered the sky, and day became night.

On the edge of town, the whine of the storm smothered the sound of cracking glass in the rows of greenhouses. Sucking winds scooped up loose wheat and detritus around the flour mills, firing the missiles against the warehouses. Fine grit found its way into every nook and cranny, affecting rich and poor alike, on both sides of the tracks. In the downtown business core, drivers blinded by the black clouds parked helter-skelter on the street. Shoppers caught outside groped their way to the doors of Eaton's, Woolworth, or any handy hiding place.

Fergus Muir later remarked to his father, Malcolm, if these storms kept on any longer, the whole of Saskatchewan would pass through Cypress Landing. Years later, people remembered the lamenting howl and grime of a black blizzard, the worst they'd seen.

When it was over, folk came out of their houses and did as they had done before; scraped away the drifts from the doors and windows, hosed down the vegetable gardens and inspected the remains of the bounty that was to keep them in food during the winter. Housewives or servants swept, cleaned, and polished inside.

City crews were out doing the same maintenance on the streets, parks, and boulevards. Industry owners inspected inventory in the open, awaiting shipment.

And early the next morning, a pottery worker approached a kiln scheduled for the first load of pottery. Grumbling to himself, he would first have to sweep up the usual detritus left by transients who had sheltered inside. What he didn't expect to find when he opened the door was a body.

2

ON the day of the storm that ravaged Cypress Landing, Cat felt driven to risk another afternoon at the Hobo Camp under the railway bridge. She dressed in a pair of Joe's overalls, tucked his cap into the bib and went into the kitchen. Her mother stood over the stove emptying the kettle into the teapot. Rose and Harley sat at the table, squabbling as usual.

"Keep your hands off my things." Rose pointed a finger at her brother. "If I find anything missing, I'll march you right down to the second-hand store, and you'll get it back."

"Who'd want your old junk?" Harley sneered. "Anything you got ain't worth a penny anyhow."

"Be quiet, both of you," her mother interrupted. "And don't say '*ain't.*' In all your sixteen years at school, you might speak proper English."

"Where's Young Charlie?" Rose asked.

Her mother pursed her lips and gently placed the teapot back on the counter and adjusted the cozy as to look undisturbed. "He's staying with Frieda Hoffman."

"Why is he at Frieda's?" Rose demanded. "Mother, have you . . ."

"No! It's for a couple of days. And you mind your manners! Frieda Hoffman is *Mrs.* Hoffman to you. You know very well that you do not dream of using first names with anyone, and I mean anyone at all, unless they're your good friends. Until then, they are Miss or Mrs. Is that clear?"

"Yes, mother. I'm sorry."

Her mother's attention focused on Cat and her overalls. "Just why are you dressed like that, young lady? The neighbors will think you don't have any dresses. Go change your clothes right now."

Cat said nothing, lowering her gaze to the floor.

"Did you hear me, Madam? What's the matter with you lately? You seem to be mesmerized."

"Cat has her tongue." Harley sniggered at his wit. "Ever since . . ."

"That's enough!"

Startled at the note of hysteria in her mother's voice, Cat looked first at her then Harley and Rose. Both were staring into their bowls as though something foreign had crept into them. Her mother raised a cup to her lips, then put it down again without drinking. "You better not be going near any hobos. Mrs. Roberts took pleasure in telling me Mr. Roberts saw you going down beneath the train bridge. I'll skin you if you bring home any bed bugs. Fine thing when the neighbors see my kids running wild, talking to those *people*."

At last, her mother took a delicate sip of her tea. "Besides, it can be dangerous."

"I'm doing garden work at the Muirs'," Cat lied. "I don't want to get my dress dirty or torn. When I bend over, people can see my pants," she added for good measure.

"We see London, we see France, we see Cat in her underpants," Harley sang.

Rose rolled her eyes. "You are such a hero."

"Do the Muirs pay you? Or do they expect you to work for nothing?"

"I get meals, and Mrs. Mann pays me if I'm there all day. Sometimes I get twenty-five cents. I'll bring you the money if they want me the whole day."

"Well, get some porridge into you." Her mother lifted the empty bowl off the counter and held it out to Cat, her expression plainly showing she wasn't totally convinced with Cat's explanation.

At the stove, Cat lifted the lid of the pot and grimaced at the sight of skin covering the porridge. Scraping the pot into her bowl, she mixed it up at the same time and sat at the table again. Harley passed her the milk bottle. The milk was almost clear. Watered down again, thought Cat, and she poured some over the oatmeal before adding a generous amount of sugar.

"While you're all here," her mother said, taking a seat at the table and inspecting her fingernails. "Don't come home till suppertime.

I am having company this afternoon, and I don't want a bunch of kids galloping all over the house."

Rose raised her eyebrows.

Harley snorted. "Does it mean we'll have eggs and bacon for breakfast tomorrow?"

Their mother's open hand shot across the table and met Harley's face with a piercing clap. Harley gasped and put his hand on the spot. Cat dropped her spoon into her porridge and sucked in her breath. Rose's mouth opened in a round '*oh*.'

"You'll get a lot worse if you don't stop the dirty insinuations!" Her hand shaking, she snatched up a napkin, dipped the tip in her tea, and began expunging invisible grime from the table top. "Why are you still sitting there anyway? Get out and find work. I can't get relief for you now you're sixteen. So either find work"—she stopped rubbing and looked Harley straight in the eye—"or go to a farm."

"No!" The word exploded out of Cat's mouth, shocking even herself. Her chest tightened. She had trouble finding air. A buzz like angry bees started in her head. Blinking back tears, Cat continued looking at her mother. "I just meant, don't send Harley away, Mama. Please. There won't be anybody left." She bit her lip, wondering what made her speak up. Why shouldn't Harley go to work on a farm? All he did was tease her. He was now looking at her, more astonished than her mother or Rose.

"You can count on me to stay away," he finally said, his tone resentful. "Carl and I can find plenty to do."

"Carl?" Rose echoed. "Is that the kid who spends his time explaining to the police why he chases young girls?"

"Now what?" Her mother said, sitting up. "What are you talking about?"

"He's a slimy hoodlum. According to Bessie Hutchinson, he can't keep his hands to himself. And she's only thirteen!"

"Ah, he isn't like that," Harley said. "A bunch of lies. He likes to tease, but he's never bothered anybody."

"Oh, well. Don't take my word for it," Rose's voice was sarcastic. "Just wait until you end up in reform school, along with him."

With a grunt of disgust, her mother threw the napkin at the table, face crumpling in self-pity. "Oh, I can't stand this much longer. What is the matter with the lot of you? You know I get upset easily. Why aren't you helping me? Women aren't meant to be both a mother and a father."

Harley's hand moved over his mother's. "Mama, I'm sorry. Couldn't I just . . ."

She moved her hand away, and Harley's eyes fluttered before hardening along with his jaw.

Cat felt a prod of sympathy for him. She wondered if she should tell him Joe had gone to find their father, but a tiny voice echoed in her head, *"Don't tell, don't tell."* Calm again, she returned to her porridge.

Unmoved by her mother's distress, Rose got up and took her bowl to the sink. "Well, I'm off," she said, smoothing her dress front. Rose worked as a maid for the Hutchinson's on First Street. She made good money, working from nine in the morning until nine at night, for fifty cents a day, with lunch and dinner thrown in. She got Sundays and one half-day a week free.

Her mother looked her up and down as if seeing her for the first time. "That looks like an expensive dress to go to work. In fact, the dress looks *too* expensive for a seventeen-year-old girl to have, or my name isn't Clara Perkins."

"Eighteen soon."

"You don't make enough to buy a dress that nice," her mother continued, eyes narrowing. "Are you doing things you shouldn't?"

Rose's face turned red, whether from guilt or humiliation, Cat couldn't tell. "It's a castoff from Mrs. Hutchison if you must know. I'll be home late tonight. Nell and I are going to the show to see Jeanette MacDonald and Nelson Eddy in Rose Marie." She headed for the door. "It'll be nice to listen to something pleasant for a change."

As soon as the door closed behind Rose, Harley rose from the table. Cat heard him rummaging around in the bedroom where she and Rose slept, searching for things he could sell on the street or at the second-hand store.

Harley soon left, with his mother's shout "get a job!" echoing behind him. Cat supposed he would head to what he called his *'trap line.'* First, to the heap of broken rejects outside the potteries.

Sometimes the large pile contained unbroken crockery, and even with a minor flaw it was still useable. Then he'd head over to the bottle factory and rummage through their pile for an unbroken bottle or phial. As a last resort, there was always the unloading area at the flour mills, where he would gather up wheat fallen to the ground to sell in the neighborhood as chicken feed. If he were caught, there would be hell to pay. Perhaps the managers believed someone might get the idea to steal a whole truckload. What money he gleaned from his efforts, he never shared. He likely spent it at Mercier's Store or the Dreamland and Monarch Theatres.

Cat slipped her bowl into the sink and left the room before her mother found something new to question. She drew the violin case out from under her mother's bed, found an old belt of her father's, and threaded it through the handle. Buckled and looped over her shoulder and under her opposite arm, the case fit snug against her back.

She headed for the hobo jungle. The camp was not cluttered chaos as might be expected when hearing the word 'jungle.' Fear of being turned out by the authorities kept a certain order in the camp. She had learned that if the men proved they had a temporary job in town, they were allowed to stay as long as it lasted. Cat followed the path under the train bridge, passing two women hanging washing between the willows, and returned their wave of greeting. The women travelled with their husbands, in charge of meals for the camp, always a daily stew to which camp people contributed what they could: meat, vegetables, or a loaf of bread.

Cat hunted through the camp, growing anxious. Had he already left on a train?

"Looking for Pete?" One woman was behind her; a clothes basket tucked on her hip. Cat knew her only as Helen, a large-framed woman whose bones stuck out at all angles. She dropped her basket and inspected the contents of a paper bag on a small table, then dug into it with a broad hand and pulled out a bunch of carrots. She smiled over them at Cat.

"You mean Sir?" Cat answered. "Have you seen him today?"

"He's down at the river, having a wash, I expect."

Cat heaved a sigh of relief. Helen waved Cat closer and indicated a canvas chair. With Cat seated, Helen inspected the carrots, then dug into the bag and pulled out a few potatoes. "You call him Sir? Why?"

Cat blushed. "When I first came down here, he rescued me from a man who bothered me. Then called me his Lady." She giggled. "I called him Sir Knight. It was like a pretend game with us. You know, the Knight who rescued his Lady?"

"Humph," Helen said. "People pretending they are what they aren't is why the country's in this mess." She studied Cat for a time. "Do you know what the Hobo Code is?"

"You mean that stuff they write on telephone poles and back fences?"

Helen laughed. "No. The Hobo Code are rules about how people should behave in the camps. It means we help one another, and do no harm, but some camps don't bother with the code. That man you mentioned. His name is Sam. Pete chased him off, but I still see him hanging around, maybe looking for you."

Cat felt a shiver down her spine. "I was scared at first," she admitted.

"You should be," Helen said. "You could have been in big trouble young lady if this was one of the bad camps. Pete makes sure everyone here obeys the code, or he runs them off. But some men don't like it and vow to get even. They are the most dangerous."

Helen put her hands on her hips, looking accusingly at Cat. Knowing sometimes it was best to say nothing, Cat just looked at the ground.

"What are you doing here anyway?" Helen continued. She sounded crabby.

"My dad has been gone so long. I have to know if he's okay. Maybe someone who comes here talked to him."

"Oh, Mercy," Helen muttered. She brought another canvas chair from the tent and sat beside Cat. "Your dad is on the rails? Where's your mother? Does she know you come down here?"

Cat blushed again, looked down at her feet and shook her head. Helen gave an exasperated sigh. "Now then, tell me. Where do you think he is?"

"He said he was heading for Vancouver."

"Vancouver. That might explain why you haven't heard from him." Helen slapped her hands against her knees, as if that settled the matter. "Poor guy. He'll be in one of those work camps. Our Prime Minister's answer to unemployment."

Another cold shiver went down Cat's back. She opened her mouth to ask if the work camp was one of the camps without the Hobo Code.

"Well, well, so here you are," a cheerful voice interrupted.

They both turned and there he was, his sturdy frame radiating security and strength, reminding Cat of her father. His smile drifted all the way up to bright blue eyes, crinkling the corners. He took off his cap, flourished it in a circle, and bowed low to Cat.

"Washed and dressed fresh. How do I look?" He grinned at Helen. "Thanks to Mistress Helen here. She cleaned and pressed my suit. A fortunate man I am. Two m'ladies at his beck and call." His eyes darkened, and Cat thought he looked sad, but the moment passed. He threw back his head and grinned at them.

"Oh, you are so full of it," Helen said, laughing. She pointed at him and whispered loudly to Cat. "He's kissed the Blarney Stone, you know."

Cat was glad to see him if only to quit answering Helen's pointed questions. Sir did indeed look pressed. He wore a blue shirt open at the neck. There was fraying around his trouser hems and jacket cuffs, but he looked neat in what her mother would call a '*suit of good cloth.*' His black curls were drooping wetly over his forehead.

Helen rose and went over to him. Her voice was low, but Cat heard her say, "She shouldn't be here."

"Ah, but the Lady is desperate to find news of her father, Helen," Sir replied. He spread out his hands. "Who are we to tell her she shouldn't? Besides, aren't I born to make sure she stays safe? If it isn't us, who and where might it be? She will only find another place where people are, well, you know, bad."

"But the townspeople might have different ideas. There'd be trouble if they think we are sheltering a kid from the town. And what about Sam?"

Sir's eyes narrowed. "What about him?"

"He wasn't happy being chased away. I've seen him around. He's got it in for you."

Sir chased her concern away with a wave. "I know that Helen, and I'm careful. And as for the town, we stay on the outskirts." His eyes dropped, but Helen read his expression and latched on to the message.

"You know this place, this city, don't you? I guessed there was something. A man like you doesn't hang around for no reason. Was there trouble?"

Sir didn't reply, only smiled again. "Right now, my priority is Cat, and her task. Besides, we're very lucky that she likes us too and having children around reminds us that life has a future. Wouldn't you agree, Helen?" Sir pulled a small package from his pocket. "Here, Mistress, a bit of meat for the stew pot."

"Where . . . ?

"Ask not, and you'll hear no lies," Sir replied, blue eyes laughing at her again.

Helen took the package and started back to her vegetables, swiping a hand at him on the way by. "You're lucky you are fine looking too, Mr . . . ah, *Sir*. Otherwise, we might run you out. I know you'll keep her safe. And she's lucky to have you too. Get lost now. I've no time to be jabbering away."

Sir began walking away, waving Cat to come with him. "She's a nice woman, that Helen, but she's too sharp sometimes. I bet she quizzed you without mercy too." He chuckled at Cat's expression, then added, "Come on. We'd best get to the Salvation Army soup kitchen at the end of East Avenue. A train gets in at noon, and the newcomers to town will be lined up for food. We might learn something about your father."

"I know another soup kitchen across town if we don't find anyone at the Sally Ann, At the Lutheran church—"

"No." Sir shook his head and said firmly, "We'll stay away from that one." He stopped talking and increased his step.

Cat hurried after him, surprised, but accepting. Perhaps he was afraid they would try and convert him into going to church.

The lineup was shortening when they arrived. Sir led her into the building and the line of counter at the front where two Salvation Army ladies in their blue uniforms were dishing out soup and bread.

Sir got a bowl filled with a soup of vegetables and bits of chicken floating on the top. The ladies gave Cat a head to foot inspection before looking at each other, their expression questioning. Sir put his hand on Cat's shoulder and at stared them until Cat was handed a bowl of soup as well. The woman had to tip the pot to get the last bit out. "We need another pot," she said to the other.

Cat and Sir continued down to the end of the hall, lined on both sides with long tables and set with spoons. Sir nodded and smiled at the men beside them and across the table, murmuring a good day. One or two nodded acknowledgement, but for the most part, the men stared blankly with hollow eyes devoid of hope, faces gaunt and dried like they'd been in the sun too long.

Cat broke a piece of the bread and pushed it into her mouth. It was still warm and crusty. She picked up her spoon. The soup smelled good too.

Two men sat down across from them. One rested his elbows on the table and held his head. The other closed his eyes and sighed, then patted his companion's shoulder in sympathy.

"Where's your soup?" asked Sir. At his tone, Cat put down her spoon without tasting hers.

"They ran out," said one. "We asked if we could sit here and rest a bit." He eyed their soup and swallowed hard.

Sir pushed his bowl and bread over. "We had a good breakfast," he said, explaining. "We don't need this as much as you do. He looked at Cat. "Do we Cat?"

Cat immediately pushed her soup and spoon across the table. "I had a piece of the bread," she apologized.

"That's no matter," said the man. "Thank you kindly."

His companion agreed. He pulled the bowl of soup close, picking up the spoon. "We ain't had nothin' to eat in two days," he mumbled through a bite of bread.

"There's another soup kitchen across the tracks along the West Avenue if you're still hungry after," Cat volunteered.

"You just arrived?" Sir asked. At the other's nod, he continued conversationally. "From where may I ask?"

"We started out from Vancouver early yesterday morning."

Sir smiled. "Well, maybe you can help us out. We're looking for a man who travelled the rails to Vancouver. His name is Charles Perkins. Have you run into a Charlie at any time?"

"Who wants to know?" the other man asked in between chews. His left arm curled around the bowl, protecting it from any intruder. He took another spoonful of soup, slurping noisily.

"Now, Russ. That's not our business," his companion said. He seemed to be the leader of the two.

"Yeah," piped up the man next to Sir. "Seeing he gave you his soup and all."

Sir laughed and waved the objection aside. "Maybe I should explain. Charlie is the father of this girl here. She hasn't heard from him since he left. We wonder if anyone has talked to him or seen him in a camp off the rails."

"That's different." Russ waved his spoon. He exchanged looks with his partner, who hesitated then nodded.

"What's his name again?" the other man said. "Perkins or Charlie? No, I wish I could say I know him, but I never ran into him. Have we Russ?"

Russ shook his head 'no' and drank up the last of his soup right out of the bowl. "Unless he's at another work camp. If he is, he's doomed."

Cat shivered and looked at Sir.

"Another work camp?" Sir asked quickly.

Russ had suddenly become talkative. The other men within earshot leaned forward to listen, some nodding their heads. "If he's in one of Bennet's work camps, he won't get out much. It's more like a slave camp."

Slave? Cat shook her head. Sir put his arm around her shoulders.

"Careful, Russ," his companion interrupted.

"Well, only what I call a slave, Missy," Russ said, a small smile creasing his tanned face. He didn't look like he smiled often. "They get twenty cents a day for a forty-four-hour week. It supposed to cover meals if that's what you call them."

"You sound familiar with the camp," Sir remarked.

"Me and Steve were in there," Russ said to sympathetic remarks from the men around them.

"I heard they were infested with bugs too," one man said. "And beatings." He got a poke in the ribs from the man beside him as Cat gasped.

"Fights between vagrants," Sir whispered to her. "Not your dad's way, is it?"

Cat sat up, defiant. "My father would never put up with being a slave," she said boldly. "And he would never fight either."

Another piped up. "A man can always leave if he can't take it. Like you two."

He got a disgusted look in return. "If you leave, they put out a vagrancy charge on you, so you have to get out of town fast. And avoid the railway bulls."

"Everybody knows about the railway bulls," said another man. Cat and Sir nodded with the rest of them.

"If they tell you to get off the train, you'd better get off running," said another, followed by murmurs of agreement all along the table.

"Didn't the government order the camps closed this year?" Sir put in.

Russ laughed. A derisive bark. "If they did, nobody told the camp bosses."

The man called Steve looked at Cat and said, "Don't worry young missy. Your dad would be mighty desperate to stay in a camp, even if he ever was in one. Maybe he took another name. A lot of us take on different names."

"My dad looks a lot like Sir, here," Cat said hopefully. "Except his eyes are brown like mine. Have you seen anybody that looks like him?"

All eyes swiveled from Cat to Sir and back to Cat again. Sir grinned at her, his blue eyes teasing. "By my faith, don't I have my very own good looks?"

"We seen a few hundred men like him. But can't recall anyone with eyes the color of yours."

"We only worked in the camp in Vancouver," Steve added. "So he could be at building roads outside Vancouver and not able to write."

Sir rose, as a signal they wouldn't learn anything else. Disappointed at another day with no success, Cat rose too. Sir reached into his trouser pocket and laid two quarters in front of the men. "I have a job," he said, waving away Steve's protest and Cat turned her face away, in case her expression reflected his lie.

By two in the afternoon, Sir and Cat walked near the pottery factory. They headed across the railroad siding, taking a shortcut to a small creek in the nearby coulee, expecting to find vagrants camping there.

Sir didn't talk as he usually did while they walked. Cat wondered if he was thinking it was time to move on. The thought depressed her. She had come to rely on him.

"I haven't said thank you yet," she began.

Sir looked at her as if surprised to find her there. "I'm sorry Cat, I've been miles away. Thank me for what?"

"For taking me along to ask about my dad. I'd never think of going to the places you've taken me. I'd probably just wait for the men to get off the trains and go to the camp." She thought about Helen's warning of the camps. "He needs to come home or . . ." She stopped.

"Or what?" asked Sir.

"There's a man who keeps coming around to the house. My mom is beginning to . . ." Cat kept her head down, knowing she shouldn't be discussing her mother with other people. But she trusted Sir to understand. "My dad always made the decisions, and now my mother thinks she has to be both mother and father. But now *he* is starting to make decisions for her. And then Alex . . ." She swallowed hard, not liking what she was thinking.

"Who is Alex?" Sir asked gently and squeezed her shoulder.

"My brother. He was twelve."

"*Was* twelve?" He cleared his throat. "What happened to Alex?"

"Mom sent him to a farm to work. He died."

Cat looked up at Sir. His eyes were closed, and his lips pinched together in anger.

"And this man who comes to your house. He had something to do with Alex being on the farm?"

"Yes. Maybe." Cat shrugged. "I don't know. That's why I have to find out where my dad is!" she burst out, rushing her words. "If people haven't seen him before, they might sometime. And they can tell him I was asking." She looked up at Sir, her face earnest. "So I have to say thank you. Besides, now, you're my best friend." She smiled up at him, wanting him to think she was joking when deep down she wasn't joking at all.

He studied her face, patiently considering all her words. "I'm your best friend, am I? I'm happy to hear that. But there's no need to thank a best friend, Cat." His mouth turned down at the corners in a way she'd never seen before, and he muttered, "For sure, best friends don't need to feel guilty because you did them a favor."

That puzzled her. She didn't feel guilty. Just grateful. She opened her mouth to tell him, but he was grinning down at her, in the old twinkling way. As if he knew all along what had been in her mind. "Anyhow, you remind me of someone I knew a long time ago." He paused and took her hand in his. "But people like me must keep moving in this city and not stay too long in one place, like the camp, or the soup kitchen, for instance. Otherwise, the police feel a duty to move us along."

Relieved somewhat, she took it to mean he wasn't moving soon, and he confirmed it, rather grimly.

"I have things to do and can't leave just yet."

"Everybody goes someday," she told him.

He looked startled. "Yes, I suppose so. But your father will return sooner or later."

"And my brother, Joe," she added without thinking. She looked at him, alarmed.

"Another brother? I've just assumed . . . well, anyway, is he older?"

"Yes," she said, resigned now it was out. "He is twenty minutes older than I am. I was a surprise. They weren't expecting mo. September is our birthday. He was my best friend before I met you."

"He's barely twelve, and he's riding the rails?"

Her head began to buzz. A small sound escaped her.

"Are you alright?"

Her throat felt clogged with dust. She forced out, "Yes," then explained, "Joe was sent to a farm, but he hopped a freight instead. He went to find my dad, to tell him to come home and be with my mom. But Joe promised to come back. He might even be back at the farm where he's supposed to go. It isn't far." The buzzing stopped, and she smiled up at him, relieved.

"Well, you'll hear soon I'm sure."

She heard the doubt in his voice and frowned. It was stupid to say Joe might have come back. If he had found their dad, he wouldn't have gone to the farm. She didn't want Sir to think she was a liar. "I miss him."

"Yes. I know," Sir said, and after a pause, added, "I had a sister," then so softly she barely heard him, "Once."

"Where is she?"

He hesitated so long she regretted asking. Finally, he shrugged. "She's gone." And before she could find out where his sister was living, he said, "Any other family at home?"

"My sister, Rose," answered Cat, grateful they were off the topic of Joe. "She's almost eighteen and has a good job. And Harley. He's sixteen." Should she say it would be nice to have a big brother if he wasn't always in a temper? "It's like he lives somewhere else," she said instead.

"He's working on a farm too?"

"No. He's at home. Mom wanted to send him to a lumberjack camp up North somewhere, but Harley won't go. He won a medal when he graduated from school, and he could go to higher school in Edmonton, but . . ."

"He's sixteen and finished school already?"

"Yes. He figures in his head. Math and Trig . . . trig."

"Trigonometry?" Sir asked, and she nodded.

"Good heavens. So why doesn't he go?"

"Mom said it would be a waste of time going on to another school if there's no jobs. He should find work, and make the best of it."

He shook his head and muttered something under his breath.

"We have another brother," Cat said, not liking the solemn mood overtaking them. "Young Charlie. He's only eight. He's named after my dad, so we call him Young Charlie. Everybody loves him. He doesn't remember the way it used to be anyway. He thinks everyone gets relief money."

They came to the tracks connecting the pottery warehouses to the main railway line. Cat nimbly scrambled up the scree of the train ballast and balanced on a rail, stepping along with her arms spread wide. She jumped off the track, and they continued together over the ties and down the other side of the ballast. A faint smell of sage radiated in the hot, dry air, and she sucked in her breath, almost tasting the spice on her tongue. They continued away from the pottery towards the creek in the coulee fifty feet ahead of them.

"Barely twelve," repeated Sir, shaking his head.

"It feels older," Cat stated. Sir patted her shoulder, and they carried on in silence.

At the coulee, they inspected a campfire beside a small creek where four vagrants poured them coffee from a pot on a makeshift spit over a small fire. "We got a few sandwiches if you care to share," a tall, thin man said, after giving them a close inspection.

Cat's stomach rumbled in response, but Sir shook his head and said they had been to the soup kitchen at the Sally Ann. They all looked blank when Sir went through his routine of questions about her father. Sitting under the shade of wild chokecherry bushes, the men sipped coffee and exchanged news.

"We caught a freight out of Central B.C.," one said. "It was full of horses and the smell ain't so nice, to use a polite word." He inclined his head sideways towards Cat. He unfolded a sheet of newspaper and began to break apart a number of cigarette butts, collecting the tobacco into a small tin. Sir reached into his pocket and handed the man a packet of cigarette paper, and he nodded his thanks. He spotted the violin case Cat carried on her back. "Can you give us a tune?"

Cat became suddenly shy. "It belongs to my brother, Joe. My mother forbids me to play. She says it is unseemly for girls to play the violin." Then, not wanting to be uncharitable with someone who had willingly answered questions and offered them food, Cat opened the violin case. "I'll do the best I can."

After a few tune-up passes, she broke into *Little Brown Jug*. The presence of the others flew from her mind as she became absorbed in the instrument. When she finished, she looked at Sir looking for approval. His expression flickered between surprise and sadness. Maybe he didn't think it was very good? Embarrassed, she turned her face away from them all and stowed the violin back into the case before they could ask her to play again.

The man with the cigarette tin asked, "How'd you learn to play like that?"

"My mother makes Joe practice in the bedroom with the door closed, and I go with him. She doesn't know I play." She blushed at the confession. *I hope Sir doesn't think I'm sneaky*, she thought.

Before they left, Sir said something to the men, and one put a hand in his well-worn carryall and brought out two sheets of writing paper and an envelope. Sir offered a cent for each, but the man waved it away, and they left, walking back along the rail spur leading to the outside kilns at the pottery. At one point, Sir stood still, eyes fixed far down the street. Cat followed his gaze and saw a man leaning against a lamp post. A brief moment later, he vanished from sight around the corner. Something in the way he moved seemed familiar. A policeman? She turned toward Sir who stared hard at the sidewalk, frowning.

"Cat," he said finally, "I need your help. It isn't very hard, or I wouldn't ask you. Do you know Mr. Muir and his son who live over by Waterloo Park?"

She nodded, eager. "Mrs. Mann is the housekeeper. I do chores for her sometimes."

"I may have to go away suddenly, you know, if the police send me on. I'd like you to go to their house and tell Mr. Muir's son about how you found me. Don't worry, you can trust him." He gave a weak smile. "I'll write a letter explaining everything. Can you do it?"

"I can."

Sir stared up at the ring around the sun, smelled the wind, and said to her with a laugh, "It seems we are in for another dust storm." He held out his arm and bowed. "Pray, my good lady, shall we make haste to shelter and stable our noble steeds before they are blown away over the moon?"

Delighted, Cat bowed her head and curtsied. "Yes, Sir Knight, lead on." Both laughing, they ran toward the large brick kilns standing in the pottery yard. At least one would be empty and cooling before they brought in the next load for firing. They didn't have to search, as a line of people were filing through the doorway, including the men they had just left by the creek.

As the storm hit with a vengeance, more people crowded into

the kiln. Sir led Cat behind two twenty gallon crocks the pottery workers had moved into the kiln out of the storm. There was just enough space just for her. She sat down with the violin beside her on the dusty floor.

"You'll be safe here, Cat. If any fighting or arguing starts, stay down and don't get caught up in it."

She saw him find a space across the kiln where he could keep an eye on her. He lit a candle and others did the same. For a while she watched the shapes drifting back and forth in the gloom as they settled down. Lulled by the soft murmurs of people, she stretched full length on the floor with her head resting on the violin case. But even as the wind whirled and moaned up against the kiln, her eyelids drooped and the next thing she knew Sir was shaking her awake.

"Storm's over, Cat. You should go home. Your mother will be worried about you."

He led her over to the door and outside into the dusty air. Most of the people had gone. "Have you far to go?" Sir asked, absently. His eyes swiveled around the whole area as if searching for someone.

Still groggy with sleep, she shook her head. "It's only a few blocks."

He turned then and ruffled her hair. "Goodbye Cat. Take care you go home right away. You've been gone all day. I don't want your mother to come after me for keeping you out." He held out her violin case. As she reached out for it, he said, "Your violin case had a tear in the lining, Cat. You should take it in to Mr. Levinson before it gets worse." He held on to the case while staring at her as if to stress its importance.

"I will first thing tomorrow," she promised, and he seemed satisfied. He gave her a little shove to get her going, giving her the impression he was anxious to be rid of her. After a few steps, she turned for a last wave, but he was already moving away.

A man alongside a neighboring kiln watched her walk down the road towards home.

Just before turning down the street leading to her house she remembered the letter Sir was going to give her for Mr. Muir. Sir must have forgotten. She turned and started back.

THE next day at the camp, she searched for him, but Helen said he had not been seen since the storm. But she looked worried. "Pete's probably moved on, Cat, and you shouldn't come here again. We're all sorry to see him leave, but nobody can dodge the police forever."

Cat's stomach convulsed into a knot. An uneasy image wormed into her consciousness but that space was already too full, and a door slammed shut against the intrusion, calming the nausea rising in her throat and leaving her in peace again.

3

WITH a stare that would freeze bullets in mid-flight, Fergus Muir scowled across his desk at his accounting student, Max Levinson.

"You accepted this inventory figure from Fred Mercier and didn't argue about it?" Fergus laid his palm on the paper laying on his desktop, barely able to resist balling it up and throwing it at the young man. Temper on the fringe of his tongue, he resisted adding his next thought. *Yesterday's storm filled your head with dirt?*

The corner of Max's mouth twitched. "I did object, but Mr. Mercier just looked around the store and said '*same thing as last year.*'" Max grinned full out, expecting Fergus to share the joke. "Maybe he's right. He'd know if his inventory had changed a great deal."

Fergus put his other hand flat on the desk and leaned over towards Max. "And what do you think now Max? If you ever have the good fortune to become a Chartered Accountant, would you accept that an inventory stays exactly the same, year after year?" He raised his brows watching his apprentice and after a pause saw that Max finally heard the deadly edge to his voice, or else he connected the redhead-temper adage. Grin fading, Max's gaze dropped downwards to the edge of Fergus's desk.

"Well, Max?" Fergus prodded, watching Max's Adam's apple bob as he swallowed.

"Nothing, Sir."

"You don't think anything Max, or you're not sure? Which is it?"

"I know Mr. Mercier's stock would not remain the same, sir," mumbled Max, feet shifting.

Fergus straightened the blotter on his desk and curbed his

irritation with difficulty. He sighed, detesting the energy it took to cool his mounting anger as much as the anger itself. But he continued, relentless.

"No, it isn't the same. Although you're willing for me, as head of this Firm, to sign off on a financial statement that says it is?" Fergus dipped his head, trying to catch Max's eyes, still lowered to the floor.

Max finally lifted his head to look at Fergus. "I'll go back and get the correct amount, sir."

Fergus slapped his hands on the desk and rose. He yanked his suit jacket from the back of his chair. "Never mind. I'll go myself."

Max stood straighter and squared his shoulders like someone facing his execution. "Am I fired, Mr. Muir?"

One arm in his suit jacket, Fergus stopped to eye Max. Sighing, he slipped his other arm inside and shrugged the jacket on. He got his straw fedora from the coat tree in the corner and let Max stew while he inspected it.

"You aren't fired Max," he said but gave no quarter. "Just use this lesson wisely. There are responsibilities . . ." He stopped, knowing whatever he said would sound preachy and returned his hat to the clothes tree. Pointing to a console table against the wall, he said, "Grab those books. It's a new garage over the river. See if you can take it to the trial balance." Fergus pushed past Max and left the office.

Less than half an hour later, he approached the grocery store at the corner of Union Avenue and Trotter Street. A shaft of sunlight followed him inside, lighting up the oiled floorboards and he inhaled the familiar aroma of cheese, tobacco, spices, and coffee beans that greeted him. Shelves lined the walls, stocked with assorted canned goods, cereals, laundry soaps, packaged baking supplies, and spices. Bags of flour and sugar were stacked on the bottom shelf. Smaller notions sat on shelves behind the counter, along with tea and coffee. Fergus spotted the shop owner ducking a small collection of pots and pans hanging from the ceiling to place a new sign on the back of the cash register that advertised '*Sugar 5 lbs. for 28 cents*' and underneath, '*Pears soap, 15 cents*.'

For a moment reality shifted, and he was ten years old again. Automatically dropping his head to shorten his six feet, he slouched along peering into the display cases lined up along the store. Nothing in the store had changed, and as he'd done those years ago, he stopped before the glass containers of bulk candy items. Licorice balls, gumballs, licorice cigars, and jawbreakers—bruisers were his favorite. He chose one, then continued toward Fred who was now threading a new roll into the wrapping paper unit next to the register and a weighing scale. Fergus displayed his licorice cigar and slapped a penny on the counter.

"Five for a penny," Fred corrected. He flapped open a paper bag and selected Chiclets gum and three jawbreakers. Fergus slid it into his pocket without comment and got down to business.

"Fred, about your inventory. You expect me to believe it never varies year after year. It isn't true, and you know it."

"The estimate is good enough." Fred finished threading the new wrapping roll and ripped a piece off the cutter for emphasis. "If the Feds want to count it, they're welcome. Bennett can do it. His so-called *New Deal* is the reason we're worse off than the East. While he's here, he might realize what his blasted policies did to us. We'll sell him a buggy."

A fleeting image of R.B. Bennett handling two horses pulling a car with a missing engine swam before Fergus's eyes. When gasoline prices rose to ten cents a gallon, farmers with larger farms had no extra money to buy the fuel for their powered machinery. What crops grew couldn't be harvested, making the farm situation worse. Horse power took over the automobiles. The result became a Bennett Buggy. The Prime Minister's irrigation project was a colossal failure. In any case, it was old news, and Fergus was tired of listening to the obvious.

"Accountants aren't magicians, Fred. There's no use grumbling. The tax collectors would love to come down on you like a ton of bricks if you don't file, or worse, don't pay up."

"Next thing there will be a tax on our beds, our meals—even the bald spot on my head. I don't sell enough to feed a coyote."

Enough to feed a whole pack of them, thought Fergus. The anger lying just below the surface began to make his head ache. The Mercier brothers, Fred and Thomas, did good business from this store and the separate meat market next door, although at a reduced profit from six years ago. Fred would know to the penny the value of goods he carried. *Either provide the needed inventory figure, Fred, or find another accountant.* He sifted the idea through his head imagining Fred's response, enjoying a reckless satisfaction that Fred might accept the dare.

Fred eyed Fergus's tightened lips. "You haven't inherited any of your father's diplomacy, have you? I guess it's true what they say about red hair and temper."

"Auburn," Fergus corrected automatically, thinking of Isobel. She always said it was the color of cinnamon.

Fred snorted. "Auburn, red. What's the difference?" He crossed his arms. "Maybe I should find a new auditor."

Fergus thought of leaping across the counter and grabbing Fred by the throat. He imagined the bushy eyebrows rising up to meet the bald dome, then immediately felt shame. Fred always blustered about something. Still, he tested him. "If you think it in your best interests."

He got a pensive stare in return, then Fred waved his hand dismissively. "Oh, just relax and eat your licorice. Wait here." He headed to the back, muttering about politicians and how the income tax was supposed to have been only temporary to pay for the war.

The door spring squeaked, and the two women came into the shop, whispering. Fergus recognized them both from the times Mrs. Mann hosted Church Auxiliary gatherings at the house. As chair, she hosted often, and Fergus always made himself scarce. Their purpose was to devise plans to raise funds to be used on good works for the church. *A bunch of old gossips.*

Remembering his manners, he put his hand up to tip his hat then realized he hadn't brought it. He saluted with a licorice pipe instead. "Ladies," he said. "Ah . . . Mrs. Fletcher and Mrs. Novak, I believe?"

"Isn't it terrible?" Mrs. Fletcher started. A round woman with a round face, she darted button eyes around as though the terrible thing might be lurking in the corner.

Fergus grunted under his breath. *Some lazy woman's washing not hung out until noon?*

"The murder!" They chorused together as if reading his unspoken thought.

"What murder?"

"The man's body at the pottery, dear. In the kiln," Mrs. Novak said a trifle louder, as though Fergus might be deaf. "Early this morning. Someone went to prepare the kiln for the next load to be fired, and found him." She flapped her tongue on the roof of her mouth. "That's what comes of letting hobos sleep there. We'll be murdered in our beds next." They leaned back, one plump, one slim, poised like a pas de deux waiting for applause.

"Probably vagrants drunk and fighting," Fergus consoled them. It would be forgotten in a few days. *The police won't bother. Their motto is walk slow to a fight, and fast to a fire.*

Fred Mercier came out from the rear of the store and handed Fergus a sheet of paper. "Try your magician stuff with this."

"Oh, you're back from holidays, then," interrupted Mrs. Fletcher, her tone implying he shouldn't be taking holidays. Fred flashed a smile at her which barely uncovered his teeth. "It's nice to see you too, Mrs. Fletcher. And what can I do for you today?"

Mrs. Novak broke in, "Have you heard about the murder in the kiln?"

Not waiting for a reply, Mrs. Fletcher repeated the news and Fergus took the opportunity to slide out the door behind them. He checked his watch, wondering if it was late enough in the day for a glass of Glenlivet. As if it mattered.

Fergus returned to his office and worked on Fred's account, producing a draft copy of the statements to his satisfaction. Through his open door, he spotted Max, his shock of black curly hair sticking up in every direction, a sure sign he was unsettled. Fergus sauntered past him to the file cabinet then stopped by Max's desk and peered over his shoulder at the worksheet spread out in front of him.

"How does the trial balance look, Max? Reasonable? You don't seem happy. Is there something out of place that catches your eye?"

Max wavered for a moment then said, "Everything looks fine, Mr. Muir. But it doesn't balance." Fergus leaned over Max's shoulder for a closer look and the young man ducked his head away.

Startled, Fergus registered the flinch. He glanced over at Miss Watts, his secretary. Back straight against her chair, blond head studiously turned toward her typewriter, she rolled a sheet of paper into it. Ignoring them, she finished centering the sheet and snapped the paper bail firmly against the platen. The sound echoed through the room.

"How much is it out?" Fergus asked calmly. An unwelcome twinge of unease intruded into the back of his mind at the status of his office relationships. *Ignore it. A little fear makes for an efficient office.*

Max paused before replying, then mumbled, "Seventy-two dollars. I can't see it anywhere."

"Ah. It's only a transposition," Fergus said. "Nothing major. If the error is divisible by nine, then you have transposed a figure somewhere. For a seventy-two-dollar error, you would have written nineteen instead of ninety-one or vice versa."

Fergus left a relieved Max and went for lunch, telling Miss Watts he'd be back at two if anyone needed him. Today as always it was above a hundred degrees, and upon exiting the building, the heat fell over him like a cloak. He pulled his hat down to shade his eyes from the dazzling sun then removed his suit jacket. Using his finger as a hook, he slung it over his shoulder and headed down Third Street and across the railroad tracks to Fifth Avenue for the twenty-minute walk to his house. When he reached the boulevards lined with old poplar and cottonwood trees, he slowed down to take advantage of shade, relishing the sun sparkling through the leaves of the tall trees whose branches arched over the road. Walking alongside the edge of Waterloo Park, he forgot the morning irritants, calmed by the swish of sprinklers tossing long streams of water over grassy areas. *Do the people in Cypress Landing appreciate all our aquifers when every other town is drought-stricken?* he wondered.

Fergus passed three young girls. One on each end of a skipping rope heaved it around in a large circle, while the third girl hopped nimbly as it passed beneath her feet.

"On the Corner, stands a Lady/Who she is, I do not know/All she wants is gold and silver/All she wants is a fine young man. So call in my sister, or my very best friend/Call in my very best friend/While I go out to play."

Good grief, thought Fergus, as he dodged past them. Where would they learn a chant like that? Yet he knew many young girls forced to leave their impoverished families did feel their only recourse was to stand on street corners to make a living.

Two blocks from his house, he spotted Lex Rideout leaning over his front gate looking toward him. Lex was early middle-aged, shorter and heavier than Fergus. What was left of his hair Lex combed forward, which Fergus thought only emphasized his receding hairline.

Fergus nodded as he passed.

"Fine day," said Lex. "Have you seen the postman yet? He's late today." His adenoidal voice made his words seem to emerge through his nose, broken during his early rugby playing days. It had likely been broken several times until it couldn't be straightened again.

"No." Fergus had never seen the postman during the lunch hour. "How's business, Lex?" He didn't really want to know. Nobody's business was great these days.

Lex was the marketing manager of Cypress Glasbottle. *'Glass for every occasion. You describe it; we'll produce it.'*

As expected, Lex waggled one hand back and forth in a so-so motion. "I see a crew of vagrants working in your yard today." He stared straight at Fergus with pale blue eyes. "You ever catch them stealing?" He grinned, revealing a row of white teeth that seemed too many for his small mouth.

"They wouldn't get past Mrs. Mann."

"You must hear the latest gossip, though. They know everything before we do." Hinting for news, his stare didn't waver from Fergus, and when Fergus's expression didn't change, he visibly relaxed. "I wouldn't use them. I'd rather care for the yard myself, especially my roses."

"Yes, I've heard the roses are champion," Fergus said.

Lex gave him an unexpected sharp look. "Who told you that?"

Surprised at the remark's attention, Fergus shrugged. "I don't know. Probably heard it from one of Mrs. Mann's church ladies," he said, not knowing what else to say. "Something about if you entered them in the annual fair, nobody else would have a chance."

"I might just do that," Lex's grin showed his delight at the prospect of winning.

Fergus matched his smile. "A champion coach of the high school rugby team and a champion grower of roses. You're a man of diverse talents, Lex."

"A man needs goals. I have to keep my mind occupied."

"Yes," said Fergus, not rising to the bait this time. Since the disappearance of his wife four or five years ago, he never missed a chance to appeal for sympathy.

"Well, let's have a game of golf soon." Lex hurried into the yard like a busy man with no time for idle chatter. Fergus continued to the end of the next block and his house, thinking of their last game of golf. Lex's competitive instinct had shown up in spades as he squared off against Fergus, showing off his score in the clubhouse as he waited for his reward of beer. Lex wasn't interested in a game just for companionship, thought Fergus now, but still, the rivalry made him increase his own efforts. He reached the wrought iron gate opening to the yard.

Although in the unfashionable north end of the Flats on Fifth Avenue, the house was well sited near the river and Waterloo Park. The large two-and-a-half story Craftsman style house lay in a half-acre plot, fenced along the street side with wrought iron railings joined to brick posts. Mature Ash and Elm trees and shrubbery provided privacy to the house and yard. A wide verandah sheltered the front and west side of the house. Tapered posts anchored to square brick pedestals shored up the overhanging roof, while baskets of geraniums spaced between the pedestals provided decoration and discouraged mosquitoes. The red brick, manufactured nearby, had weathered over the years to a mellow rose. Fergus paused, appreciating the house as though after a long absence. He could see the hollow chinks in the brick posts he and Peter had used for their slingshot target. They had broken a few flower pots with improved aim. The large elm tree in the back still had two nailed boards, grown along with the trunk, part of a ladder for the long gone tree house.

The large house was made for children, a brood of children and grandchildren, he thought. The rooms should echo with laughter and noise, the yard strewn with bikes and toys, the iron railings ringing with the clatter of sticks run along its metal rungs. Not liking the direction of his thoughts, Fergus continued into the yard and took the steps up the side veranda to the double glass doors leading into the dining room. An over-fed pale yellow Labrador retriever met him, tail wagging in ecstasy. Fergus patted him on the head—"Good boy, Duke"—and scratched the dog's ear. Straightening, he looked towards the rear of the property, at a storage shed for yard tools. Beside it stood the original carriage house now converted into a garage with an apartment up above. The home of the housekeeper, Mrs. Mann.

Fergus stopped to watch the activity in the back garden. Potatoes, turnips, and carrots, lay in heaps, ready for winter storage in the root cellar. Three men picked the remaining vegetables, while others cleared cucumber, tomato, and marrow vines or were turning over the earth. Every day, as a result of the hobo telegraph, a long line of men seeking work appeared in the alley behind the house. As a result, the garden and the yard never went without labor in return for food and a small wage.

He almost tripped over a violin case propped against the wall by the steps to the garden. Belonging to one of the worker's, he supposed. Bad fortune had made vagrants of even professionals and men with higher education. If his own father had not used an inborn sagacity and kept his investments in guaranteed blue-chip stocks, they might have been in the same boat. As it was, they lived almost better than before now prices had dropped significantly.

Mrs. Mann and a child came from the garage, each carrying a box. A faint chinking of glass against glass told him they were canning sealers. The girl caught sight of him and stopped dead. He had the strong impression he was being assessed. She was waif-like, maybe undersized, about ten he guessed. Her mess of sunlight filtered curls strewn about her head stopped his breath, the pain squeezing his chest. *Isobel.* He continued to stare after she and Mrs. Mann disappeared into the kitchen, the pain lingering. A nudge against his leg from Duke brought him back to the present. Another pat on the head and the dog went back to the shady corner of the veranda.

The dining room was pleasantly cool, a benefit of high ceilings and a shaded veranda. Fergus draped his jacket over the back of his chair and loosened his tie. His father was at the table, looking relaxed and sipping lemonade, glass held awkwardly in his knotted hands. Malcolm Muir, in his mid-sixties, had a full head of steel grey hair. His face was unlined, with a pleasant expression in spite of the obvious discomfort from dealing with crippling arthritis. He eyed Fergus with grey eyes that held a quiet acumen.

Fergus ignored his own glass of lemonade on the table and headed directly into the library and for the bottle of Glenlivet. He poured a good measure into a glass and returned to the dining room where he added water from the pitcher. He rolled the first taste around in his mouth with appreciation and sat. "Hot again."

His father nodded in reply.

Mrs. Mann entered and served the soup, a chilled version of one of her German recipes Fergus liked. She added a plate of sandwiches with an assortment of fillings in the center of the table. Minus the crusts again he noted, and idly wondered what happened to all those crusts she cut from the bread. Was there a great heap of them piling up in the pantry?

Fergus eyed his father. He seemed to be more taciturn than usual, avoiding Fergus's side of the room. "Are you feeling alright? Are you in pain?"

His father only shook his head. Mrs. Mann came from the kitchen with a tray holding a pot of tea, and a plate with slices of watermelon, fresh from the garden. Frowning at Fergus's half empty glass of scotch, she plunked the items from the tray in the middle of the table and hurried out again.

"What's the matter with her?" Fergus asked, but Malcolm never looked up, only picked up a slice of watermelon, and using his fork, began to pick out the black seeds one at a time.

Something is decidedly wrong here. Father not looking at him, Mrs. Mann not chattering away. He laid down his spoon and patted his mouth with his napkin. "Okay, I give up. What's going on?"

Malcolm looked directly at his son. The obvious pain in his eyes sent a tremor through Fergus, and he picked up his glass swallowing a good mouthful of scotch. The muscles in his father's jaw worked back and forth, and he opened his mouth to say something but shut it. Gently, he folded napkin in front of him. "The man at the kiln . . ."

Is that all it is? Relieved, Fergus twisted his mouth. "I heard about it this morning. So what?"

"Peter Davidson."

As if a hooded cobra had suddenly reared before him, Fergus sat paralyzed, face blank. His blue eyes narrowed.

His father threw down his napkin. "It's Peter Davidson," he repeated, voice now hoarse, derisive. "Your late wife's brother. You remember him? The man who saved your life in France?"

4

ORDINARY sounds—the men outside in the garden, the rattle of a dish inside—ceased, as though the world took a breath.

In the first instance, there was disbelief. "No! Not possible." Then a rush of anger as his whole being railed against this unwanted intrusion. *Why is this happening?* Finally, bile flooded his throat. Swallowing, he clenched his jaw. He pushed back from the table and put one hand over his face to shut out sparks of light dancing before his eyes. *Peter.*

"What was he doing here? I thought he was in the States." The volume and pitch of his own voice startled him, and he rose from his seat. "Why would someone do such a thing? No, you're wrong. It isn't him."

"He's been here for a week or so," said Malcolm. "Nobody knew. I don't understand why he wouldn't come to see us. I suppose it's because he's still a wanted man."

"You believe that trash? Peter stealing from his own company?"

"Are you implying that what I believe would have made a difference?" Malcolm's voice rose. "They proved there was fraud, and there's no doubt money disappeared. Sure it's trash, but Peter didn't stick around to prove them wrong, did he?" Malcolm took a sip of his lemonade and said in a calmer voice. "And there is the other thing."

"Other thing?"

"He took Lex Rideout's wife with him."

So it explained Lex waiting for him. Wanting information. He felt a momentary pity for the man before the impact of what he was hearing again overtook him. "Nuts! Another bunch of trash.

Running off with another man's wife? The whole idea is ridiculous. Peter wouldn't have changed to that extent . . ." But could he be sure? It was too late to find out. The rest of his drink went down in one gulp, and he banged the glass on the table, driving a nail into unwelcome guilt. For sixteen years, he'd deliberately cut Peter out of his life. And all for nothing. He was still living a lie.

"What about Peter's wife? You told me he married sometime after I left."

"Her name is Lois. She is in Edmonton, last I heard. Couldn't stand the whispers and stares. Moved away soon after Peter left. That's one marriage that should never have happened. In trouble right from the start."

"Why didn't you tell me all this before?"

"Why? You made it abundantly clear you weren't interested in all the gory details of our lives here at home."

"*Gory details?* Did you even bother to investigate? Or did you just accept Peter, a partner, absconded with the majority of Glasbottle's funds along with the manager's wife!"

"Of course I did!"

Fergus flushed at his scathing tone and sank back into his seat like a reprimanded child. Malcolm's features softened as the vacuum of silence sucked both their energies from the dining room. An indrawn breath at the door to the kitchen told him Mrs. Mann was listening. Of course she was.

"The company auditors were from Calgary. And he wasn't a partner. He was an employee with a minority share in Strathcona Holdings, with offices in Calgary. They bought it from the original owners who went bankrupt in '29 when Peter was the superintendent. He was being paid in shares. When Strathcona Holdings bought them out, Peter was made manager because of the value of those shares. I tried to get some information about the books so I could see what happened. I got nowhere. They refused, and why not? They are a private company . . ." Malcolm paused. "No matter how I wanted to pursue it, I wasn't well enough . . . physically." His flat tone told Fergus there was no further discussion on the matter of what he did or didn't do to investigate Peter's predicament.

Fergus ignored the message. "Who and what are Strathcona Holdings?"

Malcolm held up his hand. "I won't prattle on about the subject just to satisfy your curiosity." His grey eyes sharpened on his son. "Unless *you* plan to do something about this?"

"Me? Like what? It's a bit late isn't it?" Fergus shot Malcolm a reproachful smirk.

"Good God, Fergus. He was everything to us. You. Me. Because of him, you survived the war. You could investigate if only because he was your wife's brother. She worshiped him." Malcolm's hands trembled with emotion. "And when you left, Peter and I were consolation for each other. We had nobody else."

He reached for the teapot, then lowered his hands to his lap instead. Fergus waited in vain to hear he had willfully deserted them all with no concern for his own father and certainly not his best friend, who had no family of his own to comfort him.

The expression on his father's face conveyed his thoughts with a clarity Fergus couldn't mistake. As was his habit, he took refuge in the anger boiling up inside him. His hand closed around the crystal tumbler. He grinned in anticipation of the sound of shattered glass against the far wall. Then, as these things always do, just when he might believe that his nemesis wasn't sitting on his shoulder biding time, a familiar suffocation struck him. The room blurred, and the walls tilted, reaching for him. He looked at the windows. Were they closed? They gaped openly at him, airless, mocking. Any second now, he'd disgrace himself and make a run for the door to the open air. He gasped, shoved the tumbler away intact and squeezed both knees under the table, feeling he might vomit, forcing his breathing to slow. *Useless.*

"The police." He suggested in a low voice, his eyes closed against his pounding temples. "I know what Peter did for me"—his lips stiffening—"better than anyone. You don't have to remind me."

Beads of sweat broke out on his forehead. He forced himself to look at Malcolm. "Look. I'll check with the police, keep an eye on how the investigation goes. I'll tell them they can't treat him like some anonymous vagrant. I'll make sure they don't give up, but . . ." Fergus waved his hands sideways in a helpless gesture.

Fergus watched the last of the pale grey embers in Malcolm's eyes extinguish.

"If a thirsty man is looking for a river"—his father took one last drink and rose stiffly from his creaking chair—"he shouldn't keep returning to the desert."

He made his way out of the room in slow, limping strides, taking the last of the air with him.

5

CAT finished her morning chore, cleaning the bathroom. She scoured the tub, sink and toilet bowl with lye soap, and mopped the linoleum. Now she was helping her mother fold laundry.

Her mother handed Cat a towel. "I've laid out a fresh dress for you to put on this afternoon."

"Are we going somewhere?" Cat asked.

"Mr. Rideout is coming over soon, and I want you to stay here for a change."

"No, no, no," Cat's voice rose. "Don't make me stay. Please, Mama." She bunched up the towel and hugged it to her chest.

"Don't be silly. Mr. Rideout particularly asked that you be here. Cat, just give him a chance to know you better. Do it for me?"

"I'd rather have a hundred spiders crawl up my nose than talk to him." Cat threw down the towel and shrank away, but her mother pulled her close, challenging her.

"That's cruel and pure rot. I don't understand you anymore, Cat. You're never home, and I don't know where you are or what you're up to. You can't go running wild all through the town. People talk so."

Blinking back tears, Cat hung her head, then stood straighter, determined. "I don't care what people think because I don't run wild. You can't make me like him, and I don't know why you listen to everything he says, and never ask Rose or anybody when you decide to do something." She didn't want to push her luck by mentioning Joe or Alex. "Why do you let him tell you what to do? He isn't Daddy."

Her mother shook her roughly, face red with anger. "Stop it this instant! I won't have you talking to me like that, you hear? You'll stay here and speak nicely to him, and that's that."

"But I've promised Mr. Levinson I'd help out at the store," Cat begged. "I was supposed to be there already. Please, Mama. If I don't come, he will hire someone else. Couldn't I see Mr. Rideout the next time? Please?" She saw her mother's indecision and bolted out the door.

She wandered into the park and sat on a bench, crying. She rubbed her tears away with the heel of her hands and wandered aimlessly through the park, ending up in the alley behind the Muir house. She stood at the gate staring at the back door of the house.

An overgrown Labrador dog appeared in front of her, greeting her with a soft woof. She opened the gate and began to rub his ears. The dog's tail swished from side to side in gratitude while they grinned at each other.

The door leading to the apartment above the garage opened, and Mrs. Mann came briskly down the path to the house. A tall, thin woman with a narrow face and a pleasantly shaped mouth whose corners turned upward as if privy to a secret joke. She wore her dark hair pulled back into a knot at the nape of her neck. Cat tried to duck back through the gate before she was spotted but it was too late.

"Cat! You gave me a shock. Don't stand there, child. Come in." The housekeeper put her hand to her chest in a parody of checking her heart. "Are you looking for something to do?"

"Oh, yes, Mrs. Mann."

Mrs. Mann continued towards the kitchen door, and Cat skipped up beside her.

"It's my turn to hold the Ladies Church Auxiliary meeting tomorrow, and if you aren't busy, you can help me."

"I've never been to a grownup meeting before."

"Well, exciting is not a word I'd use," Mrs. Mann said as if reading Cat's mind. She reached for her apron and continued. "We discuss church business and explore ideas for fund-raising for the needy. You can help me with the refreshments."

Ms. Mann continued on the meeting's purpose. "Not as though any fund-raising amounts to a row of beans these days." She opened a drawer and pulling out clean dust cloths, handing one to Cat. "Most of the time, we just hope manna arrives from heaven."

Manna from heaven? Cat followed Mrs. Mann into the living room and set out dusting the porcelain ornaments. Not that any of them really needed dusting. When she came to the figure of a lady wearing an elegant blue dress and large hat, a small dog nestled at her side, Cat cradled it in her hand, carefully twisting the duster into every bend and fold, and even polished the bottom.

Mrs. Mann talked as she swept her dust cloth around. "Dust and dirt everywhere, all the time. Can't keep up. I swear it creeps in during the night like phantoms. I suppose it's the same at your house." She moved along, not bothering for a reply. While she dusted the window sill, she peered out to check on two men mowing and raking up the grass.

"Last month Mr. Muir gave me a generous amount of money to pay the men working in the yard. It was too much, and I told him so."

"What's manna?" Cat frowned, trying to visualize too much money.

Mrs. Mann stopped dusting and looked at Cat approvingly as if her favorite student in the class had finally asked the right question. She sat on the couch and patted the seat beside her, waiting for Cat before continuing. "I told him I only hire men who do an honest day's work and know the Good Lord says a man must earn his money. If we pay them too much, they would spread the word Mr. Muir was easy pickings. We'd be swamped with those only wanting a handout, and we could be in danger."

Cat thought of the Sam, the hobo Sir had driven away, and pictured him sneaking down the alley. "It wouldn't be good," she agreed.

"Mr. Muir told me to pay the men what I thought was due, then use the extra money for the soup kitchen," she said. "Unexpected gifts, Cat, or manna from heaven . . . Mr. Muir is a good man." She rose from her chair, her eyes inspecting the living room. Satisfied, Cat followed her into the kitchen.

The doorbell rang, and Mrs. Mann clucked her tongue. "Oh Lord, now who would that be?" She pointed to the shelf by the kitchen door. "Hand me my hat, if you please, Cat." She traded her apron for the hat, and Cat trailed her down the front hall, still holding the apron. Mrs. Mann stopped at the side mirror to adjust her hat, then opened the door.

A young man with a large case by his side took off his hat. "Good afternoon, madam. I've—"

"What are you selling, young man?" Mrs. Mann interrupted.

"Encyclopedias, Madam." He crooked his head towards Cat. "I'm sure your little girl would surge ahead of her schoolmates with all the knowledge included in this set of books." He patted the case on the verandah.

"I'm sorry, as you can see, I am just going out. In any case, I'm only the maid. The owner and housekeeper are not in at present. Perhaps you should make an appointment next time?" Mrs. Mann shut the door firmly before he could ask for one.

"Mmmph," she said, interpreting Cat's questioning gaze, as she took off her hat. "Saves a lot of time and the easiest way to handle the situation. If it's someone I wish to welcome, I tell them I've just come in and to wait while I take my hat off. If it's someone unwelcome like that young salesman, I say it's too bad, but unfortunately, I'm just going out, and it isn't convenient to visit. It keeps all the widows from bothering Mr. Muir as well." She pulled her face at the thought. "And I'll ask you to just keep that little piece of knowledge between you and me."

"Yes, Mrs. Mann." She covered her mouth with her hands to stifle a giggle.

Mrs. Mann smiled in return, as she switched hat with apron again. "It's proper to call first if they want to visit. Mr. Muir doesn't want to see people begging for handouts." She pressed her lips together. "As I've said before, he's too generous sometimes for his own good, and I like to think I'm here to look out for him." She clasped her hands together. "Anyway, you don't have to hear any more of that. Now, about tomorrow. What do you think we should bake for a sweet?"

"A cake maybe?" Cat couldn't think of anything sweeter than a cake.

"Yes. Maybe a boiled raisin cake? But I'm out of raisins."

So Cat found herself running the five blocks to Mercier's Grocery, for raisins and to ask if Mr. Mercier had an extra quart of milk on hand.

Returning, and just about to open the kitchen door, she froze at the sound of Mr. Muir's voice talking to Mrs. Mann.

". . . your Auxiliary meeting night?" Malcolm was saying.

"Yes?" Mrs. Mann said. "If they are any bother to you, I can arrange to have them somewhere else?"

"No, no. Far from it. No bother at all. This house is large enough to hold two meetings."

Cat strained to hear, as his voice lowered.

"I was thinking of the days when Peter would visit," she heard him say. "I miss him."

Cat sympathized with him. She missed Joe the same way. Then his voice rose, brighter, as though he had a new idea. "Your meeting," she heard. "I know what happens when a group of women get together. Well, men too, if I'm truthful," he added. Cat almost laughed out loud. The way he said it in a rush, she pictured Mrs. Mann prickling at the reference to women in groups.

Malcolm's voice became stronger, more like he was telling her, not suggesting. "I would like you to get the women talking about Peter. I mean, they hear things from people in general conversation which I would never hear. There's a mystery in Peter's death, Mrs. Mann and I don't like it. Otherwise I wouldn't suggest . . ." He coughed then, his voice trailing off, uncertain.

"Gossip, you mean?" Mrs. Mann butted in. "Gossip is all they do in this town. I don't pay it much attention, mind you."

"No, no of course not," he said. "But it might give us a clue."

Mrs. Mann agreed. "I know what you mean. Any information is better than no information. And those women make it a business to learn more than they let on. Leave it to me. If anyone knows anything about Peter Davidson, I'll get it out of them."

Cat barely heard their last words. A shiver went up and down her spine. Peter. The woman at the camp, Helen, had called him Pete. Sir hadn't gone away. He was dead. She didn't know how she knew, but she did. Her head buzzed like bees around the hive.

Groceries forgotten, Cat sat on the stoop, head bowed over her crossed arms, and that's where Mrs. Mann found her.

THE next evening, Cat returned early to the house. Mrs. Mann's head to foot inspection confirmed she was presentable in her clean dress and polished shoes. If she noticed the dress had seen better days and the shoe polish didn't quite hide the cracks, she didn't comment. Cat took the tea and coffee pots, cups, saucers, plates, and cutlery into the butler's pantry and readied them for serving. They both assembled three-tiered sandwiches with brown and white bread; ham with lettuce, peanut butter, and super thin apple slices, and cheese and pickle. Mrs. Mann cut the crusts off and divided each sandwich into three finger-sized ones. After, she placed them on a platter, covered them with wax paper and placed them in the butler's pantry.

"You may as well come in and listen, as sit and twiddle your fingers in the kitchen." Mrs. Mann told her when all was ready. "I'll give you a sign when we serve. Most importantly, Cat, even if things get a bit strange tonight, anything you see or hear must not be repeated outside this house. Do you know what I mean?"

"Yes, Mrs. Mann." Cat nodded earnestly and chose an inconspicuous corner of the room to sit.

By eight o-clock the ladies had all arrived, greeting each other by their family names as was proper. Louisa Novak and Cassie Fletcher dressed in their best arrived first.

"Well, hello there. You're new to the church, aren't you?" Mrs. Novak smiled at Cat. Mrs. Fletcher caught her arm, and whispered something Cat couldn't catch, then pulled Mrs. Novak along, but not before Mrs. Novak turned to look at Cat again. Cat's returned stare didn't waver, but inside she was stung. *Why do people give me that funny look?*

The next to arrive was Dorothy Skefington. She was in her thirties, a spinster, and owned two beauty parlors, Mesdames and Smart Coifs. Cat thought she looked elegant in her dress with its simple lines and her hair sleek in a cropped style.

Watching Mrs. Mann welcome Miss Skefington, Cat thought of Mr. Muir's remarks and remembered Rose's opinion if people want to trade gossip, a Beauty Parlor was the best place for it.

After Mrs. Mann welcomed more arrivals, she lost no time calling the meeting to order, and Cat sat up to listen.

"First order of business," she said, "Funds. We need more funds to supply the soup kitchens and the gathering of winter clothes. Winter will be here before we know it."

"Yes, it's already getting chilly at night," said Mrs. Ramsay, a plump lady with a broad face, and short nose.

Every eye turned to her in surprise. "Really?" Mrs. Fletcher said. "It was boiling all week."

"Have you read the latest on King Edward and Mrs. Simpson?" interrupted Mrs. Collins. "He's threatening to abdicate. Imagine! She's had to leave the country."

"I should hope so," said Mrs. Horn. "Imagine an American as Queen of England! And divorced too. Twice divorced! She only chased him because he's a King."

"Oh, I don't know," Miss Skefington locked her fingers together. "So romantic."

Mrs. Mann brought the topic back into focus. "Ladies. The floor is open to fund-raising ideas, unless you think the King will solve our problems."

"How about asking the grocery stores for more produce?" Mrs. Horn asked. "Things get wormy if they sit too long. Raisins or currents, or weevils in the flour. We could ask Fred Mercier. He always sounds cranky, but he has a good heart. We could ask all the stores. Our husbands can pick up and deliver."

"I'll do it," said Mrs. Novak. "I know Fred Mercier is back from holidays. Mrs. Fletcher and I were in the other day. We saw pictures of his holiday in Vancouver. Gosh, it must have been nice to get away somewhere. He has one of those new Kodak Bullet cameras. I bet he got it wholesale, cheap. Such wonderful scenery and pictures."

Mrs. Fletcher was quick to spoil the image. "All his pictures were out of focus."

"It doesn't surprise me," said Mrs. Horn. "He's always out of something. Last week it was prunes."

"And sunshine soap," said a woman Cat knew as Mrs. Magnusson. The room dissolved into titters, Cat among them.

"Ladies, please! Let's keep to the subject." Mrs. Mann rapped her knuckles on the table. "Anything else?"

"We could put a charity box in the Assiniboia Club. They have members from both rural areas and the city. If they can spend it on liquor, they can put in a few pennies for charity."

"An Odd Sock drive?" said another woman whom Cat didn't know. "We could have a tea or gala in the church hall. Admission to be an item of clothing and odd socks. We can sort them out and match them as near as possible."

"Odd socks?" Mrs. Collins retorted. "Who has odd socks to give away? Everybody makes rag rugs with them."

"Well, they can give them to charity this time." Mrs. Horn snapped at her.

The meeting progressed from there, suggestions, rejections, and delegation.

"Mrs. Mann is volunteering to do a lot," Cat heard Mrs. Novak whisper to Mrs. Fletcher.

"She'll browbeat someone to help her, don't worry. You, for instance." Mrs. Fletcher's raspy reply grated in Cat's ear. She hadn't uttered one nice word since she arrived. Cat looked around, but nobody seemed to be listening to Mrs. Fletcher. Perhaps they were used to it.

Mrs. Fletcher continued, "My mother told me there were eight children in Mrs. Mann's family and her mother kept them all busy. If any of them complained, her mother always said she wasn't keeping dogs and barking herself."

"What does that mean?" asked Mrs. Novak louder.

"*Shhh,*" hissed the women around her.

The business part of the meeting over, Cat rose and went to collect the tea settings. Two women were delegated to set up the card tables. "Set my table up here." Mrs. Mann pointed to the side of the room. "Mrs. Horn, you and Miss Skefington, Mrs. Ramsay and I will form this table. The rest of you sort yourselves out." Carrying a tray, Cat almost collided with Mrs. Mann coming through the door into the pantry. The tray wobbled, and Cat gamely held it steady while the cups and saucers rattled together. Mrs. Mann didn't notice.

She soon came back smiling broadly carrying a loaded tray of glasses filled with a reddish liquid. "I have a treat for everybody."

"Is it wine?" Mrs. Ramsay drew a lace handkerchief from her purse and waved it in front of her face. "I cannot let liquor touch these lips."

Just as Cat came by with the teacups for their table, Mrs. Novak snickered. "I'd be surprised if anything would touch those lips."

Mrs. Mann merely smiled sweetly at Mrs. Ramsay as she laid the tray on a table. "It's only my chokecherry cordial."

The women sent out pleasurable *"ahhs."* and settled in the chairs in anticipation.

"Is it someone's birthday?" Mrs. Horn asked.

Mrs. Mann busily handed out glasses. "Not that I'm aware."

She selected a somewhat larger glass sitting a space apart in the corner of the tray and handed it with a small napkin to Miss Skefington.

"I've just finished canning and preserving. So it's a celebration. Our private Thanksgiving, shall we say. Everyone has worked so hard this year, what with the soup kitchen and our other projects. The garden gave a good bounty, and it's time we gave thanks for being so blessed."

A sea of astonished eyes turned to her, some ladies sipping their cordial and others with a sandwich halfway to their mouths. This wasn't the Mrs. Mann they knew. The down-to-earth, blunt Mrs. Mann. The one who handed out good works, but at the same time called a spade a spade and had no truck with feelings.

Miss Skefington saved her. "What a very delicious cordial, Mrs. Mann. Extra nice product this year. Can I have a bit more?" She had sampled her drink, looked in her glass with pleasant surprise, upended it and downed the rest in one swallow.

Cat took Miss Skefington's glass, but Mrs. Mann hurriedly snatched it from her and took it into the butler's pantry. She returned and handed a full glass to Miss Skefington.

"Anyone else for a refill?"

"Are you all right, Mrs. Mann?" Mrs. Fletcher asked. "Nothing wrong is there?"

Mrs. Mann shot her a glance of pure malice. "What would be

wrong? Can't I be a gracious hostess without you saying there is something wrong?"

The hostess collapsed into her chair, her narrow face creased in lines of worry. "It's the poor, poor man in the kiln. Peter Davidson. I knew him, you see. I started thinking how short life can be . . . It reminded me of Ernest." Startled at Mrs. Mann's abrupt change in disposition, Cat jerked and almost dropped the napkins she was handing out.

Mrs. Horn rose and patted Mrs. Mann on the back. "There, there, Missus. We're forgetting our manners." She shot a reproving glance at Mrs. Fletcher. It was no secret Mrs. Mann's husband had joined a team of drovers herding wild horses down to the Texas Panhandle and hadn't been seen since.

"Could I bother you for another glass of cordial?" Miss Skefington's hand fanned herself. "Oh dear, I am so thirsty. The heat you know."

"Here, I'll get it," said Mrs. Novak.

"Wait!" Mrs. Mann shot out of her chair and snatched up the glass which she took into the pantry.

"She must be really upset," said Mrs. Horn to the ladies who raised eyebrows at the sight. In the midst of offering sandwiches at another table, even Cat stared open-mouthed.

"She's embarrassed we caught her being emotional," Mrs. Horn said. "And she hates showing emotion. You should be more careful," she scolded Mrs. Fletcher.

Mrs. Fletcher defended herself. "Do you think she might have some affliction she's keeping secret? Maybe even a brain tumor?" She rotated her index finger beside her temple. Cat bristled and decided she might accidentally spill tea on Mrs. Fletcher.

The topic of conversation returned and handed the full glass to Miss Skefington, who directed a silly smile somewhere in the vicinity of her hostess.

"Well, I should just forget about Peter Davidson," she said. "And memories connected with him. Dark thoughts never did anyone any good, did they? After all—"

"I don't suppose Lex Rideout feels the same," butted in Mrs. Fletcher.

At his name, Cat slumped in her chair to make herself smaller.

Mrs. Ramsay sat up and interrupted, "You'll never guess who I saw last Sunday evening." Without waiting for a question, she added, "Remember the new gospel church or whatever it is down the far end of East Avenue, where the deserted building was? The garage which went out of business? Alfred calls them the Holy Rollers." The ladies nodded. "When Alf and I went past, the place was going full blast. You can't credit such a noise."

Mrs. Mann leaned forward with the rest of them, in spite of herself.

"The preacher at the front was waving his arms around calling them all sinners and telling them to get saved before the Lord came for them. There was a line of people standing in front of him, and the preacher shouted at the first one '*Are you ready, brother?*' Then he lifted up his hand and smacked this poor fellow square against his forehead, hard enough to knock him clear into next week. The people all started hollering. Some were actually rolling on the floor yelling rubbish and calling out for the Lord. Even if He did answer, nobody would hear with all that commotion."

"What were you doing there yourself?" From her slumped position, Cat didn't bother to wonder who had asked, being too interested in the answer.

"On our way to the band concert in the park, of course. Where else?" Satisfied, they all nodded. Nearly the whole city went to the park in summer for the Sunday evening concerts.

"So, what has all this to do with Mr. Rideout?" Mrs. Mann refocused on the subject.

"The fellow the preacher knocked on the forehead? It was him—Mr. Rideout."

Cat slouched into her chair again. The ladies sat back, collectively amazed at this revelation. They buzzed among themselves for a moment.

"Man hasn't a lick of sense being there in the first place," Mrs. Horn said.

"The poor, poor man," Mrs. Ramsay continued, reveling in the limelight. "Such a gentle man. I'd have thought he didn't need saving. But there's more."

All ears tuned in.

"His house is across the alley from ours, remember," she said. "At night when we got ready for bed? I checked whether the cat was in or out. Alfred always forgets. If I've told him once, I've told him twenty times," she complained, then caught herself. "Anyhow, when I opened the kitchen door, I heard crying from his yard, but I couldn't see anything. So I went upstairs and opened the back bedroom window to investigate."

"Nosy Parker's what she is," muttered Mrs. Fletcher. Nobody paid her the slightest attention, and Cat silently applauded.

"His kitchen door was open, and the light shone right out at him," continued Mrs. Ramsay. "I could see him sitting in his yard by a little bower he built. It's covered in a mass of those lovely roses. He was sobbing and actually talking to his wife." She looked at the faces before her and nodded wisely, emphasizing her remarks.

"Sounds like the whack on the head gave him more than he bargained for," said Mrs. Collins, breaking the silence.

"No, no." Mrs. Ramsay said. "He built it for her. A shady nook with a bench to relax and read. It's covered with climbing roses. He worshiped her, and when she ran off with Peter Davidson, he was devastated. Besides the money he took with him," she added.

Miss Skefington rose unsteadily. Holding her glass, she weaved a line towards the butler's pantry. Cat stood up, wondering if she should follow. Before she could decide, Miss Skefington returned, firmly gripping her filled glass in one hand and a bottle in the other. She snaked her way back along the same track to her chair. She laid the bottle on the small table beside her, then sat down and took a healthy sip, glazed eyes directed towards the ladies' heads.

Cat made a tentative wave of her hand to catch Mrs. Mann's eye, but Mrs. Mann's attention was fixed on Mrs. Ramsay. Cat sidled towards the small table beside Miss Skefington and reached for the bottle. The young woman put her hand out gently, and they had a minor tug of war before Cat gave in and was rewarded with a wonky smile.

"I just can't fathom it! What did he say?" Mrs. Novak asked.

"I don't know, do I?" Mrs. Ramsay sounded cross. "It was hard to understand any words from two backyards away."

The ladies sat for a quiet moment, disappointed. There were general murmurs of sympathy for Lex.

"You must have seen a lot of Clarissa Rideout," said Mrs. Horn. "Although she was never a friendly sort. Quite the snob."

"We only really spoke once as I remember. Mostly it was an odd wave or nod across the back gardens. She said they planned to move across the tracks up the hill. Lex was looking for a suitable house there. I got the feeling she thought Alf and I common people. As if a manager of Glasbottle was any better than a superintendent of Ross Greenhouses, the largest in North America! Anyway, Lex Rideout was mesmerized with her. He was forever running after her wherever she went—doting on her, spoiling her." Mrs. Ramsay rolled her eyes, as though spoiled adults were an abomination. "Maybe she liked Peter Davidson because he was different. You know if something is hard to get, they want it more." Coming from Mrs. Ramsay, it was a surprisingly astute observation.

Even Mrs. Fletcher seemed taken aback for a brief moment, then said, "Well he finally gave in, since they ran off together. Who'd think he was the sort? But still waters run deep. Or perhaps it was the money what appealed to her more. I felt sorry for Lois Davidson and was glad when she left. Saved everybody a lot of trouble. Well, really," she added to the shocked silence. "How can you treat someone normally? We wouldn't be able to open our mouths, without reminding her."

"Yes," said Mrs. Collins. "And you'd think Mr. Rideout would want to sell and all. Now more than ever. But he just sits there, talking to a wife who has flown the coop, feeling sorry for himself."

Cat hardly dared to breathe. Would they mention her mother's connection to Mr. Rideout?

Mrs. Mann had had enough. She looked around the room, her bony face wreathed in smiles. "Anyone fancy a piece of boiled raisin cake? Or more sandwiches? More tea?" Cat headed out to bring in the cake slices and plates, then stopped as Mrs. Mann said, "No? Well, then, we may as well play whist." Cat turned back to her chair, wondering if all meetings were as confused as this one.

Miss Skefington made a small sound, waved her forefinger back and forth at the ladies, mumbled something indistinguishable which sounded like "*zbloomers*," then slowly melted out of her chair to the floor.

"Oh, Lord," muttered Mrs. Mann.

Uttering cries like an out of tune chorus, the ladies closed in on Miss Skefington, all talking at once, giving advice, trying to shake her awake.

Mrs. Mann spied the bottle on the small table, neatly swept it up and hurried off, muttering, "Smelling salts."

But Miss Skefington remained immune to any life-saving techniques.

"Oh, oh, the Good Lord has taken her," Mrs. Collins cried. She threw her arms to the ceiling. "Oh Lord, hear our prayers."

Mrs. Mann rose from her knees and shook her hard. "Oh, shut up, Marion," she shouted. Startled by the use of her given name, Mrs. Collins gulped and went quiet.

Just then the door burst open, and Fergus appeared. "What in the devil is going on?" He shouted. "It's bedlam in here."

Stunned into silence by the force of Fergus's powerful form and language, the ladies all stood rooted in various stances, mutely gaping at him. Cat took the opportunity to hide behind a stuffed wing-back chair and peeked around the edge. She saw Malcolm arrive behind Fergus, take in the scene, and melt back into the hallway.

Fergus glared at them all, then spotted Miss Skefington on the floor. He kneeled beside her and put a finger to her neck.

"Is she dead?" Mrs. Collins asked in a shaky voice.

"No," said Fergus. "She has a pulse." He lifted an eyelid, peered into her exposed eye, then leaned over and sniffed. He rolled back on his heels.

"She's drunk."

He lifted her to the chesterfield, and laid her against a pillow amid small cries of "never," "impossible," and "disgraceful," around the room.

Miss Skefington opened her eyes and smiled up at Fergus. Then hiccupped, said "my hero," and passed out again.

In one accord, the ladies said hasty goodbyes and scarpered into the night. An hour later, after dosing Miss Skefington with cups of strong coffee, Fergus helped her into a taxi with Mrs. Fletcher, who took her home and helped her to bed.

THE next morning, at the tail end of serving breakfast, a grumpy Mrs. Mann offered up apologies. "The worst meeting of my life. I thought if I spiked Miss Skefington's drink, she might talk about things she hears in her beauty parlors. Otherwise, she won't say anything, in case it gets back to the ladies, and she'll lose their custom if they know she gossips their business about."

"Quite right too," Malcolm agreed. She glared at his twitching lips. "I expect you will have to put up with talk if it gets about what happened."

"*If?* Oh, Mrs. Fletcher will see it gets about. But I'll say somehow the drinks got mixed up without my knowing. Thank goodness Mrs. Fletcher is a know-it-all and people don't pay her much mind. They will believe me before they believe her."

Mrs. Mann cleared the plates from the table and stood there holding them. "You know, there is something someone said which bothers me, but I can't remember what, or who said it."

"Probably a request for more—" Fergus started to say booze, but Malcolm took his arm and pushed him down the hall to the library. Inside, he closed the door and both men gave way to laughter.

Mid-morning, Cat rapped on the door and peeked through the screen at Mrs. Mann spinning the dial on the radio.

"Come in, child. Quickly, before the flies get in too."

Cat darted through the door as ordered. She stopped just inside on the small hooked mat.

"Nothing but static," Mrs. Mann said, turning off the radio.

"Is there anything I can do today, Mrs. Mann? Help clean up after yesterday, maybe?"

Mrs. Mann drew herself up, and Cat added, "I guess nothing turned out the way it was supposed to . . . uh."

"Cat. What are you trying to say?"

Cat knew honesty was best with Mrs. Mann. "I heard Mr. Muir talking to you about Mr. Davidson." She hurried on. "I couldn't get your attention when I saw Miss Skefington was drinking straight out of the bottle. I tried to grab it from her, but she wouldn't let go. I hid behind the chair when Miss Skefington fell on the floor," she finished lamely and waited in silence for a reprimand.

Mrs. Mann's expression soured. "No, not so good. And I wasted my best cordial."

Remembering how Miss Skefington looked, Cat started to giggle.

Mrs. Mann joined in, "From your view, it must have been quite a sight. Well, don't think our meetings are all like that."

Cat came farther into the kitchen. "Where would you like me to start? Should I sweep the living room floor?"

"Goodness, Cat. Why don't you spend some time playing with your friends? Go swimming or something. They have a nice new water slide at Rotary Pool."

Cat stared down at the floor and shook her head. She couldn't tell her all the girls she approached said their mothers had forbidden them to be friends with her. She supposed it was because her family was on relief or her father had gone. She pushed away the thought of Mr. Rideout coming to the house.

"I don't have a bathing suit," she said, hoping her face didn't show the truth. "But it doesn't matter. I can't swim anyway. Besides I like coming here."

"Oh! Well then." Mrs. Mann smoothed her apron. "I'm flattered that I'm the one you think of when you want company."

"You don't mind if I come here a lot?" Cat asked, remembering her mother's remark about running wild.

"Let's put it this way. I will never think of putting on my hat when you ring the doorbell." Mrs. Mann turned away to the stove, and then back again. "In any case . . . have you eaten lunch? No. Thought so. Well, let's see what we can rustle up, then get to work. Lord knows, there is always plenty to do in this house, what with two men in it." The lines around Mrs. Mann's mouth softened, and Cat felt an unexpected nudge of happiness.

Without being asked Cat went to the cupboard and got out the cutlery.

6

MALCOLM arranged for the release of Peter Davidson's body from the coroner for burial after getting the okay by the police. On a hot and airless Friday afternoon at Restside Cemetery, the mourners clustered around the Muir family plot already containing the graves of Isobel, Maggie, and Malcolm's wife, Margaret, all dead of Spanish influenza. Fergus couldn't tear his eyes away from their headstones.

Sixteen years ago, he and Peter had leaned on each other at this very spot, both betrayed by a loss at home after seeing so many on the battlefield. Fergus touched his pocket where he carried his billfold that still held a picture of his wife and a barely two-year-old daughter he had never seen. He turned to Malcolm and read the same thought in his expression. *It's just us now; the only two left.*

The minister was into his narration, but his words didn't register even as Fergus saw his lips moving. Numb, he looked around, recognizing neighbors, then Lex Rideout who met his eye and immediately looked away, a few people he didn't know, and a client who raised a hand of sympathy. A small clutch of vagrants, neatly dressed, stood off to one side, two women with them, who were wiping away tears. Mrs. Mann exchanged nods with two of the men, and Fergus supposed they were workers in the yard. *They wouldn't be here unless they knew Peter. Was one of them responsible?* He scanned the rest of the group; a couple of policemen watching the vagrants, and a reporter, notebook in hand, watching the police watching the vagrants.

Fergus realized the minister was mentioning Peter's war record, and Military Medal for bravery at the 1918 Battle of the Canal du Nord in France. The vagrants nodded as one, but others shifted their feet, no doubt comparing an image of courage to the fraud charges four years ago. Malcolm squeezed Fergus's shoulder.

The minister droned on, "We commit the body of Peter Patrick Davidson to your keep . . . ashes to ashes . . ."

Malcolm straightened over his canes.

"May the Lord bless him and keep him. May the Lord make his face to shine . . ."

Then it was done, and people drifted away. A few shook Malcolm's hand on the way out. Malcolm laid a rose against Margaret's headstone, then another at Isobel's and Maggie's.

"Come on, Dad. Let's get out of here." Fergus put out his arm, ready to help Malcolm over the uneven ground. At the car, they both turned for one last look. A child stood at the open grave, a cluster of wildflowers in her hands. She hesitated for a moment then let the flowers fall into the chasm that was Peter's resting place, then with a flash of tanned legs, ran off into the trees bordering the paths.

"She's the girl who helps Mrs. Mann," Malcolm said. "Now why is she here?"

Ferus shrugged and turned to the road. He needed a drink—to rid his senses of the cemetery's silent decay.

ISOLATED in his room, Fergus drank. Stretched out on top of the sheets,
he propped his back against the brass headboard and recalled his father laying a rose on each of the graves. So absorbed in his own misery, Fergus had never appreciated what their deaths must have meant to Malcolm. "Dad lost his own wife, a daughter in law, and a grand-daughter," he told himself. Jealousy stabbed at him, imagining Maggie with his father; being carried about, Malcolm seeing her first steps, reading stories while holding her on his knee. Besieged by his imagination and unable to control his longings, Fergus raised the glass of scotch and drank. He knew his father was disgusted at his evasive responses to Peter's death. Jerked out of his flat, but comfortable life this past week, his memories were not so easily dismissed.

Peter, Fergus, and Isobel. Growing up together, they had run free;

explored the cliffs, wandered the prairies in the spring, hunting and eating the ripe cactus berries to the point of being sick. They tied ropes to trees in the coulees, then carried the rope to the other side and swung back, screaming the Tarzan yodel. They swam in the shallows of the river, among the garter snakes, and built crude rafts which immediately sank when launched. In the winter, they had careened down the cliff sides on makeshift cardboard sleds until the cardboard fell apart. When new snow fell, they played Fox and Goose and built snow forts and organized snowball fights.

Most women in the neighborhood had voiced disapproval to Laureen Davidson. Isobel behaved like a hoyden when she should be learning domestic things like a proper young girl. Mrs. Davidson would just smile and change the subject.

What is the point when everybody is dead except me? What grand scheme could possibly exclude everybody important to me? He set his glass on the bedside table and went to the closet, groping on the top shelf for a box. He sat on the bed, opened it and took out his service revolver, turning it over relishing the feel of cold metal against his palm. As he had done so many times before, he took it apart and started cleaning it.

MALCOLM sat in his study an open book on his lap, staring at the print without seeing it. The window faced the back garden and the edges of Waterloo Park beyond. Through the open window, he heard crickets beginning their courtship ritual, their chirps enhancing that peculiar stillness in the air that always happens just at the moment when evening lets go of the day for night.

Malcolm thought of the funeral service and the line of tragedies which had befallen his longtime friends Patrick and Laureen Davidson. *And now Isobel and Peter are gone*, he thought, *If Peter had asked for help, he'd still be alive.*

In May of 1914, Peter and Isobel's parents set out for Ireland on a visit. Their ship, The Empress of Ireland, collided with the SS Storstad in the St. Lawrence River and sank, taking over a thousand passengers, including Patrick and Laureen Davidson, with it. All the responsibility of being the head of the household fell on Peter, and he struggled to wind up their affairs.

Becoming part of the family had been a given. Isobel moved into the house while Fergus and Peter moved into a new apartment in the renovated carriage house. The large house had a family.

Violin music drifted through the open window. At first, engrossed in his thoughts, his mind dismissed the idea. When the sound persisted, he seized his cane and went through the kitchen and out to the edge of the backyard bordering the park. He stopped, ears tuned to the direction and listened. The music was an introduction, simple, but it took his attention immediately and left him wanting the next phrase. When it came, it gently spiraled upward. He closed his eyes and breathed with the notes. The resonance told him it wasn't an expensive instrument, but the clarity of the notes gliding through the dusk took precedent. For a moment it was light and merry, playful almost, then shadowed, leading gently into the melody, a lullaby. Brahms' *Lullaby and Goodnight*, and incredibly sad. A child's piece, but performed with a touch like a mother's hand brushing the cheeks of an infant. The sadness emphasized by all minor notes tore at his emotions. He repeated the words under his breath.

Lullaby and goodnight, with roses, bedight, /with lilies o'er spread in baby's wee bed/Lay thee down now and rest, may thy slumber be blest.

He stood there until the last notes died, tears springing to his eyes, and then turned to see Mrs. Mann, standing at the doorway of the coach house. She lifted her shoulders, expressing the bewilderment in both their minds.

Malcolm galvanized into action. He headed across the back road into the park towards the place where he had heard the music. As he crossed the park, swarms of whining mosquitoes rose out of the grass. He alternately waved his cane and arm, brushing away all but the persistent ones. He plunged his cane deeper into the turf, staggering on the uneven ground, but determined to reach the short distance to the benches on the path overlooking the river.

A young boy, cap pulled down on his head, sat on a bench with the violin case laying across his lap, staring intently towards the path to the gate. Malcolm strolled more slowly wanting to appear as if he were just passing by. As he came to the bench, he saw not a boy, but the girl from the cemetery. "Well, well," he said, stopping in front of her. "You must be Cat. I've seen you at the house with Mrs. Mann."

She was still for a long moment, then turned towards him with a puzzled look on her face in dreamy bliss. A pair of dark amber eyes gradually took him in, and she smiled at him, saying nothing.

"I heard music," he said. "It must have been your violin. You play very well."

"Not me. Joe," she said, her voice thick, on the verge of tears. "I keep his violin for him because he is at Mr. Marchenko's farm and doesn't want anything to happen to it. Our father gave it to him, you see." She pushed the cap to the back of her head, and a few curls sprang from underneath.

Malcolm sat down beside her and put his cane between his legs, both hands resting on the handle. "Oh," he said, "Where is he now?"

"He had to go back," she answered, pointing south down the path out of the park. "I come here so I can talk to him."

Odd, thought Malcolm. *I didn't see anyone on the path.* "He's your older brother?"

"Yes, he was born twenty minutes before me. My dad said it was because they weren't expecting me and they had to have time to prepare for a special event."

Malcolm grinned. "Ah! Twins, then. I suppose he will be coming home in time for school next month?"

Cat didn't reply for a time, then said, "He's staying at the farm."

"But you can't be fourteen yet?" She shook her head. "Doesn't he have to go to school until he's fourteen?"

"That's what the lady told my mother," said Cat. "But with Dad gone, she can't afford to keep him. So she sent him to the farm anyway."

And didn't tell the truant officer where he is, I dare say. And I suppose the father has deserted them, so the family could get relief vouchers. Not that they'd stretch very far.

"Well, he's very good at the violin. Brahms," he said. "I saw you today at the cemetery."

"The music is for Sir," she explained. "So he knows he would be blessed."

Malcolm sucked in his breath. *May thy slumber be blest . . . ? What an unusual child,* he thought. She reminded him of Isobel. "How do you know him?"

"I have to go home now." She hopped off the bench and ran down the path to where her brother must have disappeared earlier, the violin case bumping against her back.

"Come to the house tomorrow," he shouted after her, but he wasn't sure she heard him. *I asked too many questions,* he berated himself. Malcolm gazed out along the river, and let the white noise of the current cleanse his mind of a day best soon forgotten, but one thought lingered. A thought of the hands that had coaxed delicate music from a violin. And those same hands laboring on a farm.

FERGUS dreamed again. Peter's death, the funeral, made the dreams all the more vivid and disturbing because they had been absent from his sleep for some time. They held no order, just a fragmented cacophony interspersed with the symphony of artillery, and stuttering machine guns, and the anguished cries of the wounded in No Man's Land alternately cursing and calling for help. When the wounded began calling their mothers, those listening knew it wouldn't be long before the man became eternally quiet.

Like waters in a stream, his dreams rippled with sudden peace. A wedding, Isobel smiling, everybody cheering, Peter grinning stupidly at them both. A honeymoon suddenly cut short and Isobel, waving goodbye at the station in Calgary, shouting, "Take care of each other!" The first adventure taken without her. Then loud explosions again, his bursting lungs gasping for air while he groped frantically in the dirt.

He awoke shouting, his body soaked, smelling of fear and sweat. Grasping the pillow from under his head, he threw it to the foot of the bed, before laying down again to stare at the ceiling, willing himself to shut out the sight of Denvers's face. Looking up at him, smiling at him. Like a movie he was forced to watch, he was there again. In the Bourlon Wood.

THEY crept along the duckboards of the forward trench, then into the sap head where each footstep raised a sucking sound in the glutinous mud. Fergus was careful to keep his balance, remembering the time his hand had gone through the wet remains of a soldier buried in the mud. They scrambled one by one over the sandbags into the field and followed the same track as the first team. Fergus had his pistol, a Webley, and he had handed a rifle to Jinks, hoping he wouldn't freeze if he had to use it. After half an hour, they spotted their objective, a ridge about half a mile off, and reached it with no problems.

Feeling along the cable put down by the first team, they found the break in a shell hole. Fergus pointed across the road ahead of them. "Fritz on the other side," he warned. They did the repairs, and Fergus checked back and received an okay from the Battery.

He made them lay down and watch the road for any action. It was quiet, and they continued on across the road. They found the bodies of the team, laying in a small shallow where they had taken cover. The Germans had stripped all three of their boots. "The Huns must be short of footwear," Fergus said to the others, smothering the anger boiling up inside. He looked at Jinks, beginning to shake. *Away with the fairies*, as Peter would say.

Fergus shook him by the shoulders, "Snap to it, Jinks. There's a good fellow. We've still got our job to do. Pick up the gear. Look for a high spot to set up the telescope. If we're lucky, we can sight some Hun positions. Move!"

They walked on, laying the communication line as they went. It was early morning by then, still and quiet, the beginning of a warm day. Finally, they came upon a deserted quarry, strewn with German clothing and equipment, *remnants of a fast dash away*, Fergus thought. Shallow dugouts dotted here and there along the walls of the quarry, and sticking out of one was a communications pole.

Fergus pointed. "A good observation spot for us" Up close, the dugout was large, about sixteen feet deep, with wooden stairs leading down. Fergus peered down them and saw the dugout was lined with zinc. A communication line led into it.

"Fancy layout," said Denvers, looking over his shoulder.

They stripped the wires of the communication line and connected their own wires to it. Pleased with himself, Fergus wired back to the Battery. "We're in place," he messaged and again got the okay back.

Fergus nodded to the other two. He took off the headset and tossed it and the speaking set into the dugout. "Okay, men, let's make ourselves at home."

He should have known it was too easy. When the bullets started whistling, shifting the air beside him, he realized the dead men were retreating, not coming forward. The bullets made a splatting sound in the bank when they hit. *Damn*, he thought, *we have no fire power, not even a Mills bomb*. He signaled the others to keep apart.

He had no time to register the whiz when the air exploded around them sending fragments of dirt and metal shrapnel bouncing off his tin hat.

"Whiz-bangs!" Fergus yelled and threw himself in the dirt. He risked a look to check on the men and saw Jinks running back to the road.

"Jinks!" called Fergus, and covered his head with his hands at another explosion, this one closer. A scream of anguish and he raised his head to see Denvers on his back, a crimson stain rapidly blossoming through the khaki of his tunic. Fergus rose and running in a stoop, grabbed him under the arms at the shoulders. Denvers squealed in protest.

"Sorry, but we can't stay here," Fergus said, dragging him towards the dugout.

Another whiz-bang landed and Fergus threw himself on top of Denvers to protect him. Seconds later he took hold of Denvers again.

"No!" Denvers gasped. "No. Leave me here."

"Not on your nelly."

Ears ringing, Fergus barely had time to register the next explosion as he pushed Denvers, screaming in pain, through the doorway. Only a reverberation against his ears, numbing his head with a crushing forward thrust, and everything went black.

7

FERGUS went quietly past his father's door and headed down the stairs to the library. He raised the window to its fullest and put his face against the screen taking in gulps of the night air. His shoulders tightened as he heard the door open and a familiar *shuffle-tap* behind him.

Fergus turned. "I woke you."

"It isn't the first time," Malcolm replied. "I listen to your dreams more often than not. Then I hear you tiptoe past my door to come down here." Malcolm eased into the leather chair he used for reading and pointed to the other. "Peter's death is bound to bring back memories. Now, don't you think it's about time we talked?"

Annoyance rising, Fergus said, "Why? Talking won't erase what happened."

Malcolm abruptly put out his hand, palm out, stopping Fergus saying more. "That's not the point. It won't erase anything, but *you* might change."

"Jesus, Dad. Not now."

"Ever since you've come home, you've stayed wrapped up in yourself, uncaring of the world around you, or people in it. I've only seen someone cynical, sarcastic, and a wee bit arrogant. Have you any idea what went on in our lives when you left? The people left in this house? Even Peter's death floats off you like straw in the wind."

Hearing his own half-formed thoughts thrown at him struck Fergus like a blow to his head. He sat down in the chair opposite Malcolm and pushed his hands up in weak protest.

"No, father, you don't know." Fergus pressed the palm of his hand against his forehead as if to push away his thoughts. "It's the only way I have control. I just can't . . ." He threw his hands up, resentful of Malcolm's intrusion. "It's hopeless. I can't make you understand."

His father said nothing for a long moment, then, "Fergus, I want to help, but you shut me out. *Help* me understand."

Fergus sat up and half rose as though he were going to run, then sank down again. "Blast it, Dad. What do you want me to say?"

"Anything! I don't care. Fergus, I only . . ." He closed his eyes and exhaled the remainder of his thoughts. "What were you thinking tonight, up in your bedroom?"

Fergus laughed without humor. "Lice," he lied. "The bloody lice. Couldn't get rid of them. Always in my uniform, in the seams, hiding in the stitches. We had to scrape them out with a knife. Hopeless. Whenever I think of the lice, I start remembering things best forgotten."

Absently, he scratched at his breast bone. "October 1916. They gave us four days' notice. Half the men were on leave, harvesting. There was a mighty scramble and men from Moose Jaw to Regina were running for the train. Isobel and I just married but we were excited. This was it. We were on our way. We sailed from Halifax on the Saxonia. At Liverpool, they sent us on to a disbursement camp, then on to Seaford camp in Sussex for training. Everything from trench fighting, mustard gas, field sanitation to grenades." Fergus snorted. "It wasn't even close to the real thing, even with live ammunition."

Malcolm nodded. "Isobel used to read parts of your letters to us." *Trying to push me along, old man? If you only knew.*

"The truth would never have gotten past the censors." Once started on his story, Fergus felt his cramped muscles loosening, his breath starting to even out. Perhaps his dad might be satisfied with parts of it—perhaps he wanted to feel the events as Fergus felt them. Fergus smiled to himself. He'd tell him the dirty bit. Life in the trenches.

"Lice wasn't the only thing. Disgusting, filthy trenches. And the rats. Brown rats as big as cats." Fergus held out his hands to describe the length like a fisherman retelling the story of the great catch that got away. "So vicious they'd eat your eyes out when you were asleep if you weren't careful. They only disappeared just before a barrage of enemy gunfire. And the reek of overflowing latrines, unwashed bodies, let alone a sweet stench of the dead out in No Man's Land. The bodies would bloat up with gas, then the gas would disappear, and the bodies just stayed in the same position as they died. You could see them; standing, kneeling as though they were praying. The stink molded to your skin and left a perpetual taste in the roof of your mouth. You forgot what clean air was like. Rain and mud up to our knees, and sometimes our hips." He gave Malcolm an accusing glance. "Try burying telephone cable seven feet deep in mud, in the dead of night, within spitting distance of the Huns. A man could go mad in the trenches if he weren't rotated frequently."

He paused, eyes glazed over. "Men got trench fever from the lice, and trench foot from the wet. They gave us whale oil to rub on our feet. Peter and I just poured the oil right into the boots. It was squishy, but we didn't get trench foot either."

"But why did you transfer to Signals? Surely, it wasn't any better?"

"Eh?" Fergus said, still in another world. "Officers came into the camps looking for men interested in communications and radios, so Peter and I volunteered. It meant we could stay in the same outfit."

Fergus smiled. "Our RSM was a Scot, and he laughed at us. *'Laddie, signalers are called suicide squads, aye? They stand in the open field waving flags aboot, telling the Hun to start firing practice.'* He told us that signalers didn't carry firearms, but Peter and I vowed we'd protect ourselves. Only officers were allowed pistols, but we managed to get one." He winked at Malcolm, and grinned. "Don't ask me how." Malcolm didn't.

"Next thing we knew we were attached to the Royal Engineers and sent for training. Simply, it was all about setting up communication between front line trenches and headquarters. Too bad it wasn't simple at all. Cables got shelled and had to be repaired. When a gun battery arrived at battle position, we had to run wire to a forward observation post, and lines to each battery section, and to headquarters. Sometimes we were forced to run phone lines over open ground, or hang them in trees, at the same time dodging fire. We found out later we had laid enough cable by September 1918 to reach from Alberta to Ontario."

"Peter and I took leave together then. Sightseeing and in the bars, blanking ourselves out. Never talked about home. Both of us superstitious enough to keep away from that topic. We got back just in in time for the preparation of the Battle of Canal du Nord."

Fergus paused, moved to the edge of his seat, then got up and went to the drinks table. He poured a finger of scotch into the glass, then raised it in inquiry to Malcolm, who took it and gripped it between both hands. Fergus considered the bottle, then left it and sat down again.

"There was a place called the Bourlon Wood. It was occupied high ground, riddled with trenches, machine gun nests, and artillery. Laying communication lines there was really difficult, and Brigade HQ wasn't getting the information they needed."

"And sure enough the Counter-Battery Staff Officer said he wanted the exact positions of the German batteries on the high ground just north of the Bourlon Wood, and to know if it was being reinforced. The last signalers sent out were incommunicado. Which meant the line was broken somewhere." He glanced at Malcolm, "You know what Counter-Batteries are?"

"I'm not so ancient as to be entirely ignorant," Malcolm replied at once. "They take out the German guns at the start of the attack. We—you, set up an observation post with equipment to get the general location of their gun flashes. And then mathematics pinpoint their exact location. If the guns are silent, you are the bait used to invite the enemy guns to fire, and so on."

"Give the man a cigar." Fergus crossed his arms, then uncrossed them. "And I was ordered to go. I looked at the two men who would go with me, and my heart sunk into my boots. One of them was at the end of his rope and should have been sent back with the last rotation. His name was Jinks if you could believe it, and the other men shunned him. Silly superstition. I tried to get him retired out for rest, but you know, worn out men were branded cowards. The other man was only a kid, about eighteen. Denvers. He was from Fort Garry and had worked for CPR telegraph. Probably lied about his age to join up. We couldn't wait for replacements and their equipment, so I told myself it was business as usual."

Fergus stopped. He laced his fingers together, rocking them back and forth in agitation.

"Just a kid, Dad. Why do they always take the kids? Full of dreams of glory and end up as cannon fodder." Early morning light crept into the room. He reached over the desk and turned off the lamp, shrouding his face into a silhouette. *Was this how Jinks felt back then?* Fergus looked beyond the room and walls to somewhere else.

He kept his voice level, carrying Malcolm along with him while he told him the story up to the point of the blast which knocked him unconscious.

"The next thing I knew I woke up, my ears ringing like Christmas bells. A pile of earth and broken wood was what was left of the door. We were buried."

"Go on," Malcolm whispered, at last getting some roots.

"I panicked. I dug and dug where the door had been. Hopeless. It took a while to calm down and then I realized I could still see. Light from a ventilation shaft carved out of the chalk, letting in just enough to take our bearings."

"Yes?" Malcolm urged when it looked like Fergus would quit.

Fergus ran his tongue along his teeth. His jaw tightened. "When I didn't return, Peter began to search. He saved me." He rose and went to the door.

"Wait." Malcolm fumbled for his cane to follow. "Peter saved you? Fergus! What about Denvers? What happened there?"

His back to Malcolm, Fergus gripped the doorframe—"He died there"—then was gone.

8

THE next morning, tantalized by the smell of new bread Fergus came into the breakfast room. Seeing him, Mrs. Mann broke off her conversation, and Fergus wondered if she and Malcolm had been talking about him, then reproached himself. His father would not break confidences.

"There's brunch," she greeted him. "Fresh sweet rolls. Bread in the oven will soon be ready. Bacon and eggs if you like."

"It's too hot for a meal. I don't know how you can stay in a hot kitchen and bake."

"I prepare it the night before and just bake it for a short time in the early morning while the shade is on that side of the house."

"Just coffee please."

Mrs. Mann pursed her lips and left the room like a soldier obeying an unwanted order. Like a General marching into battle, she returned carrying a bowl of fruit, cream and sweet rolls which she arranged in front of him. Standing before him, they waged war by eye contact until Fergus conceded defeat. Mrs. Mann poured his coffee, a fresh cup for Malcolm and returned to the kitchen. Malcolm picked up his newspaper and stared at an item on the front page, then sighed, folded the paper and placed it back on the table. He helped himself to another roll, and buttered it, then laid it back down on his plate and stared at it.

He looked tired, Fergus thought, noting dark circles under his eyes, his face pale. A twinge of guilt ran through him, followed by the familiar surge of annoyance. *Giving me the silent treatment*, he thought. He topped up his coffee cup, placed a sweet roll on the saucer and rose. "I'll be on the verandah."

Malcolm raised his eyes as though just realizing Fergus was in the room. Without acknowledgment, he picked the newspaper off the table and pushed it in Fergus's direction.

Outside, Duke padded over to Fergus the minute he sat down, nudging him and sniffed at the sweet roll laying on the saucer. "You are a nuisance, you know?" Duke thumped his tail in agreement and drooled on Fergus's pant leg. He gave him the roll, and Duke scarfed it down in two bites.

Fergus rolled up the newspaper and swatted at a fly hovering over the crumbs on his plate, then spread it apart and scanned the page. Nothing much, a crop report, storm damage, an opinion about Germany's increasing power and Hitler. Fergus read the first paragraph, and moved on down the page, stopping at the article in the bottom right-hand corner.

Was the Funeral of Local Man a Chilling Reminder of Justice?

An old picture of Peter smiled out at him. Fergus sat up, his fists gripping the edges of the paper.

The funeral yesterday of a well-known local man, Peter Davidson, might remind us in these trying times even a hero is not immune from crime.

His vision blurred as he skimmed over the words, his mind only registering a phrase here and there.

Strathcona Holdings . . . Glasbottle . . . fraud . . . evading justice and prison. Killed by persons or person unknown, but likely a fellow tramp . . . 'who by the company he keeps shall we know him.'

Fergus gave the newspaper a vicious twist and threw the revolting mass over the verandah railing. As it hit the ground, it opened, and the picture gazed up at him. Fergus could almost hear him shouting down the opening of the ventilation shaft of the dugout, ordering Fergus to get a move on, or Isobel would kill him if he came home without her husband.

Peter, Isobel, and Fergus. They had sworn a childish oath of loyalty to each other. *Loyalty.* The word echoed in Fergus's head.

Fergus left his coffee on the verandah railing and went inside and up to his room. Methodically, knowing he would be most credible if he appeared as a well-dressed professional, he shaved, then put on grey linen trousers, white shirt, light blue sports jacket and chose a blue matching tie. He tied the laces of his shoes, polished and gleaming like headlamps. Giving up on the hair, which even under threat of torture never strayed far from its ruffled appearance, he went downstairs.

Fergus opened the garage door to fetch the car, a 1933 Ford Model 40 Sedan. Winding down the window, he drove towards downtown. He crossed the railroad tracks and halted at the stop sign on Second Street. A group of pedestrians crossed in front of him, including the girl who had been in the yard with Mrs. Mann. She was carrying the violin case which Fergus recognized as the one on the veranda. She turned her head to stare at him as she passed, giving him the same odd sensation she was sizing him up. Amused at the idea, he almost waved to her. The sun dancing over her curls again brought an image of Isobel. Curious, he stayed where he was as he watched her go a short distance on West Avenue and into Levinson's Music Store. The driver in the car behind him honked him out of his musings, and he continued towards First Street to the four-story brick building which held the City Hall and Police Station. It wasn't until he maneuvered into a parking spot he realized the reminder of Isobel hadn't squeezed his heart in pain as it usually did.

The police offices were situated in the basement. The place smelled of stale tobacco, sweat, and lye soap. Three vagrants sat on a bench along the wall beside the door. An officer at a desk inside the railing interviewed a nervous-looking young man in overalls twisting a cap in his hand.

Fergus approached the desk constable. "I need to speak to the officer in charge of the investigation into Peter Davidson's death."

The constable looked him over. "The reason you wish to see him, Sir?"

"I'd appreciate knowing the progress of the investigation." Fergus lowered his voice. "If I could just see whoever is in charge. I knew him you see. Mr. Davidson I mean, and I can help with some background." Fergus felt his face flush. *This isn't going well. I sound apologetic. Don't beg, you idiot.*

A tall policeman with sergeant's stripes came towards the railing from the back. He raised the gate, held it in midair, and stared.

"Ferg Muir!"

Both Fergus and the desk constable turned. It took a few seconds before he said, "Archie? Archie Gillespie? You?"

"The same," said Archie with a broad smile as he pumped Fergus's hand up and down.

The three men on the bench looked on in interest. One poked the man beside him and grinned.

"It's alright, Collins," Archie explained to the constable. "I'll look after him." He threw the three men a stern glare and led Fergus into a room, walls painted pea green. Archie pointed to a chair at a table with a scarred brown top. "Interview room," he said as he closed the door, and took the other chair.

Fergus looked at him, in turn relieved and amazed. "I hardly recognized you. In high school, you were the smallest runt in Grade Twelve. Now you're taller than I am. What have you been eating?"

"I was a late bloomer," Archie said. "I saw you a few times from afar, but we don't run in the same circles exactly." He used his fingers to push the peak of his hat back from his forehead. "After France, I joined the Edmonton Police service. About six months ago, a promotion in Cypress Landing went begging so I took it." His voice sobered. "Shocking about Peter. The Depression turned more than a few people into bad eggs."

Fergus shook his head. "Oh no, not Peter. You knew him."

"When the money runs out, people do things they normally wouldn't do. We've had a lot of experience these last few years."

But Fergus persisted. "I wasn't here, but my father and Peter remained close. He would have noticed. Something is rotten about the whole thing." Fergus explained Malcolm's suspicions and answered Archie's questions as best he could. "What did the autopsy say?" he finally asked.

Archie turned sideways and put his boots up on the cigarette-scarred table, hands behind his head.

"Captain Embleton is very strict about procedures around here." His lips twitched. "He was a captain during the war. And he runs this place the same way. General orders posted up on the board and everything. Number one is don't discuss any police business with the public. Very serious about that one. Some have been let go because they had flapping lips."

"Is there something secret about the autopsy?" Fergus protested.

"Orders are orders." Archie brought an arm from behind his head and looked at his watch. He let his boots drop to the floor, then stood. "Sorry, Ferg, I can't help you. But if you have any new information, don't hold back." He winked. "I'm off duty soon. How about I get out of this monkey suit, and we'll have a drink or coffee for old time's sake. An hour? We can reminisce. But no shop talk." He looked pointedly at Fergus. "The Queen's or Eaton's?"

Was Archie sending him a message? "The tea room at Queen's, rather than the bar." Better to keep a clear head.

Under a dazzling sky that promised another scorching day, Fergus left the Police station and drove to his office and parked in front of the Commercial Block, a brick building in the Classic Revival style like most of the downtown buildings. The office would be empty. This was a quiet time in his practice, and he had decided there was not enough work to keep the office open six days a week. He went up the marble stairs to the second floor and his office suite. When he opened the door, he was surprised to see Max Levinson.

"It's my coursework. My next lesson is due. I hope you don't mind." Almost apologetic, he held up a paper and kept on with his excuse for being in the office. "It's too noisy at home."

"No, it's fine," Fergus assured him. *He shouldn't have to ask if I mind.* "Your mother giving music lessons today?"

Relief flooded Max's face. "And my brothers and sisters arguing." He scrunched his nose.

Fergus thought of the silence this morning at home. *It could be worse, Max. It could be too quiet.*

"Anything I can help you with?" He pointed to Max's lesson.

"Not so far, thank you, sir. This one is pretty straightforward. Not like most."

"Yes, they can be . . ." Fergus's mind went back to the company where he had articled. Wondering why he hadn't thought of it before, he said, "Max, I was thinking of starting weekly student accounting sessions. Relating to accounting principles and your lesson subjects. Would you be interested?"

Eyes lighting up, Max said, "Very much."

"Good. Think about what night best suits you, and what issues we can discuss. We had better keep things general. I am not going to do your assignments for you." He found himself smiling, softening the warning. "The Depression has brought to light a lot of questions about accounting practices, and the need for national regulations, instead of each provincial branch being a separate authority." As he talked, he warmed up to the subject. "I rather think my father will join us. We can meet at my house."

Fergus decided to leave Max alone with his lesson and wait for Archie at the Queen's tea room. Thinking that Peter's funeral had left him soft-hearted, he nevertheless left the office with a satisfied sense of accomplishing something constructive. *Makes a change,* he thought.

The Queen's Hotel was prominent on West Avenue, directly opposite the station, so people alighting from the train saw the welcoming sign first thing. Most of the hotel's sixty-three rooms boasted ensuite bathrooms, a unique feature. The Queen's had a tea room, fine dining room, drawing room, billiards room, barber shop, and a bowling alley, though the latter had closed for lack of paying customers. Fergus went up the stairs and passed through the large pillars guarding the entrance to the spacious lobby.

He chose a corner table and ordered coffee for two. "And bring one right away," he asked. Fifteen minutes later, Archie Gillespie, now dressed in street clothes joined him. Without his helmet, he displayed a head of dark brown hair and the beginnings of a bald spot.

"It's hot enough to melt lead," Archie began, wiping his sweaty face. "Sorry about back at the station. The captain is a good man, but he makes sure we never forget we are a professional organization. He's a disciplinarian. He got rid of the bad ones on the Force who thought they were entitled to *certain privileges*, if you know what I mean."

Archie waited while the waitress laid scones, jam tarts, and jam on the table. She poured coffee into both cups. Archie smiled at her, showing a row of even white teeth, and then helped himself to a scone. "He pins up general orders on the board every day." He cut his scone in half and smeared strawberry jam on it.

"Today it said, *'wear chin straps on point of chin.'* Yesterday it was, *'don't hang around bootleg joints when off duty.'* My favorite is, *'don't stand around gossiping with civilians.'*" Archie looked at Fergus and grinned. "Are we gossiping?"

"It seems to me a policeman can pick up all sorts of useful things, talking to civilians," answered Fergus, hinting.

Archie handed Fergus a tart. "I'm sorry you lost Isobel and your little girl," he said softly. "The Flu was terrible. We lost Richie too."

Fergus remembered Archie's brother, an impish kid trailing after his big brother. Shocked, he murmured his sympathies, then, "Are you married?"

"I never quite made it," admitted Archie. "I'm seeing a widow though, a nurse at the Maternity Hospital. Don't know how it will turn out." He eyed Fergus. "How about you?"

Fergus shook his head. "And now Peter's gone too. He saved my life in France at the Canal du Nord, you know. If it weren't for him, I wouldn't be sitting here now." Fergus sat back, suddenly nauseous at hearing his own words.

"I was there. In the third CMR," Archie said, then added casually, "Why are you asking questions about Davidson?"

Fergus sighed. "I'm not sure. Maybe loyalty." The word smacked up against his brain again. "Dad thinks Peter may have been deliberately killed. If I can convince him it was an accident, we can get on with our lives."

"So it isn't for excitement then Fergus? You aren't here because you get a kick out of showing us policemen we might bury a murder just to keep the peace?" Archie's tone was light but his brown eyes hard and cold.

"Believe me, Archie, I couldn't care less about excitement. A mundane life suits me just fine. But dealing with Peter's death is making Dad sick, and he isn't a well man to begin with. I tried talking him out of it, but he has a point when he says the charge doesn't make sense."

"How's that, then?"

"Peter was never greedy about money. Certainly not enough to steal. If he took it and ran off, why come back now?"

Archie looked into his empty cup as if searching for the answer.

The waitress arrived with fresh coffee. Archie waited until she moved off to the next table. "Maybe the lady who went with him spent it all, then ditched him. I heard Lex Rideout spoiled her rotten, always buying things for her."

Fergus shook his head. "It doesn't make sense, Archie. Peter was more of an old-fashioned knight, not playing Lothario and running off with women. And he wouldn't have changed his basic character that much. Dad thinks his death and the fraud charge are connected somehow, and he came back to fight it. I don't know if I agree with him. If that's true, then why didn't he come to see us? We were like his family." Fergus clenched his fists. "Damn it, Archie, I owe him some loyalty. I hate all those lies about him."

"It sounds like you don't know what you want. A boring life and at the same time you can't stop conjuring up mysteries about Peter's death. Make up your mind, Ferg," Archie summed up their conversation. A policeman's analysis, blunt and to the point.

"My only interest is to find some closure for Dad. Tell me what the autopsy said."

"Won't help much. He was hit in the temple area with something flat with a sharp edge. A brick maybe. It could have been unintended, but hit in a vulnerable spot, he was dead before he hit the ground." Archie drained the last of his coffee. "It really does seem it was a fight with another vagrant that went ugly. We talked to people staying at the camp under the bridge, and they said he had a run-in with another hobo who vowed to get even with him. A man by the name of Sam. Nobody's seen him since the day of the storm. If he did it, he's high-tailed it. After the dust storm, witnesses said everybody had left the kiln, but Peter stayed behind and could have been waiting for someone. That's about all we've got."

"Why were they in the kiln for God's sake?" Fergus asked.

"Often done. After the firing, once the kiln is emptied, they wait until it cools down before loading the next batch. It takes about eight hours, so the pottery leaves the outside doors open and lets the hobos in. It's a nice overnight place, cool in summer and warm in the winter. We like it too," Archie said. "We know where to look for people if they're wanted. So the captain's got a captive audience when we tell them to move on."

"What a life," said Fergus.

"If we let them bunch up in the camps, the union troublemakers get them all worked up by telling them the government is responsible." Archie was defensive now. "We don't want an episode like last year. The Union persuaded about a thousand men to move on to Ottawa. They got as far as Regina and rioted."

"I remember," Fergus said. One man killed and many injured.

"We aren't as bad as the railroad cops," Archie continued. "Some of those guys are real sadists. The stories the men tell; you can barely credit them. Some of the riders are just kids too. Even women. A month back, a kid got thrown off the freight. He fell under the wheels and lost his legs. Our captain is strict, but he won't stand for cruelty."

Fergus waved aside stories of hobos and riots. "Not even one eye-witness for Peter's attack?"

Archie shook his head. "Good luck with finding one. People today don't want any more trouble than they already have."

Both Archie and Fergus pushed away their plates with the food half-eaten, silent for a long moment. *This is a waste of time*, Fergus thought. *It has to be just what it looks like. An accident, a fight with a vagrant. No connection to Peter's fraud charge at all.* It was the result he craved, so why wasn't he relieved?

"There was one thing though," Archie volunteered. "A young girl. Peter was seen with her for a few days before. They thought she might be his daughter as he was very protective of her. She came into the kiln with him. After the storm, she went off somewhere, and he stayed behind."

"Protective? Sounds more like Peter. Who is she?"

"Not a clue. But we ruled her out as she'd not likely help with any new information. Captain is convinced the killer was the vagrant." He thought for a moment. "This kid. Funny thing. She had a violin case with her. Strange thing for a kid to have. Hope she didn't pinch it," finished Archie, the consummate policeman.

Fergus lifted his head, warning lights flashing. "That I do find interesting. Because I think I know who she is." He reached into his pocket and laid a crisp, blue two-dollar bill on the table and rose.

Archie's eyes rounded at the sight of Queen Mary's face staring up at him. "Thanks, Ferg. My treat next time." He picked up the unfinished scone on his plate and popped it into his mouth. His large hand shot out as Fergus was about to leave, clamping his arm in a hard grip. "Don't go off half-cocked, poking your nose into affairs that aren't your business, Ferg. The captain won't like it."

"If I find anything new, I'll let you know, Arch." An uneasy feeling gnawed at him. "But I'm curious now about the girl. She spent time with Peter and, accident or no, if she saw anything at all, it could put her in danger."

9

THE next day, after serving breakfast, Mrs. Mann attended the Lutheran Church of the Nazarene on Union Avenue. Her church was one of the oldest in Cypress Landing, founded for the most part by German-Russian settlers, her ancestors among them.

The German-Russians were originally German farmers who, at the invitation of Catherine the Great, left Germany to farm the vast Russian steppes. In the latter part of the 19th century, Mrs. Mann's grandfather sensed a restricted future in Russia and wisely became part of a mass emigration of farmers to begin a new life in the Canadian West.

Proud of her origins, Mrs. Mann was a spiritual lady who took her church seriously. Her name may have been shortened from Mannheim, but as she had repeatedly told others, she was not about to shorten her religious duty. In the years during the Great War, to mitigate open hostility, most of the German-Russians changed their names by deed or marriage. Now, in 1936 none of it mattered, but it accounted for the ethnic mix of names in the church rosters.

Today, she put on her best hat and Sunday dress and went off to church, carrying her Bible. All week long, her thoughts had centered on her failed detective attempt, and today she reached a decision. Regrettably, it involved eating crow.

Mrs. Mann settled herself at the back in a pew smooth with age and smelling of fresh bees' wax. Satisfied after locating Dorothy Skefington's smart crop haircut and stylish hat, she gazed idly around the rest of the congregation while waiting for the service to start. The choir filed in, the pastor went to the dais. Congregational murmurs shushed, a chord from the organ sounded, and everyone rose for the first hymn. For once, Mrs. Mann's attention wandered, and she barely took in the rest of the service. She looked at her handout for the title of the day's sermon. '*Trusting in Him when it's the Worst Day of your Life,*' she read and closed her eyes thinking of how she might approach her quarry.

Finally, it ended, the choir finished their last hymn, and people began filing down the aisle. Mrs. Mann waited until Miss Skefington was opposite her row and joined her as the line shuffled along outside. "Good morning" She kept her voice pleasant in spite of Miss Skefington's frigid stare. "I was wanting to speak to you sooner, but with one thing and another, the days flew by. About the other night at our meeting."

"If you don't mind," Miss Skefington interrupted archly, "I'd rather not." She brushed past the pastor with a hurried smile and went down the front steps.

Oh no you don't, thought Mrs. Mann, and after briefly acknowledging the pastor's outstretched hand, she scurried right behind her, leaving the surprised man's greeting to sink into the air.

"I only want to apologize," she cried out. Miss Skefington increased her pace.

"Oh stop, stop," pleaded Mrs. Mann after a few steps, clutching her chest dramatically and gasping for breath.

Miss Skefington muttered something and stopped. She turned and reluctantly came up to the older woman. "It's just . . . Mr. Muir . . . well, how can I ever face him again? I was so embarrassed. He's my Accountant." Her face looked like she had just been offered a dish of fried worms. "How could you get me drunk? And in public?" She glared at Mrs. Mann. "Oh, you are wicked!"

It was a bit too much for Mrs. Mann to take, eating crow aside. Her chin hardened like steel. "How was I to know you'd sneak off into the kitchen to guzzle it right out of the bottle?" She adjusted her hat with a sharp jerk, opened her mouth to say more but relented and confessed. "I did put brandy in your first glass. But only a bit! I just wanted you to be a little . . ." she sketched a small back and forth with her hand. "well . . . relaxed."

Miss Skefington stared at her in amazement. "But why, for pity's sake."

Mrs. Mann glanced around. A few church people were standing on the corner gazing in interest at the two of them, Carrie Fletcher among them. She took Miss Skefington's arm and said, "Not here. Come to the house with me. I'll put the kettle on, and we'll talk."

"No!" Miss Skefington pulled away. "Not your place. What if I run into Mr. Muir?"

"The Muirs take lunch on Sunday at the Queen's." Across the street, Carrie Fletcher separated from a group of ladies and headed towards them. Mrs. Mann grabbed Miss Skefington's arm and pulled her along the street. "Oh well, your place then. It's nearer anyway." Her voice grew insistent, sharp. "Look, Dorothy, we must talk. A man's reputation is at stake."

At the sound of her first name, Miss Skefington's brown eyes opened wide. On hearing the second statement, a spark of interest flashed in them.

"A man? What man?" But Mrs. Mann hurried her along, leaving Mrs. Fletcher behind. They soon reached Miss Skefington's small house a short two blocks from the church.

When they were both seated at the kitchen table with a full teapot and china, Miss Skefington took charge and gave Mrs. Mann the same no-nonsense look given to her girls in the beauty parlor. "So begin," she said, her tone crisp.

Mrs. Mann took in the fine china, with matching teapot and hot water pitcher. "A lovely set," she said, picking up her cup and taking a sip.

Miss Skefington's face softened. "It is, isn't it? It belonged to my grandmother. She gave it to my mother when she left England." She straightened then and glared briefly at Mrs. Mann before wagging her forefinger back and forth. "Don't think you can butter me up with compliments. Start talking. I think I'm entitled, don't you?" She helped herself to a cookie and offered the plate to her guest.

Might as well get it over with. Mrs. Mann accepted a shortbread cookie. "It's all to do with the murder of Peter Davidson. When he was accused of running off with Lex Rideout's wife and all that money, I could hardly credit it. But then after he was gone a while . . . well, I thought maybe he did it after all." Mrs. Mann paused uncertainly and twisted her teacup around in the saucer.

She clicked her tongue against her teeth, censuring herself over her lapse of conviction he was innocent. "Then he was killed, and it made me wonder why did he come back when he'd be arrested at any moment? There had to be a reason."

"So what? That has nothing to do with me." Miss Skefington's cookie brushed the air, erasing away the excuse. "I didn't know him. I knew who he was of course, and his wife, Lois. She used to come into the parlor before she moved to Edmonton, but what—"

"Well, that's just it." A flush rose up in Mrs. Mann's cheeks, and she squirmed, revealing her guilt. "Your beauty parlor. Both Mrs. Davidson and Mrs. Rideout had their hair done at your place."

"For Pete's sake, I was just beginning my shops, and times were so bad. I couldn't possibly have known what was going on, could I?"

Mrs. Mann tried again, "The other night, at the meeting, you said something just before you, ah . . . well, passed out."

Miss Skefington closed her eyes in pain, and Mrs. Mann hurried on.

"It's why I did it. So you'd relax. I realize now I didn't handle it properly, but I thought you might say something about Mrs. Rideout especially. Of course, I was aware you wouldn't talk about any of your ladies in front of everyone else, for them to gossip about, and tell tales."

"Well, I never!" Miss Skefington cried, eyes wide. "I just can't believe this!"

"Here," said Mrs. Mann, lifting the teapot. "Have a fresh cup of tea." She poured both cups, then put the pot back on the trivet. "Before you get all hot again," she assured. "I wouldn't have let it get so far as you telling secrets about just anyone. I would have stopped you if you said anything bad, I swear." Dorothy Skefington said nothing, only sharpened her accusing glare, her lips tight.

Unaccustomed to being on the wrong end of bad behavior, Mrs. Mann fought to stay calm in spite of a strong need to squirm. "I was only interested in Mrs. Rideout," she finally said, resorting to sounding cross. "She's disappeared anyway, so what difference would it make now?"

"It makes a difference to me," snapped Miss Skefington. "I don't talk about my ladies. If it got out, I'd not only lose her, but I'd lose all her friends too. In the end, I'd lose my business."

"Yes, I know. But you must know I am not the sort of giddy, irresponsible woman to coax idle gossip, especially gossip which causes harm and misery." Mrs. Mann left off being defensive and resorted to pleading. "There's much you don't understand. After Fergus left for the East, Peter Davidson came to see Mr. Muir regularly. They were both grieving, and like family to each other. Mr. Davidson was a gentle, good man, Dorothy. He saved Fergus Muir's life in France. It has to count for something." Her voice breaking with emotion, she stopped before the tears came and embarrassed them both. Miss Skefington pretended not to notice and fussed over the teapot, lifting the lid to see if it needed more water.

After a moment of uncomfortable silence, Mrs. Mann swallowed. Knowing she couldn't stop now, she continued, her words passionate. "Fergus's father is heartbroken and needs help, Dorothy. If he doesn't get answers, his health will deteriorate, and I can't stand by and watch. I think you started to say something the other night. It sounded like '*bloosers*' or '*bloomers*' to me. If it will help find whoever killed Peter Davidson, then you must tell me, and trust in me. Nobody will know what you've said." Miss Skefington stared at the table, silent. Mrs. Mann waited until finally she sighed and rose to her feet. She collected her handbag, gloves, and hat. "Thank you for your time and the tea, Dorothy."

"Wait. I'm only trying to get my thoughts together," Miss Skefington put up her hand. She motioned for Mrs. Mann to sit again. *Finally*, thought Mrs. Mann. Her legs wobbly with relief, she almost collapsed into the chair.

"I saw her bruises," said Miss Skefington after another pause. "Clarissa's, I mean. She came in one day. It was hot, and she had on a sleeveless dress with just a scarf over her shoulders. Her arms were covered with bruises. She said she had caught them in the pantry door when she was carrying things out. Any fool could see it was a lie."

"Lex Rideout beat her?" An incredulous Mrs. Mann asked. She couldn't have been more dumbfounded if she'd seen a green man from Mars. "But everyone says he treated her like a china doll."

"Well, he didn't." Miss Skefington's tone was flat and definite.

"And it wasn't the first time. She had bruises down the back of her neck, once over her shoulders and her legs. She told me she was always falling or bumping into things."

"And all the time he let everyone believe he was doting on her, he was actually abusing her." A stab of doubt shot through her, even as she tried to dismiss it. "Do you think she was telling the truth?"

"I think so," said Miss Skefington. "I wondered about it myself. Especially since it's not the Lex Rideout we all see. The high school and everyone from the mayor down believes he walks on water because of the sports glory he brings to the town's reputation. She is seen as a snob, but maybe she was too terrified to talk to people in case he flew into a rage."

"Or he kept her close because she told stories which weren't true. Who knows what people are really like when it comes down to it?"

Miss Skefington nodded. "My mother's favorite saying was if you want to know the truth about people you have to follow them home. I tried to be friendly with Clarissa, but she seemed so frightened, and I think embarrassed too. Now I feel guilty I didn't make more of an effort."

What could you do? What could anyone do? Mrs. Mann felt Clarissa Rideout's defeat, then said aloud, "She'd be grateful to you for not telling anyone, but in the end, she'd have nowhere to go." She privately thought if it were her husband, he'd get the frying pan against the side of his head. "It explains why Peter Davidson was friendly towards her."

"If Lex Rideout knew about his sympathy, think how much worse it would be for her." Miss Skefington made a sound of disdain. "Yes, for the sake of safety, she'd have no choice but to run."

They sat in companionable silence for a time, then Mrs. Mann stood and said, "Thank you, Dorothy. I'll keep your secret. It will just give both Mr. Muirs some assurance Peter Davidson was the person they thought he was, and he helped Clarissa Rideout out of pity. It's something to be glad about."

"I hope it helps," said Miss Skefington. "Poor Fergus. It was the Spanish Flu, wasn't it?"

Mrs. Mann nodded, smiling at the direct hint about Fergus.

"Just when everybody thought it was over. Nobody knew a third wave was going across the country. Isobel, Maggie and his mother Margaret went to a church celebration. They all caught it, and all three died within the week."

"How awful," Miss Skefington shuddered in shock and sympathy.

Mrs. Mann turned at the door to say goodbye. "I feel I have really only just met you, Dorothy. And made a true friend indeed."

"I still haven't quite forgiven you for spiking my cordial," replied Miss Skefington, but she smiled. "Although I did drink it too fast and perhaps too much."

Mrs. Mann laughed, "Well, when Fergus carried you to the sofa, you looked very fetching, all helpless. I don't think he minded too much. I could see him trying not to laugh. And he put you down quite softly."

"Really?" Miss Skefington's cheeks turned pink. She lowered her eyes, then ran her hand over her hair messing it up in her embarrassment. It fell back into its perfect shape. *How does she do that?* It was all Mrs. Mann could do to keep her own hair in its neat bun. *Maybe I should make an appointment at the salon for a new style.*

"I wasn't in any shape to notice," Miss Skefington giggled. "Do you think he has any women friends? See them socially I mean? He always seems so inaccessible."

"Grouchy, you mean." Mrs. Mann sniffed. "There is nobody in his sights yet, but you never know." Privately she thought he never would, but then a white lie now and then didn't hurt. "He's not a bad sort. But he can't forget the war, just like a lot of veterans." Loathe to gossip about her employers, she changed the subject. "Mrs. Collins went into hysterics because she thought you were dead, and I shook her silly." She snorted, trying not to laugh, and then both of them started.

"All the way home Mrs. Fletcher said I was shameless."

Rolling her eyes, Mrs. Mann waved it aside. "Carrie Fletcher thinks everything is shameless. She lulls herself to sleep counting shameless things instead of sheep."

Outside, an unforgiving sun beat down, hurting her eyes after the dimness of the house. She walked slowly home in the overheated, airless afternoon, her mind occupied with how she was going to tell Fergus and Malcolm what she had learned without revealing the source.

IN the study after dinner that night, Fergus poured two glasses of brandy. He handed one to his father, then related yesterday's conversation with Archie Gillespie.

"The police want Peter's death declared an accident while in a fight with another vagrant." Fergus leaned forward, his arms across his knees, looking up earnestly at his father. "I know you want me to do something, Dad, otherwise Peter's name will be in the records as a criminal, a fraudster. We . . . I . . . owe him so much. But honestly? I feel like I can't do anything about it. I don't know why."

"Yes, you do, son," Malcolm leaned back against his chair, his voice neutral. "You have to keep everything logical hoping it will control all that inner chaos you are fighting."

Fergus flushed but didn't object. "There was nothing stopping him from coming to us, Dad. But he didn't because of me. It's my fault."

Malcolm's hand shot up, palm out like a policeman directing traffic. "Stop right there," he said, almost shouting. "That's one thing you don't know. You can't be sure!" Malcolm lowered his voice. "No more guessing. Questioning the police is a beginning. Now, let's start with what we do know."

Fergus sat down behind the desk and laid out a pad of memo paper. "Okay, number one." He stared at the blank pad. "This girl . . . Cat. What about her?"

Malcolm smiled at the thought of her. "Unusual child." He told Fergus about seeing her in the park, and his questions to her about Peter. "She called him '*Sir*.' When I asked her how she knew him, she took off like a shot. There is something I can't put my finger on with the child. One minute she is talking to you and the next she is somewhere else, and then she looks like she is surprised to see you sitting there." He stared through the window, at the gold reflections of the setting sun, as if searching for inspiration. He gave up, gulped the rest of his brandy and took refuge in the usual statements of his generation. "Maybe it's the way kids behave these days, although I must admit they have it rough. Most of them with no fathers."

Fergus thought of the way Cat had stared at him when crossing the street. "Mrs. Mann might be useful there," he said. "She can get the girl over here on some excuse and pin her down somehow. She might be forthcoming if Mrs. Mann is present. She spent almost a week with Peter. She has to know something."

At the mention of Mrs. Mann, the lady herself appeared in the doorway wheeling the trolley with coffee and strudel.

"Thank you, Mrs. Mann," Malcolm said by way of dismissal, but she stood there until she had their attention.

"I spoke with someone today," she started. "I'm not going to tell you who, so you will just have to accept my word as to the facts." Her face was set into determined lines telling them it was no use questioning her. "It is about Clarissa Rideout and the reason she's gone. Mr. Davidson took her away because her husband was beating her."

"Good heavens," Malcolm said.

Fergus's eyebrows shot straight up. About to take a bite of a pastry, his mouth froze open. He stared from her to Malcolm and grinned.

"See, Dad? It's the second time today someone's said Peter was protective of people. If someone was in trouble, he was the first one there to help."

"Where did you get this information?" Malcolm asked, his grey eyes narrowed in vague suspicion.

"I can't tell you," she repeated. "I'm sorry, but I promised. I can say that the person is in a position to know the truth. The person said Clarissa Rideout had bruises everywhere. She wasn't a snob; she was afraid of her own shadow. In public Lex Rideout doted on her, so everybody thought he spoiled her, but in private he was an overbearing, possessive bully." Mrs. Mann's eyes sparked indignation. "The poor woman had to put up with him playing a happy couple in public, and treating her like a slave in private." She sniffed and drew herself up. "And then he has the nerve to sit in his garden and cry over her. Just like he was the wronged one."

"Cry?" Fergus snorted.

Mrs. Mann told them what Agnes Ramsay had seen from her back window. "Silly man." she finished. "Never miss the workhorse until it's gone."

Malcolm's face mirrored Fergus's own disgust at the thought of a man treating his wife in a brutal fashion.

"The reason why Peter ran off with her," Malcolm said dismissing Lex's grief in the garden. "It makes sense. Peter certainly would have tried to help her."

Fergus nodded, but his mind puzzled over the possibilities. "It makes sense up to a certain point. But Peter was married. Why would he run?"

"His marriage wasn't a happy one. Women know these things." Mrs. Mann was greeted with silence.

"Oh for goodness sakes," she told the two doubting faces in front of her. "I don't know how men can be so wise in business and not have any idea that women can think as well." The two expressions changed from doubt to annoyance.

Mrs. Mann threw up her hands in surrender. "The year he left, Lois Davidson worked in our soup kitchen helping to set it up. While women work, they say a lot of things, often without thinking. And they don't realize when they talk to one woman, there is a roomful listening to every word. Believe me, their marriage was not going to last. I think she was ready to move on long before she actually did. She thought she was an aristocrat while he was too conventional."

Odd sort of person for Peter to marry, Fergus thought. *Not his type at all. But there must have been a reason he did.* "Too trusting, I think," he said. "But even if his marriage were in trouble, he wouldn't abandon his responsibility. He would have helped Clarissa Rideout to get away, not run off with her."

"Well, he did." Malcolm's practicality echoed in the pause following Fergus's attempt at logic.

"Maybe he took her someplace, meaning to come back, and then something happened and he couldn't," Fergus said, still finding excuses, then sighed resigned. "Yeah, yeah, I know. You're going wonder why he took the money if he was going to come back."

"To help her get started somewhere else?" Malcolm suggested, then shook his head before Fergus could reply. "No, it makes no sense either. Peter wouldn't steal money for her."

"The only thing which makes sense is he didn't take the money, but he found out about the charges and thought it wiser to stay away until he could figure out what happened."

"And waited four years to come back? And then Lex Rideout ran into him, and killed him in a fit of rage over his wife?"

"Certainly a motive," said Fergus defensive, warming to his new theory. "But you'd think he would just want to learn where she went. Killing Peter wouldn't bring her back, and Peter never told anyone Lex Rideout beat his wife. The pieces don't fit. Do you really think he's a bully? Wouldn't we know if he was? And if he was, could he go as far as murder?"

Malcolm's face cleared at a new thought. He faced Mrs. Mann. "Could she have made it up?"

"You mean could she be the sort of woman who likes a life of drama? Of course, she could, and be a witch as well for all anyone knew. Lex may have kept a close eye on her because he didn't want people to know she was crazy."

"We have to talk to Cat," Malcolm told Mrs. Mann.

"Why? What for?" The corners of her mouth turned down and her eyes flickered between them.

"Cat spent nearly a week every day in Peter's company," Fergus told her.

"Oh Lord, I knew that." She sat down and clasped her hands together. "But I didn't think . . . well, the day before I had the Ladies Auxiliary meeting here, I found Cat on the kitchen step. She looked terrible, and I can't forget the sadness in those amber eyes of hers." Mrs. Mann put her forefinger to her lips to stop them from trembling. "I coaxed her to tell me what was wrong. She knew Mr. Davidson. She thought he'd left town and only realized he was dead when she heard us talking in the kitchen," she nodded to Malcolm. "She knew him as Sir."

A chill went through Malcolm, thinking of her in the park, and her voice telling him the violin piece was for Peter so that he'd be blessed. He groaned softly.

"I encouraged her to talk about him until she felt better." Mrs.

Mann rose and smoothed down her dress.

"What did she say about him?" Malcolm stopped her leaving.

"Just that he took her to places where they could ask the train-riders if they had seen her father. She talked about where they went, about how nice he was, that they were best friends. That's all."

A wave of heat flooded over Fergus, drowning him. He drummed his fingers on his notepad, trying to ignore the signs. *God, not now.* The desktop in front of him tilted and he clamped his jaw tight willing his mind to dwell on Cat and not Peter. He quietly sucked in deep breaths of air until he felt easy again. "Do you think she saw something she's keeping secret?" his voice was hoarse.

Mrs. Mann turned a questioning face to him.

"She was in the kiln the afternoon Peter was murdered. It now seems a good idea to find out if she saw anything."

Mrs. Mann's face went ashen. "Oh my heart, let's pray not. I can't bear to think about how it would affect her. We have to do something. What if she saw who killed him?" She put her hand up to her mouth. She turned horrified eyes to Malcolm, then Fergus, as though she wanted to say more. Instead, she grimly started stacking cups, saucers, and plates.

10

MRS. Mann disappeared with the tea trolley, and Fergus inspected the notepad in front of him then turned to a new page. "Dad, catch me up on Peter's life while I was away." In spite of trying to sound detached, his voice trembled, and he coughed to cover it up. "What about his investment in GlasBottle? If we get it on paper, something might jump out that doesn't fit."

"First, I'd rather know about you. How *you* felt about Peter." Malcolm's eyes had sharpened on Fergus, showing he had noticed the emotion. "You can't deny you went out of your way to cut ties with him when you went to York. Is there something I should know?"

"No," said Fergus. His cheeks drew in like he'd just sucked on a lemon. "You know I couldn't stand living in Cypress Landing without Isobel and Maggie. As for my feelings about Peter, I thought you knew. He was the solid one of the three of us, our leader, and my big brother even if I was only a year younger. Everything was easy for him. He took our war experiences in stride and never let it control his thinking. Don't get me wrong; I was happy it was him who saved me. At the same time, Dad . . . I wished it hadn't been necessary."

Malcolm's expression was open amazement, then fascination. He stared at Fergus as though he'd never seen him before. "Are you telling me in all those years, you were in a competition with your best friend?"

I should have known that's what he'd think. "No, Dad," Fergus said, rubbing his head in exasperation. "Not even close. It was more like whatever we did, I knew Peter was just better at it than I was. Isobel suspected it bothered me sometimes. I don't think Peter did.

But it made me a better person because I tried harder and found out I could shine just because I thought I could. Which is good, isn't it?"

"Until you just expelled him, and me, from your life. Why was that, then?"

Fergus shifted in his chair. His body heated, his heartbeat skipped. He made his voice neutral, like anyone stating a well-known fact. "I needed a new start, growing without anybody's support, owning my mistakes. Most of all, not looking at Peter every day, knowing he saved my life." After a pause, he added, "And me always trying to prove I was worth it."

"If that weren't so monstrous, I'd laugh," Malcolm said, his tone dry.

"For goodness sakes, Dad. I know that now! But you asked how I felt then. So, are you satisfied? Now, can we get on with finding answers about how he died?" Any more talk and he'd be admitting Peter still haunted him.

Malcolm considered Fergus for a long moment, then settled himself in the chair. Fergus twirled his pencil between his fingers, trying to look nonchalant while his father got his thoughts together, but he was deeply disturbed by the questions. His replies had surprised him as much as they did his father. Had he resented Peter's ability for years without admitting it? Was there competition in their relationship? Thinking back, he thought not. They had loved each other as brothers. Then why did he fear he'd see nothing but revulsion in Peter's eyes for what happened at the dugout? The room began to close in on him again, and his chest tightened. He opened his mouth.

"There's more," Mrs. Mann's voice interrupted, and the pencil flew out of his fingers. He muttered to the underside of the desk as he retrieved it. Malcolm merely looked resigned at the interruption, as if long experience told him he had naught to do but listen.

"I hate passing on second-hand gossip, but in this case . . ." She paused and took a deep breath. "And besides, I've heard it more than once Lex Rideout makes regular visits to the house of Mrs. Perkins." She blushed bright pink, which said more than words as to the purpose of those visits.

Fergus's head poked up over the top of the desk. "Uh . . . Mrs.

Perkins?"

"Clara Perkins is Charles Perkins wife," said Mrs. Mann, with the emphasis on *wife.* "Cat's mother."

Fergus got to his feet. He and Malcolm looked at each other sharing amusement at Mrs. Mann's embarrassment. But was this piece of idle gossip in any way relevant, he wondered?

Malcolm spoke for both of them, prodding, "And where is Mr. Perkins . . . Charles?"

"On a train with the rest of them, I imagine," she replied. "One week they are here, the next, not. He was one of a parcel of men let go from GlasBottle early in the spring about the same time Mr. Davidson left. I must say, I was surprised. Charles Perkins didn't seem to be the type to just leave town, but then who can trust what goes on in families these days?" Mrs. Mann left the room muttering, "And that's all I have to say."

Fergus frowned. "Well, if Lex is after the mother, he would treat Cat well, wouldn't he? To stay on Clara's good side?" But the fact that Cat's father had also worked at GlasBottle with Peter nagged at him.

"Look," he added. "I don't think there is any danger to Cat from Lex Rideout. She couldn't possibly be involved vis-a-vis Peter and Clarissa Rideout. But we should keep an eye on her. Maybe Mrs. Mann can coax her here on the pretense of helping around the house?"

"Might be an idea. If we can gain her confidence, we might learn more about Peter." Malcolm picked up his brandy glass, swirled around the last few drops and drained it, looking depressed. "We've got nowhere else to start."

Fergus held up his notebook. "Okay, now, can we avoid the personal inquisition and get on to Peter's business history?"

"GlasBottle started up in the mid-twenties," Malcolm began. "A couple of investors from Winnipeg, on the lookout for new industry opportunities stopped off at Cypress Landing on their way to the West Coast. Incentives such as free gas to start a new industry, plus all the raw materials of silica and potash just over on the Saskatchewan side made them stay. Peter had a hard time settling after the war. He was ripe for a new venture." Malcolm looked impatient now. He began to massage the swollen knuckles of his fingers. "This can't really have any interest to you. Why don't I just tell you what happened in the last year he was here?"

"Because I don't know any of this," Fergus said, tapping his pencil on his notes for emphasis. "I have to know how he got caught up in the first place."

"Peter invested some start-up capital for shares in the new company."

"Where did he get the funds? He pretty well invested everything before we enlisted."

"He liquidated them. He gave the new company the major portion and started speculating with the leftover cash."

Fergus threw down his pencil and ran his hands down both cheeks. "Oh, no. Really?"

"Peter wasn't any different from anyone else before the crash. Watching everybody making money hand over fist, buying on margin, not able to resist the excitement of investing."

"You did," said Fergus. "Fortunately."

"I wasn't about to trade in a company whose shares were at inflated prices, with no relationship to its actual worth. Nobody cared about company financing or balance sheets then, not like they do now."

"Shutting the barn door and all. Isn't hindsight grand?" Fergus picked up his pencil again. "What's next?"

"With his investment, Peter wanted a management position as well. I advised him to start learning what it takes to make bottles, let alone market them. He looked into the background of the men and used his lawyer to draw up the legal details."

"Is his lawyer still Haskell?"

"Yes. Haskell and Buckley. I saw Harold Haskell at Peter's service. He left immediately when it ended." Malcolm paused, thinking, while Fergus made notes. "Odd he didn't come over to say a word." The thought seemed to make him remember something else. He went to the desk, leaned over Fergus's shoulder and rummaged in a side drawer. He removed a large brown envelope and took it back to his chair.

Fergus wrote busily for a few moments, put down Haskell's

name then abruptly focused on Malcolm. "Shouldn't there be legal documents? Property? His shares? Did the authorities confiscate them all?"

"I don't see how." Malcolm looked irritated at the thought. "It's still is an open case. I can't see them taking his possessions without first finding him guilty. The most they could do is freeze any assets." Lips set in grim lines, Malcolm absently brushed a pastry crumb from the arm of his chair.

"What happened at the bottle plant?" Fergus prompted.

"They started construction and imported equipment," Malcolm continued. "Don't ask me what equipment, I'm no authority on the arcana of glass making. Peter lost me when he started speaking of gobs, and viscosity something or other. They had a new machine that could turn out glass jugs at half the price of pottery stoneware and would be their ace in outbidding pottery customers for the same items. They hired experienced salesmen, and Peter went with them on their marketing trips for a while, but he didn't like being an agent. He preferred the supply side, he said. He seemed happy as if he had found a purpose, after . . ." Malcolm had started to say after Isobel died but stopped.

Fergus wisely skipped to the next item. "Who did the books?"

"In the beginning it was Peter. Before you ask, there was a good deal of direction from auditors in Winnipeg, and a man to set up the system and train him. When the company went bankrupt, Peter was no longer bookkeeper, and it was sold in '29."

Did Peter have anything to do with the cause of the bankruptcy? Did he lose his investment and decide to steal it back? Fergus was immediately ashamed of his thoughts.

He looked up from his notes to find Malcolm's eyes piercing into his mind.

"It prospered for a while," Malcolm said, his voice soft. "Companies actually dropped stoneware in favor of glass bottles. But as production grew, so did delays, and the marketing end wasn't working properly. Agents hired in other provinces were miles away and weren't familiar with the production, nor the delivery system. The CPR made the delivery rules. Peter accused them of provoking competition with other companies over delivery queues. The CPR mishandled crates, and there were a lot of breakages."

"The good old CPR." Fergus's lips curled in sarcasm. "As they said at Bill Miner's trial in Kamloops, '*Bill Miner isn't so bad. He robs the CPR every two years, and the CPR robs us all every day.*'"

Malcolm relaxed and grinned. "Peter would love that. This next is the important bit, so listen. The Company went into debt and began paying Peter in shares in lieu of wages. Finally, they couldn't carry on, and they made a deal with Strathcona Holdings to take it over."

A soft knock at the side of the open door, and they both looked up.

"Did you need anything else before I go off for the night, Mr. Muir?" asked Mrs. Mann. Fatigue lay in black circles under her eyes. *She really has taken to that girl.* Fergus had not thought Mrs. Mann had emotions, and now he was mildly shocked at his assumption.

"Can you arrange for Cat to come to the house on some pretext or other?" Malcolm said. "She's got information, I'm sure, even if she isn't quite aware of it yet. She trusts you. Perhaps you can convince her to trust us as well."

"If she shows up." Mrs. Mann's slow answer reflected her reluctance. "The child comes and goes like a ghost." Her mouth turned down at the corners to indicate what she thought of parents who let their children fend for themselves.

"Strathcona Holdings bought out GlasBottle in 1929, then what?" Fergus said after Mrs. Mann took herself off to her apartment above the carriage house.

"Peter became the overall manager. With his beginning investment and what he was paid while working, he ended up with between ten or fifteen percent of the shares. Together, it was enough to declare him a minority shareholder. After the crash, they kept going by carrying large inventories, but wages soon exceeded production. Peter hired a marketing manager from the East, to sell and also write up orders."

"And he got Lex Rideout," Fergus finished, adding, "So what?"

Malcolm smiled broadly watching Fergus's face. "Lex handled everything administrative. Bookkeeping, Banking, Accounts Receivable, and Accounts Payable. The works."

Fergus laughed and groaned at the same time. "It's a joke." But he knew many companies played fast and loose with accounting methods then. Peter wasn't the only trusting soul. Honesty and integrity were what he expected from people, if only because he treated others the same. *It is amazing there weren't many more cases of fraud,* Fergus thought. *This example would be a learning opportunity for next week's discussion with Max, to point out the consequences of non-uniform accounting standards.* He made a mental note.

"Peter left himself wide open," he said quietly to Malcolm. He had learned nothing here, only discouragement that there was nothing to warrant investigation. Discouragement made worse at the thought of Peter's inevitable descent into fraud and losing everything he had, including his faith in people.

"Was it because he didn't know the details of the operations? Or was he just fed the bottom line, only the information someone wanted Peter to know? Is there a chance we might take a look at the books during his time there? If Peter was a minority shareholder, wouldn't he have the right to order an audit of the records?" Fergus knew he was grasping at straws, looking for details.

"How do you think the fraud was discovered?" Malcolm passed his hand over his eyes as though he had repeatedly asked himself the same questions. "There was an independent audit, from Strathcona's hired auditors. They are not a publicly traded company, so they don't even have to have an audit before issuing a financial statement."

Fergus yawned then gave his head a vigorous rub to wake up some ideas. "I wish we knew why he ran. Why didn't he stay and fight then? Why come back now? The whole idea has got me thinking pigs fly. What are we missing?"

For an answer, Malcolm emptied the brown envelope over the desk in front of Fergus, pulled out a file of news clippings. He selected a piece and passed it over to Fergus.

"This is all I know. What was reported. And no, pigs don't fly. Peter wouldn't have left for good without telling me. I'm convinced he didn't know anything about this. I think he found out after he left and for some reason, decided not to come back. If we only knew why, we'd be halfway there."

The news clipping was dated May 1932. "*Local Man charged with Fraud*," It outlined the case against Peter. A separate account in a Calgary branch of the Imperial Bank in Peter's name. Cash, a lot of it, deposited and taken out under his signature. The bank manager identified Peter's picture, as the man who signed the signature card. There was Peter's signature on orders which could not be traced back to an actual customer. Cut and dried case.

Fergus looked at Malcolm in disbelief, then poked at the clippings. "This report indicates someone good at financial manipulation. Day to day financial affairs are one thing, and Peter was smart." Fergus waved the clipping in the air. "But he did not have the kind of knowledge to handle this type of fraud."

"You mean you found something you were better at than Peter?" Malcolm said in mock surprise.

"This type of fraud needs a trained mind, and you know it." A new purpose swelled his mind. He trusted his knowledge and competency. "Someone picked him out and framed him. Peter didn't talk to you? About discrepancies at the plant? There has to be something! There's always something."

"He wondered why there wasn't enough money in the bank when the cash flow statements said the opposite. Peter would look at the financial statement indicating cash flow was adequate, yet he never saw it from his end. Head Office wanted him to lay off men, and keep only those who were working on actual orders. He did to a certain extent but refused to lay off too many, because when the orders came in, he couldn't fill them. And they had a lot of bad debts."

Malcolm's tone intensified. "You people in the East can't appreciate the chaos in the West in those early Depression years. Orders came in, but the money didn't. All sorts of people couldn't pay their bills. It was a vicious cycle. Every company was facing the same things. People relied on someone else to pay so they, in turn, had a chance pay their own debts."

"So did you advise him to do anything at all?" Fergus couldn't stop the accusation.

"Nothing much." Malcolm massaged his fingers again, his face wincing in pain. "I regretted later that I didn't push him. I told him to ask questions at the company's head office, but can't say if he did. God knows, my clients had troubles not much different. Many times I refused the offer to become both a consultant and auditor. You know my ethics. We can't do both and stay at arm's length."

True, thought Fergus. An auditor couldn't be objective if he was personally involved in policy-making. But Malcolm wasn't Peter's auditor, so why didn't he advise him?

Malcolm read the question in Fergus's mind. He sighed. "I lumped Peter's concerns in common with my own clients, and I'm afraid I left him to his own devices."

Fergus smiled to himself and thought, *I can handle this job. It's what I normally do.* "Well, somebody executed a wicked scheme and got away with it. I think more questions are in order, don't you? You never know what may turn up."

"Quite," said Malcolm, non-committedly, but his face reflected satisfaction and a glimmer of hope.

11

"DO I have to? Can't you send Young Charlie?"
"Don't be silly, Cat." Her mother wiped the last plate
and stacked it in the cupboard with the rest of them. "Mr. Mercier
always adds a bit more to the meat when you go." She folded the tea
towel and hung it by the stove to dry. "Now no more arguing. And
remember to say thank you."

Cat shuffled slowly down the sidewalk, hating the chore. She
hopped over the cracks in the sidewalk, quoting, "*Step on a crack,
break your mother's back.*" At the end of the block, she went inside
Mercier's Meat Market, thankful the place was empty of customers
to witness her purchase.

"Ten cents worth of hamburger, please, Mr. Mercier." Except for
his bald head, Tom Mercier didn't look like his younger and thinner
brother next door. Stout and a happy smile creasing his fat cheeks,
he viewed the world with a benevolent eye where brother Fred's
only saw suspicion.

"Good afternoon, Cat. Hamburger? What luck. I've just made
a fresh batch." He smiled at her over the top of his glasses. "*Bonte
divine!* Every time I see you, it seems you've grown an inch. It must
be all my good beef, yes?"

Cat gave him the expected laugh. "I guess so, Mr. Mercier."

Mr. Mercier slapped a scoop of hamburger on a square of waxed
paper and placed it on the weigh scale. Before the needle stopped
moving, he scooped another bit of meat, adding it to the other, then
whipped the whole bunch off the scale. "Can't ever reckon the
amount correctly the first time. I must need new glasses." He tut-
tutted as he wrapped the meat in waxed brown paper.

"Thank you, Mr. Mercier." Cat reached up and put the dime

on top of the glass meat display, hoping her embarrassment didn't show. Mr. Mercier had weighed meat for so many years, he probably didn't even have to use the scale, then told herself he must do the same for other people too. She took the parcel and scooted outside and didn't see Tom Mercier's parting smile fade and his eyes darken with sadness.

The sight of a green car parked outside her gate brought her to a halt. Unsure whether she should run or wait, the package in her hand decided for her. Heart tripping in her chest, she continued round the back of the house, and soundlessly entered the kitchen. Voices came from the front room, her mother's and then a man's. Laying the package on the table, she turned and started to tiptoe out. Her mother's voice, raised now, called, "Cat! Could you come in here please?"

Cat held her breath and waited. Her mother's voice was not strident as it usually was when she had something to say. Maybe if she didn't move, she could fool her mother into thinking she'd already left.

"Cat!"

Cat had a sudden urge to pee.

"I have to wash my hands, Mama!" She made a dash for the bathroom. After washing her hands, she remained frozen at the sink. *Joe,* she thought. *What would Joe do?* She opened the bathroom door and marched with no hesitation into the front room. Cat looked at her mother questioningly, ignoring the man sitting across from her. She imagined his eyes penetrating her head. "Yes, Mama?"

"What have you been up to young lady?"

Cat was genuinely puzzled. "What?"

"Have you been hanging around the pottery? Amongst those hobos? After I told you to stay away from there?"

"No, Mama," Cat's eyes widened to perfect circles, and she shook her head. "I have been helping Mr. Levinson in his music store. He's fixing the violin, and I'm dusting and helping him arrange his music bins."

Lex Rideout spoke from behind her. "You haven't been around the pottery kilns?" His voice was soft but persistent. "I was down there last week, and I'm sure I saw you talking to a man. A vagrant."

His voice made her head buzz like bees around a hive.

She glanced at him, then back to her mother. "No Mama. I only asked one man there if he had seen Father when he was hitching on the train. I always ask when I see them coming from the trains. They aren't bad, Mama, really. Most of them are nice." To her horror, her voice wavered on the edge of crying. "I'd like to know if Dad's okay," she finished, gulping. "I really want him to come home."

"Oh Cat, honey," her mother said, her tone exasperated. "If your father wanted us to know where he was, he'd send a letter. I haven't heard from him since he left, near on four years now. I don't expect him to come back, baby. We have to make the best of it. Mr. Rideout has been good to us, Cat. We're lucky to have him." She smiled at the man across from her. "He's sorry he had to lay off Daddy. He's helping all the men who had to be laid off. He told me he'd have hired him back by now if he'd only stayed here." She reached out and took Cat's hand. "Don't you see what people think of me when they see you talking to hobos and vagrants?" She shook Cat's arm a little and said more briskly, "They'll say I don't care about you, and you may get hurt. You have to stop making me look bad."

Lex Rideout spoke again, his voice soft. "Here." He reached out his hand to her.

Cat pretended she didn't hear, and her mother pushed her forward, whispering. "Mind your manners!"

Lex Rideout pressed a coin into her hand and closed her fingers over it, holding her hand in his, trying to pull her gaze from the floor with his own. "Buy yourself some candy."

The buzzing noise in Cat's head muted the room.

"Thank you," she whispered, and left. Dropping the nickel on the table beside the meat, she scrubbed her hand against her dress and hurried outside, letting the screen door slam behind her. She headed down the wooden walk at the side of the house until she came to the gate near the front street. She opened the gate and wedged herself in the small space where it met the corner of the fence. Curled inside, knees pulled up, she drew the gate towards her and hid.

In the weeks after her father left home, she'd taken refuge there often. Soon after he'd gone, they moved to this house because the rent was cheaper, and her mother had said it was all they could afford. But Harley told her their house had been purchased by someone, and they were told to get out or be put on the street. Cat would never forget her first sight of a family put out of their house, sitting in the street surrounded by all their furniture. She was glad now to have a place to live, but she missed the house where she and Joe had been born, and all its familiar corners, where everything in the family was solid and secure.

A memory of the day her father left forced its way into her head. She and Joe sat quietly near the swing behind the house, both scuffing at the gravel in silence as another argument raged on inside. "We have no money, Charles," their mother cried. "Nothing! You need to go back to the plant and get them to put you back to work. Go down on your knees and *beg* if you have to." The back door swung open, and their father came down the porch steps. Without seeing them, he disappeared around the side of the house. She looked at Joe then, tears welling in his eyes as he studied the corner, anticipating, as if it would come to life at any moment. The same way she had looked at the train tracks when Joe left her. . . .

The front screen door creaked open, and Cat strained to listen to the footsteps cross the porch to the front sidewalk. Her mother mentioned Cat and said she'd come around, she was just shy. Lex Rideout's voice replied something, and then her mother's voice again as they moved towards the sidewalk and his car. Cat heard Joe's name and Young Charlie's. Her own name was said again, and a longer discussion, then a car door, and the sound of the engine moving away.

"Cat!" her mother's angry voice pierced the air.

Cat held her breath until the front door closed again.

She was used to making herself small to stay out of the way. And so she sat where she was for a long while. Her thoughts turned to Sir, and she felt better. There was something she was supposed to do, she knew, but she couldn't remember what it was. She tried to focus on it, but the bees started buzzing in her head again. This time she let the buzzing carry her along. She frowned. A picture of an envelope popped into her thoughts, and the face of Mr. Muir sitting down beside her on a bench. She absently rubbed the hand which had held the nickel Mr. Rideout gave her. The feel of it was still burning a spot into her palm. Why did her mother let him put his sweaty hand on her? Had he seen the nickel on the table where she'd thrown it? Silently crying for Joe, she rose, snuck around to the front street, and started running.

MRS. Mann had just finished taking the trash to the back alley, when she spied Cat behind the garage, standing quietly, eyes red. At the look of Cat's face, she had to stop herself from rushing forward and pulling the child in close.

"Cat," she said instead. "I was wondering where you've been. Have you come to see me?"

At the girl's hesitant nod, she continued, "I was just going to sit down on the veranda with Duke and a cup of lemonade and a piece of cake. Now we have company. Isn't this nice?" She smiled at Cat as though she might be any lady she met down the street and invited in. But Mrs. Mann's sharp gaze didn't miss the disquiet on Cat's face and the arms held stiffly down the sides of her undernourished frame. *Something or someone's given her a good scare.* Mrs. Mann held open the gate, indicating Cat should go through ahead of her. With a glance behind her, Cat hesitated, her eyes wide and unfocused.

Mrs. Mann saw Malcolm heading her way, on his daily walk around the yard. He came up to the gate, looked around the corner and saw Cat.

"Well, I do declare, Mrs. Mann," Malcolm said, taking in the situation. "We seem to have Royalty coming to tea this afternoon. And a Princess by the look of her. Margaret Rose? Now, why weren't we informed so we could prepare a proper welcome?" He smiled at Cat, as he strutted forward to stand before her. "Your Royal Highness," he said, his tone formal. "Welcome to our humble cottage. We would be honored if you would take rest with us and partake of some refreshment."

He waited until he saw Cat's eyes focus with interest on him and a small smile tug at the corner of her mouth. Her rigid arms relaxed.

"If you would just take my arm, Princess? While tea is being prepared, might I show you around our small garden? You might find flowers of interest, and then we can sit out of the heat of the day with delicious delicacies." Malcolm put out his arm, and Cat laid her hand daintily on it. They both marched regally by Mrs. Mann through the gate. As they went through, Malcolm handed the housekeeper his cane and winked. "Can you take care of this, Mrs. Mann, while I entertain our royal guest?" The housekeeper stood open-mouthed while Malcolm went along the path, walking like a Prince.

Fergus arrived home in the late afternoon to find his father and Cat in the study, putting together a picture puzzle. They both looked up as Fergus sauntered in.

"May I present Miss Catherine Ann Theresa," said Malcolm formally, giving a regal wave towards his guest. "Otherwise known as Cat."

"How do you do?" Fergus took a cue from his father's expression and bowed down to shake her hand. "I'm Mr. Muir's son, otherwise known as Fergus to my friends and pretty ladies." Cat regarded him solemnly. Then as if making up her mind on something, she smiled. The smile transformed her face from grave to bewitching. She looked so much like Isobel, Fergus's heart jolted.

"I am learning how to play chess," she said.

Fergus raised his eyebrows at his father.

"She's quick, and we'll have to watch out when she really gets into it. Now we have a jigsaw puzzle. There isn't much conversation while playing chess." Malcolm's eyes sent the rest of the message.

Pulling up a chair to the table, Fergus selected a puzzle piece. He toured around the puzzle trying to fit it into various slots. Cat sighed, rolled her eyes at the ceiling and took the piece from him, moving it to the chimney of a house. It fit right in.

"Oh." Fergus gave her an exaggerated sheepish look.

"She's been doing the same all afternoon," Malcolm informed him.

"Okay, Miss Smarty-Pants." Fergus chose another piece with a neutral color and no discernable pattern. "Where does this one go?" Cat looked at the piece, then at the puzzle and pointed.

Fergus tried it, and it fit. He sighed dramatically. "I'm convinced."

He reached for another piece, making sure to keep his eyes on the game. "And where is the violin you always carry with you?"

"I left it at Mr. Levinson's music store." Cat slotted another piece to complete a duck swimming on the pond. "He's giving it new strings."

"Oh yes, I remember seeing you last Saturday," Fergus said, then met eyes with his father before adding, "You met my friend, Peter, didn't you?"

Malcolm held his breath, but Cat didn't seem disturbed. "Yes."

"How did you meet him?" Fergus asked, keeping his voice neutral.

"At the camp under the train bridge." She looked from one to the other, measuring their reactions. "My mother wouldn't like me going there."

Fergus stopped himself from saying, *who would?*

"Well, now, that's interesting." Malcolm was genuinely curious and let it show. "But why go there at all? It's a brave thing to do."

"That's what Sir said. But the people aren't bad, and they were all nice to me. I met two women and their husbands. There aren't any bedbugs either like my mother says." She rolled a puzzle piece in her fingers, then joined it to the fishing pole held by a boy. She inspected it for a moment, then said, "I wanted to ask if someone had ever seen my dad."

"And did you find anyone who did?"

She shook her head, biting her lip and looking down at the half-completed puzzle.

Fergus took over. "Well, the vagrants who work here are nice. But then if they weren't Mrs. Mann would soon sort them." He snorted, which made her smile in agreement.

"Did you ever see Sir Peter get into an argument with someone there?"

She creased her head, thinking. "Once I did. A man followed me around, and Sir chased him away. The man didn't like it, and he swore at Sir. Then Sir told me he'd stay with me and help me."

"That sounds like him. We used to be called the Three Musketeers, Peter, Me, and Isobel. She was Peter's sister. We had a lot of adventures." He chuckled, and his voice got confidential.

"We went skating on the creek one day. There had been a chinook, and the ice was soft. We were playing tag, and we got all bunched up and fell through the ice. By the time we walked home, our snow suits were frozen solid. We looked like icebergs." Cat looked wistful at such fun.

"Good Lord! I never knew that." Malcolm gave Fergus such a severe look, Cat began to laugh, and Fergus joined in.

Fergus watched Cat laughing and said, "You remind me of Isobel."

She turned to him, interested. "Sir told me I reminded him of someone. Was it her?"

Fergus nodded, a lump in his throat.

Cat continued to plug piece after piece into the rural camp scene. "He called you Gussy, and said I could trust you." she stopped and looked at them both, eyes wide.

Malcolm laid a warning hand on Fergus's arm. Fergus continued cautiously, "He did? Doesn't surprise me at all. We were good friends. Did he ask you to come and see us?" They both held their breath.

Cat's eyes squinted at the far wall. "Something about . . ." Fergus saw her hand clench, and her face pale. "I don't remember." A knuckle rubbed against the palm of the other hand.

Malcolm shot Fergus a warning glance. "Well, no matter," said Fergus. "Here you are now. My father will have you playing chess in no time, and you might even beat him. I can't."

"Are you going to tell my mother about him?"

Both men shook their heads in unison.

The three hadn't noticed Mrs. Mann come into the room. She leaned against the doorframe with her arms crossed over her chest, watching them with a smile on her face. Malcolm was the first to see her.

"Sorry to interrupt your business meeting, but thought I'd give you fair warning. Dinner in twenty minutes." She nodded to Cat. "I've set an extra place if you'd care to stay. Chicken and dumplings."

Cat immediately stood up. "I have to go home." She cast her eyes longingly around the study and the bookshelves.

Fergus noticed and before she could dash out he blurted, "Do you like books?"

"I go to the library almost every day."

"Well, perhaps you can help us out. Dad and I need a catalog of our books, and to arrange them in better order. There's some time before school starts, and you could have a job making a list. You'll find our old books too. Nancy Drew? Tom Swift?" Cat's face glowed with pleasure.

Malcolm took up the call and nodded briskly, encouraging her. "I can't do it myself, and Mrs. Mann is too busy."

Cat's eyes shone. "I'd like to do it."

Fergus stood up as if the matter was settled. "I'll drive you home and ask your mother if it would be alright if you spend the next week here. She can't mind if she knows Mrs. Mann is here too."

At the mention of her mother, Cat's eagerness waned, but the prospect of books won out. Malcolm could hear her clear voice chattering as they left.

Over dinner, served under the glowering expression of Mrs. Mann who announced to the room at large how the dumplings had fallen and the chicken overcooked and dried out, Fergus discussed the events of the afternoon.

"They live at the end of a street of row houses, over by the flour mill," said Fergus. "They are all city relief houses. The inside is clean enough. Clara Perkins is something else. She's pretty if you like the big blue eyes and the fluffy, helpless type. Cat must get those amazing eyes from her father. I told her mother my father was severely disabled." He spread his hands in apology to a startled Malcolm. "And Mrs. Mann needed the help for this project. She was all feigning '*Cat is too young to work*' and '*I need her at home*.' Right up to the time I offered to pay her some money which I said would help her with school clothes for Cat. Her tune changed then."

"We should be careful," Malcolm said. "We don't want talk around the town."

"I thought of that, and said she was right. Cat was too young to be paid outright, but perhaps the whole arrangement was best kept between us. I'm sure she won't tell anyone at all." Fergus curled his lip over the same disgust he had smothered while talking to Clara Perkins.

Malcolm told Fergus what he had learned of the family. Her brothers and older sister, Rose, who was a maid and babysitter for the Hutchison family on First Street. "Cat has a twin brother, Joe. She says her mother sent him to a farm over in Bow Valley area.

"I'm distressed that she took him out of school if you can imagine someone doing that to a twelve-year-old. He plays the violin too. I heard him in the Park, and he's very good. It's his violin Cat carries around." Malcolm ate some chicken and poked at a dumpling. "I got the impression she's not telling everything. When she told me she watched him go to the farm, it was too . . ." He waved the fork in a circle before him, looking for the right word. "*emphatic.* Almost as though she had rehearsed her story."

"What Peter said to her about us disturbs me." Fergus let his thoughts whirl in confusion, recalling what little Cat had revealed this afternoon. "I find it quite peculiar that he told her she could trust us. What can't she remember whatever it is? If she knows something, why is she blanking it out?" He dropped his eyes to his plate. Shutting out unwelcome thoughts was something he had perfected. It struck him now, with her in the car, he hadn't once felt he was suffocating, as he usually did.

"Did she tell you about her older brother? He's sixteen, and I get the impression Cat doesn't care for him much." Malcolm went on to explain Harley had been skipped two grades so he was now finished high school.

"Really? On the way, she asked me where I worked and if men were lined up when I was hired. When I told her what I did, she said, '*Harley says accounting is boring.*'"

"So what did you say?" Malcolm watched him closely. He strongly suspected Fergus felt the same way about his profession.

"What I say to everybody. The stories behind the figures aren't boring." He grinned at Malcolm. "It's funny. I used to use the line just to keep people quiet, but now with Peter's situation, it's true. A self-fulfilling thing, do you suppose?"

Malcolm said nothing but looked pleased.

Fergus speared a carrot, raised the fork to his mouth then changed his mind. "When I asked Cat about her friends, she went all silent. Which means she hasn't any. Would people shun her? Stop their children from being with her because of her mother's reputation?"

Malcolm put down his own knife and fork and sighed. "The Depression has cast a pall over every phase of people's lives. When the money ran out, their attitudes changed. They looked inward, became competitive and made new rules of living and behavior. It made them turn all common things into something special, and people find a perverse delight in their neighbor's failures."

"Like what?"

"Mrs. Mann told me one woman rose at four-thirty in the morning so when other wives got up, they would see she was the first one out hanging her wash on the clothesline."

Fergus grinned until he saw Malcolm was serious.

"They focus on anything which makes them more respectable than the next person." Malcolm pointed his fork at Fergus, nodding. "A competition of superior homemaking skills give an artificial power over hard times. And yes, mothers watch their children never associate with someone poorer or less *moral* than they believe they are themselves. It might rub off. Oh sure, there are thirty different women's organizations in the city, serving the deserving poor. It makes them feel righteous, if not holy. I wonder if the very poor really care anymore. It gives some truth to the saying 'blessed are the poor for they can act natural without fear of what people will think.'" Malcolm laid down his knife and fork and took a sip of water.

Malcolm's insight left Fergus wondering, and with a sense of shock. Not so much at Malcolm's words, but at his own lack of perception. *Why haven't I noticed people have become hypocritical?* This city which had moved forward since its inception was now standing still, substituting dark humor for well-being. Had his preoccupation with his own mood made him blind? In his worst moments, the pleasures of his childhood had given him hope that joy might once again be part of his future.

"What kind of adults will these children become? People whose security comes from constantly proving they are as good as, or better than their neighbor? Don't these people realize what kind of future they are imposing on their kids?"

"Can any one of them imagine a future different from what they have now?"

Fergus had no answer. They finished eating in silence, gripped in their own thoughts.

12

AT the turn of the century, a pair of businessmen imagined a men only, gentlemen's club in Cypress Landing. Where, by convention, dialogue was never formal, and what was uttered inside the walls was never repeated outside. And so the Assiniboia Club was born. It had since evolved into a place where city businessmen, rural farmers, and ranchers met for the mutual benefit of all. The club was a typical male bastion with the comfortable odor of nail-studded leather armchairs beside upright cigar stands, over-stuffed chesterfields in front of a large marble fireplace. In the corner stood a radio cabinet, and scattered here and there, burnt into the walls, were the brands of several area ranches. Every room was a smoking room, and this Monday evening, open windows and ceiling fans struggled to contain the haze.

Fergus and Malcolm arrived together with the planned goal of subtly delving for information about GlasBottle, Peter, and anything else that might yield clues.

"Don't go charging in like a wild bull, Fergus. The operative word here is *subtle*. Or with you, hyper-subtle. This is not the time to imitate Mrs. Mann."

"Good advice, Dad." Fergus slapped him on the back and snickered. "I'll be the soul of discretion." When Malcolm turned down his mouth at him, Fergus added soberly, "Of course I will. I do have some experience with business tact, you know."

They entered into a noisy, smoke-filled room. Fergus left Malcolm saying, "I'll get the drinks." He pushed himself into a space at the bar and tried to catch the eye of the busy bartender. *Nothing more elusive than a waiter's eye*, he thought just as the bartender looked over. Fergus held up two fingers and mouthed, "Whisky."

The barman nodded. While he waited, Fergus turned and faced the lounge. He spotted Harold Haskell, a head taller than the crowd, standing with the familiar figure of the Mayor, a short, round man with dark hair and a bald spot. The barman placed two glasses in front of Fergus, and a chit which he signed, then he returned to Malcolm. Handing him a glass, they both headed towards Haskell.

". . . heard your speech yesterday, telling everyone bad times are over," Haskell was saying, "You sounded so sincere, I almost believed you." Both men laughed heartily. Haskell moved to greet Malcolm and Fergus. "Hello, Muir," he said. "Haven't seen you in a monkey's age. I was going to check the obits to see if you were listed."

"Happy you didn't find me," replied Malcolm, saluting the other with his drink. "Since you're only a few years shy of me."

"And me," said the Mayor, laughing again. Nodding to the men, he moved off towards another group.

"So how are you these days?" Haskell glanced at Malcolm's cane and opened a pack of cigarettes. "Arthritis still acting up?"

"No, small mercies. My body seems to be holding its own this summer, if not actually winning," replied Malcolm.

Haskell presented his cigarette box to the men, both declining. "Glad to hear it." He lit up and stared at the glowing embers on the end with a frown. He nodded to Fergus. "I saw you both at Davidson's service but didn't want to intrude. I know it wasn't easy for either of you."

Relieved Haskell had opened the subject, Fergus cut across his father's murmured thank you and asked, "Do you think Peter did it?"

"No," said Haskell without hesitation. He looked around to see if they might be overheard, then lowered his voice. "I filed objections and statements of defense against the freezing of his assets, just to keep it alive, in case he came back. But with his death . . ." He shrugged and took another pull on his cigarette. He turned his head away from them while he exhaled.

Only for a brief moment, Fergus wondered if he should ask the next question. "His Will?"

Haskell shook his head. "He died intestate. I advised him many times to make a Will, but you know, people think they'll live forever. And I suppose he thought he had nobody left, so he put it off. Now my hands are tied."

"Nothing in his house?" Fergus pushed, ignoring Malcolm's frown.

"No, it was searched thoroughly for papers, although they were looking for anything relating to the charges. But I doubt he left a Will there. Now I must track down his wife and tell her she can make a claim on his estate as his only relative. She may have already filed for divorce once she settled in Edmonton. There isn't much of anything left to claim."

Gordon Hutchison appeared, before Fergus could continue. "Hello, you two. You look too serious here. Not allowed, you know." Gordon Hutchison was the manager of freight operations for the Cypress Landing CPR terminus. He nodded to Haskell and said to Malcolm, "Haven't seen you around for a coon's age, Muir. You're looking good for an old codger. Retirement too much? Thinking of coming back to work are you?"

The new arrival edged in to stand between Haskell and Fergus, who noticed the flicker of relief on Haskell's face. Stopped in his inquisition, he looked over the room and recognized Lex Rideout against the far wall by the fireplace, smoking and sipping his drink. Fergus touched Malcolm's arm, jerked his head towards Lex, and left the group. Replenishing his drink, he meandered along, weaving around various groups towards Lex, stopping to trade remarks and shake hands with men he knew before continuing on to the next group.

Conversations rumbled around the room.

"Hottest summer on record this year. Temperatures are always around 100 degrees. We don't know what rain looks like." . . . *"The new Wheat Board is offering seventy-eight cents a bushel."—"Won't help me. My crop is pretty sparse. Even the steers are nosing around the short grass looking for more"* . . . *"German troops landed in Rhineland. Goering took over the very airport the British built. Mark my words, those Nazis are going to be trouble."* . . . *"What about Aberhart saying he's going to reissue millions of dollars of Alberta Bonds at a lower rate?"—"His brain is atrophied from*

all that rarified air in Edmonton."—"Well, you voted for him." . .
. *"The four western provinces have twenty-four senators and over three million people. The Maritimes have twenty-four Senate seats and one million population. By those calculations, we should have seventy-five."—"Why have the Senate at all? A bunch of old guys. If they died in their chairs, nobody would notice."*

Fergus finally reached the front then feigned surprise, as if he had only just spotted Rideout. "Hello, Lex." He stood beside Lex and took a healthy sip of his drink. "Good turnout tonight. How's your golf game?"

"Too hot to golf."

"Well, September is almost upon us," said Fergus, casting about to keep the conversation open. "It might rain. At least we can hope." He laughed, and Lex Rideout grunted, unsmiling. Fergus studied his face. "Are you feeling alright, Lex? You aren't your jolly old self. Anything I can help you with? Work going okay?"

Lex pulled himself upright. "Rules say we aren't supposed to talk about work here,"

"The rules also say nothing said in here will be repeated outside."

Rideout shifted from one foot to the other, still studying the middle of the room. "What's work, these days? I need new equipment. We should have had it five years ago. Equipment breakdowns and the upkeep are almost bankrupting the place."

What did Lex expect when cheap labor is put with expensive machinery? Fergus kept his thoughts to himself.

"And I've been plagued with breakages by our shipping company. Totally irresponsible."

"Replace the shippers with someone else?" Fergus put his elbow on the fireplace mantel and leaned back into it, trying to appear as though he were only mildly interested in talking.

Rideout snorted. "Contract." He took another sip from his glass and scowled. "On top of that, everybody wants me to know that Peter Davidson turned up again. It brought back some pretty unpleasant memories. I would've liked a chance to ask him why he took my wife." His face turned red, and he regarded Fergus face on for the first time since their conversation started. "I bet you talked to him."

"No, I didn't." Fergus stood up straight and dropped his gaze to his glass now that Rideout's small bear eyes were on him. "I was as surprised as everyone else."

"Why do you think he did it? Entice her away? She wasn't confident and would never have gone by herself."

"I knew Peter from when we were children together," Fergus offered. "It wasn't in his character to run off." *I wonder why he doesn't say he'd like to know where she is now. He's more interested in wondering why she went. Or does he already know, and only wonders if other people do?*

"How do you know what he was like? You weren't here."

Fergus, conceded the point, fighting to keep his temper. "How did you find out they ran off together? I mean, could it have been someone else?" He looked sheepishly at Lex and held up a hand. "Just curious."

Lex gave him a withering look. "She left a note. Naming Davidson."

"Oh? That's odd." Fergus didn't hide his surprise. Why would an abused woman leave a note for her abuser? What if it had been found early? And why tell him it was Peter? If Peter was going to return and Fergus was sure he would have, it would put him in a terrible position. Was she so foolish?

"How is it odd?" Rideout said. "She told me I wasn't good enough. I guess Peter was—since he'd cleaned out the bank account." He gulped down his drink in one swallow.

"I can't get past the idea Peter was an embezzler," Fergus protested, his face set in mulish lines, openly doubting. "I read in the paper what the auditors found. But where was the second opinion?"

"A second opinion on what?"

"Auditors hired by Strathcona Holdings did the audit. Why couldn't Peter's lawyer get an independent auditor to review the books of both Strathcona Holdings and GlasBottle?"

"Nothing to do with me." Lex waved the review away. "Head Office didn't ask my opinion. Are you trying to reopen the case, Fergus? Even if I could help, I wouldn't. All the gossip would only start over, and people would call me a fool again. It's bad enough he had to come back and remind everybody."

"I'm sorry, Lex," Fergus said, meaning it. "It's a hell of a thing to happen to any man. But isn't Peter entitled to justice? The financial records are important right now. We could help each other. I get to the truth about Peter, and in the process, help you find your own answers. It would be worth it, wouldn't it?" Fergus put his glass to his mouth, half sick with his hypocrisy. He was the last one to offer advice on truth and peace.

Lex didn't reply, and after a moment, Fergus asked, "Did you keep the note?" Rideout turned horrified eyes to him, and Fergus quickly added, "I mean, I knew a fellow down East who had the same thing happen. He kept the letter and foolishly read it over and over, torturing himself. I hope you wouldn't do the same."

"Why would I be so stupid? I think about it sometimes. Who wouldn't?"

But his eyes flickered as he looked down into his empty glass. *He's lying*, thought Fergus. *About there being a note or about not keeping it?*

"Look, Muir." Rideout's voice was harsh. "I'll think about it. But, the company's my livelihood. Stir up trouble, and people start fighting back."

Fergus stared at him. Cigarette smoke lazily whirled around Rideout's face, blurring his expression. "I know you're trying to help. But to clear Davidson? I dunno."

"Right now, you're my only hope, Lex. If it wasn't Peter, then it's someone else. Wouldn't you like to know for sure? What if it were still going on?"

Lex didn't answer, but his eyes widened as though the question startled him.

A resounding gong drowned the din of voices. Dinner was announced with the meeting to follow. The men began to file into the other room.

Fergus finished off his drink and went to join Malcolm.

THE next day, started out easily enough. Cat was installed in the study with a notebook and asked to list all the book titles with authors, and think about how to section the library into categories. She settled into her task with a big smile on her face, and Duke to keep her company. Even if the job was spur of the moment, Fergus was glad of the inspiration. It was a good idea to sort their small library out. After telling Mrs. Mann he would not be home for lunch, Fergus headed to the office, walking in the morning sunshine, under brilliant blue skies. The day was already moving towards another scorcher. He had too much to drink again the night before. Also, his mind still echoed with Rideout's reference to the years of no contact with Peter, resulting in another restless night.

After a few hours at the office, he took advantage of a break to go out for a needed haircut. Rounding the corner of the hotel to the barbershop, he met Malcolm coming from the other direction. Grinning, he opened the door to the shop and waved him inside.

Fortunately, the place was empty. Eddie, the longtime barber, and sole operator, welcomed them with surprised pleasure.

"Well, as I live and breathe." He pointed to the chair and said, "The son and father. I thought you had gone to the competition." Eddie always said the same thing when Malcolm showed up; even it had been only three weeks since the last haircut.

Fergus started towards the chair. "You don't mind, Dad? I have an appointment soon, the one we talked about." The two eyed each other as he sat.

Eddie whipped the cloth around his shoulders, tucked it in and examined his cut. "The usual?" Fergus relaxed easily, under the clipping sound of scissors while they exchanged views about the weather, nothing new there, a few anecdotes about the comings and goings of visitors to the hotel, and the Depression.

"Never seems to get any better," said Eddie. "Our part of Alberta is nothing but a life of wind and grasshoppers. A farmer told me grasshoppers even eat the clothes off the clothesline. I've stopped shaving the farmers. You wouldn't believe it, but the dirt is embedded right into their faces. It dulls all my razors."

Fergus, sitting with his eyes closed, had no reply to this piece of information. The dust storms and grasshopper menace was no longer news.

Eddie continued with his scissors.

"I read about the death of Peter Davidson," he said at last. "A crying shame for him to end up that way. He came in here regularly. A nice fellow. I never believed what they said about him."

"No," said Malcolm. "Nor what they still say."

Fergus finally opened his eyes.

"I used to hear talk from the men who worked at GlasBottle." Eddie worked the scissors and comb around Fergus's ears. "They all chipped in to pay for a game of billiards. Money's scarce, but habits die hard, I guess, and who am I to say people shouldn't have a bit of enjoyment? It's better than drink. Afterwards, they would come in here and hang around while one or two got a cut. And they talked. Of course, I'd listen in."

Eddie let out his signature giggle, a deep breath, a snort, and a bray like a donkey. In his ecstasy, the comb he flourished in the air left his fingers and bounced off the chair to the floor. He exchanged his laugh for a cuss and fetched a fresh one from his work counter. "People think barbers are invisible," he continued his story. "As long as we keep our mouths shut like the barber pole outside the door, they ignore us when they talk."

"Anything interesting?" Malcolm's voice was casual.

"When things started to go bad, they were worried people might be laid off. They said the work was there alright, but wondered why nobody seemed to be getting paid . . . except for Mr. Rideout."

"What?" Fergus turned his head to look up at him, but it was forcefully put back in place.

"That's what they said to each other. Then a lot of them were laid off, and they didn't come in anymore. It was probably all sour lemons against Mr. Rideout. He's done us proud. Even paid for uniforms for the whole high school rugby team out of his own pocket. Can't get much better. It sets the boys a good example, and heaven knows young people need a good example these days."

Eddie used the brush on Fergus, held up a mirror for inspection and whipped off the wrap. Fergus paid, nodded to his father, and left. As he turned the corner along the street to his office, he saw the object of Eddie's monologue a few doors down, speaking to a woman. Curious, he examined the display in the men's wear store window while watching them. The woman looked young, had dark hair and was carrying a briefcase which she had up against her chest like a shield. She shook her head at Rideout and turned her shoulder as if to walk past him. Rideout put his hand on her arm and said something. She pushed past him and rapidly went cater-corner across the street, not minding the traffic. A crowd of young boys passed her and surrounded Rideout, laughing noisily. They all went into the coffee shop.

Fergus fought the urge to follow when he looked at his watch and hurried to his office. Sterling Matthews, an excise tax auditor at the Department of National Revenue, had just arrived and was waiting for him. His greying hair said he'd been around for a while. Fergus found him easy going, with a ready smile.

After he'd satisfied all the tax auditor's questions about the companies Fergus represented, he was able to relax. He decided earlier to raise the subject of Strathcona Holdings, hoping Sterling might pass on any information about past investigations of the company.

"Are you staying overnight in Cypress Landing?" Fergus asked him, ready to test the waters. "Would you like to come to my house for dinner?"

"No, I'm afraid I am taking the train to Calgary tonight," Sterling replied. "Next time, perhaps." He leaned back in his chair.

"Rough day?" Fergus asked, seeing the slight stretch and groan from the other man.

"Yes." Sterling laughed. "If I hear one more man today ask a sneaky question prodding for information about another company, I'll get physical with his nose."

Fergus blinked a few times and smiled. *Malcolm will enjoy hearing how my plan went*, Not wishing to embarrass them both with a blatant breach of ethics, and keep his nose intact, he chuckled and changed the subject. Resisting an impulse to offer him a drink from a bottle kept in his desk's bottom drawer, Fergus opted for coffee and biscuits brought in by Miss Watts. Small talk revealed mutual acquaintances from Fergus's time spent in Ontario.

Saying goodbye, he asked for Sterling's card. "It's handy to have a contact in Ottawa when I have tax questions needing quick answers," he said, and gave his card in return, genuinely liking the man. "Until next time, when you will find our house more comfortable that a hotel."

THE same evening, Fergus and Malcolm were still at the dining room table eating dessert and coffee when the doorbell rang.

Mrs. Mann, looking sour and wearing her hat, bustled through the kitchen. Both men watched bemused as she passed through the dining room to the front hall to answer the door. Fergus grinned at Malcolm and pointed to his head.

She soon returned and announced, "Mr. Jack Levinson says he must see you on a matter of urgency." Her face questioned the urgency part, but she stood aside while he came into the room, a bit out of breath.

"I do apologize for the interruption," he said seeing them at the table.

"Not at all," replied Fergus, rising and pointing to a chair. He hid his surprise, wondering if there was a problem with Max. "Nice to see you again, Jack. Please join us for coffee and dessert?" Mr. Levinson sketched a wave and smiled towards Malcolm and took a seat.

Fergus looked at Mrs. Mann. "Ah, Mrs. Mann. A new hat, I see. Very becoming. Could you bring another plate please, before you go out?" He grinned at her.

"I've just come in," she said, shooting an acid look at him that said he should be locked up.

Mr. Levinson sat down and waited until Mrs. Mann set a plate of strudel before him and poured his coffee. He thanked her and watched her leave the room. "Do you know of a girl named Cat Perkins?"

"Has something happened?" Both Fergus and Malcolm said at once.

"No, no." Now it was Jack's turn to be surprised at their evident alarm. He looked from one to the other then reached into his jacket pocket and pulled out a letter. "I was repairing Cat's violin today. There was a tear in the lining of the case, and inside the lining, I found this." He handed the envelope to Fergus. "I think from where

I found it, it's important. I thought you should see it right away."

It was unopened, with the notation private and confidential on it. It was addressed to Fergus. Seeing the familiar handwriting, Fergus held it out to Malcolm.

"It's from Peter," he whispered, voice unsteady.

Malcolm leaned forward. "Open it."

Swallowing, Fergus examined the envelope again, not quite believing. Hands shaking, he took a knife beside his plate and slit the envelope open. He pulled out two sheets and spread them apart.

"It's his Will," he said, scanning the nearest sheet, and handed it over to Malcolm while he took up the second closely written page. The writing on both sides of the paper was cramped and uneven, but legible.

Fergus read quickly, then again more carefully. When he finished, he gazed at Malcolm through tear-filled eyes, unable to speak.

Malcolm immediately took charge. "Mr. Levinson," he said crisply. "Can you stay for a while? I want to phone Peter's lawyer. He will want to see you."

Less than an hour later the doorbell rang again. Muttering, Mrs. Mann marched down the hall towards the front door, then ushered Harold Haskell into the dining room.

"Coffee please, Mrs. Mann." Fergus waved Haskell towards a chair.

Without preamble, Malcolm told him what had transpired and laid the documents, with the envelope, in front of him. While he read, Mrs. Mann brought in fresh coffee and quietly left again. Haskell finished reading and looked up to find three pairs of anxious eyes staring at him. He smiled.

"Excellent. We can use this. Nobody can contest it was written by Peter. Jack, I must ask you to sign a notation, explaining how you came by this letter and testify you watched Fergus open the document in front of you and attest, as far as you know, none of us were aware of the contents." He glanced at the clock. "Also the date and time. We can draft it out tonight, then have it signed and witnessed in my office. I want to study our options, so it'll be a few days."

"Gladly," replied Levinson, seeming confused at the rapid turn of events, then satisfied that his sense of urgency had proved correct.

"I want you, Fergus, and you, Malcolm to come in as well. There will be some formal documents which need your signatures."

Haskell returned the papers to the envelope and put them in his pocket. "Who is this person Cat, named as Peter's beneficiary?"

"Her name is Catherine Perkins. She twelve." Between them, Peter and Malcolm described Peter's involvement with Cat, and what they had found out about her. "Peter says here," he indicated the letter, "he'd give her a letter for us. He obviously put the envelope into her violin case shortly before he was killed."

"This is very bad news." Jack Levinson interrupted, shifting uncomfortably. "I would not like to think Cat is in harm's way."

"We are making sure that doesn't happen," Fergus said grimly. "Now more than ever."

Haskell frowned. "The question is, did she know the letter was in the case? I think at this point, we all must keep quiet about what has gone on here tonight. If your suspicions are correct, and you think this girl knows something then she may be in peril, now she has acquired ownership of Peter's shares in GlasBottle, and thus Strathcona Holdings."

Fergus's hopes took a leap. This was an important new aspect. "Given that Peter names us as trustees and Cat is now a minority shareholder, will we be able to make demands on the company?"

"We'll discuss it after I study it more in depth," Haskell replied. "It's a matter of proving the board has not acted in a minority shareholder's best interests, which means we may have to claim oppression remedy. But I must warn you now, it will take a long time."

"Can I keep the letter Peter wrote to me?" Fergus had an unbearable yearning to hold it once more but when he was alone.

Haskell dashed his hopes. "You can pick up a certified, typed copy. I'll phone you in a day or two."

There seemed to be nothing more to say on the subject, and after talking over the points he would formally set out, Haskell left with the papers.

As Jack Levinson was leaving, Malcolm asked him about the violin, curious to know more about Cat's brother and his musical talent, determined to help if he could.

"Yes, it's all repaired. Cat looks after it well. She'll soon need a more advanced violin. I will see what I can do."

"For her brother Joe? But he's at a farm, didn't you know? It's too bad. I heard him playing in the park one night. The sound and emotion expressed in such a simple piece was astonishing."

"Joe?" Jack Levinson's eyes opened wide in surprise. "No, no, no, Mr. Muir." He laughed aloud at Malcolm's confusion. "Cat is the one. Her brother does not have the passion to play the violin. But Cat, you wouldn't believe it, she has the touch as though the angels themselves guide her. I told my wife I'm giving her lessons. To waste such promise would be criminal."

"But-but, she told me herself it was Joe!"

"Something to do with the mother, I believe." Levinson's eyes rolled in disapproved of his own words. "She never allowed Cat to take violin lessons. But Cat and Joe have been resourceful." Jack Levinson chuckled again. "With her brother gone, Cat's afraid they might take the violin away, so I will hold it, and she can come to the shop to practice." He tipped his hat and said goodnight, still chortling to himself as he went down the front path.

Malcolm and Fergus talked long into the night discussing their next move. They needed the financial statements for GlasBottle and Strathcona Holdings for those years when Peter had been with both companies. Malcolm said Haskell was the person to demand them and Fergus agreed but it would take time they didn't have.

"I've asked Lex. I'll give him another day, and then push him again." He told Malcolm he had not questioned Sterling Matthews after all, and why. "But I can phone him if we come across anything worthwhile with the Board's dealings. It'll have to be enough for now."

Malcolm turned to the question of Cat. "Peter told her something. It bothers me that she would smother it."

"It's easier to forget than face it." Fergus lowered his gaze from his father. *Memories are painful to bear*, he wanted to say. His chest tightened, thinking of Cat in the same predicament. "A doctor?"

Malcolm looked worried at the idea and vetoed it. "It would frighten her more. Patience is the answer. If she feels comfortable, then she will talk. Like when she told us Peter sent her here. It just popped out. Let's just leave it and see what happens."

Relieved, Fergus agreed. That night, he dreamed of Peter again and woke in the morning, his eyes wet.

13

THE few days Haskell said he needed to prepare the trustee documents turned into a week. Almost to the day, Fergus received a phone call from Haskell's office telling him the documents were ready for signature. He telephoned Malcolm, then made his way down the block towards the law office, located on the second floor above a realtor. Fergus found the steel cage elevator— grateful Malcolm would not have to navigate the stairs. He went into the large reception area. A row of empty chairs flanking a low table with magazines and papers in a neat pile greeted him. Malcolm had not yet arrived.

At the far end of the room, two desks with typewriters formed a barrier to a bank of cabinets. A woman with her back to him, stood against an open filing cabinet, engrossed in the contents of a file. There was nobody at the desks, and he stood in silence for a moment, waiting.

"Miss?"

The woman turned, her soft brown eyes startled into the present from wherever place her mind had been a moment before. Her straight eyebrows and dark hair, worn at an unfashionable shoulder length, framed her face perfectly. Fergus stood struck for a second until he realized he'd seen her before. On the street with Lex Rideout.

"Er," he stammered. "Miss, uh, I'm Fergus Muir. Mr. Haskell is expecting me? I'm a bit early. I'll just wait for my father to arrive. If you can just tell him I'm here?" *Idiot*, he thought, *sit down and stop babbling*. He sat.

The door opened, and two girls came in, chattering. One smiled at him, as they seated themselves behind the desks. His eyes darted between them and the woman, hers beginning to crinkle with suppressed laughter as she moved towards him, still holding the file. Fergus stood again. She was tall, a mere four inches below his own height of six feet.

"Of course, Mr. Muir. I'll tell my father you've arrived," she said, eyes laughing out loud.

Father? The door opened, and Malcolm came in. He saw the two of them and smiled, "Ah, Mrs. Buckley, how nice to see you. I see you two have met." His sharp gaze read her smothered laughter and his son's bewildered expression.

"Buckley? As in Haskell and Buckley?" *A woman lawyer?*

As if reading his mind, she gave him a sharp look and said, "Oh yes, women are turning up everywhere these days."

Fergus's face grew hot.

Mrs. Buckley took pity on him and said, "You don't remember me, do you?"

Fergus took the easy route and shook his head no.

"Jean? Jean Haskell?" She prompted, her voice low and pleasant. "I was about thirteen or fourteen when you went off to war."

After a long moment, the light went on. "Richard's kid sister! All grown up without the pigtails." The two girls snickered. His father glowered at his manners. Fergus flushed again. What was the matter with him? Why should he care who she was or whether he had known her before?

The door to an inner office opened, and Haskell came out shaking hands with a client. Collecting a sheaf of papers from one of the secretaries, he waved Fergus and Malcolm into the office. Fergus breathed a sigh of relief, ducked through the door ahead of Malcolm into safe haven and sat.

"The next task is to pursue inquiries into Peter's fraud charge," Haskell told them when all the papers were signed. "I have to warn you Strathcona Holdings will respond with delaying tactics. I'll let you know how things go."

On the way out, Fergus glanced around the office, noted Jean was nowhere in sight, and almost scurried through the outside door to the street.

When he arrived home after work, Fergus found Malcolm on the veranda gazing across the yard with a contented smile on his face. He looked up and put a finger to his lips, then indicated the elm tree across the lawn. Duke and Cat were spread out in the shade of the tree's crown, Cat's head propped up against Duke, reading to him. Now and then she held the book out, showing a page to Duke who thumped his tail in appreciation. Scraps of sound from her high voice floated across the space vacillating in emotion suited to the scene. Fergus guessed the book was Tom Swift. Suddenly the excitement of the story seemed to enter dangerous waters.

"Yuggh?" Duke rolled over upsetting Cat into a heap on the lawn, sending the book flying. She burst into giggles and attempted to hug the lab while he licked her face.

Fergus and Malcolm crept quietly into the house.

"What made you acquire Duke in the first place, Dad?" Fergus asked when they were inside. "I thought you were more of a cat man."

"Peter," replied Malcolm still staring at Cat and Duke under the tree. "He brought him to me one day while Duke was still an energetic pup. He said Lois wasn't keen on keeping a dog. A dog messed up the house or some such thing. Anyway, I took him." He turned to look at Fergus. "I'm glad now. He's great company." He passed a hand over his eyes as if erasing memories then limped out of the room, all his weight on his cane.

AFTER dinner, Fergus telephoned the police station and asked for Archie Gillespie.

"Sergeant Gillespie has gone off duty, sir."

"Then I need his home phone number," Fergus said, expecting a refusal.

"We don't give out home phone numbers."

"Well then, can you relay a message to Sergeant Gillespie and tell him Fergus Muir would like him to call around? At his convenience, of course." Fergus couldn't help being sarcastic.

"For what purpose, sir?"

"Personal." Fergus put the receiver on the hook, hoping it made a loud click on the other end.

Impatient, he waited in the study and began to read his copy of Peter's letter again. Halfway through, reality poked a blunt finger and the room tilted, closing in around him. Familiar panic sent him rushing for air, reeling down the hall and through the kitchen door to the yard. Sucking air in a frenzy to force down his rising nausea, he backed up against the elm tree, hidden from the house. Peter's letter had opened a deep crack in his carefully built wall of detachment. If he couldn't control his nerves, he'd fail. Malcolm's unspoken disappointment was a given, and he'd surely go after evidence of Peter's innocence himself. Malcolm's health would suffer, and that alone would summon Mrs. Mann's contempt. Quitting was no longer an option. The nightmares and guilt would take on intolerable dimensions, and he'd never survive. There was no going back now. He had trapped himself. Fergus turned his face to the tree and let the rough bark stablize him.

He stood in the yard for some time, willing himself to breathe steadily before finding the wherewithal to make his way back into the stifling house.

A long hour later, the front doorbell rang and Mrs. Mann, her hat in her hand this time, brought Archie into the study.

"I suppose you'll want coffee?"

Fergus held up a decanter of whisky and raised his eyebrows at Archie, who rubbed his hands together and put a thumb up.

"No coffee, thank you, Mrs. Mann. Could you ask father to come down?"

Fergus poured three glasses, added water, handed the glass to Archie and got right down to it. "Peter Davidson."

Archie lifted his glass in a silent toast, took a sip and gave his attention to Fergus. Malcolm entered the room in determined strides, such as they were, nodded curtly to Archie, and sat.

Archie spoke first. "I ran our last conversation past the captain, but he is adamant the case is closed. The vagrant did it, sure as God made little people."

Fergus silently handed him Peter's letter.

"What's this?" Archie read halfway and then became all policeman. "Where did you get this? Why is it typed?"

Fergus explained how it came into his possession and enlarged on the events leading up to his phone call to Archie. "You can see the attestation from his lawyer, Harold Haskell which says it's a true and complete copy."

"My friend . . ." Archie read aloud.

". . . You must know I tried to meet you, but I'm being watched and saw no chance without someone accusing you of hiding a fugitive. Then Cat came along, and my days were taken up with this brave child. When you meet her, she will remind you of another dear to us both. Clarissa Rideout told me Lex was abusing her, and I offered her money to escape, but she said she couldn't hide money from Lex. We arranged to meet at the train station. If she missed it, Plan B would have her take a bus and meet me in Regina. I had enough money to help her get to relatives in the States. I waited nearly a week, but she never showed. Plan C? I was about to return when the papers reported I was a wanted man, accused of absconding with a bank account, and her.

After the trenches, I couldn't bear the thought of being locked up. I went east to find you. I could not draw money from my bank and had to work my way across Canada. You had already gone by the time I got to York. Why didn't I write? I confess I was ashamed, and I went into a slump. I didn't care anymore. Like you, after Isobel and Maggie died, I wanted no familiar place.

But I was drawn to home even as the men I met and rules of the road seemed nobler than the life I knew. Until I met Cat. This child, fighting her way towards survival, made clear a hope-filled existence is a shot at retaining all that's best in life. Look after her. When you see her as I do, you'll realize how special she is. Fergus, I am innocent of these charges. Rideout knows it and might help. The statements I got and the ones Strathcona Holdings made up had inconsistencies. I had not the know-how to pin it down. Strathcona's Board asked that I set up an account at the Imperial Bank in Calgary as a transfer account between Calgary office and Glasbottle.

I never made transactions, so my signature was forged. I suspected the bank made an error and so I told the Board I'd attend the next meeting. Almost immediately I was charged with fraud. I may be pushed to leave town soon, but I'll be back. Cat will bring this letter to you and Malcolm.

Help me, Gussy. One for all and all for one.

Peter."

Archie folded the letter and sighed. "You won't want to hear this, Ferg, but there is no concrete evidence here, only suspicions. And nothing indicates he was in real danger except being chased out of town by the Police." He held up his hand to forestall any objection. "It does indicate he thought he was in danger. But any lawyer could argue he was paranoid." He folded the letter and pocketed it. "I'll see what the captain thinks."

"I want you to convince your captain to re-open the case." Fergus fought to keep his voice reasonable. "Of course he had no concrete evidence. If he had, he'd have gone to the police, wouldn't he? He says he's being watched. Why? And he suggests a place to start to look for evidence. He gives a motive. And what about Clarissa Rideout? Where is she?"

Archie didn't hesitate. "She could have used Peter as a blind, and had other plans all along and wanted to divert her husband's attention. Or she could have lied about Rideout abusing her. Maybe Peter could be lying."

Fergus wanted to shake him. He walked to the drinks table and gently laid down his glass.

"Peter wasn't lying, Archie. Rideout told me his wife left a note, naming Peter." Fergus came closer to Archie, obstinate. "Why would she name Peter and deliberately put him in trouble? Peter was the only one to offer her help. It was a crass thing to do and even if she had other plans, was she so clever? I don't believe she left a note. Did you or anybody ever see one?"

For once Archie hesitated. "No. But as I said, she could have been using him as a diversion."

"Well, in truth, I knew Peter well, better than anyone, and when it comes to the true version, I'll take his any day."

Archie said nothing, but he looked down into his glass thoughtfully. Finally, he said, "Look. The captain is a fair man, and I'll talk to him. But you have to know he's dead against interference from the civilian population. That's the military coming out in him. If he decides to investigate, he won't want to hear any advice from you."

"But I can find out what's going on with the financial side! Besides, we have a responsibility." Fergus indicated Malcolm who had been silently taking in all the back and forth conversation. At Fergus's comment, he only nodded agreement.

"Peter also left a Will naming Cat as sole beneficiary, and Malcolm and me as trustees."

"Ah yes, Who is she and where does she fit in?"

"Remember the girl with the violin who was seen with Peter?" Fergus told Archie the bare details about Cat. He kept his expression neutral and didn't mention she may have seen something she shouldn't have at the kiln.

"Neither here nor there," Archie stubbornly concluded. "You better not say in public Peter was murdered by someone who framed him. Not only will it sound idiotic, but it'll rile up the captain before I can talk to him. He's on the warpath already this week. A mounted constable got drunk in the Royal Hotel while he was on duty, and forgot where he put his horse." Archie grinned. "Our captain isn't partial to the Force being the butt of public jokes. So I'd be careful if I were you. It wouldn't take much for him to make an example of you. Or me. And I wouldn't like it either." He looked hard at Fergus. "Friend or no friend."

Neither man spoke for several seconds.

"Agreed," said Fergus finally. He grinned and held up both hands, palm out. "See? No fingers crossed. Care for another drink?"

After Archie left, Fergus swore softly. "Sorry," he apologized to Malcolm. "But we're getting nowhere."

"Archie has a point, Fergus. What if it was a fight with a vagrant? Remember the hobo Peter chased away from Cat? He was angry, and could easily follow Peter to the kiln and smash his head with a brick." Malcolm picked up a newspaper. "At this point, we can't connect his death with the fraud charge. Why don't you concentrate on the concrete and ask Lex about the financial statements for Strathcona?"

Only half convinced, Fergus ran his fingers through his hair. He reminded himself of Max Levinson dealing with a problem.

They sat silently then, Malcolm reading the paper, and Fergus scribbling topic notes for Thursday's lecture period with Max. He and Malcolm had come to look forward to the discussions. Malcolm said it kept him up to date on accounting practices. Max had asked if another student from a rival firm could join in, and Fergus could tell by the way Malcolm strutted around the study that he really just reveled in playing professor.

Fergus broke the silence. "What does Jean Buckley's husband do?"

"Not sure," Malcolm said, still reading his newspaper. "They split some years back. As far as I know, he is somewhere in the East." Malcolm laid down his paper and looked up at Fergus twirling his pen between his fingers. "Why?"

"Just curious."

Malcolm went back to reading.

"Do you know why they split?"

"No. None of my business," said Malcolm pointedly, and turned the page of the paper.

"Anyone else on the horizon?"

"Haven't heard." Malcolm laid down his paper again. "Do you want me to get another haircut and find out?"

"Never mind." Fergus went back to his notes, smiling. Malcolm waited for a long moment then cautiously lifted up the newspaper again.

"Any children?"

Malcolm stretched the pages of his paper with a crisp snap.

14

MALCOLM filled the next two days doing mundane chores, with no word from Haskell or Archie Gillespie. The weather remained hot but began cooling at night, and although the leaves on the trees had not yet turned yellow, people prepared for frost now September was looming. Cat finished cataloging the books. She and Malcolm played chess and chatted, but Cat shied away from any mention of Peter, and Malcolm finally stopped trying.

"Are you looking forward to school?" Malcolm moved into safe waters.

"I'm going into Grade Six this year, and I've decided to start at Dundee School instead of Gates Street."

"Oh? But doesn't everyone have to attend school in their home area?" In his surprise, Malcolm moved his Queen without thinking.

Cat regarded him stolidly. "I don't want to go to my old school anymore."

Malcolm pursed his lips regretfully at his Queen, not meeting her gaze. *Children in a pack in the playground can be cruel,* he thought, *especially when reinforced by careless parents.* And she wouldn't have her brother Joe for support.

"Well"—he pondered the board's possibilities—"it will be a long walk in winter to and from your house. If your mother makes a bag lunch, perhaps you had better bring it here to eat with us. And any new friends who also bring lunch." He knew there was no supervision during the noon hour, so children weren't allowed to stay. School sites were planned so kids could walk home for lunch. Anyway, he suspected she made her own sandwiches.

While Malcolm worked around the house to occupy his mind,

Fergus's stayed on Jean Buckley nearly all week. An image of her standing in her office, engrossed in a file, would suddenly intrude into his work. But more, he was curious about her conversation on the street with Lex. By Friday, he decided, lifted then replaced the receiver. After following the pattern a few more times, he finally gave the operator the number of the law office and asked for her, giving his name. He tried to control his breathing while he waited. When was the last time he had felt this anxious over a woman?

"Jean Buckley here."

"Jean, it's Fergus. Fergus Muir."

"Hello, Fergus. Did you want my father?" Did he imagine it or did she have a laugh in her voice?

"No, actually, I wanted to redeem myself for not recognizing you the other day. Are you free to have dinner with me tomorrow night? Maybe take in a show later?"

There was a long pause. Was he too abrupt? "Hello? Are you there?"

"Yes," she said softly, "and yes, dinner would be lovely. What time?"

"About seven? I'll pick you up."

"Fine. Seven it is."

"Great! See you then." He nearly hung up the phone but quickly fumbled it back up to his ear. "O-oh, I need the address."

She gave it to him, and Fergus hung up, heart thudding, and took in some much-needed oxygen.

ON Saturday, at her mother's command, Cat stayed home to do chores. She swept the floors, dusted the furniture, then she and Harley harvested the remaining potato crop in the garden. Under a scorching sun, they dug potatoes and spread them on the ground to dry. She held the sacks while Harley filled them and they lugged them into the cellar situated under a trap door beneath the kitchen table. They stacked them alongside a boarded section of carrots. Cat relished the coolness of cellar after the outside heat even though she hated the dark. She always imagined the trap door falling shut, locking her in and leaving her in total blackness. She was thankful for Harley's company in spite of expecting him to tell her he saw a mouse.

Finished by late afternoon, they sat on the back step, overheated and tired.

"Fifteen cents each." Clara Perkins came outside and handed them the money. "For the early show and an extra five cents for a treat. But be home right after nine o'clock. I don't want you running around the town. Now hurry and get washed up first."

Harley took off immediately to see his friend, Carl. Cat arrived at the Monarch Theatre just before seven o'clock to find a new Charlie Chaplin film, Modern Times, was about to begin. She went down the street to join the lineup for the door when she saw Mr. Rideout at the very end. By the time she spotted him she was too close to turn and run without him seeing her.

"Hello, Cat. Your Mama told me you were coming. Want to line up with me?" He indicated a place beside him.

Frozen, she stared at him for a long moment. "No." Paralyzed with fear, she could only whisper, "I'm waiting for Harley."

"Well, we can wait together." His white teeth smiled at her, but she imagined his voice as insistent.

"I promised to save a place for them." Her breath came in small gasps. Hoping she wasn't going to cry, she began to shake, then did the only thing she could think of. She turned and darted to the front of the line and went into the theatre with a group of four, two men and two women, pretending she belonged with them. Keeping beside them through the foyer, she pushed past the usher taking tickets. She ran down the aisle to the second from the front row of seats, ducking down so she couldn't be seen from the back. She imagined cold eyes searching her out and made herself small.

Once the house lights darkened, she cautiously raised her head and looked around. She didn't see him. Relieved, she stayed hunched down in her seat and soon occupied herself in Charlie's antics with factory machines.

"I won't be home tonight for dinner," Fergus told Mrs. Mann earlier that afternoon. She looked up from the list of groceries she would need for the next week's meals and took in his expression. "Wonders never cease," she said. "Who's the lucky girl who makes you look like you ate the canary?"

About to tell her to mind her own business, he sighed in defeat instead. "Jean Buckley. Harold Haskell's daughter."

"I know who she is. I've known who she is since she was born." Her face turned stern, as though he were a teenager on his first date. "You're a nice boy. She's a nice girl who has had trouble in her life. And I know you wouldn't have thoughts about her you shouldn't have. Would you?"

"No, Mrs. Mann," said Fergus meekly, not sure he appreciated being called a boy. "Rest assured, I'll make you proud."

"Oh, be still my beating heart." And Mrs. Mann, unmoved, bent her head to her list.

Fergus rang the front doorbell promptly at seven o'clock. The house, on the hill west of the town, was a small one and a half, the front yard surrounded by beds of manicured bushes and fall flowers in bloom.

"It's open," Jean's voice called. Fergus pushed at the door and stepped into a small front hall, cluttered with packing cases. He took off his hat, just as Jean came around from the back of the house. A medium sized dog of uncertain heritage padded from behind her and stood between them.

"Oh, go sit, Ditzy," she said, pushing the dog away. "Hello, Fergus."

"Ditzy?"

"She was a stray we picked up and brought home. She was so grateful she ran around in circles showing off. Father said she was ditzy, and the name stuck."

Fergus eyed Ditzy who had one ear cocked, the other hanging down over a face covered in fuzzy fur springing out in all directions. "Suits her."

Jean looked cool in an off-white dress, contrasting with her dark hair, pulled back into a simple chignon. A string of jet beads rested elegantly over her collarbone.

He reluctantly tore his eyes away from her and indicated the packing cases. "Are you coming or going?"

"Going." She made a face. "All grown up and I'm moving in with my parents. Their house is large, and we agreed it would be of mutual financial benefit. Besides . . ." she trailed off and smiled up at him. "Shall we go?"

When they had settled in the car, Fergus turned to his date. "Chinese or Dry?"

"I favor Dry tonight," she said, laughing. Alberta Liquor Laws, enforced by Premier Aberhart, made it illegal for men and women to drink together in public, including restaurants. However, it was common knowledge the Chinese restaurants didn't give a fig for Bible Bill's liquor laws. Large numbers of people suddenly became addicted to Chinese food. Diners brought their bottles with them but followed the implicit rule to keep it concealed. Ginger Ale could be served, and nobody noticed a bottle appearing and then disappearing again under the table.

"Okay, I know a nice quiet restaurant."

They drove in companionable silence, and upon arriving at the dining room, Fergus pointed to a corner table set for two. Seated, they looked at each other as if surprised they were actually here.

"This is nice," Fergus started—"Nice here," Jean said at the same time. Embarrassed, both snickered.

"You first," said Fergus.

"I was going to make some inane remark about 'this is nice. I'm glad you asked me out.'"

A waitress came over, carrying menus, and a pitcher of ice water. Fergus took both menus then handed one to Jean while the waitress poured water into goblets. "I haven't been out to dinner with anyone but my father or clients for a while." He shook his head. "Feels strange."

"Strange?"

"Oh, no, please, not that kind of strange. Excited, different." He quit talking. "I seem to have a habit of babbling when we meet." He pursed his lips and gave a whistled version of *yeh-hoo*. "Let's start over. How long have you been in law?"

The waitress brought over a small tray with queen olives, celery, and nuts, and placed it in the middle of the table, setting small plates in front of them.

"About eight years. It's all I ever wanted to do. Richard should have been the one."

"What's he doing now?"

"Professor of History at Queen's University." She looked amused. "It looks as though my brother and I traded choices, doesn't it? Not exactly what my parents expected."

Once they had ordered, she said, "You lived in Ontario?"

"Until three years ago," Fergus paused. "After the war, I wanted to start fresh, you know? I was even reluctant to return when Dad called me. But I was lying to myself. I don't think I was ever really happy in the East. Something to do with being raised near the prairies, I suppose."

"You can't see the horizon anywhere else, or the show of a lightning storm on the prairie. After law school, I never should have stayed in Nova Scotia." She stopped suddenly, looking uncomfortable.

"You went to Dalhousie? Many women in your class?"

Her face cleared. "Yes to the first question, and no to the second. It was Dad's idea of choosing a University in the East. He wanted Richard and me to *know* Canada." Fergus waited, thinking she might comment on her marriage, but she only made a wry face and went silent.

Their food arrived. While they ate, they talked of their school days, the wild freedom growing up.

"What's the worst you ever did?" Fergus issued a challenge.

She thought for a while. "Not stopping someone when I knew it was wrong." Before he could ask what it was, she returned, "What about you?"

"Peter, Isobel, and I sucked on lemons in front of the trumpet players in the Sally Ann Band while they were playing downtown. The sight of the lemons made their mouths pucker up. They blew some queer notes."

Jean looked delighted. "Is that true?"

"Word of honor. The crowd thought it was hilarious. Our parents found out, and we had to pass the collection plate every Sunday afternoon for a month while the band played."

"Horrible kids."

When she disclosed her preference was Family Law, vital for children in the present economic conditions, he told her a bit about Cat and her family. A selection of cheeses appeared on their table, which they both ignored. Fergus glanced at his watch. "The second show starts in about half an hour. Let's drive round them all and choose one, or none." He signaled for the tab.

They drove past the Monarch and saw Charlie Chaplin's name on the marquee. Regarding each other, they agreed something silly would be a nice conclusion.

THE first show ended, and the lights came on. Cat moved down the row of seats towards the aisle. As she turned to walk to the front, she saw him. He had been sitting two rows behind her all along. She hurried then, but he quickly rose and caught her as she went past. He put his hand on her shoulder. "Looks like Harley left you. I'll take you home to make sure you get there safe and sound." He stayed with her the rest of the way up the aisle.

In the lobby, Cat ducked away from his hand, pointing to the washroom.

"Okay, Cat. I'll wait here." He stooped a bit to look at her, his expression pleading. "I know you don't like me much and worry your mom will forget your dad. But I only want to help her in a difficult time. Can't we be friends?"

She turned and darted to the washroom.

She waited a long time, then washed her hands. When she pocked her head out the door, he had his back to her, looking at the posters on the wall. She tip-toed up across the lobby and pushed the outside door just as he turned around. She ran straight out into the street and collided with Harley and his friend. In relief, she clung to him, small hands gripping his shirt so tight they turned white. He attempted to pry her off until Rideout came behind her. Lex saw Harley, shrugged an elaborate gesture of defeat and walked away.

"Can I come home with you Harley? Please?"

"Aw, no, Cat. We weren't going home just yet. Go home by yourself."

"No. Take me with you, Harley. Please. I won't be a nuisance."

Carl looked at Cat intently. He nudged Harley. "Let her come, Harley." He smiled down at her. "We'll look after you, girl."

Looking him over, aversion nagged at her. But the prospect of walking home alone was overwhelming. Still holding on to Harley, Cat threw a last look down the street where Rideout had disappeared.

The early crowd was just leaving the theatre, and Fergus searched the street for a parking space. He recognized Rideout's green sports coupe just pulling away, and he moved into the spot. Farther along the street, Cat stood with two older boys, holding on to one of them whom Fergus assumed was Harley, and pointed her out to Jean. Cat cast a glance behind her and found Fergus's eyes. For a moment he thought she wanted him, but she turned and continued down the street with the two boys.

Inside, the only seats near the back were smack in the middle. They side shuffled along the row past smiling patrons. Once they sat, Fergus glanced around the place and tried to shake off an undefined discomfort, which he blamed on the seat, and he squirmed trying to regain his relaxed mood. The movie started, the house lights dimmed, and he took hold of Jean's hand, turning to the flickering screen. An image of Cat on the street intruded into his thoughts. He turned back to Jean. "Come on, we have to go."

"Why?"

He tugged her to her feet and folded up the chair seat. "I'll explain later."

He grabbed her hand again, and without apology shuffled past now grumbling people and soft yelps protesting stepped-on feet. Pulling Jean along, he hurried up the aisle and out the door to the street.

Jean said nothing until they reached the car. "What's wrong?" she asked, as he opened the door for her. He sprinted around to the driver's side.

"I should have known," he muttered and drove off down the street. "I'm sorry," he told Jean. "It's Cat. I should have realized when I saw her face. She doesn't like Harley and yet she was holding on to his arm for dear life. Something is wrong. I have to know if she got home."

He drove through town, looking for her along the way. He told Jean in disjointed sentences about his suspicions she had seen Peter killed. "I just have a bad feeling. She gets terrified but can't say why. I'm sorry about all this, Jean," he repeated.

"Shush, Fergus. I'm a great believer in instinct. Let's just find her."

Fergus parked in front of Cat's house without seeing any trace of her along the way. Clara Perkins opened the front door and gazed at them both in surprise. "Jean Buckley, Mrs. Perkins," Fergus introduced them bluntly. "Is Cat home, Mrs. Perkins?"

"She's gone to the show."

"We saw her leaving the show with Harley," Fergus insisted. Fibbing a little, he said they seemed to be on the way home. "I thought she'd be here by now."

In spite of his effort to appear casual, Clara Perkins picked up his urgency and narrowed her eyes at him. She folded her arms in front of her. "Just why are you interested in Cat, Mr. Muir? You always want her for something or other. The child isn't your servant, you know."

"No, she isn't, Mrs. Perkins," Fergus agreed. "But that's just it. I—we," he indicated Jean, "told her we would all go together for ice cream after the show. I wouldn't want her to think we had let her down." He floundered and could feel his forehead beginning to perspire with the effort of keeping his voice calm and not shouting at the woman.

"Look," he said on impulse, "We just felt a little sorry for her, you know? She told me about Joe going off to a farm." He saw her start, and her face tighten, and he put both hands up before she could retaliate. "I know, I know, boys his age need work, especially in these times. Lucky to get work, I say. But Cat seemed so lonely, we thought to cheer her up and take her mind off Joe till he comes back. She's kind of cute too. Just like her mother, I'd say." He beamed at Clara Perkins. He could feel Jean beside him tremble and knew he'd gone too far.

But Clara Perkins didn't register his last statement. She drew in her breath sharply and stared at him. "Joe's not coming back, Mr. Muir."

"But Cat says he's coming home," protested Fergus. "I don't

understand."

"Because he's gone for good. Like everybody else," she said bitterly. "It's not my fault . . ." Clara burst into sudden, unprovoked tears.

Jean put her arm around Clara Perkins and patted her shoulder, her brown eyes looking questioningly at Fergus.

"That's strange," he thought aloud. "Cat told me she was with him when he went to the farm. Wouldn't he tell her if he wasn't coming back?" He groaned then. "He must have told her. Poor kid. That's what she's hiding."

Clara Perkins stared at him, her face wreathed in abject horror. "Went with him? Hiding? She couldn't. I could tell if she did . . ." she paused, thinking, then gave a pathetic moan. She pushed at Jean. "Go away. You're just making trouble. She isn't with Harley. She's with Lex Rideout. Get out."

"Clara?" Jean interrupted. "Why is Cat with Lex Rideout?"

Fergus gaped at Jean's pale face and tight lips.

"He's been good to us all, has Lex. He said he was going to take Cat to the show tonight as a treat, and he'd bring her home. I don't have to worry if she's with him. Oh, just go!" She slammed the door shut.

"Come on!" Fergus ran down the porch steps, almost slamming into Rose entering through the gate. She was slim, a more mature image of Cat but with darker hair. She looked from one to the other.

"What's going on? Mr. Muir, isn't it?"

"Yes. This is Jean Buckley." Rose nodded to Jean and returned her questioning face to Fergus.

"Cat." Frustration made him abrupt. "She's with Harley. She hasn't come home. And Lex Rideout . . ."

"Harley?" Rose cried. "You saw her? And Lex Rideout?"

"No, we saw her with Harley. But your mother said Rideout was looking for her too."

She gripped his arm. "Did Harley have someone with him? A short chunky boy?" Fergus nodded, and she cried, "Oh no, you have to find her!"

"Where would they go? Any place which is a favorite spot? Think, girl!"

"I am!" Rose snapped. She grasped both hands in a prayer attitude and closed her eyes, then opened them. "Ranger's Cave. It's where the slimy wretch would go. And Harley!" Rose clenched her fists. "Oh, wait till I get my hands on him."

Sweat broke out on Fergus's face at the mention of a cave. "Ranger's Cave. The cave over by the Golf Course. In the cliffs?" At Rose's nod, he added almost hopefully, "But it's quite a long way for them to walk. Would they go that far?"

"Yes, they would. And he never uses the traffic bridge. The train bridge is his personal shortcut across the river."

"The train bridge? But there's nothing but the ties to walk on. What if a train comes along? There's no place to get out of the way."

Rose snort mocked his question. "Harley loves the dare."

"And Cat would go with them?"

"Yes, she would, just to show Harley she wasn't afraid. And she can't stand to be near Mr. Rideout. She thinks he's taking Father's place, or maybe she just hates him. I don't know."

"Show us the place."

"I can't." Rose wrung her hands now. "I only came home to collect some clothes. I have to get back to the Hutchison's. They want me to stay overnight. Oh, stop asking questions. Please hurry." She turned to the house. "I can't stand any more of this. This is the last straw. I'm going to ask Mrs. Hutchison if I can move in." Her voice faded as she ran around the sidewalk leading to the back of the house.

As they drove towards the bridge, Jean directed Fergus to all the shortcuts to get them to the Golf Course. "When you get across the river, on the road to the Golf Course," she said, "there's a cutoff on the right, about half a mile on. It looks like a footpath, but it's wide enough to let a car through. It leads directly to Ranger's Cave. It's been a few years, but the path should still be there. I think the kids use it now as a lover's lane."

Fergus looked across at her but said nothing, just concentrated on driving as fast as he could, keeping an eye out for policemen around the main streets watching for speeders.

Jean smiled at him, reading his look. "In those days, we used to use it for hikes," she explained.

"That's why those skinny legs turned out just fine," he replied absently. "All the hiking."

"Hmmm . . . keep up with the flattery. It's a new sensation for me."

They left the outskirts of town, and the traffic eased off to almost none, allowing them to increase their speed. He soon spotted the turn-off, and they continued easily along the narrow road.

"No lover's lane couples tonight," he remarked. They drove for a while, silent. "I'm bothered with Clara Perkin's story about Joe," he told her after some time. "I can't put my finger on it, but why is she so sure Joe isn't coming home?"

"I sensed it too, but maybe she feels guilty for sending him to the farm. After all, he's only twelve. And she wants us to agree it's not her fault."

They were nearing the place. "I barely remember where the cave is." He strained his eyes to see further out than his headlights would allow. "Everything looks different."

"We'll have to park and walk." Jean pointed ahead, then realized it was futile. "Well, you'll know where to park because the path ends. It can't be too far ahead."

"I hate this," Fergus said to take his mind off the cave. "I knew Cat was in danger, and I was sloppy."

"Stop it right now," Jean commanded. "What we're doing this minute is what counts."

"I'm glad you said 'we.'"

Jean stared at Fergus. "Why are you so nervous?"

"I'm not nervous."

"Then why are you sweating? Come on Fergus, give."

He hesitated and then admitted, "I hate caves."

"But we all used to play in the caves. Didn't you?"

"We did," he replied lamely. She waited for more, but he drove, staring straight ahead and pressed his lips together.

Fergus felt her disapproval but thought if he opened his mouth to say more, she'd see his rising panic. They soon arrived at the end of the path. He stopped the car and closed his eyes.

Jean opened the car door, and got out. "Come on," she said briskly. "We better get going." She stooped and peered through the window at him.

"Are you okay to walk in those shoes?" he asked more to break the tension after his evasive answers than anything else.

"I'm fine, and don't even think about asking me to wait here." She started to walk away.

Fergus watched her for a moment, then threw his hat in the back seat and opened the door to follow. "Hold it," he called. He went around to the passenger side, opened the door, and then retrieved a flashlight from the glove compartment.

On impulse, he held up his hand again and returned to the car. He took the key out of the ignition and locked all the doors. She waited, her hands on her hips.

"We don't want to be stranded, do we?" He jiggled the keys above his head in defiance of her silent rebuke.

The light of the full Harvest Moon, large enough for them to reach out and touch, made their way across the prairie easy. The air was warm, under a lingering twilight, and the clear sky above them would soon be ablaze with stars. There was a faint scent of sage in the air. He found his thoughts wandering under the influence of vastness, dreaming in the familiar feeling of being just a dot in the expanse of the universe. All he needed was to hear the yip of a far-off coyote to make the fantasy real. He almost stopped to listen but then brought himself sharply back to why they were there.

They followed a well-trod footpath for about half a mile, seeing and hearing nothing. *What if they went somewhere else? Maybe Cat realized going with Harley was a bad idea and decided to go to our house*, he thought. She'd taken refuge with Mrs. Mann before, and she might just head there. They should have stopped by, to check if she had turned up.

They were nearing the cliff edge—he could see it ahead. His heart started to pound in his ears. His sweaty palm took a firmer grip on the flashlight. They heard voices ahead, carried on the clear air, and they stepped up their pace, almost running. The voices were sharper now, shouting, and the sound of scuffles. Near the very edge of the cliff, they saw Harley and another boy, pushing and shoving at each other.

"Over my dead body!" shouted Harley.

The boy pushed at Harley's chest. "You're the one who brought her here. You know the score."

"Jackass. My little sister?" Harley took a wild swing at the other boy and they both fell to the ground grappling. Fergus took a quick look around, but Cat was nowhere to be seen.

He pushed past Jean, handing her the flashlight. He danced about the two bodies crashing around and took a grip on the first neck he could grab and pulled them apart.

"That's enough," he said. Caught in surprise, both of them came apart easily enough.

"Where is she? Where's Cat? What have you done with her?"

The stocky boy pulled away in a frenzy and started running back down the path. Harley stood his ground, wiping his bleeding nose.

"I got into a fight with Carl. I told her to run. To hide in the cave." He was breathless.

"The cave?" Fergus shouted. "But it has snakes this time of year!"

"Aww, that's just a lot of tales. Besides it's too early for hibernation," he said, but he looked uncertain. "Isn't it?"

Fergus grabbed him by the front of his shirt and pulled him close to his face. "You'd better hope it is." He gave him a shove towards the cliff edge. "Lead the way."

15

AFTER a solitary dinner of roast pork with baked apple, scalloped potatoes, and beet greens, Malcolm retired to the study, looking forward to a quiet evening. He wound up the gramophone and set the needle down on Mendelssohn's *Violin Concerto*. Sighing happily, he settled in his chair with a glass of scotch and a new book, Prokosch's *The Asiatics*, just as the doorbell rang.

Harold Haskell showed up right behind Mrs. Mann at the study door, barely waiting for her to say his name. Still, he gave her a big smile as he brushed past her. "Hot as billy blue blazes out there," he said to Malcolm by way of greeting and continued over to the drinks table where he helped himself to a glass of scotch.

"You wanted me to keep you up to date on Strathcona Holdings," he reported as he poured himself a drink. "Besides." He held up his glass. "I'm out of scotch." He lifted the drink and took a healthy sip. "Fine scotch," he said looking appreciatively at his glass.

"Come in, Harold." Malcolm lifted the needle from the record. "Have a chair and a drink."

"I misplaced my liquor permit book," Haskell explained grinning. "A lot of nonsense. Why do we put up with it?"

Another one of Bible Bill's laws. This one mandated the purchase of liquor. One first had to apply for a "permit to buy" booklet. Each bottle bought was duly noted. Nobody was sure what it was for, but people said it was a method of identifying the Province's lushes, even if the said lushes were in their own homes.

"Do you think they hire people to actually count and record the number of bottles we all buy?" Haskell went over to the chair Malcolm indicated, and stood there, still pontificating. "Does everyone have a secret liquor file? Can you see me in formal court attire confronting someone like you and quoting the number of bottles of scotch you bought last year?"

Malcolm joined the trial pretense and saluted with his own glass. "What is the charge? Oh, right. Sorry sir, I forgot. I'm accused of being too drunk to tune in to his weekly diatribe, *Back to the Bible Hour.*"

"And how does the defendant plead?" Haskell asked, sternly.

"Guilty, Your Honor. . . . But does it count in my favor if I confess that I pretend to listen?"

"No." Haskell laughed and sat. He had arrived wearing a shirt and suit trousers, but minus his jacket. Malcolm noted his shirt cuffs were frayed and had already been turned once. *The law business should pay as well as the accounting profession*, Malcolm thought. He had liaised with Haskell often enough in the early days of the Depression to know that law offices spent most of their time pursuing bad debts, and foreclosures, and probably hadn't changed much. Most professional fees were paid in kind, but at least they didn't go hungry.

Curious as to Harold's real purpose, Malcolm sat back. Haskell could have telephoned the information instead of coming across town just for a drink.

"I sent an official request for the financial records for GlasBottle and Strathcona Holdings for the years 1930 to 1932. I hinted in the covering letter I would go before the courts and claim oppression. They will stall, hoping we find it all too expensive and quit. But we have to start somewhere." He paused, and Malcolm nodded without saying anything. The two sat quietly for a time.

"Cora tells me Jean has gone out with Fergus tonight," Haskell said casually.

Ah, there it is, thought Malcolm. "Yes, it seems so."

"I've heard that Fergus didn't come through the war well." Haskell turned his glass watching the liquid swirl.

"I don't suppose many of them did," Malcolm agreed, sighing. "The men who came back are all very discreet about their experiences, and he and Peter were the same."

"Peter never mentioned to you the circumstances surrounding

his medal citation?"

"Not a word. Although it involved Fergus, I never asked. It doesn't do to question these veterans. A joke in return is about all you'll get."

Haskell inspected his glass again and screwed up his lips as though wondering if he should have another. "I've heard it said Fergus has a bit of temper."

"Ah," Malcolm said, sensing where this was going. "I sound trite, but Fergus doesn't suffer fools gladly, and he's impatient and blunt, so yes, a bit quick off the mark. He'd never make a politician. Fergus is haunted by people dear to him who are gone. It's a lonely life when nobody is left to share memories. I would hazard a guess he and Jean are sharing just that very thing from childhood."

Haskell sighed and shifted his feet as though he regretted his next words. "At the moment, I don't mind saying I hope that's all it is." He raised his hand palm out, defending Malcolm's unspoken question. "I know. I know. It's Jean I worry about. She carries scars from her time living down East." He finished his drink, sat a moment, twirling the glass in his hand. "He's in prison. Her former husband."

Malcolm tried to hide his shock and failed. He cleared his throat. "I'm sorry Harold," he said gently. "You know Fergus isn't the kind of man to abuse any friendship he might have with Jean."

Haskell nodded. "It isn't news I'd like to see traded about the town. If anything comes of their friendship, Jean will tell him in her own good time."

"Of course."

"Well, I'll leave you to it." And Haskell was gone, leaving Malcolm frowning into the silence, his book forgotten.

THEY reached the cave by a steep, natural path that zigzagged down from the clifftop for about fifty feet to meet the river bank. Fergus thought of Cat making her way down there by herself, and deliberately drove the image from his mind. *One thing at a time,* he told himself. He and Peter and Isobel had done the same thing many times, and there was no reason to think Cat couldn't manage. The cave itself was actually an overhang, the sandstone carved out by rainwater and wind and had likely been used by the Natives for shelter and protection from the weather. Looking into the cave from the semi-circular entrance showed an area about eight feet wide, and Fergus remembered the width varied and dug into the cliff for another twenty feet or so.

They stopped at the mouth, the three of them strung out along the path and leaning up against the cliff wall. Overheated and sweaty, Fergus removed his suit jacket, handing it to Jean. His shirt was soon wet as well and clung to his body.

"Cat!" Harley shouted. "It's okay honey. Come out."

"She won't come, Harley," Fergus snapped. "You've tricked her too many times."

"I'll go in and get her," said Jean. She was watching Fergus, his pale face awash in sweat.

"She doesn't know you," replied Fergus, tone brusque. "Stay here, both of you."

He moved to the mouth of the cave. The roaring in his ears increased, and although reason told him otherwise, he heard explosions. Stooping to enter the cave, the familiar dank smell of dirt assaulted him at once, and he automatically began to breathe through his mouth. He stifled a moan as the walls closed in around him. Taking small darts, he forced his way quickly into one side of the cave and then weaved to the other, as if dodging bullets. He kept the flashlight beam low to the ground, watching his path.

"Cat," he called out, hoarsely, willing her to come running to him so they could get out. "It's me, Fergus. I'm here now, and you're safe. Come to me, Cat."

There was no answer, and he repeated her name every few feet. The darkness was almost complete now, the entrance only a faint glow. He hugged the wall, the explosions inside his head now joined with a clamoring of voices and screams of men in mortal agony. An almost impossible magnet drew him back to the light and safety before the walls collapsed in on him. Nauseous, his legs weak—he sucked dank air into his lungs, and sank against the limestone wall, paralyzed. *"Damn it Gussy, get going, man!"* Peter shouted at him, his voice so clear, Fergus swiveled his head to find him. Almost crying, he forced himself forward. Another ten feet in, his flashlight picked up a lighter form against the side wall. He lifted the torch up and saw Cat, her back hugging the wall as if trying to become part of it. Still as a statue, her eyes were wide with terror.

"Cat?" Fergus said, his voice tight with strain. "It's Fergus. Come to me. Follow the flashlight."

She remained immobile, nor did she look towards him.

He played his flashlight over the ground in front of her so she could see to make her way to him. There was a pool at her feet where she had wet herself in fear. About a foot in front of her he saw a mottled tree branch. Catching it up in the light, he registered the grey and brown pattern in his mind at the same time as it moved and stretched out. It was about three feet long and likely had been moving away from him, sensing his motion. So far, it hadn't been alarmed, and there was no buzzing sound.

"Don't move, Cat," he whispered unnecessarily. "Stay still and don't move."

He became calm, his mind sharp. The sounds of explosions and urgent voices evaporated. He shone the light carefully around him, behind and to the sides to see if there was anything he could use. He saw boulders but discarded the idea. If he threw and missed, he would be worse off. He looked at the snake. It was up, testing the air, sensing warmth in front of it. He had to do something before it curled up against Cat to keep warm.

He slowly took off his shirt while juggling the flashlight. He placed the flashlight down on the ground with the light pointing obliquely towards the side away from Cat. Praying to himself like he'd never prayed before, he stepped softly towards the snake. It was a huge risk, but it might give Cat a chance to run, and he couldn't think of anything else.

Totally focused on the snake's head and tail, and just as the snake gathered its body to move forward, forked tongue still flicking, he threw the shirt over it. In one motion he grasped both shirt and snake at the tail end. Quickly twisting his wrist to fold the shirt around it, he flung it as far as he could towards the end of the cave. In the next heartbeat, he caught Cat up in his arms and ran back towards the opening, snatching up the flashlight on the way.

Legs weak, he reached the outside and almost whooped with

joy as he saw Jean and Harley. Their anxious faces melted into expressions of relief.

"Are you okay, Cat?" Harley touched her arm gently.

"My head hurts," she mumbled, turning away from him and laid her head on Fergus's shoulder. Harley's face went red, and he said nothing else.

"Where's your shirt?" Jean asked.

"Keeping a rattler warm," said Fergus, sounding smug. "Let's make tracks out of here." He handed Harley the flashlight to light the way, and they went single file, with Jean in the middle and Fergus right behind, protecting her from slipping. But Jean went upward easily and sure-footed as if edging up the side of a cliff in her best dress and shoes were an everyday occurrence.

Cat weighed nothing at all, and Fergus carried her easily. In his joy, he didn't mind she hadn't spoken, but her arms were wrapped tightly around him, and he took it as a good sign.

It was getting dark now, and Harley swept the flashlight back and forth to light the path as best he could. Every so often, he'd look behind him at Cat and bite his lip. At the top, they all breathed easier and made better time. A short way to go to the parking lot, Cat turned her head towards him and said in his ear, "I saw him." and started to whimper. "I went back for the letter, and I saw him." Whimpers turned to helpless sobs.

Fergus stopped and lowered Cat to the ground. Jean turned and started to come near, but he gestured for her to stay and jerked his head at Harley. "The car." She understood immediately and reached into the side pocket of his jacket she still had over her arm. She drew out the car key and handed it to Harley.

"Go to the car and start it up. Can you see to get there?" she asked him.

Harley looked uncertainly at her and then Fergus, still subdued and pale over Cat's condition. He handed Jean the flashlight. "Sure. Don't worry about me."

When Jean turned back to Fergus, he was holding Cat close to his chest, and stroking her hair. His voice was soothing. "It's okay, Cat. You're safe."

"He hit him." Her body stiffened and drew away from him. "I

wanted to go and help Sir, but I was too scared. I ran home."

Fergus took both her hands in his. "Going home was the right thing to do, Cat."

His words only seemed to make her more distressed. "Sir told me to tell you about him. I promised him, and then I didn't remember." Eyes welling up with blame and remorse, she stifled a sob.

"Listen to me, Cat," said Fergus, bending down to look at her squarely. "It only matters that you're safe. But for now, you and I shouldn't tell anyone what you saw. Okay?"

Her nod was hesitant. She clung to him and laid her head on his shoulder as he picked her up, and he whispered softly into her ear. "Let's go home."

At the car, Fergus confronted Harley sitting in the driver's seat. "Have you got a driver's license?"

"Sure do. Got one right away when I turned sixteen."

"Drive then. And don't try to go across the train bridge."

Harley looked at him jaw unhinged, then grinned.

Before Fergus got into the car, he pulled Jean in front of him. "Cat, I want you to meet a very nice lady. Her name is Jean Buckley."

Cat had stopped crying. She snuffled once and turned a pale face past his shoulder to stare at Jean's soft brown eyes and gentle smile. Finally, she took one arm from around Fergus's neck and held it out. "How do you do, Miss Buckley? I am very pleased to meet you." Then, she bent her head and vomited all over their shoes. Her body started to shake.

Inside the car, Harley groaned something unintelligible.

Jean, holding her hand, said, "She's ice cold. She's going into shock, Fergus. We should get her to the hospital." She put the jacket around Cat. "Put her in the car. I'll hold her. Have you got a blanket in the trunk?"

Fergus ran to the back of the car and lifted the trunk. He found a blanket and tucked it around Cat huddled on Jean's lap, then ran to the driver's side. "Move over."

Harley almost jumped into the passenger seat, and Fergus turned the car around, wheels spraying dirt and grass.

16

FERGUS bundled up a semi-conscious Cat and carried her towards the door. She mumbled into his shoulder, pleading, "Too fast, it's too fast. Don't go."

"It's okay Cat," Fergus said softly. "I'm taking you to the hospital. We have to go fast." He headed into the admitting room towards a nurse behind the counter.

"This child needs attention. She's had a shock," he added lamely as if shocks were something laying around for any child to pick up.

The nurse took one look at Cat and picked up the phone. She spoke quietly, Fergus heard the word '*urgent*,' then she replaced the receiver. In a few minutes, a doctor came through some swinging doors, inspected Cat, and told the nurse at the desk to send a staff nurse to him in Room 3. As he took Cat from Fergus, she mumbled, "Joe." Feeling inadequate, Fergus watched the doctor disappear through the doors.

"Details," the nurse said, briskly.

Fergus pulled Harley forward. "This is Harley Perkins, Cat's brother," he said, nudging Harley to answer the nurse's questions.

Patiently, the nurse shifted her focus to Harley. "Where was she and what was she doing that caused you to bring her to the hospital?" Harley went red and gave a pleading look to Fergus.

Fergus gave her a shortened account of the episode in the cave. The nurse finished her notes and said crisply, "The mother's signature is required on permission forms." She again looked at Harley. "Who is responsible for payment?"

"I am," Fergus replied quickly, getting a relieved smile from Harley.

Later Harley stood in the waiting room shifting from one foot to another then looked squarely at Fergus. "I'm sorry," he said simply. "I didn't think . . ."

"No, you didn't," Fergus replied, his expression dark.

Harley nodded. "I should have made her go home. It's my fault she's here." He stuffed his hands into his pockets and inspected the floor. He closed his eyes and looked so apprehensive that Fergus almost pitied him.

Harley looked at Fergus and Jean and straightened up. "You can't hate me more than I do myself. I'm mad all the time—ever since my dad left us." Fergus opened his mouth to say that was no reason to take it out on Cat, but Harley rushed on, "I know it's no excuse, but even if you think I'm capable of doing something to hurt my sister, I wouldn't. So, please, I'll do anything to make it right . . ."

Fergus turned away and took Jean by the arm towards the chairs, suddenly weary from the strain of the last few hours. Harley followed and stood in front of Fergus. For the first time, Fergus took in Harley's face. His hair was darker than both Rose's and Cat's. His eyes were a clear blue, and intelligent. At the moment, they were free of guile, and Fergus decided to believe him, although with reservations.

"Go home Harley, and tell your mother Cat is okay. You don't have to go into the full story. I don't think your mother could take it calmly." He took Harley's wry face for agreement. "Tell her what you want, but downplay it. You will have to bring her here so she can sign permission for Cat's treatment, but try to convince her Cat will be okay, so she shouldn't panic."

"I sure will, Mr. Muir. But the first thing my mother will want to do is ask Mr. Rideout for advice."

"That's up to her," Fergus replied, then added pointedly. "But she knows Cat doesn't like him. Does he have to be involved in all her problems?"

Harley looked puzzled. "Okay, Mr. Muir. You saved Cat, and anything you say is fine with me. I'll think of something to tell my Mom."

"Okay. If you are serious, then I want you to stay with Cat through the night if she's held over. Stay in her room. Don't let anybody but the medical staff or her mother near her. Do you understand?"

"Yes." Harley's eyes narrowed, shrewd. "What's going on, Mr. Muir?"

Fergus didn't know what to reply, and he looked at Jean for help, shrugging.

"Your little sister has had a lot of shocks this past month, Harley," Jean volunteered. "It is likely Cat has either seen or is aware of, a whole raft of disturbing events which she's blocked so she won't have to think about them. If she were an adult, she would be in a worse state than she is."

"She's been acting strange ever since Joe . . ." Harley stopped.

"Your mother told me Joe isn't coming home." Fergus latched on to the subject. "But Cat says otherwise, and I wonder why. Your mother didn't tell Cat he won't be coming back." He considered Harley and said pointedly, "Is that about right?"

"What?" Harley sat down hard on a chair. "No. Yes. How do you know?" He looked past Fergus's shoulder, evasive.

"I don't know for sure, but Cat said she went with Joe when he left for the farm. And he told her he *is* coming back."

Fergus wasn't prepared for the impact of his words on Harley. They seemed to hit the boy with gale force. He made a sound, half rose from his chair then slumped back, blood draining from his face. Eyes welling with tears, he blew out a long breath. "The poor kid. I could have helped her if I'd known, but she'd never come to me because I've always teased her. I've got the brains of a jackass, Mr. Muir."

Something is screwy here. Harley's reaction is over the top, Fergus thought thinking about his mother's near hysteria earlier.

"Let's just agree that you haven't been using them to any advantage," he could only say, still inspecting Harley's face trying to analyze his reaction.

Harley gave Fergus a grateful look and stared at the floor for a long time, then almost to himself, muttered, "Out of the crooked timber of humanity . . ."

"No straight thing was ever made," finished Jean. She sat up. "Kant? You read Kant?"

Harley blushed bright red. "I was thinking of Rideout and my mom. And my dad. He's an honest man, a straight shooter, but he couldn't find a job. While crooked men have an easy time and end up with everything. If only my father were here." He didn't finish.

"Are you saying Lex Rideout is a crook?" Fergus said before Jean pursued her interest in Kant. He couldn't believe it. He could understand Cat and Harley's resentment of their mother's relationship, but calling Lex a criminal?

Harley looked mutinous at the idea he might be wrong, a frequent attitude, Fergus surmised. "Well, he might be. I go down to the bottle factory to the scrap heap and pick through it for unbroken bottles. I do the same thing at the pottery yards. I find some seconds or rejects I can sell. People don't mind a bubble in a glass bottle or a pottery piece that hasn't been glazed evenly."

He stopped, correctly reading Fergus's flash of distaste, then pity. "It's for university," he explained, his tone angry and defensive. "I don't want to stay here forever."

"There's no guard to stop people wandering around the grounds?"

"Oh sure," replied Harley, dismissively. "A drunk. I wondered why they kept a drunk, so I watched. I thought I could tell Rideout his watchman was always sleeping and drinking on the job, and I could do it. But then I thought maybe he wants a drunk watchman."

"Go on," said Fergus.

"The scrap pile is right across the field from the loading docks, so I just sort of made myself small and watched. The more I saw, the more I thought it was a funny way of conducting a loading operation. Rideout himself helped the truck driver load up the crates. He seemed to run the operation single-handed, and they didn't sign any paper. Every time I saw them loading before, the truck driver always signed some paper or other."

"Was there a name on the van of the shipping company?"

"Ready and Waiting." Harley laughed.

Fergus knew of it. It was an old trucking company first set up by two partners, Frank Ready and Harvey Waiting. Frank was dead, and Harvey retired. Fergus wasn't sure who ran it now. He thought back to the night at the Assiniboia Club when Rideout had complained about his shipper and breakages.

"He could have been personally loading the crates, so the

shipping company couldn't claim they were broken when they were picked up. Paperwork could have been arranged beforehand."

Harley didn't look convinced.

"He has no reason to steal, Harley. He'd make more money showing a good profit to Head Office."

Harley got up to leave. "All I know is I don't feel bad, finding a bottle or two from the scrap heap."

Fergus gave him money for taxi fares to and from the hospital for both him and his mother. Harley thanked him and hesitated a moment before leaving. "My mother isn't bad really, Mr. Muir. She just has this idea in her head of what life should be like. If she can't cope, she panics and takes the easy way out." Harley had the grace to blush then, recognizing his own recent actions. "She wants me gone, but I'm not going. Now she's beginning to act helpless, so other people will solve her problems. We just really need my father to come home."

Fergus had no ready answer for him. He watched Harley go on his way, trusting him to follow his instructions.

He turned to Jean, who had followed the conversation with an astonished expression. She looked at him and said, "He must be what, seventeen?"

"He's sixteen, and already graduated from high hchool. They skipped him grades."

"I can see why. But Kant?"

"I'm sorry about this," Fergus said. He rubbed his head. "What I want to know is who smashed Peter's head with a brick? And if it was the vagrant he chased away from Cat, or someone else. And if so, did she know him?"

"Will we ever know? But I believe Harley when he said Rideout is stealing from the company. What if he always did, and Peter found out, so he framed Peter and said he was stealing the very crates Rideout was stealing himself?"

"Whoa." laughed Fergus. "Hold on. Even in my worst audits, I've never come across a plot like that." She was so willing to believe Harley's opinion; an odd thing for a lawyer to take hearsay over evidence. Was she joking? Suddenly in the last hour, Lex Rideout was a different person. He tried to visualize her description with the one he knew and found it absurd.

"Some people are like sharks," she said. "You might not see the fin circling until it's too late." She looked at him sideways, and he saw teasing in her eyes. He decided she was playing with him to lighten the mood. At the same time, he felt uncomfortable. He studied her face and thought again about seeing her on the street with Rideout.

"Is Lex Rideout your client?" he asked suddenly.

Her surprise was real. "Of course not! Peter was—is our client. We don't like to represent two officials of the same company."

Why not? Fergus wondered. He let it go. His tongue felt thick. He badly wanted a drink. "Do you think Cat will be okay? I didn't dare ask her about Joe. It might have sent her over the edge."

Jean took his hand in hers. "Fergus, Cat needs professional help. I know someone. I've used her on some of my family law cases. I think I should give her a call."

"It might work," he agreed, a welcome relief flooding through him. "You can call her now? But first, I think we should each take a washroom break and clean our shoes—take some of the smell away." He grinned at her and wrinkled his nose. "I don't think we exactly smell like '*Evening in Paris*,' which isn't great anyway."

They went their separate ways. Before Jean found the washroom, she asked at the desk to use the phone.

When he came back to the waiting room, Fergus stopped at the front desk to speak to the nurse, but there was no news yet. The nurse sighed at his request to use the phone, cautioning him to make it brief, reminding him it wasn't a public telephone. Malcolm answered on the first ring.

"Dad, I'm at the hospital. I brought Cat."

"What happened to her?" Malcolm said, his alarm showing down the line.

"I can't say too much on the phone," Fergus said cautiously. Telephone operators were sworn to not listen to conversations through the central switchboard, but on a quiet night, clever people knew not to say too much.

"Don't worry, Dad. Trust me when I say it's all under control. I'll fill you in later."

Fergus sat and waited for Jean. When she came down the hall smiling and looking less weary, he rose and took her arm. "I can drive you home. You don't have to wait, you know."

"Not on your life, Fergus. I'm here for the duration."

Pleased, he put up his hands in surrender. "Are you too tired to listen to something I want to tell you?"

"Fire away," she said, sitting.

"The cave," he started, then paused.

"You were terrified."

"It was the war. I was buried in a cave. The feeling of suffocation is always there. Peter found me and rescued me." He watched her, trying to read her expression, almost waiting for derision.

"Ah," she said, finally. "And now you are repaying the debt."

"Partly," he said, relieved she understood. "But what if I can't prove he's innocent? Then what?" The prospect made him suddenly tired. He slumped forward, arms resting on his thighs, and stared down at his feet.

"Silly man." She poked him with her elbow. "You'll find a way. For Cat's sake too. I hope she didn't recognize the man who killed him. Whoever it was, it won't bring him back." She looked past his shoulder at the door.

A petite, dark-haired woman wearing a fitted suit came through the doors, stopped and looked around. She caught sight of Jean and headed their way.

"Hello, Roberta," said Jean, standing quickly and sounding relieved.

"Roberta Flower." Jean introduced Fergus. "She's a member of The Children's Aid Society. If anyone can help Cat, Roberta can."

Roberta Flower held out her hand to Fergus. She was in her fifties, he guessed, with a kind face and brilliant blue eyes. She took in his lack of shirt and smiled. The three sat again. "What's the story on the child?" she asked without preliminaries.

With Jean's prompting, Fergus told her as much as he felt she needed to know, starting with Peter's note. He kept to details relating only to Cat, leaving out mention of Peter's Will and financial affairs.

Roberta showed no emotion during the telling. She must have heard these stories many times before, Fergus thought.

"I'm familiar with the Perkins family. I've had to get the truant officers after them more than once." Roberta sighed. "You'd think people would be used to hard times. But those who came from Old Country stock revert back to apprenticing children at the age of twelve. The old system is gone thank goodness, but now they are just put out to work. The vision of children having a better future than what the parents have is lost in the necessity for living today. I never knew the father, but I hear he is riding the rails?"

The double doors leading to the hospital center opened, and the doctor came through. All three stood up at his appearance as he strode over to them.

"Dr. Anderson," said Miss Flower and gave him a winning smile.

"Miss Flower," declared Dr. Anderson. He looked at Jean and Fergus, and his smile disappeared. "Are you the parents of the child?"

"Thanks for the compliment, Doctor," said Fergus sarcastic, then contritely, "I wish we were, believe me."

The doctor's eyes wandered over the suit Fergus wore, well-tailored but shirtless.

"It's in the cave," Fergus said, reading his expression, "covering a snake."

"How is Cat?" Jean interrupted.

"Severely dehydrated," the doctor said crisply. "Too much sun and too little water. She's being given fluids right now, and her vitals have improved. We'll keep her here under observation. There's no need for you to stay." He looked at his watch, gave a tired sigh and turned to leave, then stopped. "The admission report said something about a cave. It doesn't wholly explain her confused condition." He gave his watch another glance then looked at Fergus impatiently.

"Doctor," said Roberta. "If I may have a word, please?" She turned to Fergus and Jean. "I can take it from here if you like. I'll fill in Dr. Anderson. He's very understanding. I'll spend some time with Cat when she's able, and let you know any result. Can we leave it for now?"

"Tomorrow, then?" Fergus asked the doctor.

But Roberta shook her head. "I think it's advisable for you to wait until Monday or even Tuesday. I would like a day or two to get to know Cat and gain her confidence. If she's acknowledged something repressed, she will be confused and feel guilty tomorrow. Let her recover and gain whatever inner security she lost tonight. I'll arrange everything with her mother and her family."

"Cat will freeze up with a stranger," said Fergus, reluctant to leave.

"I have some experience, and I know what I'm doing, Mr. Muir," she said firmly, but her smile took the sting off her remark. "Go. I'll phone Jean when it's okay to see her."

She moved off with Dr. Anderson, and Fergus had no choice but to take her advice.

He dropped Jean off at her house. At her door, they stared at each other for a moment, at a loss for words.

"Well, you certainly do know how to entertain a girl," Jean started. "What will you do for an encore?" She was joking, but she shivered and hugged herself.

"I hope you'll let me make it up to you. Next Saturday?"

"Oh, no you don't," said Jean. "You invited me in on this, and you can't get rid of me so easily. How about taking me with you to the hospital again? I want to know what you are going to do next."

"The first thing I am going to do is call on the police, and this time I'm going to insist I meet with the captain."

"Fergus," said Jean, her face startled then alarmed. "You can't. I'm appointing myself your legal adviser, so you should think about it."

"Hadn't I?" Fergus said, confused.

"You're tired Fergus, not thinking. Wait and see what Roberta turns up. Cat isn't out of the woods yet, but she's terrified and in no condition to tell what she saw. The police have all but decided it was a vagrant. Can you imagine the questions? In her state of mind, they will convince her to say anything, and she'll agree just for the peace of mind, truth be damned. I can sneak in tomorrow and talk to Roberta. If there is any development, I'll tell you. Right now, go home and get some sleep."

Fergus had to concede. "Right. And I have to fill in Malcolm." He smiled at her. "I can't tell you how much I appreciate all you've done tonight." He bent and kissed her cheek. They examined each other's eyes for a long moment. Then Fergus kissed her properly, his mouth moving over hers, liking its softness. She raised herself to meet his kiss, and his heart fluttered. He became more urgent, questioning. She responded, then suddenly pulled away, both hands firmly against his chest.

"It's been a long day, Fergus." Her breathing was rapid and shallow.

He dropped his arms but held on to her hands.

"Sure. But the ending was nice." The smiled at each other. "Sleep well."

She called out to him softly, as he went off down the front path. "Should I wear my country clothes next week then? And bring a big stick and a rope?"

He stopped by the car, opened the door and waved. "I'll let you know."

17

FERGUS drove down the back lane and into the garage, as quietly as he could so as to not disturb Mrs. Mann in her apartment. In the yard, lifting his face to the sky, he took a deep breath. It seemed to him the cleanest sky on earth was right there above him.

He did a little dance, whirled around, spread his arms out wide, basking in a spirit of freedom, and lifted his face again. His eyes landed on Mrs. Mann glaring at him from her window. He stayed where he was, arms splayed out from his shoulders. She took in his appearance, his wrinkled suit, his open jacket displaying his stained undershirt. She stared at him a moment, then drew down the green shade at the window, shutting out the sight of him. If it were possible for a shade to slam shut, he heard it. He giggled helplessly, then turned and entered the house through the kitchen door.

"Mrs. Mann is right now preparing to give me a lecture tomorrow," he said to Malcolm as he came through the door of the study.

Malcolm stared at Fergus, then took off his glasses as if they blurred his vision. "Has she got good reason?" He pointed his glasses at his son's appearance.

"Oh, this?" Fergus replied, nonchalant. "I used my shirt to tackle a rattler when I rescued Cat." He grinned.

Malcolm rose halfway out of his chair, then sat again.

"There was nobody else. Cat was in Ranger's Cave by herself, and she was literally scared stiff."

"Cat's fine," Fergus said reading the worried creases in Malcolm's face. "Dehydrated. And heat stroke. The doctor is keeping her for observation. She'll be safer there than at home. Just so you know, I offered to foot the bill."

"I think you'd better start at the beginning."

Fergus slumped down in the chair, his legs splayed out. He told Malcolm the whole story, starting with dinner, and seeing Cat at the theatre with Harley. He saved Cat's confession to the last. "The trauma in the cave triggered her memory. The poor kid couldn't absorb any more shocks, I think." He also told him about Roberta Flower and their plan for Cat's safety. "She seems competent. And there's another strange thing."

"Yes?"

"When I mentioned Joe to Clara Perkins, she told me he wasn't coming home. The whole family but Cat agrees he isn't coming back. I suspect Joe did tell Cat he isn't coming home again, but she's denying it. The whole family is strange. Every time I talk to any one of them, I feel like I'm in a different conversation. Then Harley . . ." He frowned and shrugged it off. "We'll find out more if Roberta Flower manages to gain her confidence."

Malcolm found he couldn't speak. Finally, he cleared his throat and said, "Cat needs to think her brother is coming back. She talks to him in her head like he is beside her. How terrible to be apart from your twin."

"Will she ever tell us whatever she knows?" Fergus looked down at his hands. "A few weeks ago we couldn't even imagine someone like Cat in our lives. Without Peter, would we have ever been aware she existed?"

"Thank goodness you decided to go after her," Malcolm said and gave a long sigh of contentment. "Should I pin a medal on Cat when this is all over?"

Thinking of the rescue, Fergus brightened. "When I went inside, it was hell. I was there, in France again, paralyzed. I imagined the walls caving in, forcing myself not to run." Again, Fergus smelt the dankness, relived a helpless feeling of suffocation in the unbearable blackness. He clenched and unclenched his fists. "Then I heard Peter's voice, right there, shouting at me like always. I couldn't disappoint him. When I saw Cat with the snake in front of her, I went absolutely calm. Getting her out was the only thing on my mind. And it worked out just fine."

"Yes, it did, didn't it? You just had to believe in yourself." Malcolm's voice quivered, but Fergus didn't seem to notice, so intent on talking.

"Jean noticed, but she didn't push," he continued. "I was terrified and ashamed at the same time. I even thought of turning around, pretending that Cat would have come here instead of going to the cliffs. When it was all over, I told Jean about being buried." Fergus finally registered Malcolm's expression at the last comment. "What is it?"

"What do you like about Jean?"

"What? Am I twelve again?"

"Of course not. I meant, what is she like? I wondered what you thought of her."

Fergus regarded his father with suspicion, but answered anyway, "She was marvelous at the cave. Didn't turn a hair. She listens, doesn't interrupt with questions when I tell her something, but has great insight. She's just nice. Is that all you want to know?"

Malcolm said nothing in reply. He shifted in his chair, folded his glasses and laid them gently along with his book on the side table. "Fergus. Tell me about France."

"France again?" Fergus stared at his father. "You're worse than the Spanish Inquisition."

Malcolm persisted. "I need to know what happened when Peter rescued you."

Fergus leaned back in the chair and closed his eyes. His euphoria disappeared, and rage took its place. He opened his eyes. "Did you harp at Peter like this? In your cozy little conversations? Did you keep on at him until he finally gave you *his* version?"

"Peter never talked about his war experiences, and I never asked." Malcolm's voice was steady, but his grey eyes narrowed at the accusation. "I need to understand what happened to you."

"Why? It has nothing to do with you. Is there some kind of judgment factor here, looking for a reason why I am like I am? Ashamed that I'm not the brave lad going off to war and coming home a hero instead of whatever it is you called me . . . arrogant, cold? Is that it?"

Malcolm put his hand up, palm out, his eyes now frigid. "Stop right there."

Both angry, they glared at each other,

"I was there all night and well into the next day," Fergus snapped, then spread his hands out in a pleading gesture, questioning. But Malcolm's expression told him he wasn't giving up.

"You were so full of yourself a moment ago," Malcolm snapped at him, furious. "If you conquered both the cave and your memory of France, then talk! Get the rest of it out! Humor an old man. I've had to put up with your highs and lows, walking on eggshells day after day, wondering what mood you're in. It's been sixteen years, Fergus. End it now, for your own sake if not for mine."

"There's nothing else to tell, Dad," Shouting in his frustration, Fergus cursed, "Bloody hell, I can't make something up just to tease your imagination. Denvers begged me to end his pain. I couldn't do it, and he cursed me, said it was my fault he was there, and I should have known it was a trap." Fergus turned pensive blue eyes to Malcolm. "What man wouldn't feel guilty about it? I had nothing to do but think. About the absolute futility of it all. Why did we agree to get involved in someone else's war?"

"We didn't agree, really," said Malcolm, unable to resist correcting him. "We were a colony of Britain then and when they declared war, Canada was automatically at war too. It's different now, but it was the right thing to do then. Men volunteered."

"Until they were stuck in the trenches and suffered the results of decisions made by fools," snapped Fergus.

"How did Peter get you free?"

Fergus stood up, hands at his sides, balled into fists.

"No more. I'm tired. It's been a long, trying day. And from now on, quit harping on about the blasted everlasting war, can't you?" Fergus snarled and beat his retreat.

CAT woke from a restless sleep. She sat up in the midst of unfamiliar surroundings and sucked in her breath, frightened, until she spotted Harley dozing in a chair by her bedside. When she whispered his name, he opened his eyes immediately and reached out to touch her arm.

"It's okay, Cat. You're in the hospital. Don't you remember Mr. Muir bringing you to the hospital?"

"Is Carl here too?" Her voice quivered.

"No, Cat. I'm finished with him. I'm sorry about him, I really am. I won't tease you anymore either. I didn't know . . . well, Mr. Muir asked me to stay with you to make sure you're . . ." about to say safe, he stopped, "not alone," he said instead.

She put her head back down on the pillow and considered him. "Did Mama come?"

"She was here, but she went home again. You know how she is. I told her I'd stay with you. So here I am." He tucked the sheet around her to prove his point.

"Don't let Mama bring Mr. Rideout here." She didn't look away from his questioning stare. She considered telling him why, then only said, "I don't like him."

"You aren't alone there." He opened his mouth to say something else but only agreed with her. "Don't worry, little sister. I told her not to tell him, that if he knew what trouble we all were, he'd want nothing more to do with us."

Satisfied, Cat laid down again and was soon asleep.

RISING

late the next morning, Fergus and Malcolm met in the breakfast room, eyeing each other edgeways, sniffing the air like two contenders, gauging temper.

"Maybe we should spend the day relaxing." Malcolm kept his voice neutral. "Take a walk, read, then visit Cat in the hospital."

"The best idea I've heard in a long time," Fergus said, hoping his father would take it as a truce, and not start another session about the war.

Malcolm looked pleased, and the stiffness retreated somewhat. It seemed both preferred to avoid last night's conversation.

Mrs. Mann, however, didn't believe in relaxation. She marched through the dining room in her hat and Sunday dress and announced, "People who get up too late for church, are welcome to make their own breakfast. The makings are in the kitchen. Put the dishes in the sink when you are done, or if you've a mind to help, one can wash, and the other can dry." She smiled at Malcolm as she said the last, and as she went out the door, shot Fergus a look full of ice, with a shade of disappointment as if he had let down the team side.

"Mrs. Mann." He felt it was time to explain. "It wasn't what you think . . ."

But Mrs. Mann marched into the hall, straightened her hat in the hall mirror and departed towards the kitchen door. They heard an audible click as she left the house.

"So remind me," said Fergus, stomach rumbling as they made their way to the kitchen. "Why do we keep her on?" It was really a rhetorical question, and he didn't expect an answer.

"This is her home," Malcolm said anyway. "She's a good cook, she works hard, she's loyal, and thrifty. And most of all, she cares about us."

"I know," said Fergus, irked, as they made their way into the kitchen. "You make the toast. I'll do the eggs, and put on the coffee pot. Is it enough?"

"Should be. We'll need lots of coffee." Malcolm's thumb pointed at the breakfast room. "Did I detect frost in the air out there?"

"When I came home last night, clothes in a mess, I played the fool dancing a little jig in the backyard. Mrs. Mann saw me from her window. She probably thinks I've ravished Jean."

Malcolm, slicing bread, threw back his head and laughed, and Fergus joined in.

After breakfast, mindful of Mrs. Mann, they cleaned up the kitchen.

"Later on, I might walk down the block to Lex Rideout's house and remind him about GlasBottle's financial records," Fergus told his father. "At the Club, he said he'd think about it. Maybe I can convince him to give them to me today."

Malcolm had just stacked the last dish in the cupboard when there was a knock on the back door.

Fergus opened the door to find Max Levinson on the back step, looking both excited and determined. He held a square box in his arms.

"Please Mr. Muir, can I come in before anyone sees me?"

Fergus stood aside. As Max sidled into the house, Fergus caught movement in the alley at the corner of the garage.

"Who's out there?" he asked, sticking his head out the door to peer into the yard. "Did someone come with you?"

"It's okay. It's Tom . . . a friend. He can't come in."

Fergus raised his eyebrows at Max. "Why not?"

Max set the box down on the floor. It had *Property of T. Eaton and Co.* written on it. His manner went from determination to indecision. "Maybe I shouldn't have come."

"Maybe you should explain first," corrected Fergus, using his office voice. "What's going on?"

"My father told me about Mr. Davidson and how you are trying to clear his name."

"Good God," sputtered Fergus, temper coming to a simmer. "How many people has he told? How many people know about the letter?"

"My father never said anything about a letter, nor would he break any confidences. He thought I might be able to help, and he asked me. Well, just hinted, really." In defense of his father, Max's mouth set in a line. "I wanted to help because of the Thursday night lectures. Even the one we've had has made a big difference to me. So I got in touch with . . ."

"Max." Malcolm held up his hand and interrupted the incoherent chatter. "Slow down. Start from the beginning."

"Okay." Max sat on a kitchen chair and took a deep breath.

"One of my friends is the bookkeeper at GlasBottle. He doesn't want me to give you his name. His boss is Lex Rideout. Tom," Max continued, naming the friend who couldn't be named, "would quit if there was another job available. But he's the sole support for his mother and brother. He says Mr. Rideout changes his reports and threatens to fire him when he questions it."

"You talk to each other about your work?" Fergus almost snarled. "Trading information about our clients?"

"Lord, no. I'd never talk." Max half stood, horrified, then sat again. "My father drummed it into my head years ago to never talk about our business customers. I told Tom you'd react this way," he said, voice rising with resentment. "This was a mistake after all."

Fergus relaxed, secretly glad of Max's spirit. "I believe you. Just tell me exactly what your father told you."

Typically, Max ran his fist through his hair. "Father said Mr. Davidson had been accused of fraud. That you could prove it was all a lie and it was a shame you couldn't see the records. I took it on myself, Mr. Muir, to meet Tom and suggest if he found some records, I could hand them over to you. After all, it was a time before Tom was hired, wasn't it?" Max kicked the box with his foot. "So, as a favor to me, he did."

Fergus and Malcolm both started and said together, "These are records from when Peter was there?"

"He has to get them back soon. Before they're missed."

"How long?"

"A day. Two days at the most."

"You realize this is highly irregular, Max? Illegal even? The lawyers have filed a request for the records, but it hasn't been approved yet. So, are you willing to proceed?" Fergus eyed his apprentice soberly, even to some extent disapproving.

Max's glance never wavered. "I am."

Fergus thought for a long minute. Did he really want to involve a student in something considered on the wrong side of ethics? Still, he couldn't help but thrill at this new opportunity. In a quandary, he looked at Malcolm, who gazed back, his face expressionless.

"You know even if we find something in the records, we cannot use them in a court of law," he said to Max, ignoring his own temptation.

Max shifted his feet. "But you might be able to use the information as leverage without revealing how you came by it."

Fergus looked at his student with dawning respect.

"Still," he acknowledged. "There is a question of how you came by these records, Max. This friend of yours, Tom. Maybe Lex changes his reports because he sees mistakes in them. Ever think of that? And whether I can in all conscience agree to it. I've a good mind to tell you to take the records back and give you a lecture to boot." He tried not to look at the box, but in the end, curiosity won. "What's in there?"

"A list of Accounts Receivable, Accounts Payable, and a GlasBottle Sales Record for '32. I know it isn't much. Only what he could lay his hands on quickly without a prolonged search, which would leave traces and look suspicious. But he managed to find the Consolidated Statements for Strathcona Holdings for 1932. They would show some relationship to GlasBottle statements."

Fergus made up his mind. "Leave the box with me. I'll ask Haskell for his opinion. Then, I'll make a decision. We've got a day or two?"

Max nodded, looking apologetic and humiliated that his offer of help might be an inexcusable blunder. He scurried to the door, fumbling for the knob on the wrong side. Blushing furiously and grinning, he corrected himself and hurried out. Malcolm raised his eyebrows, but Fergus, surprised at himself, had only wanted to tell Max he had shown an initiative Fergus wasn't aware he possessed.

"Should we really worry about ethics now when Peter's name is at stake?" Fergus said to Malcolm. "After all, we aren't sneaking records for personal gain."

Malcolm went off to phone Haskell. Fergus sat and pushed the box around with his foot, angry and feeling set up in an almost impossible position.

"Haskell said, 'sometimes justice stands in the way of the law,'" Malcolm reported, coming back into the room. "His way of saying the decision is up to you."

"I'll walk down the block and ask Lex if he has made any progress at getting financial statements. If he agrees, I'll take these back." Fergus stood, and picked up the box and headed for the study. "If he won't cooperate, I'm not refusing this chance only to find out later Haskell's formal request for records is denied."

Malcolm started towards the stairs, saying he would go out for some air, and then visit Cat at the hospital.

The back door opened and Mrs. Mann appeared. She smiled at them both, and her eyes searched around the kitchen as she took off her hat.

"Kitchen back to normal," said Fergus defensively.

"Oh, not to worry, Fergus," she said, giving him a blazing smile. "What you would like for dinner tonight? I was thinking of your favorite, wiener schnitzel with red cabbage and parsley potatoes? Strawberry tarts for dessert? Or maybe deep apple pie and thick cream?"

Malcolm grinned. Fergus shot her a guarded look, but her face was beaming at him, not at all sarcastic. "Rousing sermon at the church today, was it?"

Mrs. Mann drew her mouth together ready to snap a reply, then sighed. "Why didn't you tell me you rescued Cat from a herd of rattlesnakes and had to take her to the hospital last night?"

"A herd of rattlesnakes?"

"Lydia Horn's cousin's niece was on the admitting desk last night when you brought Cat in, and she told her mother, and her mother told Lydia what a hero you are. Why didn't you tell me? I'm the only one who didn't know in the whole Ladies Auxiliary." She implied it was downright unjust that as President of the Ladies Auxiliary, she was the last to know something about the very house she lived in.

"You didn't give me a chance."

"Well, I admit I may have been a tad hasty when I saw you reeling like a drunken hobo around the backyard. What if someone had seen you in a dirty undershirt? It would be all around town I can't wash white things white." She drew herself up in outrage, then as if remembering her contrition, added, "But I'm not one to hold a grudge, and if an apology is needed, then I am giving it to you now."

"Accepted, Mrs. Mann. But it isn't necessary. Deep down you know I'd never do anything to make you ashamed of me. We were going to tell you this afternoon anyway."

"Is she alright then? She didn't get bitten?"

"Cat is fine, and there was one snake, which I took care of with my shirt, and is the reason I didn't have it when I came home. Cat had heat stroke. They're keeping her in the hospital for a few days. You could visit her this afternoon and see for yourself."

"Why was she at the cliffs in the first place?" Mrs. Mann said, scandalized. "Running wild all over town. That mother of hers doesn't seem to care."

Fergus's eyes shot a question at Malcolm. They stared at each other for a long moment, then Malcolm said, "Tell her."

"Tell me what?" Mrs. Mann looked from one to the other.

"Sit down please," Fergus told her, laying the box on the table. "It's a complicated story, but we'll do our best. Though anything you hear from now on must be kept entirely to yourself."

Mrs. Mann sat, then half rose again, incensed. "Mr. Muir, I say here and now I never gossip about anything that goes on in this house! The very idea!"

"Yes, of course. I've repeated the same thing so often, to Jean and Harley and Roberta Flower, that it just comes out."

"Who is Roberta Flower?"

Fergus retold the story, ending with the visit to Cat's house, and about Joe, and why Jean had recommended Roberta Flower spend time with her.

Mrs. Mann's expression grew more and more disturbed as he went on. The last shocked her to the core. "Oh my, oh my, oh my. Doesn't that family ever talk to each other? They won't tell her Joe isn't coming home. And she won't tell them she knows it, but she pretends he is?"

"She isn't pretending," said Malcolm. "She believes it."

"Well, maybe her trust will bring him home. No wonder she is in a daze half the time. How much can a child take? First, her father takes off, then her brother Alex, and now she is probably afraid the same thing will happen to Joe!"

"Alex? Who's he?"

"He was sent to a farm three years ago and killed. He was around twelve years old. The paper said he was playing on the hay rack and fell through the slats, and his head caught. When he tried to get out, his neck broke, and he died."

"I remember now," Malcolm said, his shock evident. "But the name didn't mean anything. It caused quite a stir in town. There were questions about child labor on farms when there were so many unemployed men available."

The incident meant nothing to Fergus either. Did he even read about it, or perhaps he hadn't cared?

"That's not all," he said, his voice distraught "Cat was at the kiln when Peter was killed and saw the whole thing. She was in shock when she told me and by now might not remember. So keep the information tight under your hat."

"Well, why aren't you telling the police then? Did she tell you who it was?" Her voice had a tremble in it.

"No. So we can't tell the police. They'd frighten her more than she is already. If she did recognize who it was, we are her only chance to be safe from harm."

He privately thought whoever did it could be long gone and was nobody they knew. For now, Cat was safe. His concern for Peter's innocence had to take precedence. Thoughts he might fail began to plague him, and he looked at the box of records again.

FERGUS debated with himself whether to phone Lex Rideout and decided he might have a better chance of getting any financial records if he talked to him in person. The day was already another scorcher. He calculated if he went through Waterloo Park, not only would it be cooler but he would reach Rideout's house from the farther side—it would seem like he had dropped by while taking a stroll.

People with the same idea of how to spend a Sunday afternoon sauntered along the paths or conversed on park benches underneath the trees. Some had blankets spread on the lawn, eating and relaxing while the children played.

On a large grassy area near the corner where Fergus was headed, four teenaged boys tossed a rugby ball between them, one catching and the others tackling as he ran with it. Fergus changed his path and walked towards them when he recognized Lex. He ran towards Fergus carrying the ball and the boys noisily urged each other to get him. Fergus stopped to watch. Rideout caught sight of him, grinned, and tossed him the ball. Instinct drove Fergus to reach for it. For a short moment, everybody stared at each other, then Lex yelled, "Go get him, boys."

The four of them rushed at him, and Fergus tucked the ball under his arm and went towards them, intending to sidestep at the last moment. But his leather shoes slid over the grass, and before he knew it, he was prostrate on the ground with four piled on top, all pulling at the ball under him, then one ran off with it, whooping. Blood pumping in exhilaration, Fergus dusted himself off, and eyes on fire, he ran, tackled, and tossed the ball for a time, before he had to plead exhaustion. Laughing noisily, the boys left, and he and Rideout sprawled on a bench letting perspiration evaporate.

"Not bad for an old man," Rideout said, observing Fergus's soft middle. "But you have to stop sitting and get those abdominal muscles toughened up."

Fergus nodded, still trying to get his breath back. "Great fun," he said, rubbing spit on his raw elbows.

They sat in companionable silence for a while, Rideout appraising the girls walking by, either nodding or turning down his mouth. Fergus watched him and made a futile attempt to clean grass stains and a squashed grasshopper off his trousers.

"Holy mackerel, look at the stack on that one," Rideout leered towards the path. "Legs too."

Fergus followed his eyes and saw two girls. "Barely out of the cradle, Lex. You've been hanging out with your teen boys too much."

"Doesn't mean I'm blind. I can still look. But I'd never touch. My reputation in this town means a lot to me."

Fergus changed the subject. "I'm glad I ran into you today. Literally." He grinned. "Have you thought any more of letting me look at Strathcona's financial statements?" Rideout sighed and lowered his head. "I could really use your help, Lex. What I said before still stands. There's more going on than it looks."

"Not going to bring my wife back though, is it?"

"No, but you'll get some answers when we find out what really happened."

Lex stood. "Well, I did look into it, Fergus. And Head Office said no. You can understand their position. Would you give someone's records to another auditing firm?"

"Not without permission. That's why I'm asking you. And I don't want current records. Only 1930 to 1932. They're old."

"Well, I don't have those years on hand. If I did, I might consider it. I'm sorry Fergus. I can't help you."

Fergus sat on the bench and watched Rideout walk down the path towards the street. He had lied. Lex did have the records. . . . Or at least Fergus had them at home.

18

FERGUS spent a sleepless night debating ethics against justice vis-à-vis the box in the study. After a fast breakfast, he telephoned Miss Watts, who told him he had one appointment which she could reschedule for the next day. Malcolm departed for his regular massage therapy session, then lunch with a friend. Fergus shut the door of the study and lifted the box onto the desk.

It was late morning before he stopped for a break. He squirmed in his chair, bothered by painful bruises in spots where young, hard muscle had plowed into his yielding flesh in yesterday's free-for-all. He rotated his shoulders while he looked at the worksheet covered with figures.

After a quick survey, he put aside the GlasBottle records. As he expected, they only showed revenues, largely still owing by the customers. Nor was he satisfied with the Consolidated Statements of Strathcona Holdings as Peter might see it. There simply was not enough time to perform an in-depth analysis before he must return the records.

He concentrated on the auditor's report, whose name was not familiar, which also didn't surprise him. But he was bothered by an expense for consulting fees. Idly, he searched through what records he had and found a name, then got out his Calgary Directory and looked up the name of both the auditor and the consultants.

Needing a break, he wandered out the kitchen for a glass of water, tiptoeing past Mrs. Mann and her ironing board. He added some slivers of ice scraped from the icebox and drank. For a while he stood at the kitchen window, staring at three men in the yard beating the Axminster carpet from the living room. Lunch would be an hour yet, so he snatched an apple from a bowl on the sideboard, silently dodging Mrs. Mann again. Speaking when she was listening to her favorite radio drama was not allowed. She never missed an episode of the daily fifteen-minute show, boring him and Malcolm with updates, picking over the actions and personalities of the characters like they were real people. He hovered by the door to the hall and listened.

"Oh Willy, Willy," said the voice on the radio. "Where are you, son? Up to no good . . ."

"He's at the lumber yard stealing the lumber!" Mrs. Mann shouted at the radio. She banged the sad iron on the stove for emphasis and attached the wooden handle to a fresh iron. "Anyone with half a brain can see that."

Fergus snickered to himself and backed quietly into the hall. Lifting his apple for a bite, he stopped and stared into space for a long moment, then hurried to his desk. An hour later, he murmured, "Gotcha."

MALCOLM followed Fergus into the study after dinner. Mrs. Mann did the same but with a tray bearing a full pot of coffee and cups.

"I've phoned Max to pick up the box," Fergus said, feeling and sounding self-satisfied. "His pal can get it back where it belongs."

Handwritten copies of statements were pinned up against the library shelves so they could both sit back and look at them. Also pinned, were worksheets with headings and totals of accounts, with arrows and lines which corresponded to items in the statements.

They stood in front of the worksheets, and Fergus pointed out the bits of information he had been able to deduce from the records.

"No luck matching revenue with sales orders. Even allowing for Accounts Receivable, bad debts and breakages, there's a large gap." Fergus related what Harley had told him about the shipping at GlasBottle, and Rideout's remarks at the Assiniboia Club regarding breakages.

"At the Club. Lex said the equipment maintenance costs were almost bankrupting him, and it had been the same for the last five years. And the Accounts Payable list supports it." Fergus pointed his pencil at the worksheet. He moved his pointer over to the Consolidated Statement for Strathcona Holdings. "But here, look at the equipment repair expenses."

Malcolm's eyes flicked back and forth between the different statements. "They're missing."

Fergus smiled, still feeling rather smug. "Look at the Asset Account for Equipment for both GlasBottle and Strathcona."

Malcolm's mouth formed a silent 'oh.' "What kind of Companies make up the holding company?"

"I checked. GlasBottle is the only manufacturing company. The rest are real estate and commercial."

Malcolm sat back with an expression of disbelief. "But the auditors. It's all wrong, even with the loose accounting principles then."

"Strathcona chose the lowest bidder for services."

"Can't blame them. But no auditor would let that slide."

"This auditor did. See this expense for consulting services?" Fergus pointed to his worksheet again. "According to the directory, the auditors and the consulting outfit are in the same building and on the same floor. I'll bet my last red cent the auditors also have a consulting service and are collecting fees for both."

"Companies pay consultants to put the company in the best light. If the auditor is also the consulting company, he can't refuse to sign off on a financial statement which is based on his own recommendations." Malcolm looked both resigned and revolted. "Has our profession sunk to this level?"

Fergus had no argument. "It explains the so-called clearing account they asked Peter to open. An unrecorded account used as their own cookie jar. By transferring money between accounts, the Board covers up profit shortfalls then grabs juicy bonuses."

Malcolm crossed the room and poured two cups of coffee. He gave one to Fergus, and they drank while sitting in chairs, both morose.

"So there never really was any money in it for Peter to steal," Malcolm said. "They used him, and when he threatened to ask questions at the Board meeting, they decided to cover their own bank manipulations, and get rid of Peter at the same time."

"Yes." Fergus slammed his coffee down on the table, rattling the cup within the saucer, and swore softly.

Malcolm winced, but in truth he was outraged. It was brutal and unforgiving. "What are you going to do?"

"Haskell will take it from here. I'll see him tomorrow." Fergus sipped at his coffee, made a face and eyed the bottle of whisky across the room. He got up and added a dollop to his cup, and did the same for Malcolm. "Here's another twist to roil the waters," he said, sitting down again. "Strathcona is pulling a fast one on their shareholders, but GlasBottle has got one going as well. Lex's claim about breakages might be a red herring for stealing. If the thief needs a delivery system, Ready and Waiting could be the company of choice. I'm not convinced it's Lex who is stealing, but someone sure is."

"Frank Ready was an honest businessman. I hate to think his name is being used for deceit."

"Not only his," said Fergus, thinking of Peter. "And I have an idea how I can use Harley to find out."

19

WHEN Fergus arrived at the office the next morning, Max gave him a furtive thumbs-up indicating the box had been delivered safely back to Tom. His eyes had been full of questions when Fergus handed it over, but he gave no indication he'd even opened it.

Mid-morning, Archie phoned and asked to meet over lunch. His voice held a friendly note, but underneath, Fergus detected he wouldn't take no for an answer to the invitation. His suspicion was confirmed when they met at the Club Cafe.

"I didn't want to summon you to the station," Archie answered the question in Fergus's eyes. "It would be all over town by tonight. Hangers-on, and newspapermen with nothing else to do but pester every person who comes through the doors."

"I appreciate it, Archie. I was actually going to call you today anyway."

They ordered the Chinese set meal, a plate of Chicken Fried Rice with Sweet and Sour Pork with Chop Suey.

"I heard you're the hero of the hour." Archie fiddled with the band around his chopsticks. "A daring rescue at Ranger's Cave."

"Not you too," protested Fergus.

"Well, the girl was the same one you were concerned about, so I suspected there was more to the story than what's being passed around. There didn't seem to be any reason you'd fly off to the cliffs chasing a kid who was just there playing with her brother."

Archie's words were teasing, but his eyes were piercing and his expression intent. "You said you were about to call me. So, what did you want to talk about?"

Fergus looked around at the nearby tables to see who had their ears tuned to them. At the nearest table sat a Chinese family. They were busy talking in their own tongue and eating, and he was sure they were not interested in the two of them.

"Bring you up to date on what's happening. I thought if I could see the captain, I might be able to convince him the case isn't as simple as he thinks," Fergus said as their meals arrived. "It's a delicate situation." Fergus briefed him on Cat's rescue, and what she had told.

Archie said nothing, picked up his chopsticks and dug into his rice without much success. He slapped them down and picked up his fork. "Who did she see?"

"She went into shock before I could ask her."

"Well, so what? She might not have known him, and there is nothing new if she didn't. We could question her though and ask her exactly what she saw."

"No, we can't, Archie. She's teetering on the edge, and if we go battering at her with questions, we may do her considerable mental damage. When Roberta Flower talks to her, we may know more, but for now, it's imperative for people to assume Cat had heat stroke." Fergus shoveled more rice into his mouth, followed by a morsel of pork. "I have evidence which proves Peter's fraud charge was trumped up."

Archie swallowed a mouthful of food and treated Fergus to the policeman's cynicism: feigned polite interest, and ears tuned out. "What evidence?"

"Nothing I can show you until I've shown it to Peter's lawyer. Factual evidence, and it only requires formal verification, which is what I'm hoping his lawyer will get."

Archie took some time to drink from his water glass, using his napkin to dab at a drop on his tie. He looked directly at Fergus and said, "I have a few questions for you as well, Ferg. About the day of the storm. Do you remember where you were when it hit?"

"In Eaton's," Fergus said without hesitation, "buying a new shirt."

"See anybody you know while you were there?"

Fergus thought, then shrugged. "While the storm was on, I just wandered around with the other customers, looking out the windows. Then the day went black, the lights came on, and people just stood, waiting for it to be over." Fergus suddenly stopped eating and looked at Archie. "Why? What's going on?"

Archie picked up his fork then laid it down again. "The captain wants to ask you some questions. We've been interviewing people who knew Davidson and need a few points cleared up. About Davidson's murder."

"And?" Fergus's eyes narrowed. His heart picked up pace.

"This afternoon would be a good time," was all Archie said.

Fergus laid his chopsticks across his plate and pushed it away. "Why this all of a sudden, Archie? The police keep insisting it was a fight between vagrants."

Archie shrugged. "You're the one who wants the case kept open, so don't blow your wig when we ask questions."

"I have work waiting at the office, but how about five o'clock? To stop the gossips, you can invite me in as if I were your long lost friend. I want to talk to your captain too."

"I can't wait to see you two bang heads."

They left the restaurant and went in opposite directions.

Fergus returned to work in a somber mood, wondering if he'd have to prove he was in Eaton's while Peter was being killed. His store charge account would have shown his purchase, but when the storm was over, he left without the shirt and had gone home. He shrugged it off.

Miss Watts handed him a message as he entered the office. "Lex Rideout wants you to call him right away. He phoned just after you left for lunch."

"You might get a call from the police," Lex said, immediately upon saying hello. His voice was guarded as if he wasn't sure of his welcome. "I had to go to the police station this morning. They said they were questioning anyone who knew Davidson."

"Why are you telling me, Lex?" Had they found new evidence? Is that why Archie told him to come in? To share it with him?

"Well," Lex hesitated, "I'm sorry, but they wanted names of people who had contact with Davidson or knew him, and I guess I added your name to the list."

"So?"

"I just thought you should know, and that I wasn't talking about you behind your back. You can't blame me. You're the one who couldn't let the matter drop."

Fergus replaced the receiver, puzzled why Lex thought it necessary to tell Fergus he had given his name to the police. The whole town knew he and Peter had been close. *He doesn't sound as if he's sorry.* Lex sounded pleased, almost as though it were Fergus's fault the police had called him in.

Meanwhile, work waited for him. He closed his office door and brought out the card the excise tax auditor had given him the week before, with the department and telephone number. Fergus lifted up the receiver and asked for long distance.

After he'd spoken with Sterling Matthews, Fergus immediately phoned Harold Haskell's office and inquired if he could see the lawyer right away. He walked the few blocks to his office, looking forward to seeing Jean. Maybe they could meet later for a coffee break if she wasn't busy.

At any rate, he didn't have a chance to see her. Haskell met him at the door and led him straight into his office. "Anything meaningful?" he asked, closing the door behind him.

"A classic case of the Board ignoring the interests of the minor shareholders for their own," Fergus replied.

Haskell rubbed his hands together. "Ah! I suspected something of the sort. What did they do?"

"Strathcona Holdings improved their cash flow by capitalizing their equipment repairs."

"How so?"

"As you know, the cost of new equipment is put into an asset account." Fergus waved his hand around, pointing. "Like your law library or office furniture, for example. They aren't treated as a yearly expense because the assets last over a long period and benefit a business for many years. Only a certain portion of their value is used each year against revenue."

"Yes, yes, I'm familiar with assets, and yearly depreciation expense. What I want to know is what happened in *this* case?"

"GlasBottle did ordinary repairs to their equipment and could legally use those as an expense for the year. But Strathcona Holdings added those expenses to the Equipment Asset account. It meant that ordinary business expense was decreased, making their profits larger. It also inflated the original value of the piece of equipment. Dad and I are sure they only wanted their profits to look greater."

Haskell was silent while he sorted it all out in his head. "What would they gain?" he asked finally. "Big profits only mean they would pay more income tax than they would have otherwise."

"The bank gives loans based on the credibility of their finances. They grant themselves bonuses for a job well done, including stock option bonuses, which raise their ownership share. And the stock options don't show up in the books until they're exercised. Of course, they will have another set of statements for income tax purposes, which probably show a loss or very small profit at best."

"Tax avoidance. The tax department will love that." Haskell wrinkled his forehead, then frowned. "Private companies are family owned. So the Board would be comprised of the main owners, with perhaps a few outsiders for advisory purposes. What's the point of keeping bonuses a secret if they're the sole owners? Or are they trying to oust one of the others, a family member perhaps?"

Fergus smiled. "Because of the Depression, they pay their managers with shares instead of cash. It waters down their sole ownership. They are basically giving away part of the company they think is theirs alone. So to maintain their original ratio of ownership, they grant themselves stock options. As long as the share price remains flat, they're safe."

"How does Peter come into all this?"

"Remember the bank account Peter opened for them in Calgary?" Fergus explained its use as a clearing account. "It's all in the brief. Peter is in the clear."

Haskell slapped his palm down on his desk. "Evil doings. Well, I'll push for a real audit."

"Unfortunately, it means Peter's assumption that Lex Rideout knows all about it is wrong," Fergus said. "Peter wasn't the only one being cheated. Rideout was too."

"I'll start preparing new requisitions right away. I have to warn you, they will stall."

"It's okay. I thought of another way to speed things up."

"How?" Haskell eyed Fergus over his glasses, and Fergus told him.

Haskell didn't sound enthusiastic. "If you think a government department will help," was all he said, and stood.

Fergus took the hint it was time to leave. "I didn't see Jean as I came in."

"Oh, Jean is filing some papers at the courthouse, I think," Haskell said, absently shifting the report on his desk and taking up another.

On his way down the stairs, Fergus thought Haskell sounded a trifle frosty, then forgot it. After all, why would he be interested in Fergus and Jean having dinner together?

FERGUS left early before his appointment at the police station. He had a job for Harley. Something he couldn't do himself on the chance he might be recognized. He caught Harley leaving the hospital just as he got to the parking lot.

"Who's with Cat?" he asked sharply.

"Miss Flower wants some time alone with her. Cat will probably be discharged tomorrow but hasn't told Miss Flower anything about what's going on in her head. Miss Flower said I have to protect her from any harm," Harley paused, then asked Fergus, "Do you still think she's in danger?"

"Yes, I do."

"Then shouldn't I know why?"

"'That's what I'm hoping Miss Flower will find out."

"Well, I checked with Cat first, Mr. Muir, and she said it was okay to leave her with Miss Flower."

"Good." Fergus took his arm, leading him farther out into the parking lot. "I have a job for you."

They talked for some time. Harley shook hands with Fergus and took off at a fast walk.

Fergus went back to the hospital and found Cat's ward. He saw her in the corner bed, talking to Roberta Flower. She spotted him and gave a tentative smile.

"Well, Little Miss Sunshine, you look much better than when

we brought you in," he said, although it appeared she'd been crying.

Roberta shot him a dour glance. *Have I interrupted at a bad time?*

"I can go home tomorrow," Cat said. At her solemn expression, he wasn't sure if she was relieved or apprehensive.

"Are they tired of you already?" Fergus lifted his hands in mock horror. Cat giggled.

"I shall be here tomorrow morning at nine sharp to drive you home, my lady."

"Yes, please." She looked from him to Roberta, then back to him. "Thank you for coming to get me from the cave."

He nodded, a lump in his throat. He told her he would see her in the morning, said goodbye to Roberta and left for his appointment with Archie.

ON the dot of five o'clock, he approached the front desk. Archie came from the back and greeted him, saying in a voice loud enough to be heard by a news reporter lounging in a chair nearby, "I'll be ready in seconds, Ferg. Why don't you come back while I finish up? No use you sitting out here. Someone might think you're being arrested." And he laughed and opened the gate for him, giving him a hearty slap on the back as he went through.

Fergus grinned and murmured through his teeth, "No need to get carried away with the slaps."

Archie laughed even harder as if at a joke and pushed Fergus ahead of him. Once through another door and away from the front desk, Archie opened a third and signaled Fergus to enter. His smile faded.

The room was small, with a single wooden chair on one side of a table, and two on the other. The walls were painted a cheerless gray. Archie indicated the single chair to Fergus and went to the other side. The door opened, and a policeman in uniform bearing triple pips on his shoulder board came in, taking the chair beside Archie.

Fergus stood up, was introduced to Captain Embleton, and sat down again with an impulse to throw him a crisp salute.

The captain sat straight, not touching the chair slats. He was of medium height but made himself look taller with his upright posture. His uniform was impeccable. He had a square face, straight nose, and square cleft chin. He looked familiar to Fergus. Then it struck him. Captain Embleton looked like Dick Tracy, a familiar in the comic strips, and he almost grinned. His eyes darted to Archie, who stared back at him steadily. Did he detect a gleam in Archie's eye? Fergus turned to the captain and nodded politely. "Captain."

"You were an Army man?" Captain Embleton asked abruptly, in a deep voice used to command. At Fergus' nod, he added, "What outfit?"

"Signalers." His tone discouraging more questions on the subject, Fergus looked directly into the captain's grey eyes. He knew Archie would have filled him in anyway, and there was no need for the captain to pursue his history.

Embleton looked back at Fergus, appraising his face. Apparently satisfied with his conclusion, he continued, "Sergeant Gillespie has filled me in on the details concerning this man Davidson's death. What is your interest in the case?"

At the captain's reference to the '*man Davidson*,' Fergus couldn't resist a rebuttal. "First of all, his name was *Peter* Davidson. He earned a Military Medal in the war. At great risk to himself, he went under fire into enemy territory, to rescue my team. I owe him my life. He was a courageous man who only gave out kindness to others and got back treachery in exchange. We—I—the justice system owe it to him to get to the truth regarding his death and more importantly clear his name of fraud charges."

"Why is clearing his name of fraud charges more important than finding out who killed him? Or do you already know who killed him?"

"Of course not. It could have been a vagrant, as you suggested. The fraud. If I get the proper records, I can prove it one way or another. The task is within my province, my job if you like, and what I do best. The proof of his innocence might also tell us if his death was an accident or intentional."

Fergus stopped, winded. *There goes my chance,* he thought. *Charging ahead like a bull elephant, Dad would say.* "Am I wasting your time?" he said, to break the silence more than not knowing what else to say now. He started to rise from the chair.

"Mr. Muir," said Captain Embleton, and pointed his finger at the chair as if unused to people leaving without first being dismissed. The beginnings of a smile twitched at his mouth. "Now you have your diatribe off your mind, can you now tell me what evidence you have to back up your theories?"

Fergus had mentally rehearsed his speech all afternoon. "To be honest, I have a small piece of hard evidence, and some suppositions," he said, talking too fast in his eagerness. "I've known Peter Davidson my whole life. I was married to his sister. He was not the kind of man who would stoop to criminal levels no matter how bad things would get."

"You've hit on our problem, Mr. Muir," the captain said smoothly. "You say you've known Davidson all your life. But that's not strictly true, is it? Our information tells us you haven't seen or spoken to him for, what, the last sixteen years? Seems a long time for someone who was a bosom friend, a brother-in-law."

Fergus, surprised by the turn in conversation, said nothing.

"One person we questioned," the captain continued, "claimed there were bad feelings between you and Davidson. Said Davidson revealed you had known each other since childhood, and even served together in the same outfit during the war. When our witness asked Davidson if he still heard from you, he said '*no*' then clammed up. Left our witness with the impression there was a falling out over something major. What is your response?"

"Was it Lex Rideout? It's ludicrous. Peter was not my enemy."

Embleton pounced on his question. "Why would you think it was Mr. Rideout? We interviewed a few people."

"He told me he had been questioned," Fergus said, wishing he hadn't been so prompt in naming Lex. Had Lex actually accused him in words or had the police jumped on an innocent remark, widening it to suit? "If you are insinuating I wanted him dead, it's more than ludicrous. The man saved my life. Nothing will repay that kind of favour, except maybe my own for his." Surprised at his own words, he realized they were true. He would do whatever it took to prove him innocent. He sat up straighter and watched as Archie and the captain exchanged glances.

"We might have a different point of view. Let's look at the whole picture. The two of you have a disagreement major enough that you leave town. There is no contact for sixteen years, and you only feel it's safe to return when Davidson leaves Cypress Landing. Life proceeds smoothly until one day Peter Davidson comes back to town. You take the opportunity to right a wrong and get your own back for that major disagreement."

Fergus felt his gorge rising. "I was the one who came to the police to assert it might have been intentional. You've suddenly done a turnaround. You were the ones who kept insisting on a fight between vagrants." He looked at Archie, whose expression remained fixed.

"You might have wanted to know how the case was being handled by the police. Was it murder? Accident? Was there any evidence left behind? A guilty man would like to know all those things. The easiest way to find out is to ask."

Fergus shook his head. "You are wrong, Captain. My wife worshipped her brother. And I loved my wife. I would never tarnish her memory by killing him."

His emotion didn't impress the captain who only stared at him stone-faced. "You don't deny you and Davidson had no contact after you left town. That is strange in itself considering the relationship you were known to have. I read Davidson's letter. The '*one for all*' bit. What's that about?"

The room tilted. The familiar feeling of being closed in surrounded Fergus. Horrified, he fought the panic and the urge to run which always followed. Perspiration ran over his forehead.

"Did you need a glass of water, Mr. Muir?" Captain Embleton asked, eyes gleaming, sensing victory.

Fergus didn't answer. He thought he caught a flicker of sympathy in Archie's eyes, and he concentrated on his breathing.

"You know what it was like coming home after the war," he said as calmly as he could. "Our old way of life seemed lost, and I had to consider a new life. There was nothing sinister about it. It was replaced by my education and the presence of new things. Anyhow, my father kept me informed of how things were going at home, so I didn't completely lose contact with what was happening."

He stared down the captain, his eyes not wavering, determined he wouldn't be treated as a subordinate.

"I hated the war, Captain, and I had lost my wife and daughter. I believed a new place would help me forget. That's all it was." He dared another glance at Archie, who stared straight ahead, his mouth set in a thin line.

The captain stayed silent for a time, staring at the wall behind Fergus. Noises came from the hall outside, a cough, shuffle of feet, protestations by someone led past their door.

Finally, the captain tore his gaze away and considered Fergus. "Okay, just to be clear on points, let's go through it one more time. Start with where you were when the storm was on and what you were doing about the time Davidson was being killed."

For the next hour, Fergus endured the same questions asked in a new way, hoping he gave the same answers. He considered and rejected an impulse to ask for Haskell, thinking it might show he had something to hide.

Finally, Captain Embleton slapped both hands flat on the table and said, "Okay. We'll call it a day. Thank you for coming in, and helping us with our investigation. We'll be in touch if we need anything more. We appreciate your patience, Mr. Muir. If you can show us any *evidence* when you investigate Mr. Davidson's fraud charge, we'd be happy to hear it.' His expression told Fergus he doubted it.

Straight-backed, the captain marched from the room. Standing, Archie gathered his notes together, then waved Fergus out the door. "He doesn't accept your dodge about being out of contact with Pete." As Fergus went by, he whispered, "and neither do I."

20

ANTICIPATING the task set for him by Fergus, Harley took his familiar shortcut over the train bridge which spanned the river and followed the tracks leading directly to the GlasBottle factory.

He arrived at the plant and found a spot behind the caragana hedge, bordering the property along the road. The sparse shrubbery gave him both cover and a good view of the loading docks and scrap heap. He studied the dock, noting its layout. An ordinary man door at the side gave entry into the plant, while the loading dock itself had two sliding wooden doors at the building end, large enough for a good-sized loading cart to pass in and out. Beside the dock on the ground were several crates, empty he supposed, ready to be taken inside.

He sat down in partial shade, in full view of the road. If anyone were to see him, they would assume he was just another vagrant. He opened up a bag, took out a jam sandwich and a small glass canning sealer filled with water, and waited.

Half an hour later, a Ready and Waiting van drove past Harley and into the entrance to the plant. It stopped, then reversed up to the edge of the loading dock, and the driver got out and went through a side door. A few minutes later, the loading dock sliding door opened, and two men and the driver appeared. Harley half stood in a low crouch, watching. The driver and one man started loading crates into the back of the truck, while the other man pointed a pencil at each one, apparently counting. He looked at the paper in his hand evidently comparing figures and made a mark. When they had finished loading, the driver signed the sheet, got into the truck and drove away. The two men disappeared into the plant, and the doors were pulled closed.

Disappointed, Harley stepped through a break in the hedge, and walked to the scrap heap. He searched around the pile, looking for intact bottles or glass containers. The guard, sitting in the small shack he used to keep out of the weather, sneezed. Through the open door, Harley saw the guard's attention focused on a magazine. He lifted a bottle to his mouth, then smacked his lips. Something his father had said echoed in his mind, '*a man should give every job honest value, no matter if he thinks it beneath his abilities.*' He scowled at the guard. *I should apply for his job.* Then he spotted a nice green tonic phial and picked it up. A bubble in the bottom gave it a bit of pizzazz—he could sell it for at least fifteen cents.

Not for the first time, Harley wondered what it would be like going to university in Edmonton. Taking advanced mathematics instead of spending his free time rummaging through refuse.

"Buzz off," the guard shouted, ripping Harley from his daydream.

"I'm not hurting anything," Harley barked his defiance.

"If you cut yourself on broken glass, don't expect any sympathy from the factory. Shake a leg or I'll call the police."

Harley thought about challenging him, but remembered why he was here and so went slowly back to his vantage point, going through the gate this time. "Hope the guy drinks himself to death," he muttered, tired of the inactivity.

He heard the sound of a truck coming down the road and hastily grabbed his jar of water, lifting it to his mouth. The driver from Ready and Waiting drove by him without a glance, and turned towards the loading dock again, the truck performing the same maneuvers before stopping. This time, whoever was inside sat and waited for so long Harley wondered if he'd fallen asleep. Finally, the driver and a passenger got out. Harley expected them to go inside to look for the dock manager, but the two men headed to where the empty crates were piled. The men lifted one and placed it on the dock and repeated, not stopping until Harley counted six. Both men vaulted up to the dock and moved them into the back of the truck. *Only a bunch of empty crates*, Harley thought. Then watching the effort the men used to lift them, he realized they were not empty after all. There was no sign of the guard. Probably out cold on the floor by now.

Harley didn't wait to see more. He ran down the road towards the railroad bridge and headed for the warehouse of Ready and Waiting. Usually, the shipments of GlasBottle crates were taken directly to the CPR yards and loaded on rail cars ready for transportation. If these particular crates were unloaded at the company's warehouse, then they were destined for someone local. If he could get into the warehouse, he could mark the crates somehow, so he could tell them again if and when they appeared.

Harley viewed the world in numbers. When asked how he got the solution to problems so quickly, he told his high school math teacher he could just see it. When asked what he saw, he had described number patterns to the teacher whose face became more puzzled the longer Harley talked. Hurrying down the street now, he decided the odds of getting into the warehouse were favorable. But first, he had to make sure it was the van's destination.

FROM her bed, Cat watched Roberta Flower and Dr. Anderson in deep conversation at the door of the ward. Her eyes wandered to a bed nearby and a boy of Young Charlie's age. His parents were sitting one on either side of the bed, his mother holding his hand. The father said something which made the boy giggle. Cat watched for a minute then looked away, feeling sad, thinking how nice it would be when her father came home.

Cat saw Miss Flower nod to the doctor and come towards her, smiling and giving the thumbs up. "Good news! You can go home tomorrow. The Doctor sees no reason why not." She poked her hand into a large bag and held up a square box for Cat to see. Her eyes lit up. The new Monopoly game.

"How about us making a start on this? I challenge you to beat me."

Half an hour later, they were well into it. Shaking the dice, Miss Flower started talking. "Dr. Anderson tells me you were a bit delirious when you came in. Sunstroke does that to a person. Do you remember any of it?"

Cat watched Roberta move her metal shoe five paces down the

board, and she shook her head.

"Your move." Roberta handed the dice to Cat. "Apparently you kept saying *'too fast, it's going too fast.'* Then you said *'Joe.'* Who is Joe?"

Cat threw the dice. Two fives. She moved her dog and bought a hotel. "My twin brother." Her lip trembled. "I promised him I wouldn't tell."

Roberta didn't seem to care. She shook the dice and tossed them across the board. "Golly, another five—What gives here? You wouldn't tell what?"

Cat hesitated for a long pause, considering, then said in a low voice, "He was supposed to go to the farm, but he jumped the train instead."

"Oops, I got the Utility, I guess I owe you some rent." Roberta paid up and continued. "Wow, that was a brave thing to do. Where did he go?"

Cat looked down at the rent money in her hand, silent.

"I won't tell anyone else if you say so," she heard Roberta say. "You don't have to tell me, but sometimes everything feels better when you do. Your move."

Cat added the money to her stack and took the dice, then laid them down again. Deep inside her identity, in that barren wasteland where Joe resided, something stirred. With a silent apology to Joe, she broke her promise.

"He wanted to go to Vancouver to look for my dad. So he could tell him he had to come home." She looked down the ward to the little boy's bed. The parents were kissing him goodbye.

"Did he change his mind then?"

Cat examined the metal dog play piece in her hand. It looked like their dog Buster, who had disappeared one day. Maybe he had followed her dad when he left. She squeezed her eyes shut. A tear rolled down her cheek.

"It's okay, Cat. You don't have to say if you'd rather not. Joe and your father will come back one day."

Cat opened her eyes and brushed the tear away with the back of her hand. Still looking at the metal piece, she shook her head and sniffed.

"No. Joe isn't coming home. The train was going faster all the time, and he ran along beside it. He grabbed the ladder, then fell off."

She heard a quick intake of breath. Roberta pulled Cat close. Cat sagged against her shoulder, looking at the boy down the ward. After a long pause, Roberta released her, cleared her throat, and looked at her. "Did you see him?"

Cat saw only sympathy in Roberta's face—like she understood why Cat had to be there with Joe. "I saw him grab the ladder. But there was no ledge . . . no ledge."

"No ledge? What do you mean?"

"He knew how to do it. He practiced. Catch the ladder, put his foot on the ledge and push himself up the ladder. But when he put his foot under the boxcar, nothing was there. One second he was there, and then he wasn't. Because there was no ledge."

Cat felt Roberta's hand on hers, squeezing. "What did you do then, Cat?"

"I only remember I was scared, and maybe it was all a mistake. My head hurt so much I had to close my eyes and wait for it to stop. I heard Joe reminding me not to say anything, just that he was on the farm." Her tears were falling free now. "It was my fault. I shouldn't have gone with him. He might have changed his mind."

"Good Heavens no," Roberta said, putting her arm around Cat again, and cradled her head against her chest. "We never know how people decide to do anything. Joe made up his mind to go. I bet he was the kind of brother you couldn't persuade to do anything. Am I right?"

Cat lifted her head and had to admit it was so. She spotted Fergus at the door of the ward looking around. Following her eyes, Roberta took her arm away and quickly gathered up the monopoly board and shoved it into the box. "There's Fergus come to see you." She didn't look happy he was there, Cat thought. She quickly wiped the last of her tears away, not wanting him to see.

When she told him she was going home the next day, Fergus promised to come for her. He even made a joke about going home, which told her he wasn't cross with her for going into the cave.

Which is what Roberta wanted to talk about when Fergus left.

The cave.

"Fergus was puzzled by something you said when he rescued you from the cave. About Mr. Davidson, the man you call, Sir. Do you remember what you said?"

"No." Cat made her voice emphatic.

"You said something about going back to the kiln where they found Mr—ah, Sir, and you saw somebody hit him. Fergus wants to know who you saw. Can you tell me?"

Flutters started up in her stomach, and she shivered. "No. I don't remember."

Miss Flower looked at her for a long moment, then nodded and smiled. "Oh well, it isn't important now. What matters most is you're safe." She sighed. "I will miss your company when you leave. I hope you'll still have time for me then. I'd love to stay here the rest of the day, but I have to get back to the office before it closes up. Anyway, you'll get one of those lovely dinner trays soon." Cat thought the meals were heavenly, but she laughed when Roberta rolled her eyes.

FERGUS arrived home to a late dinner with Malcolm, cranky and half angry at Archie for not preparing him for the nonstop questioning, stopping just short of a direct indictment he had killed Peter. He would never again doubt an innocent man could be hung for murder if he was unable to provide an unbreakable alibi for the crucial moment.

"It must have been Lex," he said. He gave Malcolm the short version of his interrogation. "Why would he make such an accusation? He probably did it to make sure I won't have time to focus on financial statements. It wasn't enough he'd already said he wouldn't let me see them."

Mrs. Mann fussed around the dinner table, removing the lid from a casserole dish, unleashing a rich aroma of stew, then left and came back with a mound of hot buttermilk biscuits. She stood for a moment and asked if there was anything else they required. At the negative answer, she found things to do at the sideboard, arranging dessert plates and cups and saucers. Malcolm shot Fergus an amused glance and put his finger to his lips, in a signal to say nothing. They dug into the stew and began to eat. Finally, Mrs. Mann departed into the kitchen, mumbling something unintelligible.

"Can you prove you were at Eaton's?"

"No. Unless one of the clerks remembers me. It's ridiculous."

"Don't be too sure," Malcolm replied, thinking about Fergus taking the blame for Peter not coming to see them just before he was killed. He hoped Fergus hadn't shared that bit with the police. It could be taken out of context with the whole story, and give them more dirt to pile on him.

"We've both seen what the Army Brass can do to make themselves look good," Malcolm said, showing his dislike of where events were leading them. "I'm sure he used some of the techniques during the war. And if he doesn't like the vagrancy excuse for Peter's death, he has you instead."

"I don't know, Dad. I think he may be one of the other few. He strikes me as the sort of person who goes where the evidence leads him. Archie says he is fair and honest. We'll just have to trust him to find out it's all supposition when it comes to me. What else can we do?"

Malcolm sighed, agreeing. "What did Archie say after your meeting?"

"Nothing." He lied, thinking that he would never have guessed his reasons for leaving Cypress Landing would be questioned after all this time.

After a short hesitation, Fergus said, "Dad, Cat is being released tomorrow morning, and I told her I'd take her home. She was with Roberta Flower. From the look on her face, I think I came at a bad time. Now I'm worried she won't learn anything before Cat's released."

Malcolm carefully laid his knife and fork down. "Well, you were there at the cave when she told you. Was there something that makes you think she might've been wrong?"

Fergus shook his head. "Not really. I mean to ask her if she knew who it was she saw at the kiln. I wondered if it could have been Lex. He hated Peter for taking his wife away, but if he confronted him, Peter would have made sure Lex knew the truth. So Lex would have no reason to kill him."

"But there is nobody else she might have left with. Unless she went by herself."

Fergus remained silent, pushing his stew around on the plate. "There is one person. Cat's father, Charlie Perkins. Didn't he leave about the same time? And he worked at GlasBottle, so it's possible he knew Rideout's wife."

Mrs. Mann came into the dining room with a tray bearing coffee. She went to the sideboard and busied herself with the dessert.

"What did you do with yourself today, Dad?" Fergus changed the subject, while Mrs. Mann brought plates and small bowls of raisin bread pudding covered with thick cream to the table.

"I spent most of the afternoon at the library," replied Malcolm.

"Find any new books?"

"Just browsing," Malcolm said evasively, while his eyes followed Mrs. Mann back to the kitchen, then called to her. She put her head round the door, eyes daring one of them to provoke her.

"I'm sorry we made dinner late for you Mrs. Mann," Malcolm said. "Were you going to visit Cat at the hospital tonight?"

"I went this afternoon." She came the rest of the way into the room. "Miss Flower was playing a game with her. I only stayed a short while, but I told her we were all looking forward to seeing her at the house again, and we missed her." She gave them a reassuring look. "I mentioned nothing else."

Before Malcolm could reply, the doorbell rang. Mrs. Mann, forgetting her hat, hurried to answer. She soon came into the dining room all smiles and announced Jean Buckley and Roberta Flower were in the living room.

"Come in and listen too, Mrs. Mann," Malcolm told her as she made to leave the room.

"May as well listen here as behind the door."

"I hope we aren't disturbing your dinner," Jean apologized, "but Roberta says she has news."

Fergus sat by Jean and ignored everyone else. They put their heads together and began to speak in low tones. Roberta Flower looked from one to the other and then came over to Malcolm, her hand out. "Hello. I'm Roberta Flower. Cat speaks of you. I'm happy to meet you." They shook hands. She nodded to Mrs. Mann having already met her at the hospital.

"Has there been any progress"? Malcolm asked, indicating the chesterfield. She chose an upholstered chair instead. "Will she be alright at home?"

Roberta absently smoothed her skirt while she thought. "I think so. I've talked to her mother you know. I've impressed upon her Cat is frail at the moment, and I cautioned her if Cat's condition does not improve, I would see she was taken from the house."

Both Malcolm and Mrs. Mann looked alarmed at this statement. "Surely not," Malcolm said.

Patience showed in Roberta's smile. "The threat is often enough for the parent to realize the child is the important issue right now. School starts in a few days," Roberta moved on, "and she says you have invited her to come here every day for lunch."

"I did," admitted Malcolm, and Mrs. Mann brightened at the news, smiled gratefully at him, and added with determination, "We'll make sure she stays safe."

"Were you able to help Cat?" Fergus said. He saw her small face again, alternating between fear and bewilderment when he brought her out of the cave.

"Helping her will take more time than I have at the moment," Roberta replied. "She seems so alone." Her expression was sober, regret twisting her mouth down. "Cat has had to process things a child shouldn't. Joe . . ." Roberta stopped.

"Did she clear up all the confusion about Joe?" Fergus encouraged.

She considered him for a long moment, then drew them all into her space. All eyes locked on Roberta now, apprehension in each face echoing her hesitation.

Roberta nodded. "But it's not what you think. Joe was supposed to wait for the farmer to pick him up. Her mother sent him there so the authorities couldn't force her to keep him in school. She'd done it once, and the truant officer told her Joe had to remain until he was fourteen. So she hired him out to a farm, where they couldn't find him. He decided to hop a freight train to Vancouver to find their father."

"Good grief," Mrs. Mann started, then stopped silent at Roberta Flower's expression.

Roberta took a deep breath and told them the rest.

"Cat went with him trying to talk him out of going. He didn't listen. He tried to hop the freight and fell off. The train ran over him."

Mrs. Mann made a choking sound and covered her mouth with her hand.

Fergus swore. "They all knew. The whole family. That's what I couldn't figure out. They knew he was dead and kept it from her. It's why they were so stunned when they found out Cat had gone with him. They realized she saw it."

Malcolm stared down at his tightly clasped hands in his lap as if they held some remedy to the news. *Is there never an end to the tragedy?* He hadn't felt such sadness since Margaret had died. "But the funeral," he said aloud. "There must have been a funeral."

Roberta closed her eyes as though shutting out an image. "There was not. I talked to my director this afternoon." She paused, swallowing hard, pressing her fingers against her lips to stop emotion. "If Joe had not been a child, he would have just stayed where he fell, but he was slight, and the train carried him along. A crew inspecting the boxcars . . . *found* him." Voice trailing off, her expressive eyes told Fergus what she didn't say. There wouldn't be much left to bury, and there would have been the animals, coyotes. Fergus willed his thoughts back to the room.

"With no identification, they buried him there, in Seven Persons. The CPR police tracked back along the rails to discover where it happened, and ultimately they found . . . things. Clothing, and a book with his name and address on the flyleaf."

"And the CPR would keep it from the newspapers, in case they were accused of throwing him off the train." Malcolm's bitterness showed as plain as sour apples.

There was nothing left to say. The silence in the room told its own story.

"Cat said something about there being no ledge," Roberta continued in a soft voice. "When Joe tried to catch his foot on the ledge, it wasn't there."

"Some boxcars have them, and some don't," said Fergus. "With the train moving, he wouldn't be strong enough to pull himself up."

"I asked her what happened then," Roberta added, and Mrs. Mann shuddered. "She said she got a headache and only remembered he made her promise she wouldn't tell anyone."

"She told me in the park when I asked where Joe was." Malcolm envisioned her sitting on the park bench again, speaking of Joe. "I thought she sounded odd. Like she was reciting something, but I assumed she was missing her twin." He shook his head. "When I questioned her, she ran off."

Roberta nodded. "Joe wanted her to stay home, but she insisted. She thinks he would have lost his nerve in the end, but with her there, he couldn't back down."

Fergus sat up. "She thinks it's her fault?"

"Children often think they are the cause of things happening to their families, Fergus," replied Roberta, showing her experience in these matters. "Family arguments, family accident, anything."

"Yes," said Malcolm pointedly. "People can believe they are responsible even when it is impossible to save someone else."

Fergus felt his face flush. He turned to Jean and knew she had caught the interchange. A strange expression flitted over her face which quickly disappeared as she met his eyes. *Almost like Malcolm's remark had hit home*, he thought and turned his attention back to Roberta.

"I assured her she couldn't know," Roberta continued. "It is just as reasonable to assume Joe wouldn't change his mind. Cat acknowledged it, but I'm not sure she totally accepts the explanation."

Fergus opened his mouth to ask Roberta if Cat had said who she saw at the kiln with Peter, then instinct told him to wait. He'd ask Cat tomorrow when he picked her up at the hospital. *It might be safer for Cat if not everyone knew she recognized the person.*

They were all silent for a while, each sorting out the information and drawing conclusions. Mrs. Mann put her hand to her face and said something which sounded like "Oh, *liebchen*."

Malcolm broke the silence. "First, she saw her brother fall under a train. Then Peter, her friend, killed. How much can the child take?

No wonder her mind shut down."

Fergus looked inward and didn't like what he saw. He felt her arms clinging to him as he brought her out of the cave. Trusting, innocent. Pushing rising nausea back, he became aware of Roberta speaking, but whatever it was she said, he missed it.

He thought about the day he found Malcolm and Cat putting together the jigsaw puzzle and Cat blurting out that Peter had told her to come to them. Malcolm had described Cat's terrified appearance when they found her in the alley that day. What or who had made her run to them? There was so much more they didn't know, and Cat was smack in the middle of it.

21

THE next morning, Fergus drove to the hospital. Cat was dressed and waiting for him, with Clara Perkins beside her.

"It's good of you to take us home." Clara gave Fergus a friendly smile, apparently forgetting her former malice. "The nurse told me you had arranged payment, and I thank you. I hope Cat has apologized for the trouble she gave you."

Fergus glanced from her to Cat's worried face. "No need for apologies, Mrs. Perkins," he said dismayed at seeing her. "Anyone would have done the same in my place. Cat wasn't to know she had sunstroke, or I'm sure she would have stayed home instead of going to the show." Cat gave him a grateful smile. "Shall we go?"

As he drove down the street, Fergus lapsed into silence, trying to think of an excuse to question Cat without her mother present. He stopped the car in front of the house and went around to open the passenger door for Clara Perkins. She gave him her hand and daintily stepped to the curb, Cat following from the back seat. Helplessly, he watched them enter the gate. As they went up the porch steps, Cat said something to her mother and ran back to him.

"I'm supposed to say another thank you," she told him.

He stooped to face her. "There's something I need to know, Cat. It's important, and I don't think we have much time. At the cave, you told me you saw the man who hit Peter. Do you remember?"

"Yes. I was too scared to tell Miss Flower. He's here all the time, and always asking me about the kiln. If he sees me now, he'll know I saw him there. I don't know what to do."

Shock jerked Fergus upright. He bent again in case Clara Perkins was watching from the window. "Cat? Did you see Mr. Rideout hit

Peter?"

Clara Perkins opened the front door and called out, "Cat? Are you finished? You'll have a relapse if you stay out there."

Fergus straightened up and smiled. "Just a funny story about a patient at the hospital, Mrs. Perkins. She won't be long."

His smile faded as he stooped down to Cat again. "Cat?"

"Sir was nice. He went with me to ask people if they'd seen my dad. There was a storm, and we went into the kiln. He told me he wanted me to take a letter to you, and I forgot. I went back to get it, and I saw them fighting. Sir fell down and got pulled by the arms into the kiln. When he came out, I saw it was Mr. Rideout." Cat started to cry. "I was scared, so I ran home. I couldn't tell Mama because she told me not to go near any vagrants. Then I forgot. Until I was in the cave." She rubbed at her eyes. "Are you mad at me?"

Fergus laughed certain Clara Perkins would be at the window. "What an idea. I could never in this world be mad at you, Cat. You've told me now. But you have to be absolutely sure. It *was* Mr. Rideout?" He was dismayed when she nodded vigorously with no hesitation.

"Okay, we have to make sure you don't meet up with him. Harley will take you to school and pick you up. And you will come to our house for lunch. Now, you'd better go inside. If Mr. Rideout comes today, pretend you're tired and go to bed."

He went to work, confused thoughts going in all directions, not noticing that Max followed him into his office until he closed the door.

"Lex Rideout found out about the books," Max blurted out. "Tom was fired—or will be."

Fergus sat down hard, hoping his face didn't seem as concerned as he felt. "Are we the only people that know what Tom did? Did he tell anybody else?"

"I don't know," Max said, his face pinched. "Tom denied everything, but Rideout said it had to be him. Tom told him nobody had been in the storage room and told Rideout to go and look if he didn't believe him. Thank goodness he had put them back and they didn't look disturbed, but Rideout said you must have seen the books, and fired him. Then he changed his mind and told Tom to take two weeks off without pay. Rideout said he'd find out the truth in the meantime." Max sat down across from Fergus and ran his knuckles over his head.

Fergus searched his memory. He had delivered a report to Harold Haskell, but nobody in the office knew about it, and it was only yesterday. Who had known about the books for Rideout to react so fast?

"From what you've told me, it sounds like Rideout isn't really sure about the books," Fergus said, more to soothe Max than anything else. "He's heard something, somewhere, and jumped to conclusions. He's seen the records are still where they are supposed to be, and he won't find anything in the next two weeks. So Tom will be back at work. Let's wait and see."

"My father will kill me," Max lamented. He put his hands up to rub his head, then thought better of it, and slapped them against his sides instead.

Miss Watts rapped on the office door and simultaneously opened it. "Mr. Haskell is on the telephone for you, Mr. Muir."

Fergus picked up the receiver, said hello and nodded to Max, who went back to his desk.

"We had a break-in last night," Haskell grumbled. Before Fergus could say anything, he added, "Quite sneaky. Someone familiar with lock-picking, as we found scratches on the door lock. We might have never noticed except my secretary spotted some current files messed up in the filing cabinet."

What's next, thought Fergus, not quite keeping up with turn rapid events. "Someone was looking for something in particular?" was all he said, keeping in tune with Haskell's reticence on an open line. The financial report?

"Very likely, but whoever it was didn't get anything important. All my important files are secured in the vault. A copy of a certain letter is missing though. It's not happened to me before. My office is at least safer than what people might have *in their house*."

Fergus got the message. *Anything in my house or office had better be secure.* "Well, I don't know about your other clients, but as for me, I have nothing in my house worth looking at. Do you have any idea who broke in? Did you call the police?"

"No to both questions. I suppose there are plenty of vagrants for hire who might have a talent for burglary. I'm looking at what has been tampered with to see if there might be a connection to any client. If I find one, I'll have to inform the client involved of course."

"Of course." Fergus hung up frowning, trying to make sense of the call. Someone wanted to find a report which could only have been prepared from Fergus's direct examination of records. A copy of Peter's letter to him missing, and whoever took it would now be aware that Cat was Peter's beneficiary. Who would benefit from knowing? Strathcona Holdings, but they knew nothing of the report unless someone alerted them. Was it connected with the police's accusation against him?

He wondered if Harley had found anything worthwhile when Fergus had sent him to spy on GlasBottle. After bragging to Captain Embleton, he desperately needed a plan

Later, Fergus told Malcolm about the break-in, who said, "You were wise to get the records back the same day."

Fergus agreed, "I don't like Max being involved. Thankfully, he's not sure I opened the box. I'll let him think I kept my ethics and just returned it unopened." Fergus rubbed his head with his knuckles. "Dad, I can't help but think Jean is involved. She's made several veiled remarks about Lex, and she said he isn't what he seems."

"There is something, Fergus." Malcolm pursed his mouth, looked undecided for a moment and sighed. "The night you went into the cave, Harold came over. One thing led to another, but he really wanted to know why you were seeing Jean—what your motives were. I don't remember what I said, something to reassure him because he seemed so protective of her. Then he told me Jean's husband is in prison."

"Prison?" Fergus repeated, voice rising, questioning if he had heard right. "What for?"

"He didn't say. Just said Jean would tell you in her own good time, and I didn't ask."

"Though you decided not to tell me?"

"It wasn't my place Fergus, and it has nothing to do with Rideout or Peter. But, for my own interest, I went down to the library wondering if they had old Nova Scotia newspapers, but I didn't find anything pertinent." At that Malcolm slapped his thighs, indicating the end of the matter. He rose and headed for the drinks table.

Fergus was at a loss for anything to say. His mind was taken up with Cat's revelation. The more he thought about it, the more he doubted her. Did she accuse Rideout because she didn't want him to come near her mother anymore? Was it her way of hoping Fergus got rid of him? After all, she blamed him for her mother's decision to send Joe away. Considering everything, Fergus was becoming more convinced the vagrant chased away from Cat had finally taken his revenge on Peter.

Visions of Cat in the cave, her trust in him, and his exuberance when he rescued her overcame him. Those visions turned to others. A child who witnessed her brother falling beneath the train, and how she had coped. Searching for a trace of her father. All the pictures suddenly reeled in kaleidoscope fashion in his mind, one after the other, then all together. It was almost too much for him to bear knowing she had also witnessed Peter killed. A man he could now admit he loved like a brother. The room tilted and his balance with it.

He sat down, put his head in his hands and groaned aloud.

"Peter shot him, and I let him do it."

In the middle of pouring a glass of scotch, Malcolm froze, as if afraid to make any sudden movement where Fergus would spook and run. Cautiously, he poured a second glass and handed it to Fergus. Sitting across from his son, he waited.

"Every man in war has a baptism of fire which either makes him a soldier or not. I failed mine." Fergus's voice was matter of fact.

A full day and night passed, and Fergus did what he could to make Denvers comfortable, both aware a stomach wound was a kiss of death unless treated medically.

He gathered everything he could find, loose soil, the pieces of wood which had been the door and stairs, and heaped it underneath the ventilation shaft. In the end, the mound was high enough for him to reach into the opening almost to his waist. It was just a few inches wider than his shoulders. Could he lift himself enough to climb the shaft? It looked impossible.

"Hello," he shouted up the shaft. "Help. Anybody there?"

He kept it up intermittently for what seemed like hours.

Just about to give up, he heard rifle fire and then some small arms fire. Not caring who it was as long as he was heard, he renewed his yelling.

"Fergus?" Peter's voice shouted.

"I'm here! There's a ventilation shaft."

A moment later, Peter's face appeared above him.

"God, you are the most welcome sight I've ever seen," Fergus told him. "I've got a wounded man here. We need a rope."

"No rope," Peter said. "I didn't expect to find you buried. I've got a man who can hold my legs, and I can come part way down. You'll have to climb so I can reach you."

"Can't you widen the shaft so I can get Denvers out?" He got his answer when he heard the chatter of small arms fire.

"Get a move on," Peter told him. "Before they start sending whiz bangs. Jones here, can give us cover. Get up here, and we'll figure out how to get Denvers out." Peter disappeared from sight as another volley sounded, then poked his head over the shaft again. "Step on it, Fergus."

Fergus turned to Denvers, whose every breath rasped—his face flushed with fever. Fergus thought of peritonitis, and Denvers read it on his face.

"Shoot me or give me the pistol," Denvers pleaded between gasps. "Please, Sergeant."

"We'll get you out. Hang on and give us a chance."

Denvers just looked at him. "For God's sake, do it now."

Fergus about to say no, hesitated, then recoiled in horror at his temptation. Reaching up, he gouged out a handhold in the wall, one on each side. Then he swung, his feet scrabbling the air for some purchase. The pressure on his arms was exhausting, and he barely made it. It was worse up the rest of the shaft. He placed his back against one side, feet on the other and dug handholds with his fingers, inching his way. If he slipped only a bit, he'd never be able to start again.

"Think out each move. Remember the cliffs." Peter sounded encouraging, but Fergus heard the nerves in his voice. The Germans must have had reinforcements; the barrage was more intense now, and Pete's face disappeared more often as he took cover.

His arms and legs refused to move. His bloody fingertips felt like mush. "I have to rest or I'm lost!" Fergus shouted.

"Bloody hell, Gussy, do it! Just a little more."

Fergus told himself, "Just one more," repeating, "Just one more," until he saw Peter's hands within reach. He made a desperate lunge and felt hands on his wrists. Fergus put his last weight on his legs and rooted them against the walls. Whoever it was holding Peter by the waist pulled back, and with a last tug they both caught his arms at the shoulders, and he was up.

Gratefully, and with deep breaths, Fergus lay on his back gazing up at the sky, oblivious to the bullets whizzing overhead. It was beginning to rain. He welcomed the spatters on his face and smiled.

"Denvers," he said, finally. He tried to stand, but his legs collapsed. He crawled over to Peter. "We have to get him out. Don't you have reels of cable?"

"No. We only came to find you."

"Did Jinks report us?"

"This morning, Division said the lines had been cut off, so I went looking for you and ran into Jinks wandering around the secondary trench, dazed and incoherent. I grabbed him and finally got out of him what happened. I made him show me where. Then I sent him back with orders to see the medics."

The rifle fire died down. *Not a good sign*, Fergus thought. The Krauts were waiting for artillery shells to finish the job. A few long moments of quiet, then the first salvo fell short.

In a panic, Fergus grabbed the spade and started digging. Jones took it from him and went at it. A big man with hefty shoulders and arms showed Fergus why he had been hauled the last foot up the shaft so smoothly. The rain was heavier now, the soil turning to mud. Fergus went to his knees by the shaft opening and ignoring the pain in his hands, scooped mud away. The German guns were starting to get their range. Peter and Jones had forged a small hollow by the opening giving them a bit of cover from the fire, but it soon wouldn't be enough. Fergus spotted Denvers just below the opening, looking up at him, eyes full of hate. He had managed to pull himself up against the pile of wood and earth. His voice was weak, but Fergus heard every word. "Damn you, Sergeant. You can't leave me like this!"

The Germans now had their range, and the shells were coming very close. Peter bent over Fergus, rain dripping off his hat and face. "We have to leave, Gussy, or get cut off."

Fergus knew it wasn't a choice. He looked down the shaft, drew a long shuddering breath and raised his pistol. Then Denvers smiled at him, and he wavered.

The earth exploded, and they threw themselves flat.

Ears ringing, Fergus raised his head and found his body covering the shaft opening. He stared down at his calf where a piece of metal protruded and reached to tug it out. He hadn't even felt it. Peter knocked his hand away, shaking his head. Fergus thought he said, "It'll bleed."

"Gussy! Move!"

"Do something!" Jones shouted, his voice frantic. "The next one will get us all!"

The words hovered over Fergus as unintelligible, drawn-out vowels, fading in and out like a palm alternately clamping and releasing over his ears. Dazed, his brain tried to decipher the words, all the while thinking there was something he had to do. *What was it?*

Peter rushed at Fergus, simultaneously threw him aside, drew his own pistol and fired down the opening.

"Let's go!" Peter's strength lifted him upright. He pushed him forward, saying "Don't bunch up." Fergus was only half aware of the three of them stumbling down the same path Jinks had taken.

MALCOLM'S face contained a mixture of horror, consternation, and pity. "Fergus, what else was there to do? Stay and die with him?"

"Sometimes I think it might have been better."

"Fergus, listen to me. Men in war are trained to become killers.

But none of you are that man forever and never will be again. Soldiers become inured to killing because there is never a face attached to the enemy. You hesitated because Denvers had a face. Men who go to war may never be the same, but they learn to live with it.

"But it's not all," said Fergus flatly. "I came home, and found Mother, Isobel, and Maggie had died. My punishment. An eye for an eye."

"You can't actually believe that!"

"I did then. Now I realize I used it as another reason to despise myself and reinforce guilt. But guilt is not so easy to dismiss."

"Do you ever think you have confused guilt with regret? Son, enough is enough."

Fergus ignored Malcolm's interruption. "You wonder why Peter didn't get in touch with us? Because he knew I failed. I let him carry out what should have been my job. He always knew I failed. Whenever I looked at Peter, that man in the Bourlon Wood was always between us."

"Bollocks," muttered Malcolm, his face grey with disapproval.

"Still, whatever you say . . . I know he never came near us because he doubted he could count on me."

"Denvers was saved from a hideous death," Malcolm snapped back. "What would you feel today if he'd been left there to die in agony? I will not stand by while you heap punishment on yourself for split-second decisions made under fire, during a war. It's like someone who is sea-sick, yearning for land but refusing to get off the boat!"

Fergus stared at Malcolm then began to snicker. The snicker turned into a laugh and soon became an uncontrolled, mocking, manic kind of laughter which happens between friends who have just shared the worst joke in the world. He lifted his pant leg and inspected a raised four-inch jagged welt on his calf, which Malcolm hadn't known was there.

"And poor Jinks." His laughter trailed off in a gulp of breath. "They shot him for being a coward. The poor bugger was shell-shocked, and they shot him."

22

THE first week in September, schools opened all over the city. The days were becoming shorter, and the last two nights had seen a touch of frost. Still, the Indian summer held plenty of heat without being oppressive.

Cat woke early and dressed herself in a freshly ironed dress, polished shoes over clean socks, and presented herself to the Grade Six class in Dundee School. She hadn't told her mother about her new school. Harley had prepared toast for breakfast, her mother being still in bed, and they did not disturb her. When he started down the familiar route to her school, she told him she had decided to go to Dundee.

Harley stopped and gawked at her. "Does Mom know?"

She shook her head. Harley said nothing more, and they turned back in the opposite direction. "What if the teacher wants to know where you live?" Harley asked after they had gone a block.

"They never care where we live as long as we are in a desk," Cat said. But if they ask, I'll say we're moving to a new house next month, and my mother thought I'd better start the new school now as later."

Harley snorted. "It'll work," he said, then chuckled. His support told her she had made the right decision.

"Harley, are you going to go rail-riding?"

"Not if I can help it," Harley said, and then grimaced with distaste. "I don't fancy a life like that, Cat."

"Everybody's gone, but it would be nice if you stayed."

Harley stopped, and Cat saw pleasure wash over his face. With Joe gone, Harley was the only person not considered grown up. Rose was apt to go away soon, leaving her with nobody. She didn't ever want to be alone again. They continued in comfortable silence to the schoolyard.

"I'll pick you up after school," Harley reminded her, then cautioned, "The first day, they might let you out early, and if they do, go to the Muir house. I'll come by at four o'clock."

He turned to leave, but she stopped him. "Harley, would you go to Mr. Levinson's music store and pick up my violin? Lessons start on Saturday, and I have to practice."

Harley gazed at her, mouth open, then realization dawned. "It wasn't Joe. It's been you all along, hasn't it?"

She nodded shyly, then grinned at him. "If you pick it up, you won't sell it, will you?"

"I won't sell it, Cat." He bent down close to her face and grinned. "All this time, Mom bragged about Joe playing the violin. You really are as bad as I am."

"Are you going to tell her?"

"No. I'll let her find out for herself. I hope I'm there to see her face."

The morning passed as Cat knew it would. She blended in with other new students, and the teachers concentrated on making sure the attendance record was correct, rather than individuals.

At noon, not seeing Harley, Cat ran all the way to the house for her promised lunch. Mrs. Mann was all smiles, and Cat was full of chatter about her teacher, whom she liked. The hour passed quickly, and Mrs. Mann bustled happily to the kitchen to fetch her hat to accompany her back to school.

Walking back to work after lunch, Fergus wondered why he hadn't heard from Harley by now, and he hoped he wasn't ignoring him. The rest of the way to the office, he planned ways to punish Harley if he had reverted to old habits.

AFTER leaving Cat in the morning, Harley walked towards the premises of Ready and Waiting. The job he was doing for Fergus made him feel valued. He had seen the boys of rich families go off to university when they were neither clever nor enthusiastic, hating them, and then his father for leaving.

His new responsibility for Cat gave him a purpose even if short term, university being the long term goal. The future somehow didn't seem so elusive. Scenes of snitching fruit from the corner store and saving his money for himself when the family needed it flew into his head. He cringed in shame, knowing his behavior would disgust his father.

He lounged across the street for the next hour watching the activities in the company's assembly yard hoping it might give him an idea of how he might get in. He decided to go down the alleyway to explore possibilities but had no success. A high fence bordered the property, with only a door to the alley to access the large garbage containers. He jumped up and down, but couldn't see over the fence into the yard.

He went to the end of the alley and the street again. Hands in pockets, he studied the other businesses located there. A garage, smelling of oil and gasoline, the open door showing the mechanic inside banging away at a dented fender. A second-hand store with dirty windows hiding whatever used goods were inside, then an empty space with a *'For Rent'* sign in the window. Further along, he came upon a man whitewashing the front of the church everyone called the Holy Rollers and stopped to watch for a minute.

Back at the shipping office, he came upon the popular sign, *'NO Men Wanted'* printed on it. Numbers began churning in his mind. Abruptly, he turned and went back down the street to the church. On the way, he dirtied his hands, smudged his face, messed his hair up, then tugged the back of his shirt from his trousers.

When he got to the front of the church, he stopped, shifting from one foot to the other. The painter dipped his brush into the pail and gave him a friendly grin. Harley returned it with a shy nod and shuffled his feet uncertainly.

"Looking to be saved brother? You've come to the right place if you're in need of salvation."

"Can I help you finish your painting, sir?" Harley asked.

"Sure, son," the man said. Harley wondered if he was the preacher who smacked his congregation in the head. A burly man with a tanned round face, and thinning hair. He didn't have one of those round collars, just shabby pants, and an open-neck shirt. "But

I can't pay you."

"My mum won't mind." Harley took the broad whitewash brush handed to him. "As long as I'm doing something useful."

The afternoon was beginning to fade by the time they were finished. The preacher, Harley had decided that's who he was, wiped his face and hands on a paint rag, and Harley asked him, "Do you know the time?"

"Fifteen minutes before four o'clock."

Perfect, Harley had just enough time to finish his final task and report to Mr. Muir.

"Thank you, son. The fellow who was supposed to help didn't show up. But the Good Lord always comes through to those in need."

"Not at all," replied Harley, mumbling, speaking to the sidewalk. "If you want, I could take the rest of the whitewash off your hands. I mean, wash the bucket and brushes for you. I'll put it on the doorstep."

"Kind of you. I confess I'm tired. Go down between the buildings to the back. There's a hose. All you have to do is rinse the out bucket. You might want to wash your face as well." He finished wiping his hands and studied Harley, a glint forming in his eyes. "Have you been saved, my boy?"

"I dunno," replied Harley, stepping back a pace, afraid the man might smack his head.

"You have to be saved. What would you do if the Lord was to come for you?"

"I couldn't go." Harley picked up the bucket of whitewash and the paintbrushes and started around the back, calling, "My mum wouldn't like it. She makes me ask permission before I go anywhere."

FERGUS rose early the next morning and rummaged around in his closet for the bibbed overalls he used for general repair work around the house and yard. Thanks to Mrs. Mann they were washed and folded, so they looked clean at least. He tucked a plaid shirt inside. On top of the overalls, he added an old sweater, then found the boots he used for rough work. A cap pulled down over his head completed the look of someone down on his luck, but with enough pride to keep his clothes neat and presentable.

By the time Harley and Fergus showed up at the shipping offices at nine in the morning, there were at least a hundred men lined up, pushing into the docking area, more men coming down the street behind them. Ten jobs were not often advertised, and the hobo telegraph had worked overtime.

Harley was dressed as well as he could be and had slicked back his hair with mineral oil, so it lay plastered to his head. It shone black in the light. A pair of spectacles would have completed his disguise, but it'd have to do. Harley pushed a way through the men and sidled over to the edge of the crowd, where he could see crates lined up ready to load. Slow moving trucks, horns blaring, slowly divided the crowd of men; some belonged to the company, and others to customers waiting to receive merchandise.

The office manager came out of the side office and with a voice like thunder shouted, "What's going on here? This is not a public area."

"We're here about the jobs," A man in the front, said loudly. "How would you like the men to line up for interviews?" He jabbed his finger at a man pushing ahead of him. "Wait your turn!"

"There are no jobs here," shouted the manager, and waved them back. "Can't you read the sign?"

"The sign says you need ten men."

"What the blazes? I don't even need one man. I'm telling you now, there are no jobs going here. You can all leave."

Rumblings began in the crowd as the message was passed to the back. The shouting got louder as some protested. New men coming into the yard pushed the others forward. The crowd of men swelled, and they milled about in a disorganized way. The manager pushed through to the loading dock and climbed up so he could face the horde. He held up his hands for silence. Nobody paid any attention. More to and fro shoving and loud protests came from the back.

Harley and Fergus edged unnoticed to the front of the loading dock where customers and employees gathered. All eyes focused on the manager. Harley swiftly indicated the crates, and Fergus noted which ones originated from GlasBottle and read the customers names attached.

Two men neared, and Harley put his hands into his pockets and studied the manager who was still attempting to speak. Fergus moved a few spaces to put another in the crowd between him and the men and tugged his cap down over his eyes.

"These are the ones," said one man. "Help me load them now, while everyone is busy."

The other man protested, "Are you crazy? The manager is right there. Come back later."

"My money is in your pocket, and I want the crates now. After all, they're just breakages, aren't they?" He laughed. "If he asks, I'm just taking them away."

Fergus heard nothing then, and he squinted at them from the corner of his eye. They were both looking at Harley, who was putting his whole attention on the manager as if nothing else in the world mattered.

"That's just a kid, trying to look like a man," Fergus heard. "Nothing to get jumpy over. How many boxes do I get this time?"

"Two . . . Don't look at me like that. We have other customers besides you. Don't worry. There'll be more next week."

Fergus kept his attention on Harley for the next few minutes in case the two were scanning the crowd. Harley turned and jerked his head sideways, indicating the men. Fergus's gaze carried past Harley, and he saw the men wheeling a dray towards the crates at the side of the loading dock. They each loaded a crate on the dray. One pushed, while the other pulled it towards a truck, acting like business as usual. He saw no reference to business ownership written on the truck. He glanced at Harley and shrugged his shoulders. Harley nodded and grinned, and Fergus realized he must know who owned the van. Fergus remembered Harley sold bottles and pottery which he found in scrap heaps to second-hand stores. *He recognizes the man.* Fergus grinned and almost gave Harley a thumbs up, then remembered where he was.

By this time, more men had crowded into the yard, bringing it to near capacity. A reporter pushed his way to the front and looked up at the manager, notebook and pencil poised. "Who in your company advertised for jobs? Can you give me a statement?"

"Please, listen," shouted the manager. Fergus almost felt sorry for him. "There are no jobs. I wish there were. Someone's played a dirty joke on all of you. If you don't all leave now, I will phone the police. I don't want to, but if you all persist in holding up business, then I will." There were a few more rumbles, but for the vagrants in the crowd, the prospect of police did it. Grumbling men shuffled towards the gate, and like lemmings, the rest followed.

One of the first out, Fergus walked quickly away. At the corner, he stopped and looked back. He saw Harley and another man at the gate. Harley tore the sign down in a dramatic show of bravado, ripping it in two and handing half to the man beside him. He gleefully ripped his part as well, and both went down the street together, jostling each other and laughing.

THURSDAY was the night set aside for the student lectures. Two more students asked to join, and Fergus consented, surprised at how popular his idea had become. To his relief, Malcolm volunteered to take over the planning and development so Fergus could concentrate on Peter's case. When the class was over, Malcolm saw by their faces they were satisfied with what they had learned and pleased with their new-found brotherhood with each other. Clearing up his notes Malcolm had a sense of accomplishment, something that had eluded him since he'd been forced to retire.

With the house quiet again, Fergus and Malcolm sat in the study to relax and wind down. The traded sections of the paper to read.

Fergus laughed aloud, and said, "Did you read this bit about the near riot at Ready and Waiting?"

"I did. Their business must be improving. Ads for workers always attract a long line of applicants."

"But there were no jobs going, according to the manager. A sign outside advertised jobs for ten men, but he said the only sign they posted had stated there were no jobs at all. You get it? *'No men wanted,'* changed to *'ten men wanted.'*"

"I don't follow."

"Think of the printed word NO in capital letters. All one has to do is take off a down-stroke and the angled line. You'd be left with 10." Malcolm laid down his paper, still looking puzzled. Fergus laughed again.

"I don't have experience with factories, Mr. Muir," Harley said. "But I can count. I know how many milk bottles a crate holds and what it would bring in the market. It doesn't take a wacko to know it's a lot of money, even at a lower price."

Fergus sat behind his desk and studied Harley, who had shown up at the office. He had looked around the outer waiting room, and Fergus suspected curiosity had brought him.

"It was you, wasn't it? You changed the sign," Fergus said. "It was a brilliant idea and got us in the yard. You know who owned the van that picked up the crates?"

"It belongs to the man who owns the second-hand store on East Avenue."

"We just have to find out who is behind it at GlasBottle."

"Lex Rideout of course. So, now what?"

Fergus didn't caution him against making assumptions. "We can't go to the police without revealing how we know. I want you to come with me to see Mr. Haskell. He was Peter Davidson's lawyer and now Cat's." Harley looked startled at the inclusion of Cat's name, and Fergus continued rapidly before he could ask questions. "You can repeat what you saw to Mr. Haskell."

Harley nodded. "And what I found out when I went back."

Confused, Fergus asked, "Went back?"

"Well, you asked me to watch and see if there were any crates coming into GlasBottle."

"Yes, I did," Fergus said. It had slipped his mind. "I wanted to know if GlasBottle's products were being returned because of breakages, and who received them."

"I went back yesterday," Harley said. "I asked the dock foreman if he could help me with a paper I had to write for school homework. He said he'd be glad to help. So, I asked if the bottles got broken when they shipped them out, would they be replaced or would the buyer have to pay for the load. He told me about freight rules, FOB destination, or whatever, and said it was GlasBottle's policy to replace broken shipments. I asked him did they have to bring the bottles back to prove they were broken. He said if the shipment was broken during the transport, the shipper had to give a list of the names of the customers involved. After I said thank you and all that stuff you know, I asked if customers got mad when their stuff got broken all the time?" Harley stopped, explaining, "I didn't want him to think I was only interested in his place."

"And?"

"He said most companies were the same, but their shipping company wasn't very careful, and had a lot of breakages." Harley snorted. "But they wouldn't give GlasBottle the customer's names, only a list of items which needed replacing. He said it was because shippers didn't want the customers to think they were always breaking their products. The foreman kind of smirked and said in a sarcastic way, '*It wouldn't do to annoy the customers would it?*' Meaning he didn't believe it himself."

"Preposterous," grunted Fergus. "It just points to under the table customers. The list of replacement items is actually an order list, which they can sell at a price below the going rate."

"The way I see it, what's the difference if the shipper's customers did get annoyed, when they never paid their bills anyway?"

Fergus acknowledged the statement with a smile and thanked Harley. He looked at Fergus uncertainly, as though he might say more.

"Go on, Harley, say it."

Harley squirmed in his seat then looked squarely at Fergus. "I've spent a lot of time with Cat this last week, and she told me everything."

"That she knows about Joe?" Fergus hoped that's all she had admitted.

Harley nodded. "When you told me she went with Joe. I knew she had seen him killed. I can't imagine anything so awful. Two men from the CPR came to tell my mother. She thought she could hide it from Cat. I told her flat out Cat already knows, and she blames herself. My mom made a bad decision about Joe, but I feel sorry for her. Without my dad . . ." Harley stopped and swallowed. "It was Mr. Rideout who made Mom send Joe away. Someone has to face up to him. If my father were here, he would do it. Now it's up to me. My family has to be safe."

Fergus stood up, alarmed.

"No, Harley, you can't. You don't know for sure if Mr. Rideout is involved. I can understand you want him gone from your life, but if you challenge him, you could mess everything up. Other things are involved you don't know about."

Fergus assumed he was getting a reluctant agreement when Harley said, "Well, I'd better pick up Cat."

"Please, Harley, don't repeat our conversation with anyone before we know what's going on for sure."

Haskell telephoned him just as he was about to leave for the day. "The police have just left me. Asking questions about you. What have you been up to?"

"What questions?"

"About your relationship with Peter Davidson, and if there had been any bad feelings between you when you moved to Ontario."

"What did you tell them?"

"Nothing. Privileged information between Davidson and myself. They weren't too happy. Anything you can talk about?"

"Not at the moment." Fergus paused hoping Haskell would pick up on his reluctance to say anything over the phone.

"I understand. They have to show they are doing their job I suppose." Haskell laughed and rang off.

Fergus finally escaped into the late summer afternoon. The sun, now lower in the sky, sparkled through the trees and made small patterns against the sidewalk. The bulk of pesky mosquitoes had gone. House flies were still everywhere, but at this time of the year, they were too lazy and bloated to do anything but accumulate en-masse on whatever surface they found, mostly screen doors.

At home, he fetched himself a drink and told Malcolm the police had questioned Haskell. "I wonder who else they've bothered? You know how rumors fly in this town."

If the police had a list, Fergus's name was next, and a few minutes later, he was invited to come to the police station. At his convenience, the policeman added, which seemed to mean at ten o'clock sharp the following morning.

"Who was your spy? Was he involved in that trick at Ready and Waiting, almost causing a riot?"

The interrogation room was beginning to feel like home, thought Fergus, as he faced Captain Embleton and Archie, sitting across from him the next day. Without giving them the details of how he knew, he admitted he had evidence of Peter's innocence, and he suspected Lex Rideout of stealing from the company.

The questions came thick and fast.

"Where is the proof?" Captain Embleton said.

"Who else could it be? He says himself the company is almost bankrupt. Yet, he can buy the rugby team new uniforms. Where did the money come from?"

"He has business contacts. He's well-liked and knows a lot of people. Maybe they chipped in, or maybe he made a deal with a supply company. Or he used his own money which you know nothing about."

"Most of his salary is on a commission basis or paid in shares by the head office. In this market, it'd be difficult to sell his shares for cash."

Captain Embleton narrowed his eyes at him. "Are you trying to focus interest on him instead of yourself? Right now, you're the best candidate we have for Davidson's murder. Your excuse for losing touch with Davidson." Embleton almost snorted. "He was here a couple of weeks before he died. Did he get in touch with you?"

Fergus had to admit Peter did not.

"Such good friends and he doesn't even try to say hello when he comes back. Why is that?"

"If I had known he was in town, I would have reached out to him. You saw his letter. He said he was being watched, and it was a safety matter. I don't know what he was talking about. But he says Lex Rideout knows he was innocent. I'm as much in the dark about it as you are."

"But it doesn't stop you from acting on your *suppositions*," Captain Embleton said, his voice putting quotation marks around the word.

"Of course," Fergus said, frustrated. "When you have a case, you must start out with suppositions. Isn't that why it's called investigation?"

For a moment, Fergus was sure he saw a twitch of a smile at the corner of Captain Embelton's mouth before he stood. "You can go, for now, Mr. Muir. I caution you about taking matters into your own hands. I know the reputation of the Signalers for going off and doing whatever strikes them at the moment. I won't stand for anything which makes this police force look ridiculous, nor will I take any blame if you get yourself into trouble with the folks in this city." He nodded to Archie and left the room.

You might stop asking people questions about me, Fergus wanted to say. *Before rumors start swirling.*

He looked at Archie's face and realized what he had done. Gathered information Archie would have preferred to have come across in his own investigation. Hampered by a captain who would rather bet on sure things to keep his record spotless, Archie could only sit and watch. Not a good feeling for someone whose pride was wrapped up in a career of detection and crime prevention.

"Look, Archie, I'm sorry. Dad always tells me I get ahead of myself. I was going to see you this weekend. I thought I'd approach Lex for a facedown, but I need your knowledge and experience with how these things are planned, and what are the dangers to watch out for. I need you, Arch."

"Facing Rideout is the last thing you should be doing, Fergus. I'm sorry, I can't help you. You don't seem to appreciate you can be arrested any time now. Take my advice, and think of your own defense."

Fergus left for home and walked through the door just in time to answer the ringing phone.

"Do you like to dance?" Jean said on the other end.

"I do."

"Really?"

Fergus could almost hear her raised eyebrow through the phone. "Do I seem like someone who won't dance?"

"No." They both laughed at her lie. "There is a barn dance going on Saturday night out by the Old Rose Mill."

"I'm game if you are. I haven't been to a barn dance since I can't remember when."

Malcolm heard him tell Mrs. Mann he was going out for the evening and would not be home for dinner. "Are you going to continue to see Jean?"

Fergus shot him a 'so-what?' glare, and Malcolm had the grace to look uncomfortable. "Dad, I'm forty-one years old. It's a bit late to start asking what my intentions are. Do I have to have a reason?"

"The very fact you asked if you have to have a reason is troubling. According to her father, Jean's marriage was not a happy experience. Harold has a right to wonder." He paused and switched his cane from one hand to the next, plainly uncomfortable. "You should understand I am not accusing you of scheming. I know my son better."

"When I saw her with Rideout on the street, she didn't look happy either," Fergus retorted. "So, yes, after her warning, I wonder even more. I want to know why." Fergus scowled, then brightened. "But she's intelligent, compassionate, didn't shrink from rescuing Cat at the cave, and that's the reason I'll see her again."

Malcolm rose, ending the conversation. "I'm going for my stroll while it's still light."

Fergus had one last question. "You said Rideout was from the East when he was hired by Strathcona Holdings. Do you know from where?"

"No," Malcolm said, his tone final.

Trying to forget his interview with the police, Fergus chose a book from the study. Relaxing on the couch in the living room, he sipped his drink and was soon lost in *A Tale of Two Cities*.

Mrs. Mann poked her head around the corner of the door. "What is that dog barking about?"

Paris transmuted into a living room and a barking dog. Rising, Fergus followed Mrs. Mann and opened the front door. At the sight of them, Duke's bark became hysterical. He turned in circles, first to the street, then back to them.

"Come here, Duke. What's the matter?"

Mrs. Mann looked out to the street then turned to Fergus, her face worried. "Where's your father?"

"Out for his walk. He's back now. Isn't he?"

Mrs. Mann's hands flew up, her eyes wide.

Fergus started towards Duke who ran down the steps, down the path to the street, and turning, came back to Fergus and then back to the street again.

"Okay, Duke. Take me to him." He took the steps in leaps towards Duke, who headed down the street, not looking to see if Fergus was following. Two blocks from the house, Fergus caught up to Duke lying on the boulevard, whining.

"Where is he, Duke? What have you got?" He bent and lifted Malcolm's hat from beneath the lab's paws.

23

OH *please, no,* Fergus prayed. The grass was trampled at the curb, already drying turf torn away from the boulevard by tire tracks which continued along for a few feet before going to the road. Shocked, he stared down the silent street for a moment, then turned and ran back to the house. Duke laid his face on his paws and stayed where he was.

Mrs. Mann was standing at the gate, her face pinched and fearful.

"He's gone," Fergus said. "How could I have been so witless to realize Cat might not be the only one in danger?" He continued into the house and went to the telephone.

Mrs. Mann followed him, flapping her apron. "Gone? Danger? Will he be hurt? Oh, my Lord. I told them to watch the house! I didn't tell them to watch Mr. Muir."

Fergus hung up the receiver and turned to her. "What have you done?"

"I hired some of the men to watch the house when Cat was here, just in case. They're sleeping in the garage. I told them to keep an eye on the house, but I should have told them to watch your father too. Who would dream anyone would harm him!"

Fergus turned to the telephone again. "I didn't think it either." Hands shaking, grimly fighting for control, he jiggled the switch hook, and he asked for the police station when the operator came on.

"How long has he been missing, sir?" the desk constable asked.

"Is Archie Gillespie there?" Fergus snapped refusing to waste time trading words.

"No, sir. He's finished his shift. Just calm down, and tell me how long he's been gone?"

"About two hours. I found his hat. And there are tire tracks on the boulevard where he was taken." Fergus took a long breath. "Look, my father's not a young man. If you just telephone Sergeant Gillespie and tell him it's Fergus Muir, he'll understand."

"Two hours isn't a very long time, sir. If you just wait, he'll turn up, I'm sure."

Fergus ground his teeth and forced himself to speak calmly. "If you would just give the word to Sergeant Gillespie. It won't take much of your time. He'll want to know, I assure you."

"I'll see what I can do." The constable wasn't enthusiastic, and rather than argue, Fergus hung up. All he could do was hope he'd notify Archie.

He and Mrs. Mann stared at each other helplessly. She twisted her apron in her hands, her face a mixture of anger and fear.

Fergus had more anger than fear. "Well, we can't just stand here twiddling our thumbs. Those men you hired. They're vagrants right?"

She nodded.

"They're here now? In the garage?"

She nodded again.

"They know people in the camps. Let's see if they have any advice."

Mrs. Mann brightened and marched to the kitchen and out the back door. Fergus sat at the kitchen table and waited.

She brought back three men, entering the room uncertainly, apologizing to Mrs. Mann, "So sorry . . . all our fault, we thought it was just the girl."

"Never mind now," Fergus said, quieting them. "I want to know if there is any way of finding out who took him. You know the kind of people I mean. Somebody must have seen something."

One of the men spoke up, "A job like this would be hired out. There are a few men who would do anything for money, and something dirty like this can't be kept secret. Campers will know if someone has a bit of extra money. We can always tell." He paused, his eyes full of pity. "It would help if we knew if Mr. Muir might be harmed. Do you know why he was taken?"

"Someone wants to send me a message," said Fergus, face bright red with anger and worry. "I don't know what will happen to my father, but I'm hoping it will be nothing, for God help me, if my father is harmed it's a whole new horse race."

"Come on, boys," said a man, his voice commanding. The others seemed to accept him as their leader. "Let's get to work. Best we split up. Mr. Malcolm is a decent man and none of us will be pleased he might be harmed. "

Fergus stood. "I'm coming too."

The man turned back to him. Gently, but firmly as though used to giving orders, he said, "You'd best stay here in case you get a phone call." When Fergus shook his head, he cautioned, "You'll only hinder what we have to do. Every minute counts. The longer they have him, the more he's in danger."

Frustrated, Fergus yielded, "Let me know immediately if you find something. Any time of the day or night." He watched them leave and then slammed his fist down on the table. Mrs. Mann didn't even cringe.

Eventually, the bell rang, and they raced one another to get to the door. Without preamble, Archie and a constable came past them into the foyer. "Talk to me," Archie commanded.

Fergus spoke rapidly, in short, incomplete sentences, but total information. "Two blocks over on Poplar Street. You'll find the boulevard has tire ruts, torn grass and gravel where they made a fast getaway. Duke was with him and led me to his hat. There's no doubt he was forced."

Archie turned to the constable. "Go there."

"Duke will still be there," Fergus added.

"Scour the site," Archie instructed. "Then go back to the station and have them post the message to every patrolman when he reports in with the call box. Tell them to look for anything out of the ordinary, a nervous speeder, someone who looks as though he is driving a car too new for him. Get another constable and go back and canvass the neighborhood around the area. Ask if anyone saw him on his walk or heard something." The constable went off. Archie walked into the living room and sat on the couch.

"Is that all we're going to do?" Fergus asked as he and Mrs. Mann followed him.

"For the moment," Archie replied and took out a notebook and pencil. "I want you to sit down and tell me everything you did from this morning on."

"You know very well where I spent most of the day," Fergus said, his bitterness showing. "The point is that Dad will have been missing less than an hour before Mrs. Mann heard Duke's barking. Duke may have stayed where he was before running back home."

Fergus shot his arm out and gave a pointed look at his watch. "You can tack on another hour by the time your desk man decided to let you in on my phone call."

"I worked in the kitchen, where I usually am." Mrs. Mann's expression plainly showed impatience.

"What about the dog, Duke? Would he have protected Malcolm? Attack?"

"He would. But on walks, he tends to chase his nose, then catches up. If he was close by, someone *will* have bite marks."

"It's lucky the vagrants I hired to . . . er . . . work in the yard have gone off to see what they can find out," Mrs. Mann added.

"Whoa," Archie said. "They volunteered to go? What time did they start out?"

"About fifteen minutes before you showed up," Fergus said.

Fergus expected Archie to object to the involvement of the vagrants. Instead, he said, "It's a good idea. They'll get faster answers in the camps than we would. The vagrants clam up tighter than a drum when the police show up." Archie tucked his notebook into his jacket pocket. "Sit down and try to relax. It may be some time before we hear anything."

"I think it's Rideout sending me a message to give up. Why don't I go over there and wring his fat neck until he tells me where Dad is?"

"Fergus, Rideout might not be involved at all. Vagrants looking for money," Archie said, but not looking convinced at his own words.

Mrs. Mann flapped her hands. "If that's all you're going to do, I'll make some coffee." She marched out of the room, mumbling to herself, leaving Archie and Fergus to stare across the room at each other. Fergus looked at the clock, picked his book up, then laid it down again. The doorbell rang, and the front door opened at the same time, bringing in the constable.

"Found this at the site, Sergeant," he said to Archie and handed him a cane.

"Dad's cane," Fergus said, reaching for it. "My God, they took him without his cane."

"Can he manage without it?" Archie asked.

"For a brief time. But not if he has to walk or stand for long."

Fergus acknowledged Archie's wry smile, knowing it wouldn't be likely Malcolm would be walking far unless he escaped from wherever he had been taken. Fergus rubbed his knuckles back and forth over his head, refusing to think of the possibility Malcolm might have no use for a cane if he were dead. If Malcolm died, there would be no limit to Fergus's wrath, and he consoled himself with the thought that whoever ordered Malcolm kidnapped knew it.

"The station had a report of a stolen car, Sergeant," the constable said. "A dark blue 1929 Model A Sedan, License Plate 57-182. Stolen this afternoon. Not been seen since."

"Good work, Constable," Archie congratulated the man, who grinned.

Mrs. Mann brought a tray holding coffee, cream, and cups into the room, rattling quietly in her shaking grip. She laid the tray on the small table in front of the sofa and left the room without a word, returning with a plate of sandwiches. Giving Fergus a doleful look, she went out of the room again. Fergus stared at the food and went to the study, bringing back a bottle and scotch. He poured a small amount for them both, then put his glass on the table, untouched.

He went to the front verandah and peered up and down the street. Feeling a nudge against his hand, he turned to find Duke. He fondled the dog's ears for a time, then went back into the living room, leaving Duke to sit by the front steps watching the street.

Another hour and the telephone rang, loud in the silence. Fergus jumped. Mrs. Mann came back into the room.

"Fergus, did I get the time wrong?" Jean asked when he answered.

"Jean." Fergus glanced at Archie, choking on his disappointment. Mrs. Mann flapped a tea towel and went back to the kitchen. "No, I forgot."

"What is it?" Her voice was sharp.

"It's Dad," said Fergus. "He's missing. And we should talk," he snapped out the last word, his anger clear.

He heard indrawn breath. "I'll come over." And a half-hour later she came into the house without knocking. Fergus looked up at her from where he was sitting, and she took a step back at the blatant rage in his eyes. "Fergus?"

He stood as did Archie. Mrs. Mann came in from the kitchen and went to Jean, taking her hand. The very action stopped Fergus from saying anything, and instead, he nodded, waving her to a chair and sat again. There were a dozen questions he wanted to fling at her but knew it would require more explanations to Archie and Mrs. Mann. *You told me not to trust Lex Rideout. You implied that like a shark, he is dangerous. If you had given me a reason then, we might not be sitting here wondering where my father is. What are you hiding? I saw you and Lex on the street. What was that all about? Have you betrayed us—me?* Unbidden tears of frustration made him lower his gaze at the carpet pattern until he was under control again.

Jean's gaze went back and forth from Fergus to Mrs. Mann, who related the events of the afternoon. She asked no questions, just looked dumbly at both of them and at the end she looked at Archie, raising her eyebrows.

"Everything is being done which can be done," Archie said, interpreting her silent question.

"Have you spoken to Lex Rideout today, by any chance?" Fergus couldn't resist asking.

She paled but looked back at him steadily. "No, Fergus, I have not."

Mrs. Mann frowned at Fergus's rudeness, and Archie said, his tone cautionary, "The atmosphere just got very thick in here. I hope it's nothing I should know."

Fergus sighed, and relaxed. "No, Archie, I'm on edge. I'm taking it out on everybody else. It's all this inaction." He got up and paced to the end of the living room, then returned. "I need some air. Do you mind if I go outside for a bit?" He made his tone pleasant. "Jean, come and keep me company, will you?"

Jean immediately rose, and they went through the kitchen to the backyard.

The night sky was an explosion of stars. The warmth of the day, serenaded by a chorus of cricket chirps, had muted to a mere caress on the skin. Oblivious to the night's lure, Fergus led Jean away from the house, feet crunching the dry autumn leaves. He stopped at his sanctuary, under the elm tree next to the garage. When he turned to face her, she was already looking at him, holding up both hands, palms out, before he had a chance to speak.

"First of all, I had nothing to do with Malcolm's disappearance. It's an insult if you think I would condone such an action." She came closer to him and stared up into his eyes. "Don't say anything Fergus, and I'll tell you everything up straight. God knows I've tried to tell you before, but something always got in the way."

"I'm listening now," he said coldly. She flinched.

"You have to keep quiet until I've finished. I can't do it otherwise. It's not an excuse. It's just because I've been trying to keep it all straight myself, wondering why and how I have allowed . . . everything to get this far."

Fergus stifled the impulse to hold her hands and instead stuffed them into his pockets with unconcealed anger, wanting her to get on with it.

"I married in June '28 shortly after I graduated from Dalhousie," she started quietly. "I was just starting to work at a law office to get ready for the bar exams. Jim was a stockbroker. We only knew each other for a short time, but were in love and couldn't wait."

An unreasonable jealousy twisted through Fergus. He leaned up against the tree trunk, welcoming the pain from a knob against his back.

"One of our clients was the owner of an industrial glass manufacturing company. He was having trouble with lease contracts, and the law firm gave the file to me to sort. I saved him a bundle of money, and he was grateful. His name is irrelevant. He was well-known in Halifax and involved in a lot of charitable functions. He invited me to them, more because it showed he was a modern man who championed women in the professions than anything else." Her mouth curled into a sneer at all condescending men. Fergus had a twinge of guilt, feeling himself lumped in with the kind of man who didn't look on a woman in business as a peer.

She paused, and then said in a stronger voice, "My law firm thought it would be good publicity if I attended as their representative. Lex Rideout was the glass company's marketing manager. He was ingratiating, always making snide sexual innuendoes. He had been a big rugby star. 'The King' they called him. 'Lex the Rex.' Just waiting for women to fall at his feet. By that time, I was used to being a woman in a man's world, so I just avoided him."

She searched Fergus's face, inviting a reaction at this point.

"You told me to say nothing." He shrugged his shoulders with a tension loud enough to say what he could not.

"Yes, well, the client invited me to an anniversary celebration at his house, and I was told to bring my husband along." Jean lifted both hands and massaged each side of her jaw with her fingertips. She let out a deep sigh. "I'd do anything to take back the moment when I accepted." She looked at Fergus and asked, "Do you think we have these moments thrown at us when one decision changes the whole path of our lives?"

Her question startled Fergus, and he stood up straight. An image hurtled into his mind of the ventilation shaft—hearing Peter say they had to leave. Seeing Denvers smiling at him. He could only nod at Jean, his face rigid. She took a step back, and he knew she'd mistaken his expression for an accusation.

It crossed his mind to alleviate her thoughts, but instead, he let the tension linger.

Jean blinked at his silence, then dropped her gaze to the ground and continued, "We planned to stay only until we could decently leave," she said. "I introduced Jim to our client. You know how those gatherings go, we circulated, talked to people, picked at the food, drank cocktails, and listened to the speeches. Just as we decided we could leave, our host came over and dragged Jim off for 'a little conversation,' he said. I took a glass, pretended to drink and waited by the door to the hallway. Lex sidled up to me and made some disgusting inference Jim was soliciting customers, and putting his hand on my arm. I was a little drunk, and I told Lex to take a hike; I was too good for him. About ten minutes later, Jim showed up, stuffing papers into his pocket. We said our goodbyes, and left.

"I told Jim about Lex's accusation, waiting for him to deny it. But he said our client had actually given him a portion of his investment portfolio, asked him to look it over and see if he could produce better results. I was furious." Taken back to that moment, Jean was angry, her words tumbling over one another. "It was unethical, and I could lose my job if the former stockbroker accused our firm of association with intent to solicit his trade customers." She slapped the side of her hand in the palm of the other. "Jim didn't agree. I misunderstood, I didn't want him to succeed. All that junk men say when they revert to offence instead of defence. The client would vouch for him, Jim told me. It was his big chance to make a name, and advance his career as a stockbroker."

"And was he good at his job?" Fergus couldn't help asking.

"It seemed to work out. Nobody questioned it. The next year, I passed my exams and was admitted to the Bar. We were excited, planning a secure future. Then the stock market crashed, and Jim was in big trouble."

"The Crash could hardly be Jim's fault," Fergus said.

"You know the story, Fergus. Investing was a national pastime, whether people had money or not. Jim started to worry at the beginning of October. The Toronto Stock exchange had dropped a good bit, losing millions. People, including Jim, began buying, thinking they were getting a bargain. The market did rally somewhat, but by the last week of October, the U.S. market crashed for good." Tears started in Jean's eyes and began to track down her face. She didn't bother to wipe them away. "Jim was frantic by this time, frightened, unreachable, ranting it had all gone wrong. It wasn't until our client charged him that I found out what he'd done."

"Bought on margin like everyone else did then?"

"Worse. He'd taken the client's stocks, which were mostly solid blue-chip, cashed them in to buy bargains, and resold them after a few days at large profits."

"But it would be your client's fault," Fergus started, and hesitated, a terrible suspicion overtaking what he was about to say.

Jean read his expression and nodded. "He didn't have permission.

The client was often out of town, and Jim saw bargains too good to miss. You know how the stock market went up and up in just hours. He thought he could sell and buy and sell again in a matter of days, and the client wouldn't complain when he saw the profits."

"And not complain at Jim's commission," Fergus said drily.

"Right. But the client was enraged, of course. And that's when Lex Rideout saw his chance. He told the client I had known about the whole thing and used my position at the law firm to introduce Jim and influence the client to change stockbrokers. The client wanted me disbarred, conveniently forgetting he was the one who has solicited Jim. Thank God our law firm stood by me and even took on Jim's defence. They managed to quash the charge against me, but because of Jim's freelancing, the client lost a great deal of money, Jim was struck off and sentenced to seven years in prison. . . . The term is up next year."

"And Rideout?"

"I came home to start over, but a bad penny returns, doesn't it? Rideout was hired by Strathcona Holdings to market GlasBottle, and I was shocked when he appeared on the street one day. He asked me if our law clients knew about my life back East, and what it would do to our client base if they knew they were trusting their secrets to a criminal's wife."

"So he blackmailed you," Fergus stated, his tone flat. He forced out a laugh, daylight dawning, where it was all leading. "When I started investigating Peter's fraud, you kept Rideout informed, like telling him I had written a financial report on his business? And also tried to persuade me to give up. You even went out with me because you had to find out what I knew, didn't you?"

"To my shame, I did," admitted Jean. She blushed, but her eyes were steady. "It wasn't the whole reason I went out with you. I liked—like you. Rideout didn't hear it from me about the financial report. When he demanded to know where you were in the investigation, I taunted him and said a chartered accountant could find ways to examine financial statements, and sooner or later a dismal record would be found. It hit a nerve, I could tell. He asked me why you and Cat were so friendly, and I told him Cat didn't like him hanging around with her mother. He laughed then, but now I think he truly believes it's the only reason she avoids him."

"But he got the letter Peter wrote," said Fergus, rage starting to boil over.

"Yes, but I didn't tell him there was a letter." Jean turned away. "I'm not proud of myself, Fergus. I tried to mitigate any information, but have to admit I-I . . . chose the easy way."

Fergus let it all out, "Whatever you said wasn't enough! Rideout assumed I had some records available, and he is scared enough to kidnap Dad to stop me. Because of you, Dad is in grave danger, not to mention Cat! She's only a child!" He resisted the temptation to slam his fist into the tree.

Jean lashed out at his accusation, "Whatever Rideout is doing, it's because he's desperate. Before I even came on the scene." She opened her mouth to say something else, then bit it back. Her tone resigned, she only said, "You cannot say for sure he kidnapped your father."

"Who else could it be?" But Fergus knew she was right. Could he blame her for Rideout's actions? He had gone after Rideout and neglected the wisdom that a desperate person can only become more so.

Fergus's head snapped up as the kitchen door opened. Jean swiped at her eyes before turning. Archie came out onto the back step. "Your friends are back."

24

IT was well past midnight by the time they reached Blackwater, a small town ten miles southeast of Cypress Landing. The men had returned to the house triumphant, but weary, and Fergus realized they must have actively searched every campsite and talked to every vagrant in the city, without pause. But in the end, they had a good lead. Fergus and Archie hadn't wasted time asking questions about their methods, and instead immediately began planning how to get Malcolm back. There'd be time for details and rewards later.

Cypress Landing's police service did not extend to Blackwater.

"I'd better bring the captain up to date," Archie told Fergus, anxious to help. Fergus stood, impatient to get started. Archie said nothing but yes and no, then hung up. "He said that whatever I did on my own time was my business unless it gave the Force a bad name." Archie shot Fergus a delighted grin. "He even arranged a car for the trip."

"Thanks, Archie. I need you." *And I'll act regardless of what your captain wants.*

An hour later, Fergus parked his car on a side street a block down from the house. The car carrying Archie, along with two additional vagrants, cruised slowly past Fergus. Archie signaled he would park down the next block. Fergus nodded, knowing two strange cars parked together would raise curiosity. Although the street was quiet and houses dark, best not to take a chance someone might not be in bed and peer out a window.

Fergus got out of the car along with the three men whom Mrs. Mann had hired. They closed the card doors with a soft click and moved just as silently towards the house. The man who had taken on the role of leader of the three came close to Fergus.

"We'll give the others about ten minutes to get in place at the back," he whispered.

Fergus realized he didn't know the man's name. "We never got the chance to formally introduce ourselves." Fergus extended his hand to the man who grinned at the inanity of the timing.

"Bertram Harrison the Third."

About to take a step forward, Fergus stopped and studied the man. "The Third?"

"Just call me Bert."

Fergus thought briefly about the class disparity of men who rode the rails. "Are we ready?" he asked the men. They shook hands all around and continued towards the house. A car was parked two doors down. A blue A-Model Ford.

"It's the stolen car," Fergus whispered.

At the front door, Fergus waited while two of the men disappeared in different directions to each side of the house. He gave a series of rapid knocks as if he were in a panic.

There was no answer, and Fergus rapped louder. He heard a scuff and whispering. "Who's there?" asked a man's voice.

"I need help," replied Fergus. "Someone's after me," he rattled the doorknob. Just as he thought, the door was flimsy.

"Go away," said the voice.

Fergus rested his hand on Bert's shoulder for support, raised his leg and shot out his foot with all the force he could muster. The door flew open. In the same instant, Bert and Fergus rushed inside, greeting two startled faces which rapidly turned to angry ones. The men started forward, cursing. Seconds later, their bluster became confusion as the other two came in the door behind Fergus. The first man stopped and backed up against the other then they both turned and ran, crashing into a muscular third man coming through a bedroom door, clutching the lowered suspenders on his pants. The two shoved him up against the wall and hurried towards the back door, only to meet Archie and his two men coming through it. At the sight of the lot of them, the two men quickly sat on the floor and raised their hands.

The third man pulled his suspenders up over his muscular arms, and demanded, "What's going on? This is a private house. We have nothing to rob. Get out now, and I won't tell the Mounties." He seemed to favor his left leg as he pulled himself up into a confident stance, both hands on his hips.

Fergus recognized his father's shoes. He yanked the man by his suspenders and roughly pulled him forward, shoving his face up against him. "Where is he?"

"Where is who?" the man said, but his eyes shifted to the two on the floor. "Who are you?"

"You don't have to tell the police because we are the police," Fergus said through his teeth. Over the man's shoulder, he saw Archie give him a dismayed look. The man tried to jerk free. "I'll only ask once more," Fergus held him tighter. "Where is he?" The man only shook his head.

"Search the house," Archie said, then, and in his best police voice added, "Hold these two, and get them ready for transport." Bert went off to search.

"Hey! Wait! We don't know what you are talking about." His eyes shifted again as if to signal the other two to shut up. He widened his stance, then winced as his left foot hit the floor.

"He's not here." Bert came back and told Fergus. His face said Malcolm might have been left somewhere else. Fergus went cold, his gut twisting in spasm. Unbelieving, Bert walked down the hall looking into each room again.

"I told you!" Suspenders shouted. But he sounded too victorious, not relieved as he should have been.

Fergus rounded on him and pointed to the man's leg. "Dog bites can be dangerous if not cared for. Gangrene sets in fast." The man instinctively glanced down at his leg.

"Where is he?" Fergus shoved him against the wall and raised a rounded fist at him.

"Ah, wait," Archie said. He ordered the others to guard the three and Fergus followed Archie outside to the back of the house. "I saw it when we came around from the alley," he said. He stopped at a pair of green wooden doors set into the ground beside the house and pointed. "A root cellar."

Fergus bent over the doors and pulled out a long bolt shot through the fastener. He and Archie pulled both doors up and let them fall on the ground. The dank smell of urine and rotting vegetables wafted up. Fergus saw only the top of the stairs going down; the rest was pitch black. Archie brought out a flashlight from a deep pocket, turned it on and pushed it into Fergus's hand. He led the way down the steps. "Dad?"

At the entrance, he stooped and pointed the light around the walls. At the far end, clad only in shirt and underpants, Malcolm stared at them, his eyes wincing as they adjusted to the light. He mumbled through a cloth tied around his mouth and strained at the ties binding his hands and feet to the metal rim.

Fergus groaned, and bending double under the low ceiling, he and Archie hurried to Malcolm.

"It's about time," mumbled Malcolm as Fergus removed the dirty rag from his mouth. Malcolm rubbed at his wrists coaxing circulation, shivering with cold.

"Take it easy, Dad. It's alright now. We're going home. Mrs. Mann is having fits."

Malcolm's face was pale, and he winced when his legs refused to hold him as he stood up.

They half carried him up the steps to the yard. "Get Bert, Archie," Fergus said, "We'll get Dad to the car, while you deal with the people inside. Get them to tell you who ordered it."

"Which one is Bert?" Archie asked.

"The one who does all the talking."

Archie left, Bert came out, and Fergus gave him the keys to the car. Fergus put his arm around Malcolm as they waited for Bert to bring the car around. Together the two men helped Malcolm to the back seat, covering him with a blanket. Fergus took a flask from the door pocket of the car, unscrewed the top and handed it to his father. About to drink, Malcolm held on to Fergus's arm as he backed out the car door. "Fergus," Malcolm whispered. "I know what you felt like. Buried in a dugout."

Fergus patted his father's arm, not trusting himself to speak. He shut the car door carefully. "Stay with him?" he said to Bert then went back to the house, clenching and unclenching his fists.

Archie met him at the front door. "They don't know who ordered the kidnap," he told Fergus. "It was done through a third person. Another vagrant. I know who he is, known for fighting and robbery. We'll get him if he hasn't left town already. These three," he indicated the men, now sitting on the kitchen floor, hands behind their heads, "it was all for the money. Paid up front, they said."

Fergus went in the kitchen and pulled the burly man to his feet. "Get those pants off. And the shoes." The man hastened to obey. When he was down to his dirty underpants, Fergus pushed him back into the chair. "You put an elderly man in a root cellar and left him, tied up, unable to move, so he had to soil himself. The cold would have killed him if he'd been there much longer."

"We put him in there to keep him quiet," whined the man, frightened now. "He was a nuisance, trying to escape, wouldn't shut up. If you hadn't shown up, he would have been back in the house. We were told not to harm him, and only keep him a day, then return him back to where we got him."

"You will be arrested for attempted murder if I have anything to say about it." Fergus turned away and motioned Archie out to in the hall. "Can't you look the other way while I bash him?"

Archie looked sympathetic. "It won't make you feel better, Ferg. Leave them to me."

"What are we going to do with them?" Fergus asked, thinking of the next step. "I don't want whoever took him to find out he's free."

Archie agreed, "Take the car and Bert and get your dad home. The rest of us will fit in mine. Leave these hoodlums to me. I've got an idea."

Fergus left. As he went out the door, he heard Archie say, "Get them up, boys."

Malcolm refused to go to the hospital, and so they brought him to the house, saw he had a hot bath then put him in bed and called his doctor. Mrs. Mann waited anxiously by the front door for the doctor and bustled him right upstairs when he arrived, complaining about pneumonia and heaven knows what else he picked up. The doctor told them Malcolm was exhausted, but in good health, considering, and left after giving them pills for pain if he should need them.

Jean had remained behind, and now Fergus watched as she said goodbye to Mrs. Mann then looked at Fergus as if she expected him to say something before she left. Suddenly weary, and in no mood to examine his feelings, Fergus said nothing. She paused a moment, then brushed past him and left.

"I want to know everything," Mrs. Mann demanded when Fergus followed her into the kitchen. He gave a brief version while she heated up broth for Malcolm and a hot drink for Fergus.

"I told Bert and the others to come around tomorrow for a celebration," he finished.

"Thank you, Fergus," she said. Fergus balked when he thought she might hug him, but she only patted his shoulder, sniffed noisily and turned her back to him while setting out a tray for Malcolm.

25

ASSURED Malcolm had not suffered any lasting damage, Fergus dropped off to sleep immediately. He awoke energized the next morning, barely even remembering getting into bed. Rolling over to look at the bedside clock, he realized he'd only slept a few hours.

He came downstairs and found Mrs. Mann dressed in her Sunday hat.

"You're going to church this morning." He'd have thought she would stay home to look after Malcolm considering the night before. She must have gotten even less sleep than him.

"I'm off to offer up thanks, Mr. Muir is up there in his bed, instead of a cellar like live bait waiting for the bugs to start chewing."

Just after noon, Mrs. Mann returned and with Jean's help, had a table on the verandah laden with plates of roasted chicken, vegetables, rolls, condiments, fruit, and a cake. A large bowl of punch sat at the end, surrounded by glasses which sparkled in the sun.

How'd she get all this food so quickly, Fergus wondered then realized she had probably been baking to occupy the hours while waiting for word of Malcolm. *There's enough here for the whole block.*

Malcolm sat in an easy chair surrounded with cushions, his hands resting on his cane. A few neighbors had shown up, drawn by the chatter and smell of roast chicken. Mrs. Mann was trying to put a blanket over his legs, but he wasn't having any of it and pushed it aside.

"We got them plenty scared," Bert was saying, laughing, while the others joined in. "Best fun I've had in a long time," said another, then sobered, "Begging your pardon, Mr. Muir, we know it weren't no fun for you."

"Never mind," Malcolm waved his apology aside. "I'm sorry I wasn't in on the end. I would have liked to get a few licks in myself."

Archie appeared beside Fergus, and they joined in time to hear how Malcolm had been traced.

"The hobo grapevine was working overtime, and we pieced together one clue after another," Bert said, giving the rest a warning look, and they all stared at Archie for a moment. "Most everybody we know has worked here, and Mrs. Mann has been very fair to us." They all nodded. "And no cheating us, like some."

"Well, how did you trace him to Blackwater?" Archie asked, and was met with silence, and shuffling feet. He was wise enough to drop the subject.

"What did you do with the three men, Archie?" Fergus asked.

"We put them on a passing freight." He said. The other men chuckled. "We were bad policemen and very open to bribes on the condition they never return." Archie and the men grinned at Fergus's sour face.

"They had most of the money they got for the kidnapping and offered it up. We relieved them of close to one hundred dollars."

"Archie told us to divide the works between us," Bert hurried to explain.

"One hundred dollars? They didn't even feed me." Rather than be complimented by the large amount, Malcolm was offended.

Mrs. Mann announced the food was ready and everybody moved towards the tables.

Fergus pulled Jean aside. "I was cruel when we spoke, and I'm sorry."

"I planned to tell you at the dance anyway. You know I wouldn't hurt Malcolm for anything . . . I had a chat with him about it."

"I'm the last one to talk about secrets, Jean, as you know. I have nightmares about what I did, and *didn't* do in the war. I'll always have them, but they don't have power over me anymore because I found someone who shares them and listens to my rants. With me, it's Father. With you, Jean Haskell . . . it's me. So we'll keep each other's secrets. What are you going to do when he gets out?"

She smiled at him, acknowledging her name as Haskell. "I'm hoping he's up to arranging a divorce. It's too late for anything else."

Over her shoulder, his attention centered on a police constable arriving at the front gate. Eyes searching the yard, he spotted Archie who saw the constable at the same time and the two headed towards each other meeting halfway. They put their heads close together while the constable spoke. Archie stiffened, turned the constable, so their backs were to anyone watching, and spoke for some time. The constable nodded, saluted, and Archie watched him march off down the street. Turning, he saw Fergus and waved to him.

For no reason, Fergus felt uneasy, as if he had been deliberately found. He patted Jean's arm then pushed along the verandah, putting distance and bodies between himself and Archie.

"I'm just going in the house for half an hour or so," he whispered to Mrs. Mann.

She gave him a questioning glance, then turned to offer chicken to Bert. Seeing his chance, Fergus slipped inside and went to his room. He tucked his pistol into his belt and snatched up his jacket before sneaking out through the back gate into the alley.

A few doors before he came to the front of Lex Rideout's house, he saw Miss Skefington coming towards him, carrying a dish covered in wax paper.

"Hello, Dorothy," he greeted her warmly. "On the way to my house?"

She nodded, blushing. "Clemmie—Mrs. Mann, said at church this morning you were having a little get together and asked me to join in."

"It's a cake?" Fergus asked, peering under the wrapper. "Chocolate too. My favorite. I just have to talk to Lex for a moment." Hoping he made it sound as though he wouldn't be long, he added, "Don't drink anything Mrs. Mann hands you."

"I won't." She laughed with him. A nice laugh, he thought, wondering why he had only now noticed she was an attractive woman.

He stopped at Rideout's gate. *Here goes*, he thought, feeling the pistol tucked behind his back. Ignoring the front door, he chose the path around the side of the house to the back. The grass was uncut and weeds sprouted in the joints of the sidewalk. The area once used for a garden was covered with dead stinkweed. Two peony bushes in dire need of water, uncut blossoms drooping, flanked each side of the back porch. The only corner showing some life was a small bower-like area, a trellis covered with climbing roses and bordered on two sides by rose bushes. Lex Rideout, pruning shears in his hand, stood watching Fergus as he came around the back. The perfume of cut roses and green stems filled the air. Fergus stopped without greeting and waited. They eyed each other for a long moment.

Rideout relaxed then. "Sorry about the mess here. I should hire hobos like you do." He tossed a handful of dead-heads into a garbage bin and cleaned his hands on his overalls. "Aren't you having a party, some sort of celebration or something? Did you come to invite me?"

"Can't do anything in this town without everyone knowing," Fergus observed, and made apologetic noises. "I'm after a bit of peace. Mrs. Mann asked over a bunch of ladies hoping to match me up."

Lex laughed. "Come on in the house, and we'll have a drink." He looked Fergus straight in the eye. "And talk." Rideout's lips curved into a half-smile. "How's your father?"

He stood aside and waved Fergus through the door and into a spotless kitchen.

A contrast to the yard, Fergus thought. He feigned surprise. "He's just fine. Why do you ask?"

Rideout raised his eyebrows in surprise, and his eyes grew puzzled. "I heard he had an accident."

"Someone's got their wires crossed." *So, Lex is responsible after all. I hope he thinks the men took his money and ran.* Fergus hid a rush of anger. Rideout moved closer; his eyes narrowed. Fergus saw they were bloodshot. "Your dad's really okay?"

"Not ten minutes ago, he was enjoying the party." Up close, Fergus saw the change in Rideout. His face was lined, eyes ringed with black circles. Even his clothes hung loosely as if he had lost weight. *He looks haunted,* thought Fergus.

Rideout led him into the living room and pointed to a chair. Fergus sat.

"So what's the real reason you're here?" Rideout eyed Fergus again. "Fess up, Muir."

"First, get us the drink you promised. It's too hot to beat about the bush, Lex. I think you know what I've found out about you and GlasBottle. What if I tell you what I know, and you can tell me if I'm right?"

"You're not here about Davidson, then? Or what the police got out of me?" Lex went to the small table and showed Fergus a bottle. Fergus nodded.

Lex made a show of noticing his dirt-stained hands. "I'll just wash my hands first. Won't be a minute."

Fergus heard the water running somewhere down the hall. He took the opportunity to look around the room at the Art Deco furniture. Surprisingly, the place was neat, the furniture tasteful with clean lines, all neutral colors, and a contrasting carpet with a geometric border of red and green. He wondered if Lex or Clarissa had selected it. Two pictures perched on the table beside him of Lex and the rugby team holding up the championship trophy for last year and the year before. Across the room, Fergus saw an Art Deco statue of a Roman soldier with sword and shield. It looked like bronze, and expensive. Just as he was about to get up for a closer examination, Rideout came back into the room.

"Not unless you want to confess about Davidson too," Fergus picked up the conversation.

"Confess to what?" Lex fixed them both a drink, handed one to Fergus then sat across from him. "I suppose the kid said I killed Davidson," he said calmly. "But she isn't sure, is she? That, or the police won't believe the lying little sneak."

Impotent rage rose like bile and Fergus fought to control it. For a dangerous moment, he let himself be distracted by an image of Peter and Cat. He forced his mind back to the reason he was here.

"You're wasting your time, Muir," Rideout continued. "I'm not confessing to something I haven't done. I had no reason to kill Davidson, and from what I hear, you are the prime suspect. You and Davidson had something going on between you. Why is it so secret, Fergus? Davidson have something on you and was blackmailing you?" Rideout leaned closer, grinning. "You can tell me."

"Blackmail is more your game than mine," Fergus said, picturing Archie's short talk with the policeman at the gate. "Jean Haskell, for instance?"

Rideout waved his glass in dismissal. "Chicken feed. She told me you found financial irregularities, that's all. Women shouldn't be in business. Not reliable."

"Speaking of financials, Lex—"

Rideout interrupted with a wave of his hand. "Let's talk about the money Davidson stole. You can't excuse him for that."

"It's what I'm trying to tell you, Lex. There was nothing to steal. The fraud was all organized by Strathcona Holdings."

"You don't know what you're talking about." Rideout took a drink from his glass, gripping it so tight his knuckles turned white.

"The Board members were manipulating the accounts and making up statements showing a profit when there was none. You probably thought the profits came from their other holdings, but most of it came by manipulating GlasBottle records. They only gave you the correct statements, and they always showed losses. Peter noticed their statements kept recording good cash flow when he never saw it. He made the mistake of telling them he found some errors. They forged his signature on bank withdrawals to cover it up and charged him with stealing the money they gave themselves."

Rideout's eyes went round with surprise, then narrowed again in disbelief. "You have a great imagination for an accountant."

"It's sad but true, and I feel for you. The stock options they gave themselves have also watered down your own share of the company. Tit for tat, eh Lex?" Fergus grinned at him, and Rideout's eyes radiated shock. Fergus took a sip from his glass. *For someone with such expensive taste he sure buys cheap scotch. I should have brought a bottle of Glenlivet with me.*

"If it's true, I sure had nothing to do with it," Rideout said.

"Well, Peter was quite sure you were stealing from GlasBottle too, Lex. And you haven't stopped stealing even now. With help from Ready and Waiting Shipping." Rideout's eyes blinked, telling Fergus he had hit a nerve. "Both of you with your own customer list. Strathcona Holdings will be upset when they find out. Which they will, very soon . . . unless I help you."

"What?" Lex was thrown off balance by the offer.

"I don't think you stole for yourself, Lex. Maybe gave a little to Clara Perkins, but most of it went for upkeep of the Rugby team, right? It raised the team's morale, enough to win the Junior Championship, and your name in the city went up in lights. Your reputation means a lot, doesn't it, Lex?"

"Appearances mean everything, as the English say," Lex acknowledged, his manner showing satisfaction rather than guilt. "Appearances are what Cypress Landing is all about, or haven't you noticed?" He went to the table, refilled his drink, and sat back down.

"You really aren't an evil man," Fergus said, hoping he didn't sound deferential. "Even if you didn't know Strathcona was cheating you, it wasn't greed which prompted you to take a few crates of glass, was it? Everybody has to make a living these days. So I can keep quiet about it." Nervousness made Fergus take a larger sip than he intended. It really was terrible scotch.

"In return for what?"

"Admit you killed Peter," Fergus said matter-of-factly.

Rideout threw back his head and laughed, then cut it short. "I'd rather be accused of stealing than hang." He lifted his glass to his mouth, then changed his mind. "Cat told you she saw me at the kiln, didn't she?"

"Yes, she did, Lex," Fergus said, suddenly tired, wanting to finish. "And I doubted her. I thought she just wanted you out of her mother's life. She watched you convince her mother she needed you for support and make decisions for her. And she believes you are the reason her brothers were sent away, one by one. Both brothers dead, and you didn't care. It might not be true, but children have odd ideas, Lex, and Cat has a point. Like you say, it's all in the appearance. Your wife and her mother even have similar names. Clara . . . Clarissa."

All the time, Rideout watched him over the rim of his glass, saying nothing.

"Don't you think I'd rather Davidson was alive to tell me where my wife is?" he finally asked in a halfhearted way, as if no longer interested.

"You killed him because he didn't run off with Clarissa," Fergus replied. "To be honest, Lex, I believe it was an accident. I think you wanted him to leave town, and your fight went wrong."

Rideout watched Fergus take another swallow of his glass, then abruptly, he put his own glass on the floor at his feet and started sobbing. Surprised by Lex's sudden emotion, Fergus sat back in his chair trying to separate himself from it.

"God, Muir, you can't know how it has affected me. I can't take it anymore. I'll tell you what happened. I saw him one day and followed him for days to get him alone. He got angry with me, took a swing at me, and the next thing I knew, he was on the ground, dead. I think I picked something up and hit him. I couldn't understand it. I just wanted to talk to him."

Still crying, Lex sat on the floor, elbows on his knees and his hands covering his face. "You have to believe me. Please, Fergus. You're a good friend, aren't you? God, it's haunted me ever since. I can't work, can't sleep. I had to find out where Clarissa was!" To Fergus's horror, Lex started towards him on his knees, pleading.

Fergus pushed his chair back, creating more distance. "You know she never went with him, Lex. You were afraid Peter might tell everybody why she wanted to get away from you. You kept her a virtual prisoner in this house, kept her from making friends, and if she rebelled, you beat her. All the while, in public you played the loving husband, and pretended to dote on her."

Lex still on his knees shook his head. "No, you've got it all backwards. She made it all up. She was crazy—nuts. I had to watch her all the time because she told stories. About me. Ruining my good name. I needed to know where she was so I could be sure she wasn't coming back to tell her wild stories!"

Fergus quit talking, suddenly ill, his senses numbing. The taste of bad scotch in his mouth. It must have been ninety proof because he felt drunk, his eyesight wavering. Not unfamiliar, like the usual start of a panic episode. Lex Rideout's face blurred and faded in and out.

"The drink," he began, and blackness closed in.

26

"WAKE up, Ferg."
As if coming out of a deep dream, he saw two fuzzy faces peering down at him. He sat up, tongue thick in his mouth. The room spun, and he struggled to arrange his thoughts together.

"What in hell," he said, focusing on Archie and the constable. "Did you get him? Rideout?"

They both looked at him as if he was some old wino on a bench in the park.

"What are you doing here? Where's Rideout?"

"I have an order to arrest you, but I thought it would be nicer to wait until after the party." Archie gave a thumbs down as if Fergus had betrayed him. "Then you disappeared. Mrs. Mann told me you were in the house, but a lady said she saw you on the street and you told her you were going to Rideout's. Sure enough, you weren't inside your house at all." Archie shook his head.

Fergus sat up and held his head until the dizziness passed. The two helped him to his feet. "He drugged my drink, Archie. We have to find him. He killed Peter."

Archie sighed and held Fergus by the arm. "We have to bring you in. I'm sorry but I have a warrant for your arrest . . . for killing Peter. It's better if we just go to the Station and you can tell us all about it there." He began to say things about lawyers and rights.

Fergus pulled away. "No, Archie. For God's sake. He's getting away while we stand here! You can't believe I did it."

"It doesn't matter what I believe, and you know it. We can sort it all out at the Station. I don't have a choice, Ferg."

Fergus swore, and clasped both hands over the top of his head, and shook it back and forth in denial. He straightened his jacket over his shoulders, and suddenly had an ominous feeling. *My Pistol.* He casually put his hand behind him pretending to give himself a back massage. It was gone.

"Did you see Rideout on your way over here?" he asked without hope. "I don't know how long I was out cold."

"I saw him turning onto Union Avenue," said the constable. "You can't miss his green sports job."

Fergus swore again, getting an exasperated look from Archie who took his arm. "Let's go, Fergus."

"Cat!" Fergus's felt like he was talking through cotton. "He's after Cat." He shook off Archie's hand. "I told him Cat saw him kill Peter. Please, Archie. He's headed there. If he gets to her . . ."

The constable shuffled his feet and watched Archie.

Fergus tried again, "Archie, if anything happens to her, you'd never forgive yourself. Her mother won't be able to protect her. You know me. I promise I'll go to the moon if you want, but after we know she's safe. We have to go now!"

Archie shook his head stubbornly, but his eyes were suddenly unsure. He hunched his shoulders a little, and Fergus could almost see him weighing pros and cons and gave Archie another pleading look. Archie sighed loudly and gave in, "Okay. Let's go." The constable pressed his lips together in disapproval.

WHEN they arrived, two constables were already there, trying to make sense of Harley's babble. Doors popped open in concert along the street, spewing out neighbors asking excited questions. Harley rushed towards Fergus.

"I told you he was a crook, but you wouldn't listen. Do something! My mom's in there with Cat and Charlie!"

"Easy boy," Archie said, as though he were calming a horse. "Talk slowly."

Harley stopped, then wilted. "Cat and I were in the backyard. She went inside the house, and I heard my mother yelling. When I tried to get in, the door was locked. So was the front. When I saw him through the window, I ran down to Mercier's store and banged on the door until Fred opened it. He called the police."

Archie took charge. He ordered a constable into the backyard, and the other two were set to street duty. "Move all these rubberneckers from the boulevard and keep them across the street, away from here."

Turning his attention to the house, Archie knocked on the front door, listened and knocked again. "Police!" he said, his voice strong. "Open the door please." There was no answer. The house was quiet. Archie came back to stand by Fergus.

"Should I mention what caused all this, Ferg?" he said quietly, but Fergus heard the anger. "But now isn't the time, is it? If you've got a remedy, I'm open to hear it."

Harley ran up to the door and pounded on it. "Get out of my house, Rideout!"

Archie sighed and went forward to get Harley, calming him again. "That's not helping son. Come with me and let's see if we can come up with a plan." Harley meekly followed Archie back to Fergus.

"I can break a window and crawl in," Harley suggested, his fists clenching and unclenching.

"He'd panic and do something stupid when he heard you," Fergus said, thinking of Cat. "He's pretty desperate."

On cue, they heard a scream and an angry voice. The screaming stopped.

"That's my mom!" Harley's voice trilled with anxiety. "She's the one liable to do something she shouldn't. Go off the deep end and take the easy way out, maybe even give up Cat." Harley's voice was unsteady. He looked at Archie. "You're the police and you're just standing there!"

Fergus put his arm around his shoulders.

"Look, son," Archie's voice was still calm. "Bad things happen when people rush headlong just for the sake of action. You just said you're afraid your mom might do the same thing."

Harley's answer was to jerk away from Fergus's arm. He went off to one side and kicked a stone, which rattled down the sidewalk.

Fergus moved down the walk nearer the front of the house and squinted his eyes, examining the lock on the door. He went back to

Archie's side. "An ordinary skeleton key type lock," he said. "Kick it in?"

"This situation isn't like the house at Blackwater."

"How about getting Roberta Flower down here? She might be able to talk him out."

"She'd have to wait for authority from her boss. Too long," Archie said. "And he's at the point of no return. He hasn't anything to lose. He can't go back, only forward. Let's hope he doesn't take anybody with him."

Fergus caught the hidden accusation. *If your captain had only listened to me in the first place,* Fergus thought, his mouth clamped into a thin line. *I had to act, not wait to be arrested.* But theorizing *'what if'* wouldn't help them now.

Fergus blinked his eyes and yawned. Whatever Rideout put in his whisky was still with him. His sleeping pills? He shook his head to clear off a lingering fog and wondered if he should tell Archie about the pistol. Archie disappeared around the side of the house and was soon heard at the back door. For the next fifteen minutes, Fergus and Harley heard a quiet conversation, but no clear words.

Archie came around the front, wiping his forehead. He shook his head at Fergus.

"My turn," said Fergus, and traced Archie's path. The police constable was in the alley moving people along.

Fergus put his ear to the door. "Lex," he called out, "talk to me."

"What now?" Rideout answered finally.

"Think what you're doing here, Lex. Give it up. Anything from now on will really go against you and make everything worse."

"Things can't get much worse, Muir. As it is, your only witness is right here with me, isn't she?"

Fergus felt a chill. He looked around to make sure nobody was listening. "Did you take my pistol? It won't help, Lex. The way things are, any lawyer can convince a jury Peter's death was an accident, manslaughter. And a lot of character witnesses will vouch for you. They love you in this town and appreciate everything you've done. If you hurt those children and their mother, opinions will change fast. You can't stay here forever. Come out now!"

There was no reply, and Fergus hoped Rideout was considering what he said.

Finally, he heard a thump, like a body relaxing against the door. Was he going to give up? The surge of relief Fergus felt was physical.

"It's too late, Muir." Rideout's tone was resigned. "Everything is too late."

"No! Rideout. Come on." But Fergus heard no more, and he returned to the others.

The lack of action was beginning to bore the crowd across the street. Their murmurs were loud, meant to antagonize.

"That's what she gets for letting anybody into the house. . . ."

"No concern for the kids. . . ."

"Well, what can you expect from her kind . . . ?"

Harley turned red and faced the crowd across the street, "Go tend to *your* own kind!" he shouted. "I've seen what they are, stealing other people's food."

"Just close your ears, Harley," Fergus said.

"Supercilious nuts." Harley spit, a teen image of scorn. "As if you can tell a crook just by looking at him. They are great ones to talk. One of them stole our food delivery right off the back porch."

"Sorry, Harley," Fergus said, revolted at the idea of neighbors stealing food from a family who needed it. Not even vagrants stooped that low. The thought gave him an idea.

He beckoned to Archie, and said to Harley, "Run to my house and ask for a vagrant called Bert. They are all in the yard." He told Harley what to say. "Tell him it's got to happen now." A curtain twitched in the front window. "Rideout is watching, so I'm going to push you away. Act like you don't want to go." Harley brightened, then glowered and played a game of push and shove before reluctantly sidling away. Fergus watched him almost hopping down the street, then told Archie what he had in mind. For the first time, Archie grinned at him.

The crowd across the street lessened, then swelled again, and new ones arrived, some even brought sandwiches and sat on the boulevard picnic style, eating and ogling the entertainment. Fergus secretly inspected them all, not recognizing anyone. They all seemed to be from this area of town, and he was thankful the word hadn't spread. Things were bad enough as it is without it becoming a spectator sport. He glanced at his watch. It was only twenty minutes after subtracting an estimation of Harley's arrival at the house.

"Don't get fidgety," Archie said, noticing the anxious glance at the watch. "This is actually ideal because Rideout will think we are trying to wear him down with time. Right now, he's probably boasting the inaction will give him a rest. But in the end, playing the waiting game has effect." In silence, they passed the time pacing back and forth along the sidewalk in front of the house.

Not half an hour later, Fergus recognized the car turning the corner at the end of the street. The car slowed as it neared the mob of people then made a sharp turn and parked a few doors down. A man he didn't know got out of the driver's seat, and went around to the other side, arriving too late to open the door for his passenger. Mrs. Mann already stood on the running board looking over the neighborhood. Ignoring the man's hand, she stepped down, straightened her hat and started towards Fergus with a stride which made the man beside her scurry to catch up.

With a mere nod to Fergus and Archie, she headed for the front door. Archie made to follow, but Fergus put out his hand. "Stay, Archie." The sergeant turned his back to the door, then watched over his shoulder.

The man took something from his pocket and bent down to the door keyhole. A tall, woman with tightly curled blond hair, separated herself from the crowd and crossed the street.

"My name is Mrs. Hoffman. I'm here for Clara, and I'm going in there too." Pushing past Archie's arm, she ran up to the front and exchanged a few words with Mrs. Mann. At that point, the man bent over the door straightened and grinning at the women, turned the doorknob. Mrs. Mann squared her shoulders, opened the door and the two marched in. The door slammed shut behind them.

Archie's eyebrows hit his hairline.

27

A stale odor of sweat and panic greeted them in the hot and airless house. Freda Hoffmann made a choking sound then waved her hand in front of her nose.

Lex Rideout stood in the kitchen doorway. "What the . . . ?" He stared past them ready to attack whoever followed. Cat ducked under his arm and ran to Mrs. Mann, threw her arms around her waist and buried her head in her dress.

Young Charlie did the same with Mrs. Hoffman. "There, there, lovey," she whispered and stroked his hair.

"I'm not scared." Cat's eyes didn't echo her statement. "I'm looking after Charlie."

Mrs. Mann patted Cat's shoulder. "Where's your mother?"

"In the kitchen. She . . . doesn't feel very good," Cat said. "I'm glad you're here Mrs. Mann. He's got a—"

"Enough talk." Lex picked up a ladder-back chair and pushed it under the front door knob. "Now, get into the kitchen so we can watch the back door in case someone else gets ideas." He gripped Mrs. Mann by the elbow, and with his other hand gave Mrs. Hoffman a push towards the kitchen. "If you have to butt your nose in, you can join Clara."

Holding Charlie's hand, Mrs. Hoffman started for the kitchen, then stopped when Mrs. Mann stayed put. "Just keep your hands to yourself, Mr. Rideout." With both hands, she pushed him away. "This family is leaving here. And I'll not put up with any nonsense from you."

"And you and whose army is going to make me?" Lex's lip curled into a sneer.

Mrs. Mann turned away from him and said briskly, "Cat, gather whatever you and your brother and mother need. We'll be leaving when you're ready."

Lex drew a pistol from his trouser pocket. Freda gasped and clutched Young Charlie.

Lex used it to gesture towards the kitchen. "Move!"

Mrs. Mann, a nervous look in her eye, examined the pistol then smiled a little and said to Cat. "Your mother's in there?" Cat nodded. "Then, in any case, we must go in to get her." After a glance up at her, Cat obeyed.

The first thing Mrs. Mann did was push up on the window, opening it wide. Freda Hoffmann immediately went to Clara Perkins sitting at the table and stooped to peer into her face. "Clara. It's me." Clara Perkins sat before a round of pastry, hugging a rolling pin to her chest. A bowl with four apples was at one end of the table. She gave no indication she'd heard anything.

"That's better." Mrs. Mann came from the window and towards Clara Perkins.

"Hello, Mrs. Perkins," she said. "My name is Clemmie Mann. Mrs. Hoffman and I have come to rescue you and the children." Mrs. Mann gently touched Mrs. Perkins on the shoulder. Cat saw pity in her eyes and then anger as her gaze switched to Lex.

"Put the kettle on, Cat, and we'll have tea. While the water boils, you can see about gathering the things you'll need when we leave."

"Clara isn't going anywhere, are you Clara?" Lex said. Mrs. Perkins just cradled the rolling pin, vacant eyes staring into an abyss only she could see. Freda Hoffman choked back a sob and clutched Young Charlie close.

Lex laughed. "Cat will not leave without her mother, and so neither of them are going anywhere." Lex levelled the pistol at Mrs. Mann, his pale blue eyes cold and confident. "You made a big mistake pushing your nosy face in here, and I'll make you sorry you did. If Cat knows what's good for her family, she will admit she didn't see me hit Davidson. It's her imagination."

Mrs. Hoffman put Charlie behind her, shielding him. Charlie didn't seem worried and peeked around her hip at the scene.

Mrs. Mann turned to Cat's mother. "Listen to me, Mrs. Perkins. Don't pay that intruder any mind, do you hear? You are not obliged to stay here. You and your children can leave anytime you wish."

Clara Perkins remained mute, but her grip on the rolling pin slackened.

Mrs. Mann moved around the table from Lex so he had his back to the door.

"You just get it through your thick skull, Mr. Rideout." Mrs. Mann pointed towards the front door. "Everybody out there knows Cat told the truth and badgering her won't change it. This twelve-year-old has seen things no child should ever experience, and shame on you for adding to her family's grief. You even had Mr. Muir kidnapped, an innocent man, who would have died if he hadn't been found. Your bullying days are over. It's time you go outside and take whatever comes next like a man. Whatever you face now is nothing compared to what will happen to you if we are harmed. Everyone will turn against you. Sooner or later, you have to give up."

"You have rocks in your head if you think I'll just walk out of here. It's too late."

"It's never too late." Mrs. Mann's eyes sharpened on him. "Unless there is something we don't know about."

Lex only waved the pistol at her, his face lopsided in desperation now.

Mrs. Mann's expression grew wary. "Is there something else, Mr. Rideout?"

"Shut up." Lex put both hands on the pistol, and arms straight out, pointed it at her.

Mrs. Mann flapped the back of her hands at him like she was shooing off a nuisance. "Put that thing away, for goodness sakes," she snapped. "I know that pistol. It's been in the back of Fergus Muir's closet for years. Heaven knows why he keeps it, but at least he has the good sense to make sure it isn't loaded."

"What?" In his shock, Lex lowered his hand.

"I said it isn't loaded, or haven't you noticed? Any fool can see that just by looking at it. Some gunman you are." Mrs. Mann looked over his head at the back door, and a great smile lit up her face. "As you are about to find out."

Lex whirled around to face the back door. In a flash, Mrs. Mann yanked the rolling pin out of Clara's hand and whacked him on the side of his head. Lex fell to the floor without a sound. Mrs. Mann came the rest of the way around the table and sat on his back. "Quick!" she snapped at Mrs. Hoffman, who let go of Charlie and sat on his legs.

"Cat, can you find a piece of rope?" Mrs. Mann said.

Cat dropped the kettle on the stove and disappeared returning with her skipping rope. Between them, Mrs. Mann and Mrs. Hoffman tied Lex's hands and looped the end over his ankles, effectively hog-tying him. Delighted at this new game, Young Charlie danced around them, searching for a space to sit on him too.

Lex groaned and made an effort to rise. Mrs. Mann lifted the rolling pin high above his head. He cursed at her, calling her what sounded like '*bloody witch*.'

Freda Hoffman grimaced at Mrs. Mann "Did you just hear what I did? Vile man."

In reply, Mrs. Mann gave Lex another tap of the rolling pin. "There are children about."

Clara Perkins raised her eyes at the noise and looked on with detached interest.

FROM the opposite end of the street, Harley trotted up to Fergus and Archie. He turned and looked at the crowd on the boulevard, now standing and taking in the latest event.

"There's a gang of hobos, going up and down the alley looking in everybody's yard." Harley gave a loud laugh. "They are knocking on the doors, and when nobody answers, they open them up. But nothing to worry about I guess. Nobody's got anything valuable anyways. Maybe a bit of food."

There was silence for a full second or two. "I seen them chalking their marks on the telephone poles along the way." Harley almost danced in his glee.

The idea of hobos leaving codes which told every vagrant in the country secrets of the neighborhood was the last straw. A few people gave hopeful looks at the constable, before giving up and joining the exodus. Minutes later, the street was empty, except for a reporter holding a notepad.

Harley went round the back to the alley, carrying the same message and he soon returned with a thumbs up. Fergus held his breath and watched, praying.

The front door opened, and Mrs. Mann came out with her arm around Cat. Freda Hoffman had her arm around Clara Perkins as if she were leading the blind. Young Charlie held his mother's hand, not looking disturbed a bit. Five people rushed to meet them, Archie and the constable passing and going inside the house. Young Charlie stood and stared curiously at them all, while Harley held on to him, his eyes wet with relief. Fergus's eyes went straight to Cat inspecting her face.

She smiled at him and said, "Guess what? I wasn't afraid one bit. I remember Sir telling me if we face our fears head on, they aren't as bad as we thought. I looked after Mama and Charlie until Mrs. Mann came."

Fergus put his arms around her, unable to say a word.

The Perkins family went along with Freda Hoffman to her house. Lex Rideout was kept inside until transportation was arranged. The constable came over to Archie and handed him something that made Fergus pale. Finally, Archie and Fergus were alone.

"Where did Lex get the pistol, Fergus?" Archie said quietly.

"I was going to tell you," Fergus said, his face red. "I took it over to Lex's house, and when he drugged me, he stole it."

"You are in a peck of trouble, Ferg. Keeping a firearm that's not registered. You've put me in a pickle. I can't keep this quiet."

"It was never loaded, Arch. I only wanted to scare him into a confession, and in the end, I never did use it. Am I still under arrest?"

"No. You will have to come back with me though, and make a formal statement about what happened at Rideout's house . . . among other things." He lifted the pistol and pointed it at Fergus.

Fergus peered inside the barrel. "Are we still friends?"

Archie lowered the pistol. "You'll have to take the consequences of the firearm. But okay. Only if you promise never to pull anything else like this again."

"Scout's honour," Fergus put up two fingers in the scout salute.

He grinned at Archie, then added in a tone he hoped was casual, "There is one thing, though."

Archie turned to Fergus and growled with real menace. "What now?"

"Lex Rideout's wife, Clarissa. I know where she is."

Archie threw his hands up in the air. "I knew it! Fergus, I swear I'm going to commit murder myself."

"Hear me out, Archie. When I took my turn trying to talk Lex out of the house? After I said my piece, I got a distinct feeling he was about to give up. But then he said it was too late and it made me wonder why. We always assumed Lex was worried Peter might convince people Clarissa Rideout didn't go with him."

"I thought you said it's why he killed Peter."

"Well, yes, but he was more worried people might start wondering if she didn't go with Peter, then where was she? That's why he said it was too late."

"And what feeling came over you when he said it was too late?"

"Watch your blood pressure, Arch." Fergus took a deep breath. With each word, Archie's face became more and more infused with blood.

"I've a good mind to arrest you again, Fergus. You'd better pray the captain likes your story. Let's go."

28

WHEN he arrived home, Malcolm met him at the door, anxious for news. The first thing Fergus did was praise Mrs. Mann. She drew herself up, and said, "That man got my dander up, let me tell you. When he saw us, his face looked like a slapped backside. But I told him what's what, plump and plain." She told them what had taken place. Malcolm and Fergus listened, summoning up visions of the encounter.

"What made you think of Mrs. Mann and the vagrants?" Malcolm asked when she went back to the kitchen.

"We needed a diversion and a frontal attack. Who else but our friends and Mrs. Mann? When she delivers her *plump and plain* speech, whole nations tremble." They grinned at each other, then Fergus frowned. "I'm worried about the newspaper, Dad. A reporter was there. If the story is splashed all over the paper and the parents of the kids at Cat's new school read a version, what will happen to her? You know what people are like."

Malcolm thought. "She'd be ostracized again. And I know just the person to phone. I'll be right back." And he was, looking satisfied.

"I talked to Jack Levinson. He attends the same synagogue as the publisher and owner of the newspaper. Tom Rubins, who used to be Tomas Rubinowski until he changed his name. As soon I mentioned our mutual friend and talented violin player and said a news article would damage her name, Jack understood. I don't think we have to worry."

The next morning, Fergus came into the office and stopped in front of Miss Watts.

"Good morning, Patricia. You've got a new hairstyle. Suits you."

"Thank you, Mr. Muir," whispered Miss Watts, brown eyes wide. She couldn't resist pulling at a blond curl. Across the room, Max was grinning at her.

"What appointments do I have today?" Fergus continued pretending not to notice her stunned expression.

"You had three," she said.

"Had?"

"They cancelled." She paused. "Stiles' Styles said you had been arrested for murder."

"And the others?" His good mood vaporized at her nod. "We'll see about that." Fergus stomped into his office, sat at his desk and pulled the phone over.

"Even if it isn't true, and I guess it isn't, seeing as you are talking to me," said Albert Stiles, "how does it look when my customers know my accountant is under arrest? They'll think I am a crook too."

Fergus was furious and let fly. "How would it look? Think how you might feel if you showed them you had guts to think for yourself instead of following like a lemming. Without proof, I might add," he snarled irrationally and slammed the receiver down.

Miss Watts appeared at the door. "I didn't get a chance to tell you, Fred Mercier left a message this morning."

"He thinks I'm a crook too?"

"On the contrary. To congratulate you for sticking up for the little guy and saving the Perkins family. He said courage was a scarce commodity in this town, and you showed them up." She laughed, showing him a thumbs up.

"Oh, well then," Fergus said, at a loss for words.

"So what if a few clients left? When the news gets around, we'll more than make up for it with new ones." Miss Watts went back to her desk, leaving Fergus with a strange new feeling. A sense of acceptance.

Morning turned to midday and Fergus had still not heard anything from Archie, nor was there any news on the streets. The worry they had found nothing clenched at his insides. Deciding work was useless, he told Max and Miss Watts to enjoy an afternoon off, then left for home. He walked by Rideout's house. A police constable glared and waved him on as Fergus slowed, hoping to hear or see anything from the backyard. He didn't.

After lunch, he left the house after telling Malcolm he had a few errands, letting him assume it was business. At the high school, he asked to speak to the principal.

When he returned, he joined Malcolm who was pacing around the yard closely followed by Duke. Affection lurched at his chest. Although recognizing a reluctant gratitude Rideout had given orders to keep Malcolm unharmed, Fergus couldn't excuse the fact he'd used third-party assailants, making the outcome uncontrollable. Fergus didn't like to think of the result if Malcolm had been found later in a cold cellar, the vagrants gone.

They went to bed very late still awaiting news.

ALL along the street people were huddled in groups reading newspapers when Fergus parked in front of the office the next morning. Inside, he joined Max and Miss Watts in reading the report. Lex Rideout, the popular high school rugby coach, had been charged with the second-degree murder of his wife. More information was to come. Fergus was disappointed there was no mention of Peter Davidson, and thankful there was nothing regarding a hostage incident.

Archie came to the house after lunch on his way home for some needed sleep. "We hammered at Rideout all night. Finally, he said Clarissa taunted him she was running away." Archie ignored a disgusted snort from Fergus, and continued, "More likely, he caught her as she was about to leave. He only remembers his rage. I suppose the autopsy report will confirm how she died. When he calmed down, she was lying dead at his feet. Then when fraud charges were laid against Peter, Lex took advantage of his absence to accuse him of taking Clarissa. Like you thought, Fergus. He buried her in the rose arbor."

"What about Peter's murder?"

"Another accident. He wanted Peter to leave town, even offered him a bribe to go, but Peter refused and said he was going to stick around and clear his name of the fraud charges. Rideout says Peter kept asking him about Clarissa and was he still beating up women? Rideout hit him with a brick, and Peter just dropped. He dragged him into the kiln."

Archie went to the door, saying they still had some items to clean up before they were finished. He sketched a wave and then was gone.

Malcolm and Fergus told Mrs. Mann the latest news. She shuddered and wiped her hands on her apron. "What times we live in. Men beat their wives, and people do nothing. Husbands disappear, and families never hear from them."

Fergus wondered if she was referring to her own husband.

"I knew Charlie Perkins, and he loved his family. Four years is a long time with no word. I really believe he is dead." She dabbed at her eye with her apron and added, "Poor Cat. She's become the daughter I never had."

Fergus shared some information with Malcolm at dinner. "I went to the high school yesterday and talked to the principal about Harley Perkins. Whether there might be any financial help available for him. It turns out Harley had been offered a scholarship to study mathematics at the University of Alberta, but he turned it down. Harley's mother talked him out of it."

"A shame," Malcolm replied. "She wants him gone, then when he has a real chance, she puts the kibosh on it. No wonder he's an angry young man."

"Well, apparently, the scholarship is still on offer. I want to help him, Dad. I've got a feeling young men like him will be needed in the years to come." At his father's probing glance, Fergus added, somewhat defensive, "I read the papers too. Up to now, I haven't wanted to think about foreign politics."

"Isn't it too late for university this year?" Malcolm only replied.

"The principal said they'll be glad to get him once they know he's near genius. If he works summers at the office, and we help him pay for room and board, he will be able to do it. The scholarship is for one year, but if he takes top marks, and the principal said he could do it with one hand tied behind his back so to speak, there will be others."

"Well, Harley should have the opportunity," Malcolm grinned.

"Get on with it, son."

But an hour later Harley rocked Fergus back on his heels when he turned it down.

"You're refusing a place at university? Here's your chance, Harley!"

"I can't," said Harley, almost crying in his misery. "Mom is sick. She couldn't get over what happened. All she did was stare out of the window. All day. The doctor took her to Ponoka for treatment. He's keeping it quiet so nobody can yell at us about our crazy mother. We're pretending she's gone to work in Lethbridge."

"Why can't Rose take charge?"

"The Hutchisons were transferred to Montreal, and Rose is going with them. Mrs. Hoffman took Young Charlie. It's just Cat and me now. We can collect relief for the rest of the month, but I'm not considered an adult. I have to find a job. They can't take Cat away, Mr. Muir."

Fergus hadn't considered this outcome, and he could only stand with his jaw agape. "Why didn't you come to see me?"

Harley just shook his head, voice quivering. "I'll work and save enough money to go to university someday. I appreciate everything you've done, but it's not possible now."

"Okay, Harley, I respect your decision." They sat beside each other on the back step, both silent, keeping each other company. Finally, Fergus stood. "If I can help you find a job, let me know." He stared down at Harley another while, troubled, but unable to think of a solution, then quietly left for home.

"Well, I've had it," he told Malcolm later. "We can't solve everybody's problems. We just have to leave people to get on with their lives."

Mrs. Mann came into the living room. She handed them tea and a slice of cake, waiting for someone to enlarge on the last part of the conversation she had interrupted.

Finally, exasperated, she said, "Who's getting on with their lives? What now? Am I allowed to know, or am I just a waitress in this house or something?"

"Never just a waitress, Mrs. Mann," Fergus said, unable to joke this time. "You are our life's blood, and my life for one would be a dust bowl the moment you left this house."

"Oh get on with you. You'll get a cup of tea over the head in a minute." threatened Mrs. Mann, but she smiled.

Fergus told her about Harley.

"The poor woman. How much more can she and those kids take without being permanently damaged?"

She bustled over to the tray and brought them some more cake which they didn't need, not having tasted the first piece.

"I know what I'm going to do, and there will be no arguments from either of you." She glared at both of them. "I am going to take her in, above the carriage house. She's coming home to live with me. And I'll hear nothing against it from either of you." Defiantly, she brandished the teapot at them—tea drops erupting from the spout.

Both men opened their mouths to reply. Mrs. Mann waved them down.

"Fergus." She pointed to the hall and the phone. "Hop to it and get that Flower person on the phone."

The next few days were a mania of movement, comings, and goings. Harley entered university with a suitcase of new clothes, vowing to work hard, and come back every summer and every holiday. He might even manage the odd weekend. Don't worry, he'd hitchhike or coax a ride with someone who was coming this way. Young Charlie expressed his preference to stay with Mrs. Hoffman, becoming one with her own brood. Cat told him she'd visit every day.

In the midst of the pandemonium, Fergus almost missed a newspaper article relegated to page two, which he immediately brought to the attention of Malcolm.

'After a surprise audit, the Department of National Revenue have laid charges, jointly and severally, against the Calgary company, Strathcona Holdings, for tax fraud including alleged tax evasion by a number of the Board members. It is of interest in Cypress Landing because of the connection to GlasBottle and its manager, Lex Rideout, who stands accused of two murders, his wife, Clarissa, and Peter Davidson. Our readers will remember Davidson has outstanding fraud charges against him. The case is to be re-opened in light of the

recent developments and investigation is expected to result in clearing the late Peter Davidson of all charges. We regret the man cannot be here for the good news.'

Harold Haskell confirmed the report. "I received a shareholder's letter. The investigation includes all the share options they gave themselves, and anything detrimental to the interests of minority shareholders. It will benefit Cat when it's all settled."

Fergus had a nervous moment, wondering if the letters had cited him as the source of the information which had prompted the audit by the tax department. "Was there any mention of how they got the information?"

"They never reveal sources," replied Haskell. "But I heard an excise auditor was nosing around the plant a couple of weeks ago. A summary of the charges was just about the same as the conclusions you gave me." After a pause, Haskell asked, "How is your dad after his ordeal?"

"He'll be okay, thank goodness," Fergus said, glad to be off the subject of information sources. "And he has a busy future planned." He told Haskell about the lectures he and Malcolm had started. "Dad's planning to ask for space in the evening from the business college and set up sessions for accounting students according to their year of study. If it proves a success, he'll register the sessions with the Dominion Association of Chartered Accountants."

"Sly dog." Haskell chuckled, admiration in his voice. "And here I thought he was out to pasture. Let me know if you need any help persuading the college to cooperate."

Fergus had one more question. "I'm concerned GlasBottle will be shut down. Heaven forbid the men lose their jobs."

"They still have a general manager at Strathcona. He's appointed a man from Calgary to take over GlasBottle until further notice. And he has re-hired a bookkeeper Rideout let go because he was becoming too curious about shortages of glass products."

ON the first official morning of Cat's residency, she and Mrs. Mann came into the house before she left for school to show off her new clothes. A blue dress with a pleated front and white round collar, and black shoes with a button strap.

"I'm going to join C.G.I.T.," Cat told Fergus, her eyes shining.

"Canadian Girls in Training," Mrs. Mann explained, looking proud. "A group for teenage girls."

Both of them watched Cat start off to school. "What about the money she'll get now Mr. Davidson has been found innocent? Will her family take advantage of her?"

"Cat will insist on helping her mother. As trustees, we are already sending monthly upkeep for Young Charlie."

Mrs. Mann's face turned gloomy. "She misses her family, and so she should. I thought she'd be happy here, and I hate to say it, but she isn't. Not really. I've never known Cat to be moody. She doesn't play the violin as much either."

Fergus reflected on Mrs. Mann's remarks all the way to the office and purposely came home right about the time school let out. He joined Mrs. Mann who was watching Cat rocking back and forth on the small swing on the verandah.

"We can't expect things will ever be the same for her," Mrs. Mann remarked to him. "Is she hiding something again?"

"No," Fergus tried to cheer her up. "Not hiding, exactly."

29

CAT slumped against the swing cushions, watching Duke pad about in the yard, snuffling and peering under bushes for any stray cats. Lately, her chest always felt like she hadn't chewed her food properly. She swallowed trying to push down the lump.

Fergus came out the dining room door and headed towards her. "Mind if I sit?"

In answer, she straightened and moved aside to give him room.

They sat in silence for a moment, then Fergus said, his voice bright, "Want to hear a story?"

Cat sat up, interested. "Okay."

"Once upon a time"—they smiled at each other as he began with the familiar line—"there was a prince who lived in a place, not unlike Cypress Landing."

"Was he a handsome prince?"

"Some people might say so. He was tall, young, and strong. He has great teeth." Fergus flashed her a wide, toothy smile.

Cat showed her own then, and asked, "Did he have red hair?"

"Cinnamon," agreed Fergus, and he settled in to begin.

ONE day the Prince found a peculiar bottle on the riverbank. It was pear-shaped, and things swirled around on the inside in a formless mist. The Prince tried to see it through the glass but the shape was illusive, so he opened the bottle. As his fingers worked the stopper, it suddenly flew up. Whatever was inside hurled itself away into the air howling like a banshee.

"You've unleashed a terrible demon," said a voice beside him.

Startled, the Prince looked around.

"Down here," coaxed the voice. The Prince glanced down and saw a gnome. A real live gnome with wrinkled skin and ears that twitched in opposite directions.

"What demon?" asked the Prince.

"The one I'm guarding," the gnome said. "You only have until sunrise tomorrow to get it back in the bottle. You let the demon out, and now it's bound to you. It will harm everything it meets, and for the rest of your life you'll blame yourself. The longer it is free, the more powerful it gets. So you can understand why there's no time to lose."

"Why don't you get it yourself, since you're supposed to guard it? I don't even know what it looks like."

The gnome began to laugh. He fell to the ground and rolled around. The Prince shouted at him to stop and threatened to hold him down in the river until he drowned.

"I can only help you catch it," the gnome finally said, gasping for breath.

"So, start helping, then, instead of twitching your ears and talking about blame."

The gnome picked himself up. His fingers snapped like firecrackers, and before the Prince could take a breath, he was spinning through the air. He landed with a painful thump. "Ouch," the Prince yelled and caught the bottle as it fell into his lap.

"Welcome to Dark Dugout," said the gnome chuckling. "I'll give you a magic wand to help you capture the demon. Use it wisely because you only have one command." He beckoned the Prince to follow, saying, "You can call me Don."

The bottle gave off a glow which the Prince used to light his path. Don found the demon's trail so quickly, the Prince was sure he was about to trick him. He almost told the gnome to get lost, when he heard pitiful sobbing in the dark. He shone his bottle light in the direction and saw a boy with thin and wasted legs huddled against the cave wall.

"The demon took away my wheelchair and left me here knowing I can't move. I want to go home." The boy sobbed bitterly, holding out his arms to the Prince.

The Prince ignored him. What could he do? If he carried the boy, it would slow him down, and he would never find the demon. If he used his one trick, he'd lose the only way to get the demon back into the bottle. Waiting, Don's beady eyes bored into the Prince's.

"Give him a wand, so he can make his own wish," the Prince told Don.

"You have to do it. I can't."

The Prince turned to the boy. "After I find the demon, I can come back for you," he suggested hopefully.

Suddenly, water began gushing through the floor. Don and the Prince jumped to higher ground and watched as the water bubbled and slurped towards the boy. Terrified, the boy cringed against the wall to avoid the river's relentless charge.

"Time is short." Don's ears twitched, and he began to laugh mightily.

The Prince gritted his teeth, then pointed his wand, but he couldn't make himself give the command. He handed the wand to Don. "You have to decide. I can't."

"I need your permission," Don said, and the Prince, nodded full of shame. A ship, sails unfurled, appeared in a shaft of light. After a short stop, the ship navigated a route down the river, sails glowing like molten gold. On the deck, the boy sat in his wheelchair, waving.

The Prince sank down, crying out in mortal despair. "The sun is rising, and it's too late to get the demon. We're doomed, and I'll never forgive myself."

"Look again," Don said. "The demon is back in the bottle. The boy was saved from a terrible death."

"But I let you rescue him because I was too cowardly to decide to do it myself."

"It doesn't matter about your motive," Don confided. "You sacrificed the only wish, and the demon had no choice."

He nodded wisely at the Prince. The world dissolved with another sickening spin and the Prince was back on the riverbank. Don had disappeared, but the bottle gave a little quiver when the Prince held it up.

"THE end?" Cat asked after a long pause.

"The end," Fergus agreed.

"What happened to the bottle?"

For a moment, Fergus looked sad. "The Prince kept it for many years thinking he was a coward and blaming himself for letting a demon loose. Until one day, he realized he had turned his back on all those who loved him, and his heart had turned to stone. When he finally believed the Gnome's words that he wasn't a bad person, the bottle vanished in a puff of smoke, and the Prince was happy again."

Satisfied, Cat cuddled up, leaning her head against his arm.

"Your mother is going to be alright, Cat," Fergus's voice was full of sympathy. "She needs rest and professional help before she can come home again."

"I know," Cat said, not looking at him, afraid she might start crying. She swallowed a big knot in her throat. "I was so scared, I didn't tell anyone about Sir. Did he die because I ran away and didn't tell anyone? Will I get a heart of stone?"

"Cat, believe me, nothing could have helped Sir. In the end, you remembered, and the demon went back into the bottle."

"For real?" Cat asked. The lump in her chest eased.

"Cross my heart," Fergus said. They linked pinkie fingers and shook on it. The pain had disappeared, and she felt a burst of happiness.

"Peter would thank you for helping, just like the boy thanked the magician," Fergus continued to console her.

Cat shot up straight, suspicious. "A magician? You said he was a Prince."

Fergus blushed and bit his lip. "Well, he became a magician so he wouldn't look silly carrying around a demon in a bottle."

Duke bounded up the steps towards them, a ball in his mouth.

Cat giggled at him. There was enough time to play her new violin piece, *Salut d'Amour* for Malcolm, before helping with dinner. "He should have stayed a Prince and then met a Princess," she declared and wrestled the ball from Duke's mouth. Duke turned and raced her for the yard. She thought Fergus said something about '*one thing at a time,*' but she couldn't be sure.

- THE END -

ACKNOWLEDGMENTS

For Research: I'm immensely grateful to the staff of the Medicine Hat Public Library, who tirelessly found newspapers and numerous historical documents of the 1930's relating to the area of Southeastern Alberta. (One surprising fact: Inspecting newspaper publications for the entire year of 1936 I found the dominant theme was Senate Reform. Perhaps proving the old adage of the more things change, the more they remain the same.)

A special thanks to Mr. Kris Samraj of the Non-Fiction Services section of the MHPL, who made copies of old maps and other documents, and pushed me in the right direction for more obscure historical facts which proved invaluable.

For Encouragement: To my friends and family, you know who you are, who, in the early stages, patiently listened to my drafts and offered suggestions. To my daughter, Brenda Roath, who designed the cover and read and re-read chapters aloud and pointed out conspicuous errors while listening to my gripes and groans.

To my editor, Tessa Barron, who spent endless hours in progressively complex edits and patiently argued changes which ultimately ended in a better novel.

To my Publisher, Bear Hill Publishing, whose staff explained, with patience and kindness, all the workings of publication, marketing, and sales.

It's been a journey.

Historical Note

September 2018 will mark the 100th anniversary of the Battle of the Canal Du Nord, 1918.

Fergus suffers from PTSD. During and after WW1, there was no recognition for the shock, anxiety, and guilt veterans suffered upon return to civilian life. Soldiers who broke down in battle, who suffered "shell shock," or refused to follow ridiculous orders, were executed as cowards. WW1 veterans took up their lives after as best they could, and few ever spoke about their personal experiences. I concentrated my research on the last 100 days of WW 1, when Fergus would have seen the most action as a signalman.

The crossing of the Canal du Nord stands as one of the most impressive Canadian tactical operations of WW1. It was a risky battle plan, which emphasized combined arms operations while utilizing the Canadian Engineers. Historians agree that the battle stands as a benchmark for the evolution of 20th century combat. Although sustaining high casualties, the Canadian Corps overcame one of the strongest German defensive positions along the Western Front. It was part of what was called the 100 days final push by the Allies which ended in the Armistice of November 11, 1918. As part of the Engineers, Fergus takes part in the battle, although his part is purely a product of my imagination.

Fergus's conversation with Malcolm touched upon problems that signalers and the system of communication faced, much to do with methods and "ownership" of the equipment. Every signaler and battery had their own equipment and when they were relieved from duty, the next team would have to exchange and set up again. This volume of wireless sets meant that a certain amount of 'friendly jamming' was inevitable. Diaries and reports are quite damning. At least 95% of messages were sent unclear, with many references to the disadvantages of enciphering and deciphering as a key reason. The Canadian Corps blamed this phenomenon on poorly trained telegraphists but the statement was probably made to deflect blame away from the main issues, which were lack of Corps control and the use of fixed wavelengths.

By the time Amiens came along, some of the Artillery brigades were given continuous-wave wireless sets. But not all the divisions used them. The farther down the chain of command, the more difficult it was to convince. It was an everlasting battle of improving and updating methods and equipment. I mention Amiens because my uncle lied about his age and enlisted with the third CMR of Medicine Hat. He was awarded the Military Medal at the Battle of Amiens.

- F. Nelson Smith.

F. NELSON SMITH spent her career submerged in the numbers, working as a Certified Management Accountant. She now lives in Red Deer, Alberta, drowning in words, writing mystery novels. *No Straight Thing* is her debut from Bear Hill Publishing.

Learn more at *fnelsonsmith.com*

Read on for an excerpt from

Perpetual Check

June 1985. Stuttgart, Germany.

The man standing in the hallway outside Miss Schiller's door looked more like a sumo wrestler in a suit than a policeman. His bulk strained the seams of his suit to crucial levels, and when he used his handkerchief to mop his damp face, she swore she heard the seams creak.

She backed into her neat front hall as Sumo Man stepped in and seized the space. Face red, sweat stains marring his jacket—his breath made whistling noises through his teeth from the effort of walking up the flight of stairs to her apartment door. For a second, she wondered if he might have a heart attack.

Another policeman, this one in the immaculate green and tan uniform of a Municipal Police Sergeant, managed to squeeze by him, and she learned Sumo Man was Herr Mueller from the Landeskriminalamt, or LKA. Miss Schiller compared the face on the ID card with the one in front of her. His eyes, almost hidden in the upper folds of his cheeks, regarded her with ill-concealed impatience, so she deliberately held the card an extra few seconds to show him she might be a spinster secretarin, but she was not intimidated.

Finally, curiosity taking over, she returned his worn leather folder.

"What do you wish, Herr Mueller?" she asked, glancing pointedly at her watch. "Important items are waiting at the office. I don't wish to be late. It sets a bad example for the others."

"Please, Miss Schiller, I think we'd be more comfortable if we sat." He studied her face, and she grimaced, not hiding her distaste at dealing with a Kripo. "If you don't mind?" His voice was surprisingly tenor for such a big man.

Floorboards screaming, he followed her into her sitting room and waited while she sat in an armchair, its seat covered with embroidered velvet upholstery.

Mueller declined to sit, perhaps noticing her lack of hospitality or not trusting the chair to remain in one piece. The young sergeant stood with military correctness by the door to the hallway.

"Your employer is Joseph Dittmahn, Vice-President of Redstadt

Electroniks. With offices in the Schlossplatz."

Ida nodded in reply, though the statement made it clear he wasn't looking for confirmation. Mueller's bulk spread out in front of her, looking like a jovial Kaufmann about to take her order.

"You said he's away. Where was he supposed to be, please?" Fingers like sausages held his pencil to his notebook.

Her chin jerked in reflexively to the question. She raised her eyebrows, then cinched them together between her pale blue eyes. "He's in Munich. Until the day after tomorrow. Friday."

Mueller waited, as though expecting her to ask the obvious. Abruptly, he smiled, showing an unexpected array of white, even teeth. "His wife accompanied him?"

"No. She's visiting relations in England," answered Miss Schiller, her eyes glinting. "Has something happened to her?"

The policeman pursed his fat lips in a gentle reproof, then let the air wheeze through them, as though regretful of what was to come.

"Not his wife, Miss Schiller. We were unable to locate her and that's why we've come to you. Early this morning, Herr Dittmahn was found in his car. Unfortunately, dead."

He waited, watching shrewdly from under sleepy lids. Miss Schiller's face turned white. One hand reached out as if to push his statement away. Her grip tightened on the arm of the straight-backed chair.

"In his car?" she whispered.

"A highway maintenance crew found him at the side of the road, forty miles north of Stuttgart." He inhaled another labored breath and added, "He'd been shot twice in the head. At close range."

Miss Schiller choked off an incredulous cry. Her face twisted at his blunt words. "No! He's in Munich. He had reservations on the train from Stuttgart." Her expression obstinate, she repeated, "No. It's a mistake."

"There is no mistake," cooed the detective.

She endured his sympathetic murmurs with the same impatience of one forced to listen to a bad sermon. He required her help. Time was important. Robbery could be a motive. Did she have objections to a few more questions?

"Did Herr Dittmahn carry large sums of money or other

valuables on his person? Was he in the habit of picking up hitch-hikers?"

"Robbery!" Ida Schiller dismissed the word like a puff of steam. "But whatever was he doing in the North?"

Mueller waited while she stared at her hands, forehead creased.

Finally, she sighed. "Perhaps he did pick up someone and offer to drive out of his way. It would be like him. Charitable, but foolish." She pressed her thin lips together. "Well, a robber wouldn't get much. Herr Dittmahn carries little money. He uses credit cards. Easier to account for his expenses if the banks do his bookkeeping for him."

The policeman shifted on his dusty shoes. "Miss Schiller, you've been with the company, how long?"

"Twenty-one years."

Mueller's tone turned admiring. "I imagine Dittmahn left many things in your care, and you must know a great deal about the company's affairs. Everything was going well there?"

"You suspect a person in the company shot him?"

"I'm trying to get a background, that's all. Every possible angle, you understand."

Miss Schiller gazed back at him with penetrating eyes. "Everything is operating smoothly at the company," she said.

"The Company deals in electronic components only?"

She nodded.

"You do not deal in tractor parts?"

"Tractor parts?" she repeated. "Of course not."

"Yet, there have been shipments of tractor parts that disappeared after they arrived at their destination."

Miss Schiller's expression cleared. "Ah, you have tractor parts confused with electronic components. Herr Dittmahn mentioned that a shipment of computer components went to our subsidiary in Austria by mistake. But somewhere along the way someone had stolen the equipment and filled the crates with sand. It's odd, but . . ." She stopped.

"Yes?"

"Nothing." Miss Schiller slumped in her chair. "It's nothing to do with us. Herr Dittmahn . . . I can't grasp it. It seems impossible."

"Indeed." He stared at her for a moment longer. "Maybe something else occurred to you? About the shipment of components, perhaps."

Mueller pushed his head forward and sideways, exposing his right ear to her as if waiting for an answer from an addled toddler. It was patronizing even if encouraging, and she resented it. She pursed her mouth, looked past, and ignored him.

He tried again. "Redstadt Electroniks receives shipments of computer components from Britain and the United States, do they not Miss Schiller?"

Miss Schiller shrugged, then as if realizing the direction of his questions, gave him a peircing stare. "Why are you asking these questions, Herr Mueller?"

He held up his pudgy hand, palm outward. "Please, Miss Schiller, only a few more minutes." His voice hardened. "The Company's business is computer components. Yet some of the customs declarations on shipments arriving from Britain and the US state the containers hold tractor parts. You are perhaps not aware that your company forwards these particular crates on to Austria. It is strange, is it not, Miss Schiller? Now you say one of the same shipments contains only sand. Shortly thereafter, Herr Dittmahn is murdered."

"Rubbish!" She smiled, mocking him. "You are saying there is something untoward going on with the shipments. Secrets. But he doesn't approve of secrets. You don't know him. He believes in fairness and justice. Always. I would know if it were otherwise."

Suddenly aware she was speaking of her employer as though he were not dead, emotion boiled up. She pressed her tongue against the back of her teeth to keep her jaw from quivering and showing her anguish.

"What was Dittmahn's business in Munich?" persisted Herr Mueller, either oblivious to or ignoring her obvious discomfort.

"He told me he was going to meet with a representative from Head Office," she said, regaining control.

Mueller raised his eyebrows, and licked his pencil again. "He told you? You don't arrange his appointment book?" He didn't so much as a glance up from his notebook.

She flushed. "It was last minute. He took the notification himself, and then told me. Did you think there was something furtive about it?"

When his flickering eyelids betrayed his line of thought, her lips twitched an almost imperceptible smile at catching him off guard.

She answered the rest of his questions; Dittmahn's business acquaintances; the address of his wife's relations in England.

Only when she was sure the two policemen were not coming back, did she permit herself to shed bitter tears. After a phone call to the office, she did an uncharacteristic thing. She slipped into her bedroom like a ghost and pushed the door closed behind her with the very tips of her fingers, listening for the soft click of the latch. After a moment, she moved to the bed where she stretched out and stared at the ceiling, not caring that her shoes marked the white bedspread.

Later that same evening, she went downstairs and found a bulky brown envelope on the floor under the mail flap. She took it into the sitting room and with a small knife from her corner desk, slit the envelope in the same way she had opened a thousand like it before. Turning it upside down she tapped the open end on her palm. A letter with the handwriting of her late employer slid out. Another shake of the brown envelope, and a wad of money followed by a square of microfiche tumbled to the floor at her feet.

The letter explained the envelope's contents, and outlined detailed instructions of what she was to do. A scant two hours later, she backed her Volkswagen from its parking place and sped off into the darkness.

For the first time in her life, she knew real fear.

Far across Stuttgart at that moment, in a hotel suite with windows facing a spacious green park, a man spoke on the telephone. Thin parchment-like skin barely covered the knuckles which stood out on the hand holding the receiver. The same economy of skin. covering high cheekbones. stretched the man's mouth to a thin slit. Lustrous brown hair combed back from his forehead only served to emphasize his death's head appearance.

"Nothing was found in the office?" His quiet voice faded as he paused to listen. "And you searched his home . . . ? No—my informant is certain the document was in his office two days ago. . . . He didn't go near a bank. You found no receipts for packages or envelopes?" This time he listened a moment longer. "Ah, so? Naturally, an invoice for a microfiche. Herr Dittmahn was shrewd. A thick package becomes a thin package. Now, where would he hide it . . . ? He has a secretary who's disgustingly loyal. In love with her employer, I suspect." His lips twisted in a sneer.

Then his voice sharpened, the words insistent. "Go to her place. But be sure you have the documents before you tidy up the loose ends. Do I make myself understood . . . ? *Gut.* I will await your report."

The man replaced the receiver then poured two drinks from a crystal decanter placed on the sideboard. He picked them up and offered one to his companion.

Perpetual Check

by F. Nelson Smith

Available September 2018